Sherlock Holmes *and the* Hapsburg Tiara

Alan Vanneman

An Otto Penzler Book

Carroll & Graf Publishers
New York

SHERLOCK HOLMES AND THE HAPSBURG TIARA

Carroll & Graf Publishers
An Imprint of Avalon Publishing Group Inc.
245 West 17th Street
New York, NY 10011

AVALON
publishing group incorporated

Library of Congress Cataloging-in-Publication Data is available.

ISBN: 0-7867-1509-X

10 9 8 7 6 5 4 3 2 1

Printed in the United States of America
Distributed by Publishers Group West

PART I

The Vanishing Duke

CHAPTER 1

An Unusual Request

THE HANSOM LOOMED SUDDENLY out of the fog and pulled against the curb.

"Are you Dr. Watson?" the driver demanded.

To be accosted in such a peremptory manner, on a dark and deserted London street late at night, was scarcely to my liking.

"State your business," I responded.

"Are you Dr. Watson?" the fellow repeated.

I disdained a reply, but all at once the cab's door flew open, and a dark figure descended to the sidewalk. His hat was pulled low over his eyes, and a scarf muffled his face.

"Come along, Doctor. You're wanted."

"Is that you, Lestrade?" I asked, responding more to his voice than his face.

"Please, sir, we're in a great hurry."

He stepped forward and put his hand on my arm. Despite the faint light, I was able to assure myself that the man before me was in fact a Scotland Yard inspector and not one of the many members of London's criminal element that might wish me ill for my association with the celebrated detective Sherlock Holmes.

"What's all this about, Lestrade?" I said rather sharply as I stepped into the cab.

"I'm not at liberty to say, sir," he said, closing the door with a firm hand.

As soon as the cab's door slammed shut I heard the crack of the driver's whip. We were off, and at no mean pace. I sat back on the worn leather seat and strained to see my companion in the darkness, for Lestrade had drawn the curtains of the cab, and the interior offered scarcely more illumination than a grave.

"Where are we going?" I demanded.

"I'm not at liberty to say," he repeated.

"Is that how you're going to respond to my every question?"

"I—please, Dr. Watson, ask me no questions, for I can give you no answers."

"Very well. You will excuse me if I smoke a cigar."

"Of course, sir. But please leave the curtains drawn, sir. My orders are very strict on that point."

I lit my cigar in silence. There was something in Lestrade's tone, at once firm and apologetic, that dissipated my anger toward the man. I was clearly being summoned on some official case of great importance, and Lestrade was an agent rather than a principal in the matter. I cast my mind over the public events of the past several weeks in the hope of deriving some idea as to the nature of the emergency, but nothing suggested itself. The mystery, complete as it was, would assuredly resolve itself in the near future.

However, I could not but regret the timing of the case, for I was unfortunately somewhat the worse for wear. Earlier in the evening I had attended a party at my club, the Galenians, for a gathering of physicians to celebrate the elevation of one of our number to a position as assistant chief of surgery at Charing Cross Hospital. At the conclusion of the festivities, I had departed with an unopened magnum of champagne, obtained with the assistance of Betty, a most charming young lady who filled in at the bar from time to time. We repaired to Betty's house, only to find that Eunice, her mother, who operated a rooming house, was still awake, and possessed of a substantial thirst for both champagne and company, due in large part to the misbehavior of Bert, a licensed victualer of whom she was extremely fond. Common courtesy and hopes for the future required me to commiserate with Eunice for almost two hours, during which time the magnum was, of course, entirely consumed, and the opportunities for a congenial *tête-à-tête* with Betty, entirely exhausted. And thus I found myself on the streets of an unprepossessing section of London on a cold night at almost two in the morning, charged with more alcohol and less amatory satisfaction than I could have wished.

Under the circumstances, a rapid cab ride through London was the last thing I could have desired, but I was forced to endure it for almost forty minutes, when the cab suddenly slowed. We appeared to have left the main roads, for I could hear the horse picking his way along, and the cab itself was subject to strange, sudden jolts, as though the roadway were deeply marred. At last the cab came to a halt, and Lestrade opened the door.

"Here you are, sir. I apologize for any inconvenience."

"No apologies are needed, Lestrade," I said, stepping from the cab. I was about to say more, but as soon as I was fairly on the ground the door slammed shut once more and the cab drove off at a slow but determined rate of speed. Whatever this case was, Lestrade had evidently no wish but to be done with it as soon as possible.

I found myself on a railroad siding, confronting a large locomotive, which, upon my alighting, issued forth a vast cloud of steam. The driver of the great engine, sticking his head out the window of the cab, shouted something that I could not well make out over the hissing vapor. I observed that there was a single carriage attached to the locomotive and concluded that, for some reason, this extravagant conveyance had been placed entirely at my disposal.

Because there was no platform, I gained admittance to the first compartment of the carriage with some difficulty. The door was unlocked, but opening it while maintaining my balance on the carriage's small iron steps required no little ingenuity. Once I had the door open I braced against it with my left hand and sprang into the carriage.

"Ah, there you are, Watson. You may go, Sergeant. Watson and I can fend for ourselves from now on."

"Yes, Mr. Holmes."

The curtains of the compartment were as tightly shut as those of the hansom, but once I had closed the door an electric light illuminated the scene. Sherlock Holmes sat before me in his deerstalker and his traveling cloak, addressing a bluff London bobby who was in the act of departing the compartment through the interior door.

"If you gentlemen require anything, I will be in the compartment directly behind this one," the sergeant announced as he made his departure.

"Holmes," I said, seating myself, "what is this all about?"

"We cannot accuse the British government of a lack of imagination, can we?" said Holmes with a smile. "Here you are. I doubt that this will prove useful, but I took the precaution of bringing it with me nonetheless."

So saying, he handed me my service revolver. As he did so, a piercing whistle and an explosive blast of steam from our engine's cylinders announced our departure.

"You think we are in danger?" I asked, fitting my revolver in my jacket pocket.

"The government seems to thinks so, or at least they would have us think they think so. I think rather that it is a case of bureaucratic nerves. Clearly, something is up, and Scotland Yard is determined to take every precaution. When Sir Robert and Inspector Gregson appeared at Baker Street three hours ago, demanding that I depart with them instantly, I responded that I would not unless accompanied by both Watson and his revolver."

"Sir Robert Johnson? The head of the Yard? Is he here?"

"I believe not, though I have not been allowed to inspect the train. It appears, Watson, that we are embarked on very delicate matters, ones that require private hands rather than public ones."

"Why do you say that?"

"Sir Robert has never been one of my admirers. I think it unlikely that he would engage me in a case if he had control over the matter. Yet if we are given our own locomotive this can be no small case."

"Yes. Do you have any idea where we are?"

"We are, or were, about three miles outside of Marylebone Station. I traveled in a closed coach, but could make the journey blindfolded myself. The driver was in too great a hurry to follow a circuitous route. As for our destination, I have no certain opinion, but we should not be surprised to find ourselves among the privileged classes."

"Some sort of country house, you mean?"

"Yes. Only the high aristocracy could use the machinery of government for their own purposes in such a manner. If it were an official case, the Yard would never come to me until they had made an utter botch of things. But there has been nothing in the papers. I presume you had departed from your club?"

"Yes."

"Otherwise, they would have found you more quickly. You have led them on quite a chase, Watson. Since it is now a quarter of four, I suggest that we attempt to get some rest before we arrive at our destination, wherever it might be. Unless you prefer to read."

"I should prefer to sleep."

"Of course. This carriage is most fortunately equipped with the unspeakable luxury of private sleeping compartments. I was able to pack your portmanteau with necessaries sufficient for a journey of several days. You will find it stowed in the forward sleeping compartment, directly opposite to this one. If you find yourself in need of something, you may direct your requests to Sergeant Madden. I myself will retire shortly. You are not hungry?"

"No."

"Then I will see you perhaps in a few hours. We shall know more in the morning, Watson."

Despite his apparent languor, I sensed in Holmes's words a distinct thrill of intellectual pleasure. I concluded that to have been brought in on an official case in such a dramatic manner appealed in no small way to that hidden yet profound vanity that so often drove him to heights of deductive brilliance that none could follow and that had made him renowned throughout Europe and indeed the entire civilized world. For my own part, I confess I longed more for rest than enlightenment. Upon entering the sleeping compartment, I found to my satisfaction that it offered all the amenities of a modern hotel room, ingeniously miniaturized to fit the limits of a railway carriage. I undressed quickly and in a few minutes fell fast asleep beneath warm flannel sheets and a fine wool blanket.

I was not, however, destined to enjoy their comfort for long. I awakened only a few hours later to a persistent knocking on the door.

"Dr. Watson, sir?"

"Yes," I cried, "what is it?"

"It's Sergeant Madden, sir. We'll be arriving shortly, sir. There's a shower at the rear of the carriage, sir."

"What time is it, Sergeant?"

"Seven-thirty, sir. We should be arriving in forty minutes."

I opened the curtains on the window to discover that the first light of dawn was barely visible over the horizon. For a moment I watched the English countryside slipping by, dark and anonymous in the faint light. Then I clad myself in bathrobe and slippers and made the journey to the bathroom, where I enjoyed a warm shower, though the pleasure scarcely compensated for my sleepless condition. After shaving, I returned to my compartment and made myself as presentable as I could under the circumstances. I then crossed to the sitting compartment, where I found Holmes deep in contemplation, his long legs stretched out, his chin upon his chest, and the amber mouthpiece of his stained calabash between his lips. He did not rouse himself until the train actually halted.

"Journey's end, Watson," he said, rising to his feet. "One can only hope we have started a proper hare."

We stepped out on a platform of a rural station whose

signs, absurdly enough, had been obscured with black cloth. The platform itself was bare of people, and Sergeant Madden rapidly directed us to a waiting carriage, whose curtains were securely drawn. Holmes and I seated ourselves inside, while Sergeant Madden perched himself with the driver.

"They seem to keep us in ignorance to the very end," said Holmes, glancing at the curtains with an amused smile.

"Do you have any idea where we are?"

"Perhaps a hundred and fifty miles due north of London, judging from the time of sunrise. Beyond that I would not make a guess. I fear my knowledge of England's great houses is limited. We may as well humor our captors until the very end."

We rode at a steady pace for a full hour perhaps two hours before coming at last to a halt. Sergeant Madden opened the door of the carriage and we stepped out before the entrance of a truly grand home, decorated in an extraordinary manner with a pair of enormous elephant tusks arching over the doorway. We were quickly ushered inside, where a distinguished, white-haired butler in scarlet livery led us down a long hall hung with ancient armor and up an enormous marble staircase. We were so dwarfed by our surroundings that it was difficult indeed to imagine that this structure could be inhabited by creatures as small as human beings. The butler led us down a second hallway, whose gilt ceilings towered twenty feet above our heads. We then turned down yet another hallway, whose dimensions at last bore some resemblance to the human frame, though the woodwork of both the walls and the ceiling was intricate beyond measure. Finally the servant opened a heavy door and ushered us into a large, darkened room and bid us to seat ourselves on a large sofa, whose gilt elegance proclaimed it to be a precious relic of past centuries. The servant then withdrew, shutting the door behind him.

The darkness was broken by a pair of candelabra, each holding three thick tapers, by whose light I was able to determine that we were in a sort of sitting room, though of such opulence as I had never encountered. To our right was a high, old-fashioned fireplace, whose carved mantel bore the two light sources. Close by the fireplace was a small writing desk upon which rested several stout, worn volumes bound in leather. The walls were hung with large paintings in ornate gilt frames, but the paintings themselves were so dark that it was quite impossible to determine their subjects. Over the writing desk there was a small frame of modern design, containing a black-and-white document that I deduced to be an advertisement of some sort, for I could make out an offered price of "£25." Above the fireplace I observed a curved sword that could only be a cavalry saber, and its scabbard.

All of this I noted later, for as I entered the room my attention was focused entirely on a strange figure seated some distance away from us in an armchair set against the opposite wall. This individual was fashionably dressed and had the figure of a rather short and slender young man, but as to his identity it was impossible to say, for his head was entirely covered with a thick hood of black cloth!

"Mr. Holmes. Dr. Watson. You will excuse this fanciful garb. I cannot apologize for bringing you here in such a manner, for necessities of state—matters that I cannot discuss with you—override all considerations. For the same reasons, my identity must remain a secret, both now and in the future. The enormity of the mystery with which you are required to assist Her Majesty's government requires no less."

"Surely, Mr. Churchill," my friend said, "if mysteries are to be solved, facts must be brought to light rather than deliberately concealed."

The young man leaped from the chair and tore the hood from his head.

"How the deuce did you know my name?" he shouted in obvious vexation.

I stared, amazed, for the young man before us was indeed Winston Churchill, son of the late Conservative leader Lord Randolph Churchill, the young man whose exploits as a cavalry officer in Her Majesty's service in Africa had made his face and name famous to millions, due to the appearance of a near-infinite number of articles in the popular press, many of them written by Mr. Churchill himself.

"You should have chosen a room other than your own in which to conduct this interview," said Holmes, who I suspect was not at all averse to eliciting the response from Mr. Churchill that he had in fact obtained.

"I took every precaution!" Mr. Churchill cried, seeming to address himself as much as the two of us.

"Not entirely," said Holmes. "Would it be too much trouble to obtain some coffee? Neither Dr. Watson nor I have had what can be called a proper night's sleep, and we are both in need of a stimulant."

"Yes, we shall have coffee and breakfast as well. I myself have been up since six o'clock with nothing to eat whatsoever."

He said the last as though it constituted an enormous deprivation, though I knew from his own account of his dramatic escape from captivity at the hands of the Boers in South Africa that he was inured to every form of hardship. Mr. Churchill strode about the room for a moment as though lost in thought, running his fingers through his hair, before reaching for a bell pull to summon a servant.

"We'll have breakfast here, if you don't mind," Mr. Churchill said. "The rest of the house is not aware of your presence, and I'd prefer to keep it that way until the proper time."

"Whatever you think is best," said Holmes.

Mr. Churchill was on the verge of saying something else when the liveried servant who had conducted us to the room appeared at the door.

"What do you require, sir?" the servant asked.

"Bring us breakfast, Jensen," said Mr. Churchill. "We'll have it here."

"Very good, sir."

Once the servant had disappeared, our host turned his attention to my friend once more.

"Now, Mr. Holmes," he said, "how did you know it was I?"

"As I remarked earlier," said Holmes, "you should not have conducted this interview in your own room. When Watson and I first entered, I was struck by the asymmetrical development of your limbs. Despite the excellence of your tailor, the disproportionate size of your right forearm and hand is unmistakable. There are a variety of activities that can produce such a condition, but in this case the mute testimony of a cavalry saber is all but overwhelming. I am far from a connoisseur of such weapons, but when I observe the simplicity and utilitarian design of the specimen that hangs here on the wall, I am encouraged to conclude that it is an emblem of current service rather than past glory. This hypothesis is further supported by the fact that your hands are deeply tanned, and of course it is in the tropic colonies such as India and Africa that the saber still retains some value as a weapon in war."

"I fear you overlook the brilliant use of the French cavalry at Sedan!" said Mr. Churchill hotly, though the source of his indignation was not at all clear to me.

"No doubt," said Holmes. "I am not a military man."

"The cavalry shall always be the fairest and fiercest flower of battle!" exclaimed Mr. Churchill. "These are military matters, and must be decided by military men!"

"Of course," said Holmes. "I bow to your superior knowledge."

"Very well. Perhaps I gave myself away, to an extent, since you are so clever. What else did you see?"

"The books on your writing table," said Holmes. "The binding of one of the volumes is visible, upon which I can read the single word 'Marlborough'—obviously a biography of your great ancestor Sir John Churchill, the first duke. It is possible, of course, that an aristocratic young cavalry officer might choose to read about the duke without being his descendant. However, I also observe upon the wall above the desk a recently framed poster or advertisement of some sort, utterly out of keeping with the rest of the room. Most of the document is obscure in this light, but I am able to make out the boldface sum "£25." I am given to understand from your own account of your activities in the current war that you so far vexed the Boers that they offered that sum for your capture."

"Dead or alive!" crowed Mr. Churchill, who obviously took the keenest delight in recalling the experience.

"Yes," said Holmes. "So you see, Mr. Churchill, how very difficult it is to keep a secret."

"You shall not catch me out again!" Mr. Churchill asserted

defiantly. Before he could continue, the door opened and half a dozen servants entered. Half of them bore polished mahogany folding tables, which they set before us, and half brought trays laden with all sorts of nourishment, as well as silver pots of coffee and porcelain ones of tea. I helped myself to scrambled eggs and salmon filets poached in a sort of cream sauce. Mr. Churchill chose kippers and poached eggs, while my friend contented himself with bread and butter.

"Excellent butter, this," said Holmes, after we had had some opportunity to gratify our hunger. "Mr. Rhodes must be pleased with his dairy."

"Now, how did you know that we are at Loch Rannoch?" said Mr. Churchill.

"I could hardly fail to notice the crossed elephant tusks at the entrance, while my plate bears an obviously Scottish motif, the letters "LH" intertwined with heather and thistles. The deduction is a simple one."

My friend took a sip of coffee and sat back in his chair. He arranged his long fingers in a pyramid and looked at Mr. Churchill.

"Now, Mr. Churchill," he said, "you have brought us here at great difficulty and expense. Perhaps you could tell us why."

CHAPTER 2

The Vanishing Duke

MR. CHURCHILL EVIDENTLY FOUND it difficult to speak and remain seated at the same time. He sprang from his chair and went to the door, locking it and placing the key in his pocket. He drank the last of his coffee from his cup and then began to stride nervously about the room.

"What I am about to tell you," he said, "must be kept an absolute secret. Before I can continue I must have your word as British subjects that you will reveal nothing of what you are about to hear."

Holmes seemed amused.

"You can be assured that Watson and I will be utterly discreet, Mr. Churchill," he said. "Please continue."

Mr. Churchill finally seated himself and leaned forward, gripping his knees with his hands.

"Have you ever," he said, "heard the name of Josef Anton Salvator, the young archduke-palatine of Austria?"

"I read a brief account of his recent arrival in this country more than three weeks ago, and have seen casual references to him in the society pages since," said Holmes. "Other than that, I know nothing. What about you, Watson?"

I shook my head. "I fear my ignorance is even greater than yours," I replied.

"He is not well known in this country," said Mr. Churchill. "The palatinate is one of the ancient principalities of the Austrian Empire. Josef only acceded to the title in the past year, after the death of his father from a sudden illness. The family, though illustrious in its connections, has suffered severe financial reverses in the past decades and has declined remarkably from its former prominence."

Mr. Churchill paused to open a polished mahogany humidor that sat on the table beside him.

"I fear this may take some time," he said. "May I offer you gentlemen a cigar? They're excellent, and straight from Havana. I brought them myself."

"I believe I shall," said Holmes.

"Excellent. And you, Dr. Watson?"

I acceded as well, struck by the changeable nature of our host, who treated us with condescension at one moment and good-natured generosity the next.

"The archduke," he said, when his cigar was properly lit, "is precisely four years my senior. He served in India as an observer with my unit, the 77th Lancers, and we shared rooms together. He wanted to improve his English, while I wanted to improve my French, and his was impeccable. However, we were only together for a short time. Six weeks after he arrived, I was transferred to a more forward position, while he remained with the main detachment, for a reason that I will explain to you later. We corresponded on occasion, up until the outbreak of the Boer War.

"As you know, I have been in service in the war up until the present. But I have returned to England, secretly, on matters of state, for I intend to stand for Parliament in the coming election. I arrived only last week, traveling incognito. I was staying with friends at a hunting lodge nearby when someone happened to mention that Lord Camden was staying at Cecil Rhodes's house."

"Lord Camden is one of the wealthiest young men in England," murmured Holmes.

"Yes. Johnnie and I had been in the Transvaal together, and he had offered to back me if I ran for Parliament. A fellow in his first race can always use an extra thousand, so I thought I'd stop by and see if Johnnie was still good for it. When I arrived I was told that the young archduke of the palatinate was a house guest, and naturally I wished to renew our acquaintance, though I felt a great deal of trepidation as well."

Mr. Churchill paused and turned restlessly in his chair.

"I should like a cup of tea," he announced loudly.

There was no servant in the room, and none responded to his demand from outside, so I rose from the sofa and poured a cup, which I then handed to Mr. Churchill. He drank it down in a single gulp and placed the cup on the folding table at his side.

"This is a difficult story to tell, Mr. Holmes," he announced. "I must ask you to keep every word of it entirely private."

"Watson and I are used to keeping secrets," my friend responded, as though he had not offered precisely the same assurance only minutes before.

"Quite," said Mr. Churchill. "Well, let me begin. Josef and I were both fond of fencing. One night, while he was out, I had been drinking, rather too freely, I am afraid, for I had been given a severe dressing-down by my superior officer at the conclusion of the day. At first my mood was quite irritable, but as the evening progressed, my spirits improved. Josef and I had placed a fencing dummy in our rooms for practicing purposes, and after perhaps half a dozen brandies I took out my foil."

Mr. Churchill stood up abruptly and then sat down again. He picked up his cigar and then placed it down.

"Naturally, given my spirits, I imagined my captain as my opponent. In my ill temper I removed the button from my foil and attacked him mercilessly. But as I continued both to drink and fence, I became so caught up in the activity that I imagined I had made some remarkable advance in the art of fencing, a method of attack that no defense could parry. It was absurd, of course, but it suited my mood, and I belabored the dummy with one furious assault after another.

"At that unfortunate moment, Josef chose to return from his dinner. To his amazement, I began to assault him, in sport of course, but carelessly. Too carelessly."

Mr. Churchill flushed a bright red. He was evidently in a state of deep embarrassment.

"I was a fool," he said furiously. "Irresponsible! Irresponsible! To handle a weapon in such a manner is unforgivable!"

He struck his hand fiercely on the arm of his chair and then paused for a moment, trembling, before resuming speech.

"I wounded him," he said. "In the hand. He caught the tip of my foil with the heel of his left hand, but the point went slashing across his palm. I could easily have crippled him for life, even killed him! Can you imagine the disgrace, the injury to England?"

"A young man's error," said Holmes.

"Error! An outrage! He bled terribly, but fortunately I was able to summon the surgeon without delay. Although not deep, the wound tore his flesh severely, and his hand required more than twenty stitches. The wound was so broad that the doctor had a great deal of difficulty closing it, and I had to assist him. I had no doubt that my folly had given him a substantial and permanent scar. I was fortunate indeed, I was very fortunate, that the muscles of his hand suffered no impairment."

"When did this incident occur?" asked Holmes.

"Almost a month after Josef had arrived."

"And when were you transferred?"

"A week later. Josef assured me that the injury was nothing, but I am not sure that I believed him. I confess that we were not close. We had given the doctor a story, claiming that the injury occurred during a conventional fencing match, though I doubt if he believed us. I obtained a transfer out of India to Africa only several months after the incident. I fear my commanding officer was not sorry to see my departure."

"And you never saw the archduke again until arriving at Loch Rannoch?"

"No."

"When did you arrive?"

"On the seventh."

"And today is the eleventh. So tell us, Mr. Churchill, what was so remarkable about you meeting with the archduke?"

"Through a variety of mishaps, I arrived late in the evening. I was almost embarrassed to call at all, except that, due to the remote location of Mr. Rhodes's estate, there was no place else to spend the evening. Fortunately, I had alerted Johnnie—Lord Camden—of my arrival, and he met me at the door.

"Mr. Rhodes had already retired. He is, as you may have heard, a most casual host. He gives his guests the run of his house and often occupies himself with business for days on end. Johnnie took me down to the billiard room. He said 'We've got a real archduke here, all the way from Vienna.' That was the first I knew of Josef's presence.

"When we entered the room there were four men standing around the table. Johnnie introduced me all around. There was Lord Catsworth and Dickie Emmons, whom I had known slightly at Sandhurst, for he was in the class after my own, and Freddie Madden-Bonsbright, as well as the archduke. When Johnnie introduced me, I felt vaguely uncomfortable, because I scarcely recognized the man. He resembled the Josef I had known, resembled him quite closely, but I am sure if I had met him on the street I would not have known him for Josef."

"How would you describe his manner toward you?" asked Holmes.

"He was very much at ease, though quite formal. Josef was always quite formal. But he asked me about India, congratulated me on South Africa, and expressed regret that our correspondence had lapsed."

"What happened after that?"

"We played billiards for several hours. During that time I reassured myself that this man was the man I had known in India, although I continued to find the experience unsettling. I particularly noticed a large signet ring on the third finger of the man's right hand, which bore the double-headed eagle of the Hapsburgs. Josef had shown it to me in India, saying that it had once belonged to Charles V."

"And this was the same ring?"

"So it appeared."

"And you continued to converse with him while the five of you played billiards?"

"Yes. And just as we were about to retire, I noticed that he had sort of a stick with him, two pieces of fine polished walnut fitted together, somewhat less than two feet long, like a swagger stick. I made some remark and he told me it was a 'coup stick,' and as he said that word he smiled, as though it were a private joke."

"A coup stick?"

"He said it was an American Indian term, which appeared to amuse him all the more. I could not understand why. He seemed to be having a private joke at my expense, which I did not appreciate. I think somehow I felt he was making a reference to the injury I had done him, which served to prime me for what was to follow."

"And what did follow?"

"He offered me the stick, which I was already half reaching to grasp. As he handed it to me, it so happened that he turned up the palm of his left hand, and I could see that it was utterly unmarked. I was caught off guard, and I stared at that hand for what seemed to be several seconds. And when I lifted my gaze, Mr. Holmes, I was looking directly into the man's eyes. And then I knew. This man was not the archduke!"

"You are sure of this?" said Holmes.

"Absolutely. His hand clenched as our eyes met, and he withdrew the stick from my grasp. I knew he was a fraud, and he knew I knew. No man can call me a coward, Mr. Holmes, but I own that I took a step backward when I looked into those eyes. I have never seen such anger. Those were the eyes of a cornered and an enraged beast. He twisted the stick furiously in his hand and seemed about to separate the two pieces. And then in an instant his manner shifted. He became the Archduke Josef once more, formal, charming, and entirely at his ease."

"Amazing," said Holmes. "You must excuse me, Mr. Churchill, but I know very little of the ways of the members of your class. This could not have been some sort of charade or other amusement?"

"This was no amusement, Mr. Holmes. I felt as though I had lifted the lid on a box of cobras."

"It was not possible that your gaze had reminded him of the accidental injury you had done him, and that this memory was what provoked him?"

"I cannot believe that such an angry wound could have healed without a trace," said Mr. Churchill, somewhat evading the question. "But that is of little matter, for this man who called himself the archduke has vanished without a trace, and none can find him. And, furthermore, his valet has disappeared as well, as has a servant boy."

"This is most disturbing," said Holmes. "Please, finish your story. What did you do after you had this remarkable encounter?"

"There was little I could do, for the moment. The hour was late. The four other gentlemen I was with were all the worse for drink. The only one I knew well was Johnnie. Johnnie's a fine fellow on a horse, none better, but much better on a horse than off. I went to bed full of confusion. In the morning, I wakened early, but could find no one about until midmorning. At that time I discovered that Mr. Rhodes was not even in the house, and not expected back until evening."

"Did you encounter this man who for simplicity's sake we will call the archduke?" asked Holmes.

"No, I did not. A few of Mr. Rhodes's longtime associates were at the house—Charles Metcalf and Lewis Mitchell, as well as Dr. Jameson of the Jameson Raid. Sir Samuel Jenkins, the chief solicitor for De Beers in London, had departed with Mr. Rhodes. None of the gentlemen who remained, I felt, could be trusted with a matter of this delicacy."

"Had you met Mr. Rhodes before?" said Holmes.

"Yes. I have been a guest here twice in the past, once with Mr. Rhodes himself and once as the guest of his younger brother, Colonel Elmhirst Rhodes. And I had met Mr. Rhodes in both London and Cape Town, where I was a guest in his house."

"And so you waited until Mr. Rhodes arrived."

"Yes. I did not speak with him until after ten in the evening. He took my concerns seriously, and after talking the matter over we went to the archduke's suite. We knocked, but no one answered. We knocked for some time, and finally entered using the butler's key. The suite was deserted. After some discussion with the staff, we pieced together the following information: First, that a horse and saddle had been missing since morning. Second, the archduke's valet had been sent by the archduke that morning to take the train to London on some errand. Third, the servant boy, who slept in a small closet at the rear of the archduke's suite, had not been seen for the entire day."

"No one at the stable knew what had become of the horse?"

"No. It was gone before first light. But it is not unusual at Loch Rannoch for a guest to take out a horse on his own. Mr. Rhodes maintains several hunting lodges farther north, in the Grampian Hills. Country living in South Africa is not so formal as it is here."

"And so you had no information."

"None. On the following day the horse reappeared, brought back by a villager who concluded from the quality of the horse that it must have come from here. The horse was found near Blair Atholl, which is the nearest village on the railway, perhaps fifteen miles from here."

"The same town to which Watson and I were delivered this morning."

"Yes."

"Did you speak with the stationmaster?"

"We did. A man answering to the description of the valet had taken the twelve-fifteen the day before, which would bring him into London by the late evening."

"What about the archduke?"

"It is possible for a traveler to catch an early morning train, the four thirty-five, which originates in Inverness, before the arrival of the stationmaster. We were unable to locate the conductor who might have been on that train."

"And there was no trace of the servant boy?"

"None. And there has been no information regarding any of these three individuals since that time."

"I see. And where is Mr. Rhodes?"

Mr. Churchill appeared to be caught off guard by the question.

"Why, he has had some business to handle in Edinburgh. He departed last night by special train."

"And that was some hours after you had completed your investigation?"

"Yes."

"And were you and Mr. Rhodes together for this entire time?"

"Of course not. Why are you worrying me with these questions?"

"I am sorry. I fear that once I begin asking questions I do not know when to stop."

"You certainly do not. The important thing now is to find this scoundrel before a scandal ensues."

"It will be difficult to keep this a private matter," said Holmes. "I do not wish to be an alarmist, but I very much fear that the servant boy will not be found alive. In addition, there is the matter of the true archduke. I find it almost inconceivable that the impostor whom you met four days ago was resident in the Austro-Hungarian embassy for two weeks. Either the true archduke is dead, a statement that I shudder to make, or he is in some manner an accomplice to this deception, a possibility that I must regard with almost equal dismay."

Mr. Churchill stared at my friend in horror.

"That is nonsense!" he proclaimed loudly. "It cannot be! You defame a descendant from one of the proudest families of Europe!"

"I only ask that we confront the realities before us, Mr. Churchill," said Holmes. "And perhaps we should hear from you on the matter of the archduke. You are, perhaps, the only man in England who knows him well."

This statement seemed to strike home. Mr. Churchill lost some of his pugnacity and stared awkwardly at the floor.

"I hardly know what I have to contribute," he said.

"Come now, it's not so bad as that," said Holmes, warming

to the inquiry. "You lived with him for a month. Your remorse over your behavior is understandable, but I suggest that it may be clouding your judgment. What was your opinion of the archduke before the incident?"

"Truthfully, I did not much care for him," said Mr. Churchill reluctantly. "There was a coldness to him that put me off. I felt it my duty to treat him with the utmost courtesy, but I always felt that he held an inner resentment. In particular, he spoke of his father in an ironical manner that I found inappropriate."

"A man of exalted rank but limited prospects might be expected to nurse such an emotion."

"Yes, I suppose. He could be irritating. He would frequently praise me for my lineage, but in such a way as to lead me to believe that he sought me out for no other reason than my rank. And then he would talk of his own family as much greater than mine."

"Not the best form of flattery, perhaps."

To his credit, Mr. Churchill smiled at this remark.

"No, perhaps not. He informed me more than once that he was directly descended from two princely houses—Hapsburg of Austria and Bourbon-Parma of Italy."

"Really?"

"Yes, as though it were not my duty to inform myself of his lineage beforehand as an act of military courtesy."

"You said that his particular branch of the family had suffered reverses. Did he speak to you of these matters?"

"No, but my commander, Colonel Kensington, mentioned this earlier to me. Josef's father, the Archduke Josef Salvator, had, fifteen or twenty years earlier, been a member of the emperor's inner council of advisers, but some sort of financial disaster had forced him to sell the family's palace in Vienna. This reduced the family's position at court."

"So one would imagine."

"Yes. And I recall one incident when Josef received a letter from the diplomatic pouch. It was quite a large envelope, and addressed with such an elegant script that I could only assume it was from his father. He opened it impatiently and began reading. When he reached the second page I saw his face go almost white with rage. I made some small excuse, which I scarcely think he heard, and disappeared as quickly as I could. But before I was well down the hall I could hear him shouting angrily in German. I was horrified. Anyone in the building could have heard him."

Holmes reached out his hand and poured himself a cup of tea.

"Did the gentleman ever discuss this incident with you at a later time?" he asked.

"No. I chose not to return until very late that night, when I could be confident that he would have retired. In the morning, he acted as though nothing had happened—that is, his manner was as bland and as unruffled as ever. I had not the slightest sense of awkwardness or unease on his part."

"So that after this one outburst, his self-possession, which you had observed from the first, returned."

"Yes, and I never saw, or heard, him display such anger again."

"But this incident, I imagine, only confirmed your belief that the gentleman nursed a profound rancor toward his father."

"It did indeed. I felt he was absolutely determined to restore his family to the position it had once enjoyed, though how he intended to do that I could not imagine."

Holmes finished his tea and returned the cup to its saucer.

"This information has been most helpful," he said. "But now perhaps we ought to concern ourselves with the missing boy. Perhaps one of the servants could give us some information. I would also like to inspect the archduke's suite."

"Of course," said Mr. Churchill, reaching for the bell pull. "Jensen can give us the proper details."

A minute later the liveried butler who had met us at the door appeared.

"Jensen," said Mr. Churchill, "our guests would like to inspect the rooms occupied by the archduke. In addition, we would like to speak with someone regarding the missing boy."

"Yes, sir," said the butler. "You will need to speak with Sarah, sir. She is the boy's aunt."

"It would be convenient to conduct the interview in the archduke's rooms," said Holmes.

"Of course, sir," the butler replied. "Please follow me."

Our journey to the archduke's rooms consumed the better part of half an hour as we marched through corridors and up staircases of unlimited opulence until we finally arrived at an elegant suite that, absent a few modern conveniences, had few pieces that were less than one hundred years old. The walls were hung with fine paintings of stags and horses and dogs, and an extraordinary marble fireplace, perhaps six feet high, poured a welcome heat into the chilly rooms.

"You were the first to inspect the rooms when it was discovered that the archduke was missing?" asked Holmes of Mr. Churchill.

"Yes. We questioned the servants at the time. They had been told beforehand that the archduke's valet would tend to all his needs, and that no servant was to enter the suite unless summoned."

Holmes nodded. He opened a large armoire and discovered half a dozen fine suits, along with shirts, ties, shoes, and all the other accoutrements of a gentleman's personal apparel.

"The finest quality, of course," said Holmes, inspecting a coat sleeve with his lens. "And all brand new, I should imagine. I doubt very much if our gentleman was so kind as to leave us any clues. Is this room just as you found it?"

"Yes. Except that a window was open."

"Really? Now, that is interesting. Which one?"

"The large one by the bed."

"Wide open or just a crack?"

"Wide open. But it would be impossible to escape in such a manner."

Holmes went to the window and opened it. We were a good forty feet from the ground, and there was no ornamentation on the severe stone walls that would have allowed a man to climb down.

"Did anyone inspect the ground below?" Holmes asked.

"No. But as you see, the distance is too great."

"Perhaps. But these rooms can hardly be called stuffy, and the winds of the Scottish highlands at this time of year in winter are less than balmy. Why would a man open a window under such conditions?"

"I cannot imagine," said Mr. Churchill rather testily, for he was a man more comfortable asking questions than answering them.

"Excuse me, gentlemen. You wished to see Sarah."

We turned and confronted the butler, who was accompanied by a plain Scottish woman in the dress of a housemaid. Her simple, honest face wore a look of such distress that it was painful to observe her.

"Sirs, you wished to speak to me?" she said with a deep curtsy.

"Yes, Sarah," said Holmes. "I want you to tell me everything you can about the missing boy."

"That would be Jonathan, sir," she said. "My poor sister Mary's boy. She died when he was born, sir, and poor Will, he died not two years later, so I took him in. He's eight years old, sir, and he helps about the house."

"Did he wait upon the archduke?"

"Oh, no, sir. He's just a lad. He wouldn't be fit for such fine service."

"Did the archduke have any contact with him at all?"

The woman's face reddened with pain and embarrassment.

"He did, sir, and that's what worries me so much. You see, one day the gentleman came into his room and he found Jonathan right there on the floor, stretched out with his eyes closed. He made a terrible fuss."

"I should imagine," said Holmes. "Did the boy give an explanation?"

"Well, sir, he said it smelled like hay. That's what he said. He said it smelled like they was cutting in the fields. You see, sir, he spent quite a bit of time in the barns for a while, and he did like the hay."

"Indeed. Perhaps we had better have a look at the room where the boy slept."

"It's not much of a room, sir," the woman said. "It's just a nook."

We exited the archduke's grand suite to enter a servants' hallway, plain and lit only the cold gray light admitted by a single round window at the end of the corridor. The boy's nook was nothing more than the space beneath the back stairs, most of which was given over to storage. His bed was a pair of blankets on the floor. A bare, round candleholder sat beside them.

"There appears to be no sign of violence," said Holmes, kneeling by the blankets and inspecting them. "The boy was not in the habit of disappearing?"

"Oh, no, sir. Jonathan was always a good boy. We never had to scold him."

"Of course not," said Holmes, rising to his feet. "Thank you, Sarah. You have been very helpful."

"Sir, do you think anything's happened to Jonathan?"

"I cannot be certain," said Holmes, "but I do not think you should trouble yourself unduly."

"Oh, thank you, sir, thank you," said the woman, her voice trembling.

"Yes. That will be all, Sarah," said Mr. Churchill with some impatience.

Sarah departed down the stairs while we returned to the archduke's suite. From the expression on Holmes's face, I doubted that his expectations for the boy's fate were nearly as sanguine as he had intimated.

"This is not a pleasant affair," said Holmes, once we were securely within the archduke's suite once more. "I fear that we must have the road from here to the railway station well searched. In the meantime, I must first give these rooms the closest inspection, after which I would like to speak to all the guests."

From the expression on Mr. Churchill's face, I doubted that he regarded my friend's words with much relish, though I could not see what other course of action was possible. The young aristocrat was just about to speak when the door opened, and we were at once in the presence of one of the most famous men alive, the Colossus of Africa, Mr. Cecil Rhodes.

In his appearance, Cecil Rhodes offered perhaps the most extraordinary union of opposites that I have ever beheld in a human being. He was a short, heavyset man, dressed in a dark, wrinkled suit that scarcely fitted him, entirely without the elegance or even the comfort that one might have expected from one of the wealthiest men in the world. From his face blazed forth an almost inhuman energy, a raw, demanding passion that was yet linked with the most desperate ill health. His face was bloated and purplish, and the least effort caused him to gasp for air, infallible symptoms of a heart on the verge of collapse. The sudden, bizarre specter of this dying giant brought our conversation to an immediate halt.

"Good afternoon, Mr. Rhodes," cried Mr. Churchill, springing to his feet. "As you can see, Mr. Holmes has arrived. I felt it appropriate, given the unique issues at hand, to speak with him prior to your arrival."

"A word, Winston," muttered Mr. Rhodes, in a painful voice. "A word with you in private."

"Of course, Mr. Rhodes," said Mr. Churchill. "You gentlemen will excuse me."

The two men exited the room immediately, and as they did so I could hear the key click in the lock. I was about to remark on this impertinence to Holmes when he raised his finger to his lips with an amused look. We heard at first some low muttering from Mr. Rhodes, followed by a terrible fit of coughing, and then more unintelligible speech from Mr. Rhodes, punctuated by an occasional high-pitched shout of protest that could only have come from Mr. Churchill. After the second or third shout the voices faded entirely, as though the two men, fearing that we might overhear them, had advanced farther down the hall. At this point I was about to speak a second time, but once more Holmes dissuaded me. We then waited in silence for a long ten minutes, with nothing better to do than enjoy Mr. Churchill's cigars. At length the two men returned, with a silent and mysterious air.

"There has been an error," Mr. Rhodes told us in his heavy, labored voice. "You men will return to London. I have arranged for you to travel to Blair Atholl by closed carriage, where you will able to catch an afternoon train. We will provide you both with first-class fares."

"But Mr. Rhodes," said Holmes, "I must begin my investigation. The servant boy, whom I very much fear is dead, must be located. The suite and personal effects of the impostor must be thoroughly examined. The effects of the valet as well. There are any number of details that must be attended to before we can even think of returning to London."

"There will be no investigation," said Rhodes harshly. "There is nothing to investigate."

"I confess that I am at a loss, Mr. Rhodes," my friend replied. "Mr. Churchill described for us the terrible scandal that the disappearance of Archduke Josef will create. And there is the matter of the servant boy as well. I greatly fear that the boy has been murdered."

"The archduke has not vanished, Mr. Holmes, and I am sure the servant boy will be found. I fear you misunderstood Winston. He acted in all good faith."

"I fear that it is you that I do not understand," said Holmes. "An impostor entered your house claiming to be the Archduke Josef of Austria. Both the real archduke and the impostor have disappeared. One of your servants has disappeared. This is clearly an extraordinary game, played for very high stakes indeed. The man whom Mr. Churchill has described to us is hardly one to balk at murder, and I very much fear that he has committed at least one already."

"Nonsense!" snapped Mr. Rhodes, his face flushing even a deeper shade of purple as he spoke. "A troublesome servant boy has run away from home. I shall not miss him. Now, Mr. Holmes, you are on my property, and you must go."

Holmes rose to his full height, clearly stung by the rudeness of our host.

"I shall quit your property with the utmost pleasure, Mr. Rhodes," he began, "but Mr. Churchill has given me evidence of a grave conspiracy that involves matters of state. Archduke Josef has disappeared—"

"Archduke Josef has not disappeared, Mr. Holmes," interrupted Mr. Churchill. "You may see for yourself."

As he spoke, he took a copy of the morning's *Times* from his pocket and unfolded it before our eyes. A double-column story bore the headline "Archduke Josef to Depart after Successful Visit." The story that succeeded described an elaborate ball in the archduke's honor, held at the Austro-Hungarian embassy at the conclusion of the archduke's visit to England. "Few of the aristocracy of his nation," the reporter announced, "have made so favorable an impression on London society. His departure is sorely regretted and his return greatly desired."

Holmes stared at the newspaper as if amazed.

"This is remarkable," he said. "Remarkable."

"I have had enough," said Mr. Rhodes. "Winston, see that they leave."

And with that, the Colossus of Africa shambled from our presence, struck by another ugly fit of coughing. Seldom, I must say, have I felt less sympathy for a man in such ill health. For his part, Mr. Churchill glowered under the casual brutality of Rhodes's speech. Clearly, the grandson of a duke was unused to being spoken to in such a manner.

"I apologize for the confusion," he told us awkwardly. "I must ask you, of course, that is, I must warn you, not to speak of this to anyone. For there is nothing here to be discussed. I should be glad to pay you a fee, if that would be appropriate."

"There will be no fee," said Holmes coldly. "And now, Mr. Churchill, Dr. Watson and I are most anxious to make our departure."

It was now Mr. Churchill's turn to flush. Caught between Mr. Rhodes's boorishness and my friend's unflinching integrity, he was afforded no avenue of escape.

"Very well," he said, angrily. "Please follow me."

Mr. Churchill led us back down the long corridors we had taken but two hours before, marching in silence before us at a great pace, intending, no doubt, to vex and exhaust us. We quickly arrived at the great hallway and entrance to the house and exited thence into the enormous courtyard, where a carriage awaited us, its curtains once more drawn. A servant held open the door for us and I stepped inside, but Holmes paused and turned to Mr. Churchill.

"Mr. Churchill," he said, "I tell you now that this is a most unsatisfactory matter, and most dangerous. Mr. Rhodes will, soon enough, be brought to that great accounting that none of us may escape, but you have your whole life and career before you."

"I do," said Mr. Churchill hotly as he glared up at my friend, "and a gentleman such as myself has scant need of advice from a commoner such as you!"

I could not but wince, merely to be in the presence of such a contemptuous rebuff, but Holmes only fixed Mr. Churchill with a colder stare.

"Very well," he said icily, "but I warn you, Mr. Churchill, that this is a bad penny you spend today, a very bad penny indeed, and it shall return, bearing a tarnish not at all to your liking."

And with that, he stepped into the carriage and pulled the door shut behind him. The servant gave a shout, and we were off.

CHAPTER 3

The Baker Street Irregulars

HOLMES SPOKE NOT ONE word for the duration of our carriage journey to the railway station, and continued his silence once we made our connection. When the train paused at Glasgow, he dashed out and returned with an armload of papers, which he perused intently for further news of the archduke's departure. We arrived in London almost exactly twenty-four hours after we had left—that is to say, in the early hours of the morning. When we returned to Baker Street I went, of course, to bed, but Holmes, clearly stung to the quick by his treatment at the hands of Cecil Rhodes, plunged at once into research of the case.

I saw little of Holmes on a day-to-day basis at that time. The living arrangements that we had known for many years had changed dramatically in the new century. I had spent much of 1900 in South Africa, for my skills in military surgery, limited as they were, were in enormous demand due to the horrible casualties produced in that tragic conflict known as the Boer War. When I returned to London I continued to work full-time at Charing Cross Hospital with invalided soldiers, although most of my efforts were in fact devoted to repairing the effects of disease, principally enteric fever, which proved even more cruel than the deadly Mauser rifles wielded by the Boers. I tended to take dinner at my club, where an easy if sometimes shallow conviviality relieved the grim tedium of the day.

My hours had thus become far more regular than they had been in the past, and contrasted ever more sharply with Holmes's bohemian schedule. I was quite surprised to discover him at the breakfast table the next morning, fully dressed and prepared for an outing.

"Good morning, Watson," he said. "I hope you are well rested."

"Quite reasonably," I said. "Have you been up all night?"

"No. I confess at first I was quite perturbed, but have managed to soothe my rancor. Have you time to join me this morning on a visit?"

"I have nothing pressing at surgery. Does this have a bearing on the events in Scotland?"

"One can only hope so. An item in the paper caught my eye several weeks ago. The assistant manager of the firm of Huperman & Co., a Mr. Jonas White, was run down in the street and trampled by horses. The individual responsible has not been apprehended."

"And what would this have to do with our recent visit to Loch Rannoch?"

"Huperman & Co. is the manufacturer of the finest vaults and safes in England. When I saw the item it occurred to me that Mr. White's death might not have been an accident. I made the suggestion to Lestrade, but whether he acted on it I do not know."

"Does Cecil Rhodes have such a safe?"

"Perhaps, and perhaps not. It is a long shot, but the only one we have. I have made an appointment for ten o'clock. I suggest that you go first to Charing Cross and then to Huperman. I believe that Scotland Yard has placed us under observation, to further dissuade me from continuing to investigate this case. I think it unlikely that they will follow you, but they will follow me, and I can more easily elude them if I am on my own."

I departed for Charing Cross with an uneasy mind, not at all sure that Holmes was being reasonable in his suspicions. In any event, if I was being followed, the skill of my pursuers exceeded my ability to detect them. When I arrived I entered quickly and, after reviewing the charts of my patients, departed through a side exit, flagging down a growler and proceeding to Huperman & Co., which proved to be the most discreet of firms. Fashionably located on Bond Street, one could not guess from the exterior the nature of its business. A highly polished brass plate bearing the inscription "Huperman & Co. Appointments Only" is the only indication to the prospective customer that he has in fact reached his intended destination.

When we entered we were greeted by Mr. Huperman himself. He was a short, round man with a genial, almost obsequious manner.

"Mr. Holmes!" he cried. "It is such an honor to have a man of your reputation in my shop."

My friend gave a modest bow.

"Thank you. Mr. Huperman, this is my friend Dr. Watson."

"Ah, Dr. Watson. I have read your accounts faithfully. Never, I believe, have any of the rogues brought to justice by you and your distinguished friend ever violated the integrity of a Huperman safe or vault."

"I believe not," Holmes said dryly. "Now, Mr. Huperman," he continued, glancing about the premises, "you must understand that I must conduct my business with you in the utmost confidence."

"I understand entirely, Mr. Holmes," said the shopkeeper, his voice sinking to a whisper. "All our consultations are, as you know, by appointment only. What passes among the three of us will be overheard by no one and will be repeated by no one. Our clients' privacy, after all, is our single concern."

"Indeed," said Holmes. "That is reassuring to hear. You see, Mr. Huperman, I have in my own work come to possess many secrets. I have in the past been perhaps rather too casual in guarding them. Recently, however, I have enjoyed, shall I say, a substantial improvement in my financial situation, with excellent prospects for continued improvement if only I choose to order my affairs in a more businesslike manner."

I could hardly forbear from smiling at the tones of innocent greed with which Holmes spoke. Mr. Huperman was naturally most sympathetic.

"A gentleman of your unique talents deserves unique financial rewards," he said. "Huperman would be honored to provide you with any assistance in these matters, even the slightest."

"I require, of course, a freestanding safe rather than a vault, but of the most secure design. It will be located in a basement with a secure foundation, so that weight itself should not be a consideration. It should be commodious, for I expect a continuous expansion of my business, and it should be absolutely secure."

"Yes, Mr. Holmes. We have a number of models to which I could direct your attention, but I suggest that we begin with our superlative model, the Goliath 1000."

Mr. Huperman directed us into the back room, which was lined with safes of various sizes, and led us to the "Goliath," a massive steel cube that must have measured at least eight feet in each of its dimensions.

"Beautiful steel," said Mr. Huperman proudly, swinging open the door. "You won't find better on a battleship, and more than a foot thick. The hinges, you see, are entirely recessed within the body of the safe, while the pins themselves are four inches in diameter. To reach them, you must penetrate the entire wall of the safe."

"And the walls, base, and roof are all of the same thickness?" asked Holmes.

"Indeed they are, sir. Inside, you see, we have a large open compartment that can be arranged in a variety of ways, and a number of separate secure drawers."

Holmes examined the secure drawers with extreme care, so much so that Mr. Huperman began to evince some faint signs of distress.

"The finest steel, sir," he said.

"Yes, and excellent locks. The combinations are set by the owner, I should imagine?"

"Of course, Mr. Holmes."

My friend placed his ear almost directly on one of the drawers and turned the mechanism. "Almost inaudible," he said. "Superb work. Even a first-rate cracksman would have to spend twenty minutes on each of these drawers, at a minimum."

"Yes, Mr. Holmes. But no cracksman would ever get the chance. For the outer door is impenetrable. The interior locks only serve to prevent theft by employees."

"Impenetrable, you say," said Holmes, turning his attention to the outer door. "And how is that accomplished?"

"A time lock, Mr. Holmes, controlled by a mechanism concealed within the base of the safe and controlled by these knobs set here. Access through the outer door may be limited to a single hour a day, or as many as twelve. That schedule is set before the safe is shipped, and cannot be altered, unless the owner wishes to set the lock to prohibit entry completely for a given period of time. After that, the regular schedule is resumed."

"Ingenious," said Holmes. "So that the owner himself, even if under duress, could not explain how to open the safe prior to the scheduled hour."

"Yes, Mr. Holmes."

"Ingenious," my friend repeated. "But is there any provision for a true emergency? A profession like mine knows no hours. Suppose it were absolutely necessary to open the safe in the middle of the night."

"In that case, Mr. Holmes, you could summon me, for there is an override—complex, and different for each safe. I could not, and do not, carry such information in my head. But I could obtain it, and come to your assistance. Of course, we would make arrangements suitable to yourself to ensure that this procedure could not be abused."

"Excellent," said Holmes. "Yes, this is a remarkable mechanism. I only wish I had more experience in these matters."

"Trust me, Mr. Holmes. This safe is worthy of your highest consideration."

"I am sure that is so," said Holmes, though his expression and tone belied his words. "The cost, I fear, must be considerable."

"The finest is always costly, but in the end the only true bargain," said Mr. Huperman.

"Well said, Mr. Huperman, well said," my friend replied. But he still studied the safe with a doubtful air.

"I should not tell you this, Mr. Holmes, but when I consider your great reputation, I feel confident. Two of these safes were recently purchased by none other than Mr. Cecil Rhodes himself."

"Really?" exclaimed Holmes. "Now, that is remarkable."

Mr. Huperman rubbed his hands together, pleased with himself. "Yes, excellent testimony indeed," he said.

"What do you think, Watson?" said Holmes. "Shall we inspect Mrs. Hudson's basement to see if we can prepare there a proper reception for this remarkable safe?"

"I think we should," I said.

"We can prepare the contract right now," said Mr. Huperman. "It is quite possible to undertake construction of your safe on the premises. It is, in fact, recommended."

"Indeed," said Holmes. "But there a few matters that must be attended to first. I confess I did not adequately consider the dimensions of such a device. Yet I do think it possible. Still, I must be sure. The masonry may need repair, and I have doubts about the door."

In such a manner Holmes and I made our retreat from the eager Mr. Huperman.

"We shall hear from him in the future," said Holmes as we stepped out into a dull, gray autumn afternoon that held very little memory of summer.

"You did not ask him about Jonas White," I said.

"If I had, he would have told us nothing. I am confident that the impostor who disappeared from Loch Rannoch was a cunning thief and almost surely the murderer of poor Mr. White, who I suspect badly betrayed his employer's trust."

"You think that this Jonas White revealed the secret of the overrides for the safes purchased by Cecil Rhodes?"

"Yes, and paid for it with his life. I am tempted to visit

Mrs. White, though I fear to do so might draw the attention of the Yard."

"Why would they be concerned?"

"My dear Watson, Scotland Yard is now as concerned to prevent us from investigating this case as they once were for having us solve it. I believe I have obtained information sufficient for one day."

As we were engaged in this conversation we observed a young girl, occupied as a crossing sweeper, industriously moving the mounds of manure deposited by passing horses out of the way of passersby.

"Is that you, Jennie?" asked Holmes, bending over to contemplate the little ragamuffin. "I hardly recognized you in that bonnet."

"Do you like it, Mr. Holmes?" the girl replied coquettishly, though she could hardly be more than nine. With her face upturned I could now recognize her as a new recruit to the Baker Street Irregulars, a scarcely reputable collection of street urchins whom my friend relied on from time to time as sources of information in London.

"I do indeed, Jennie. Have you had enough of sweeping today? I've got a case, and a good one, for the lot of you."

"I dunno, Mr. Holmes," the young girl said. "I've got a box of pennies, and it's scarcely dinner."

To demonstrate, she held up the worn, stiff pocketbook that hung from a string around her thin shoulders and rattled it vigorously.

"There's more than pennies in this case," said Holmes. "I'll give you a shilling to round up the lot and bring them to 221-B by noon."

"You want us all at once?" the girl asked.

"Yes, everyone, for there is much to see. Tell them it's a shilling all around if everyone's in by two."

"But what about me? Ain't you giving me extra?"

"Here's two pennies now and a shilling later. Now stop talking, Jennie, for there's no time to waste."

Holmes gave the girl two pennies, which she put gleefully into her pocketbook.

"Thank you, Mr. Holmes," the girl said with an impish curtsy. "Thank you very much."

And with that she shouldered her broom and headed off rapidly down the street.

"What do you expect from those urchins?" I asked.

"Another long shot, Watson," Holmes said, pausing to light a cigar. "But there must have been a moment when the true archduke became the false one. I confess at this point that I cannot imagine how it was done, or how the deception was maintained. But one possibility is that the true archduke had been hiding in a hotel until the night before last. I do not know if he would dare to trust the Austrian embassy to acquiesce in his deception. Then there is the matter of the valet. An accomplice or a dupe? Is he alive or dead? At any rate, I believe that for a short time both the false archduke and the true one were in London together, though surely not in public."

Holmes broke off his discussion to raise his hand to hail a passing hansom. Once inside, rather than continuing our conversation, he sank back in his seat with his cigar, deep in thought. I followed his example, and, as we wheeled through London's teeming streets, I stared through the window at the passing scene and wondered at Holmes's prospects for solving the case. Who was the mysterious individual who apparently had impersonated the Archduke Josef? What was the purpose of the impersonation? Holmes had implied that as many as three murders had been committed, but for what purpose, when Mr. Rhodes insisted that there had been no crime? And what was the role of the true archduke?

I had no answer to any of these questions when our carriage halted in Baker Street. I had several matters to attend to before leaving for my afternoon rounds at Charing Cross. I hoped to arrange for my departure prior to the arrival of the Irregulars, but a shout of dismay from Mrs. Hudson informed me that I had failed to do so.

"Will you show in our visitors, Watson?" Holmes asked. "Mrs. Hudson, so it appears, is overwhelmed."

"Of course."

I went to the entrance and discovered a pack of perhaps

half a dozen dirty, sharp-eyed children. Jennie, the child we had earlier encountered, was the only girl among them.

"Are you Dr. Watson?" the tallest said to me in an almost accusatory tone.

"Yes, I am," I replied.

"I thought so," he said. "You can tell Mr. Holmes that the Baker Street Irregulars are here."

"I can see that for myself," I said sharply. "Wipe your feet carefully and come inside, and don't touch anything."

At the words "come inside" I heard another shout from Mrs. Hudson. However, I carefully supervised the foot cleaning and led the pack of them up to our rooms.

"Ah, there you are, Watson," said Holmes. "I believe we will hold our little meeting in the dining room."

Fortunately, Mrs. Hudson was not available to hear Holmes's last remark. He led the way into the dining room, where he had arranged eight chairs around our table. The children took their places at the table with commendable promptness, while Holmes sat before them at its head, a large leather notebook in his hands. The spectacle of one of the supreme intellects of Europe addressing such an assembly was hardly one to miss, and I stood in the doorway, watching.

"Now, children," said Holmes, placing the notebook on the table and taking out his cherrywood, "this is a most remarkable case. There is only a slim chance that there is information to be obtained, but we must take that chance. There are two points on which I require your assistance. Did you all hear about the fellow run down in Pritchard Street?"

His question elicited a chorus of affirmative exclamations from the children, who evidently had an exceptional memory for any incident in the London streets that involved violent death.

"They say he was trampled proper, so they do," pronounced the tall boy. "Busted his insides all over, they say."

The children appeared delighted by this detail.

"So it would seem, Jenkins," said Holmes. "If this case had been investigated properly at the time, much might have been done. It is still possible that we can determine who it was who drove the carriage. We are looking for that man, and we are looking for a second man. We are looking for two men who look almost exactly alike."

Holmes paused to stuff his cherrywood with navy cut and struck a match. He lit the pipe and drew upon it heavily. The children watched in silence.

"One of the men we are seeking," he said, once he had the cherrywood properly lit, "is a high aristocrat from Europe. This is not the man who was driving the carriage. I will not tell you his name, for I don't wish you to use it, or even where he is from, but this is his picture."

Holmes took out a formal photograph of the archduke, showing him in court finery and looking every inch an aristocrat. The picture showed a young man with regular features, a high, aquiline nose, large, clear eyes, and carefully tended side whiskers that echoed, in subdued fashion, the full beard of the emperor himself.

"Now, that is a toff," exclaimed one of the Irregulars, passing the photograph to Jennie.

"Cor, look at the b——y b——d!" she cried with excitement, the final words of her statement casting a slur upon the parenting of the archduke with such pungency that I have in all good conscience no choice but to omit them from the pages of this narrative.

"Quite," said Holmes. "Here are several pictures more, that are not so clear but show him in more conventional dress."

Holmes passed out several photographs of the archduke, cut from periodicals, and the children studied them with absolute absorption.

"He's got a fancy ring, hasn't he, Mr. Holmes?" asked Jennie as she studied one of the photographs.

"Yes, Jennie, that is a detail worth mentioning, and it was clever of you to notice. It is an unusual ring, and it looks like this."

Holmes took a paper from the folder that bore the image of the crest of the Hapsburgs.

"Now, children, don't ask anyone if they've seen a fellow with a two-headed eagle on his ring. Let them tell you. Do you understand?"

"Right," said Jenkins with a knowledgeable tone. "Don't give up nothing. Let them do the talking, and you do the listening."

"Yes, Jenkins. If only Scotland Yard were half so astute."

The lad swelled with pleasure at Holmes's remarks.

"So, Mr. Holmes," he said grandly, "what's this fellow done?"

"That's a good question," said Holmes. "I do not know precisely what he has done, but I do know what he has enabled another man to do. For, as I mentioned to you, there is a second man, who looks so like this first one that they could be twins. I do not know this man's name. I suspect he uses more than one. But I can tell you this: he is the man who drove the carriage. He is a murderer twice over, and would cut your throats in an instant."

"A murderer?" cried Jennie, even more pleased.

"Yes, Jennie," said Holmes, "and that is why I am not going to tell you the first man's name. I do not want it known, either third- or fourth-hand, that you have been looking for him. Now, both gentlemen arrived in London approximately one month ago, but they did not travel together. I believe that one took a suite of rooms in a fine hotel, while the other stayed in a private mansion. Then, one day, the gentleman in the hotel left for Scotland, and, quite possibly, the second man replaced him at the hotel. If he did not, the second man surely found elegant private lodgings of some sort and stayed hidden away for several weeks. It is almost impossible that either man should still be in London."

"What do you want us to do, then?" asked Jenkins.

"I want you to find anyone who knows anything about a gentleman in hiding, a gentleman who looks like the gentleman in the picture."

"You want us to find a man that hasn't been seen, and isn't here now, is that it?" the urchin replied.

"That is precisely what I want," said Holmes. "You must talk to the lowest people in the highest places, the scullery maids and the slop boys, to learn whatever you can."

"That's a tall order, Mr. Holmes," said Jenkins, with surprising shrewdness. "There ain't many in a fine hotel that would talk to the likes of us."

"I understand that," said Holmes. "But there is a story here, if you can find the person to tell it, and if you've got the ears to hear it. Whoever can help me will receive a crown, and two shillings each for the rest."

The mention of a sum of money so vast as a crown created a great intake of breath among the children. Even Jenkins appeared moved.

"A crown!" he exclaimed. "We'll find your toff, Mr. Holmes, don't you worry!"

"Excellent," said Holmes.

The children filed out, provoking another shout from Mrs. Hudson as they descended the stairs.

"Do you really think they can provide you with useful information?" I asked Holmes, once they had departed.

"Of course they can," said Holmes as we walked into the sitting room. He took a chair by the fire and exchanged the cherrywood for his churchwarden.

"Whether they can obtain it is another," he said, extending his long legs to rest on the footstool before the hearth. "Our false archduke must have had an alias of some sort. No doubt he has discarded it by now, but even to have some idea of his past movements would be worthwhile. Anything is better than idleness. Now I fear I must request a measure of solitude, Watson. I have been so anxious to obtain new information that I have not had the full opportunity to consider fully the knowledge I already have."

I did not bother to reply. Holmes's concentration was such that he took no notice of my departure, as indeed was his habit more frequently than not. Once I entered Charing Cross I quickly lost myself in the day's routine and worked until eight, when I departed for dinner at the Galenians. I did not return to Baker Street until after ten, but when I arrived, there was no sign of Holmes. I was relaxing with a glass of brandy and a copy of the *Times* when Holmes entered, wearing a reddish-orange check suit of such appalling vulgarity that I could not restrain my mirth.

"My dear fellow," I cried, "where did you obtain such a garment?"

"It is frightful," he said, "but it has served me remarkably well. After several hours of thought, I decided that I must pay a visit to Mrs. White after all, though as a correspondent for the *Daily Mail* rather than as myself."

"And what did Mrs. White have to say?"

"She had nothing to say, for she no longer resides at her former address. She now makes her home in the south of France."

"The south of France?"

"Yes. I obtained this information, and a great deal more, from Miss Gwladys Soames, a near neighbor of the Whites, in return for a fine dinner of sprats and oysters at Molesworth's. Apparently the couple argued frequently, but in recent months had achieved a reconciliation of sorts. By purest chance, Miss Soames obtained information of their purchase of a small villa in Cannes. It appeared that the couple was planning to retire there when Mr. White was struck down."

"And do you think that this suggests that Jonas White was bribed to provide knowledge of the override?"

"I do."

"Yet you have no real evidence that either of the safes that Cecil Rhodes purchased was placed in Loch Rannoch."

"No, I do not. But I am confident that that information will come. There are many areas of this case that can be explored surreptitiously, Watson, without arousing the attention of Mr. Churchill or Mr. Rhodes, and I intend to do so."

Holmes's determination to continue his investigation was confirmed a week later by the delivery of a stout bundle of newspapers, a full year's output for the *Cape Town Gazette,* for the year 1890. Subsequent bundles followed, which so filled our sitting room that navigation became close to impossible. Holmes also arranged to receive several current Scottish newspapers by mail and spent long hours in conversation with his brother Mycroft at the Diogenes, to learn from that remarkable, and remarkably diffident, intellect all that it was possible for an Englishman to know regarding the affairs of the aristocratic houses of Austria-Hungary. During this time he also made far more frequent use of his Stradivarius than was his custom, to the extent that it was not uncommon for me to wake to its melancholy and fantastic strains. Yet for all that, I had no real inkling of the depth of Holmes's emotions regarding the case until a Saturday perhaps four weeks after we had journeyed to Loch Rannoch. I was enjoying an afternoon cigar when Holmes entered the room and flung down one of his Scottish papers with an oath.

"There you are, Watson!" he cried. "British justice at its finest!"

I picked up the paper and, after finding the article that must have offended him, read it aloud:

"Proceedings of the Coroner's Court. The death of one Jonathan McPherson, from internal bleeding, which occurred in the past month, has been ruled an accident. The boy, age eight, was a servant at the house of Mr. Cecil Rhodes. The body was found at the base of a cliff several miles from Mr. Rhodes's estate at Loch Rannoch. The injuries to the boy's head have been ruled consistent with a fall, which could have produced the internal bleeding. Prolonged inquiry has failed to discover the least evidence of foul play."

"Prolonged inquiry," snapped Holmes. "It has taken them a month, they mean, to construct this absurd and shameless tissue of lies."

"What do you propose to do?" I asked.

"What *can* I do? Other than making a public nuisance of myself, which would simply play into their hands. I never saw the body, after all. I can offer no direct evidence of any kind. I could only recount the circumstances of our visit to Loch Rannoch, which would be denied by all involved."

"Have you discussed your suspicions regarding the death of Jonas White with the Yard?"

"I have explored a variety of approaches with regard to this matter, Watson," said Holmes with some asperity. "They have all failed."

"Perhaps a personal appeal to Sir Robert would be in order."

My remarks, though well intended, were mere tinder to Holmes's wrath.

"A personal appeal to Sir Robert would in all likelihood fetch me an extended period of confinement at Dartmoor, which, under the circumstances, might be an improvement. Now, if you will excuse me, I have much to consider."

CHAPTER 4

A Crown for Jennie

HOLMES'S MANNER OF SPEECH was so peremptory that I felt it best to take my leave. Since the morning displayed a rare clemency for late October, I chose to take a stroll in the park with Betty, with whom I had fortunately become more closely acquainted. I did not return to Baker Street until the early hours of the morning. Scarcely had I retired but I was awakened by an indistinct yet persistent commotion that seemed to be coming from the stairwell beneath our flat. By the time I had put on my robe and slippers I could identify the voice and occasionally the words of Mrs. Hudson, whose tone betrayed a justifiable irritation at being awakened at such an hour. I hurried to assist the good woman with whatever intruder might be distressing her. Imagine my surprise when I descended the stairs to discover her assailant to be none other than the street urchin Jennie!

"Dr. Watson!" the child cried at my approach. "Tell Mr. Holmes I've found his toff! I want my crown!"

I instantly realized from Jennie's exultant manner that however unlikely her assertion and however inappropriate the hour, no voice but Holmes's could cause her to withdraw her claims. Reluctantly I took her hand, which was far from clean and terribly cold, for the temperature had fallen sharply since the morning, and led her past Mrs. Hudson, who I think in all the years that Holmes and I had been resident at Baker Street had never regretted our presence more intensely than at that moment. Fortunately, by the time I arrived at our door, Holmes was already awakened.

"Good morning, Jennie," he said, adjusting the gas jet. "You say you have good news?"

"I've found your toff, Mr. Holmes. He's in London right now."

"Right now, Jennie? Are you sure? That hardly seems possible."

"But he *is,* Mr. Holmes. I know all about it."

"Have you seen him, Jennie? Please have a seat, here by the fire. Watson, if at all possible, could you prevail on Mrs. Hudson for some coffee, and perhaps some milk and bread and butter for the child? Perhaps we could provide her with an extra guinea this month for her troubles."

I set off in search of Mrs. Hudson, resolving, however, to make the sweetener two guineas rather than one. When I returned, Holmes was engaged in splitting a lump of coal in the fire with the poker to enhance its combustion, while Jennie, wrapped in a blanket, huddled before the hearth.

"It is hardly a night to be out and about, dressed as you are, Jennie," Holmes said, giving the coal a final blow.

"It's a proper time for fancy folk," said Jennie. "You know, Mr. Holmes, when you told us about this feller, I thought, a fancy feller like that, he might fancy a fancy lady. So I went round to Dolly Marigold's. I know a girl, Nellie, who does her laundry. There ain't no laundry like Dolly Marigold's, Mr. Holmes. Have you ever seen it?"

"No, Jennie, not precisely."

"It's lovely stuff, Mr. Holmes. But Nellie didn't have nothing to tell me. But I come across her last night, and she says 'Do you remember those two fellers that you was asking about that was twins?' And I says yes I do, and she says they was here, because she heard a couple of Dolly's girls talking about them, how one of them was come back. And so I went round."

"You went to Dolly Marigold's?"

"In the alleyway, Mr. Holmes. I couldn't go during the day, not me, could I? I had to wait."

"And what did you learn, Jennie?"

"I didn't learn nothing, for a copper run me off. The coppers take good care of Dolly, they do."

"Yes, Jennie."

"And so I come here. I figured you'd want to know. And I want my crown."

"And you shall have it, Jennie, if this information is correct. But tell me, what precisely did Nellie say about the twins, as she called them?"

"She said it was a couple of Dolly's girls. She didn't know their names. She said these twins had a couple of girls at the Metropole and now one of them was back looking for them."

"When was this, Jennie? Today is Wednesday morning. When did you have this conversation with Nellie?"

"It wasn't yesterday, Mr. Holmes, because I come over to Dolly's yesterday, and I come over here today. So it was the day before yesterday."

"Ah. Unfortunately, now is not the time to call on the estimable Miss Marigold. We must wait a few hours at least. But here is Mrs. Hudson. Would you care for some breakfast, Jennie?"

Mrs. Hudson set the tray before us. Holmes poured a glass of milk and passed it to Jennie, along with a plate of bread and butter. He then poured coffee for the two of us. I watched Jennie eat with mingled delight and horror, for she had the appetite of a grenadier and no more manners than an infant. As I saw the black on her fingers blend with the butter on her bread I realized for the first time the utter brutality of her environment. This child lived, in the greatest city in the world, a life as scarcely touched by the ameliorative hand of civilization as that of the basest African savage.

"How would you spend a crown?" I asked her when she had completed her assault on the bread and butter.

"I'll buy me a fine new dress and coat, I will," she said. "And sticky buns all day, won't I?"

"But where do you live, Jennie?"

"Live? I live wheres I can, Dr. Watson. A girl lives where she can. Don't worry about me. I'm too smart for the coppers."

She grinned widely as she delivered this last piece of information. Holmes, I knew, must have been following my thought processes. I was about to speak when he forestalled me.

"Jennie," he said, "it occurs to me that you are a valuable witness for this case. I think it would be better if you remained here for the time being."

"Here!" she cried in horror and amazement. "Why?"

"I have told you that this fellow is a murderer twice over. He has killed a boy younger than you. Having once started, he is not about to stop."

"But how will I spend my crown?"

"Dr. Watson and I will purchase your new clothes. In the meantime, Dr. Watson will give you a bath and you shall have one of my shirts for a dress."

These new domestic arrangements, foisted upon Jennie with so little warning, were far from her liking, but we gave her no choice. The notion of cleanliness I fear was utterly foreign to Jennie's spirit. I do not believe she had ever had contact with soap and water in her life. She howled at every outrage, protesting the cleaning of her ears with particular vehemence. When she was clean at last I discarded her rags and clothed her in one of Holmes's shirts. Then I brought her into the sitting room, where she curled in a chair by the fire, stunned by the transformation that had been visited upon her.

"You look much better, Jennie," I told her.

"I don't feel better," she remarked sullenly. "I want back my clothes."

"You shall have fine new clothes," I said.

"I want my old clothes," she breathed.

"Your life has changed, Jennie," I told her. "You shall sleep here. You will have the pageboy's bed under the stairs. You shall have a bed at night and three meals a day."

Her little face betrayed no pleasure at the riches we were bestowing on her. Holmes suddenly returned, bearing a sticky bun he had no doubt obtained from a vendor near the entrance of the underground. He handed it to Jennie, who consumed the confection in a bitter and aggrieved silence. Holmes and I then retreated to the hallway, where we had a brief discussion regarding Jennie's immediate future. Mrs. Hudson's reservations, however numerous, could surely be overborne with cash. I told Holmes that I would arrange for one of the nurses at Charing Cross to obtain several changes of clothes appropriate for a child of Jennie's age, and that for the long term I would approach Betty on the possibility of assuming long-term responsibility for Jennie, perhaps as a servant girl for her mother, Eunice. I had in fact significant doubts as to Jennie's enthusiasm for such service, but one could hope that after a few weeks of civilization she would be willing to endure much to retain its comforts. Once these arrangements were settled, Holmes and I departed for Miss Dolly Marigold's, to determine if the story that Jennie had brought to us could be corroborated in fact.

Miss Marigold resided in a charming, discreet home on the far side of Regent's Park, erected by the Duke of Rutland in the time of George II. She was well known among both the upper and lower classes, though her career, and that of women like her, was a complete mystery to those in the middle, who at that time preferred to believe that sensual pleasure, if such a thing existed at all, could only be found in France.

We were received by Miss Marigold at ten o'clock in the morning. It was, unsurprisingly, not easy to obtain an impromptu interview with such a person, requiring no small amount of firmness on Holmes's part to convince the powerfully built footmen at the entrance that they should disturb their mistress with his note at such an unreasonable hour. And once the note was accepted, we were obliged to wait some twenty minutes before being taken into the great lady's presence.

Dolly Marigold was a tall, blond woman, somewhat theatrical in manner, but with a remarkable shrewdness that one might expect in a woman who had risen to the top of such a precarious and ambiguous profession. Her spacious apartment, furnished entirely in period antiques, commanded an excellent view of the park.

"Mr. Holmes," she said, rising, "it is so good to see you again. And you are Dr. Watson?"

"Yes," I said, nodding.

"Please, have a seat," she said, gesturing to a pair of gilt armchairs.

Once we were seated, Miss Marigold turned her attention to my friend.

"You said in your note, Mr. Holmes, that this was a matter of extreme urgency."

"Indeed it is," said Holmes. "These are the facts as I have them. Please tell me if I have been misinformed. Somewhat more than a month ago, two of your young ladies attended to two men, who appeared to be twins, at the Metropole. In the past few days, one of those gentlemen has returned. I strongly suspect that he has asked for the same two girls again."

"Yes," said Miss Marigold.

"Where are they now?"

"I am not sure, Mr. Holmes. The gentleman, to all accounts, is very highly placed. I agreed to put matters entirely in his hands."

"When did they depart?"

"The day before yesterday."

"We must speak with whomever saw them last."

Miss Marigold paused. With jeweled fingers, she removed a cigarette from a golden cigarette box and lit it with a golden lighter. Then she confronted my friend and smiled.

"You have a great reputation, Mr. Holmes," she said. "We have collaborated on a number of occasions, I believe, to mutual satisfaction."

"Your assistance in the Argentine matter was most helpful," said Holmes.

"As was yours in that unfortunate affair involving the Duke of York," said Miss Marigold. "But our interests do not always run on parallel lines. My clients desire two things, discretion and beauty, and I strive to provide both without measure. You say there is danger. I must demand that you convince me of that."

Now it was my friend's turn to pause. As he did so, Miss Marigold placed the cigarette box before us.

"Please, gentlemen," she said, "help yourself to my tobacco. It is quite masculine, and, I assure you, without affectation or adulteration of any kind. I am a poor hostess to greet you thus. We will have tea."

Miss Marigold rose and rang for a servant. Almost instantly, an extremely attractive though somewhat awkward young woman appeared, wearing a French maid's costume of irresistible severity.

"Helen," Miss Marigold said, "we will have tea."

"Yes, madam," the girl replied, in an accent that seemed to waver uncertainly between Cheapside and Kensington. "Will you prefer the gold service or the red?"

"The gold, Helen," Miss Marigold said, struggling to repress a smile, for it appeared that not even her elegant imperturbability of manner was proof against the girl's naive charm.

"So innocent and yet so eager," she remarked, once the maid had departed. But there was, I fear, cool if not heartless cunning in the depths of her voice. Despite all her charms, Miss Marigold was a woman of business in the most elemental sense of the term.

"Quite," said Holmes. "To return to the issue at hand."

"You are most insistent, Mr. Holmes."

"I am. I understand your intense desire not to offend a client, particularly those of exalted pedigree. But I assure you that I am motivated entirely by my concern for the well-being of the employees."

"Really, Mr. Holmes," said Miss Marigold. "In our past dealings, you have always been so scrupulous to respect the privacy of my clients. Why now do you insist on frightening me?"

"Because, Miss Marigold, I am convinced that we are dealing with dangerous and ruthless men. Is it not your custom to interview your girls after such an elaborate affair?"

"I like to ensure that everything went smoothly," said the lady.

"And what did the young ladies have to say of their clients? Did they, perhaps, make reference to a certain viciousness in their manner?"

It was clear from the expression on Miss Marigold's face that my friend's last inquiry had hit home. Gratefully, she welcomed the distraction afforded by Helen's arrival with the tea service, whose golden opulence seemed to blaze like a miniature sun.

"Just place it on the table, Helen," Miss Marigold said. "I so prefer the Mandarin at this time of day, Mr. Holmes. I hope you do not object."

"The Mandarin is excellent," said Holmes, taking the golden cup and saucer in hand and passing it to me. "Such extraordinary porcelain. Where did you obtain it?"

"I am so glad you like it," she said. "It was a gift of a very generous man, very highly placed. It gave him a great deal of pleasure to see it in use. He said it reminded him of his mother. Please, have a biscuit."

The biscuits, needless to say, were as sugared as every other aspect of Miss Marigold's abode. I ate one and drained my cup, which Miss Marigold then quickly refilled.

"The two gentlemen," said Holmes, returning to his topic once more. "Did the girls have anything to say?"

"Nothing, I fear, for the ears of an outsider," said Miss Marigold almost primly. "You really cannot expect me to violate the privacy of a client, Mr. Holmes. And the girls did not hesitate to go again."

"Then I only ask you to hold what they told you in mind," said Holmes. "Several weeks ago, Dr. Watson and I were summoned, in the middle of the night, on an errand at the behest of a very high personage. He spoke of a visit from a distinguished foreign visitor, and of his distressed discovery that the gentleman was not whom he appeared to be, but rather an impostor. What he told me then, and what I have deduced since, have convinced me that both gentlemen were involved in a remarkable conspiracy, whose full dimensions I cannot yet discover. But I can tell you this, that at least two people have already died as a result of this conspiracy, and I would be remiss if I did not tell you that I believe the lives of your two young women to be in danger."

"You know, Mr. Holmes, that I have a very great horror of the police."

"No doubt. But surely you have an equal horror of deadly violence directed against your girls."

At last Miss Marigold's immaculate self-confidence seemed to falter.

"Are you convinced there is danger?" she asked, lowering her eyes.

"I am. The essence of this conspiracy is that no one must know that there are two gentlemen rather than one. They have gone to remarkable and so far successful lengths to cover their deception. I fear that the ultimate goal of this second rendezvous is to maintain their position by eliminating the last possible witnesses."

"This personage you speak of, Mr. Holmes. May I have his name?"

"I am reluctant to discuss that. However, I will say that I was called to the case by Sir Robert Johnson, in person."

"I see. You understand, to interrupt a client is the most unforgivable of transgressions."

"I do understand. Yet, as you have been so kind to mention, in the few instances in the past when our paths have crossed, we have been able to achieve resolutions that were mutually satisfactory."

"That is very true."

"Then I can only ask you to have faith in my judgment on the basis of past experience."

Miss Marigold paused for a long minute and then reached for the bell rope, giving it two very swift tugs. Helen entered almost immediately.

"Helen," Miss Marigold said, "I am trying to determine the whereabouts of Daisy and Patricia. Do you know where they are?"

"Well, madam, they're out."

"Of course they are out. Do you know where?"

"No, madam," Helen cried, looking distraught.

"No, of course not, Helen. I am not angry with you. However, it is important that we find them. When did you see them last?"

"It was a quarter to ten on Monday, madam. The gentleman sent a carriage round. It was ever so splendid."

"Please, tell us more about the vehicle's appearance," said Holmes.

The girl seemed disturbed by the sudden demand.

"Comply with the gentleman's wish," said Miss Marigold crisply.

The poor girl, whose duties, one may assume, never before included the close description of carriages, was reduced to a stammer.

"It was ever so large," she began.

"What was the color?" Holmes snapped.

"Oh, dark blue, like madam's shoes."

"Gilt on the wheel spokes?" asked Holmes.

"Why, yes, sir. It was so pleasant. I do like gilt."

"And a crest on the door? Gilt as well?"

"There were a bit of a crown, sir. That's what it was. A bit of a crown. And all gold, like you say."

"Harrison's," said Holmes. "Finest equipage in London. What about the driver? Did you see him?"

"The driver, sir?"

"Yes. Did he get down to help the ladies?"

"I don't believe he did, sir. The girls, they was all giggling. Daisy and Patricia, they're so lively. So the driver, I don't think he got down."

"I see. Now tell us about Daisy and Patricia. What do they look like, and what were they wearing?"

"Oh, sweet," said the girl, with a touch, I thought, of skepticism, for it is my experience that young ladies are not uniformly generous in their descriptions of one another.

"English," said Miss Marigold abruptly. "Foreign gentlemen often express an interest in English girls."

"Quite blond, then, one may assume, with blue eyes and pink cheeks?" asked Holmes.

"Well, Patricia, she's a bit pale, you know," said the maid. "She tries to cover it up, all right. And she's got that mole by her mouth."

"Tell us about their clothes, Helen," interrupted Miss Marigold.

"Yes, madam," said the girl, flushing a bit. "Well, Daisy, she had on that lemon-yellow frock. She does look sweet, all right, and her calf shoes, the black ones, all laced up tight. The gentlemen do like that, I know. And Patricia, she was very pink, with her fringed scarf from Paris. That's pink as well, you know."

"What about luggage?" asked Holmes.

"Oh, boxes and boxes," said the girl.

"The gentleman expressed an interest in clothes," said Miss Marigold. "I believe that on his first visit he purchased many items for Daisy and Patricia."

"And perhaps he wanted them back," said Holmes. "Helen, one last thing: Are you sure that the girls didn't say anything about where they were going?"

"Oh, I'm positive, sir. They didn't say. It was a secret."

"Very well. Did the driver say anything?"

"Well, he did, sir, now that you mention it. One of the boxes fell off and the girls were all laughing and the driver said 'Here now, you'd better be sharp if you want to make the eleven-ten at Paddington.' "

"Thank you, Helen," said Holmes. "You have been very helpful."

"That will be all, Helen," said Miss Marigold.

"Yes, madam," said the girl, retreating uncomfortably.

"Watson and I must be off," said Holmes once Helen had disappeared. "You may be sure that we will exercise the utmost in caution."

"Please do so, Mr. Holmes," said Miss Marigold with a slight edge to her voice. "Our relations have been mutually beneficial in the past. I should very much hope for them to remain so in the future."

"I entirely agree. Now, Watson, we must make haste for Paddington."

We made our departure and engaged a hansom.

"The madam has given us remarkable entry," said Holmes as we headed toward the railway station.

"You think she can be trusted?" I asked.

"Oh, she has a natural fear of compromising a client's privacy. I fear there is no danger of that."

"You believe the women are dead, then."

Holmes gazed out the window.

"I do. The extraordinary coincidence of Mr. Churchill's appearance at Loch Rannoch was a severe blow to this scheme, whatever it is. They have repaired the damage, but now must eliminate all traces of the impersonation. I cannot imagine that this individual, whoever he is, would engage these girls a second time for merely sensual purposes. No, they are witnesses. I think it unlikely that we will discover them alive."

"You are confident that we can discover their destination?"

"Yes. There is a reasonable chance that the arrival of a fine coach bearing two attractively dressed young ladies with a gift for display would not go unnoticed, particularly if they used the first-class entrance."

Holmes's surmise proved to be correct. The attendant at the first-class entrance remembered the young ladies vividly, and made a point of assisting them to their compartment personally, aboard the eleven-ten with tickets to Southend-on-Sea. Holmes and I then boarded the twelve-twenty for the same destination, a trip that, owing to a derailment on the line ahead, took almost three hours to complete. After finally arriving at that rather raffish port, we learned from the stationmaster that two very attractive young ladies had departed the station by four-wheeler two days before. A search for the driver consumed the better part of four hours. We finally discovered the man, much the worse for gin, in a disreputable public house. For two shillings he provided us with an address but adamantly refused to assist us in finding the place, describing it only as "a lovely house on the water." Even the prospect of a gold sovereign failed to change his purpose, so intent was he to complete his inebriation.

Although, as Holmes said, the trail had grown dangerously cold, we persisted in our search. The hour was approaching midnight when, with the assistance of an honest constable, we approached a home that was indeed "a lovely house on the water." However, as we approached the gate the simple fellow naturally gave rein to his trepidation at the prospect of disturbing the residents of a fine house.

"See here, Mr. Holmes," he said as my friend sought to gain access, "I've brought you here, but now I see no sign of wrongdoing. To be disturbing honest folk in their beds is no part of my job. This can wait until tomorrow."

Holmes stared at the dark house that loomed before us.

"I am sure you are right," he said. "Perhaps my friend and I should obtain a few hours' rest, if that is possible, and return here in the morning. When do you get off watch?"

"I'll be in bed by four o'clock, but Sergeant Simms in the stationhouse will be glad to lend you a hand. If you gentlemen will go to the Black Prince you can find yourselves a room."

"Thank you, Constable," said Holmes. "Your assistance has been invaluable. Perhaps I can offer you a cigar in return for your help."

Holmes quickly produced a large Cuban from his cigar case and handed it to the man.

"Now, this is a cigar, Mr. Holmes," the fellow said.

"It is indeed," said Holmes, "and a fit companion for a lonely night such as this. Allow me to light it for you."

The man bit the tip from the cigar and accepted the match my friend offered him.

"Thank you again, Mr. Holmes," said the constable as he strolled off. "Sergeant Simms will help you in the morning."

"The spark of that cigar should inform us of the good constable's whereabouts," said Holmes once the man was out of earshot. "Let us walk up a block and then return."

We proceeded as Holmes suggested. When we returned, the street was deserted. We passed through the gate and up a winding gravel drive, lined with boxwood.

"Our quarry did not stint on the setting for his crimes," Holmes said, quickening his pace once we were beyond the sight of passersby on the street. "It is a pity the weather has been so fine. I fear he must be across the Channel by now."

When we approached the door itself we discovered that the boxwoods shielded it entirely from the road.

"A discreet house indeed," said Holmes, removing an electric torch from his pocket. "I do not doubt that it has been the site of assignations past. Well, let us have a look at the lock.

Ah, a Chubbs, and one of the newer models. Fortunately, I have made a study of this design. Perhaps you would care to hold the light, Watson."

I held the torch while Holmes took a small leather case from the breast pocket of his suit. He unfolded the case and removed what looked like long steel needles.

"Superb instruments," he said to me, holding them up to the light. "Made from the best Sheffield steel. A gift, though unwilling, from John Apply."

"The Aldershot cracksman?"

"Yes. He had them specially manufactured by his brother-in-law. The fineness of the metal allows the least tremor of the mechanism to be transmitted. Yes! There we are. You see, Watson, the value of having the proper equipment."

The large door swung silently open and we entered the darkened room. The pale moonlight, streaming in the open doorway, provided the only illumination. Looking about, we could see in faint outline an elegantly decorated entrance hall. When Holmes shut the door, we were plunged into utter darkness.

"I think it safe to use the torch," Holmes said to me. "Both the shutters and the curtains are drawn."

I did so, playing the beam of light around the hallway. Large, dark rooms lay to both left and right, while a curved stairway of polished mahogany stood before us.

"Upstairs, I believe, Watson," said Holmes. "You have your revolver?"

I took the torch in my left hand and my revolver in my right while Holmes armed himself as well. We advanced quickly up the broad, carpeted steps and along a landing that led into a large room. Inside, the stale air was thick with tobacco smoke, perfume, and a very definite scent of opium. The flickering beams of light from our torches discovered a large table that bore the remains of a sumptuous, intimate feast. Broad silver bowls laden with fruit gleamed faintly in the darkness, along with champagne glasses, linen napkins, silverware, a half-eaten cake, and the skeletons of a pair of roast pheasant.

"We must risk the lights," said Holmes. "The drapes seem secure."

So saying, he lit the gas at one fixture and then another. In a corner of the room, behind a sofa, we discovered two bodies beneath the gleaming folds of a white silk sheet.

"I greatly fear, Watson . . ." said Holmes, reaching his hand down and placing it on the throat of one of the girls.

"Here! What are you about?"

The young lady stirred convulsively and sat upright, staring into our eyes with honest rage!

"Who are you? There'll be trouble, you two coming in here unwanted! I'll have the law on you!"

"We *are* the law," said Holmes.

"You ain't no coppers," she replied, still furious. "There ain't no coppers fool enough to mess with Miss Marigold's girls. Daisy, wake up! We've got company!"

Daisy, who was noticeably less alert than her voluble companion, stirred beneath the sheet for a moment but then relapsed into slumber.

"Get up, will you?!" cried the first woman. "You two get out of here and leave an honest girl alone, or our gentleman will fix you both!"

"From what Miss Marigold told us, you must be Patricia," said Holmes. "I wonder that you are still alive."

"You wonder! You'll wonder a sight more when Miss Marigold's fellows get ahold of you. Daisy! Get up!"

With that statement, Patricia rose to her feet and pulled the sheet from the still-sleeping Daisy. To Holmes's and my consternation, both young ladies proved to be entirely naked.

"This is entirely improper," said Holmes.

"Oh, it is?" continued the young lady, whose lack of shame, like her capacity for verbal jousting, appeared to be without limit. "What's improper is you blokes coming in here and sneaking up on a defenseless girl. Well, you've got what you come for. Now get out!"

She delivered this speech with greatest satisfaction, for she well knew how difficult it is for a man to confront such insolent provocation without giving way to either anger or desire.

"We came here to save your lives," Holmes said at last. "We spoke with Miss Marigold because we have conclusive evidence that your gentleman, as you call him, is a ruthless killer. I am greatly surprised that you are alive."

"What time is it?" groaned Daisy, rolling over and exposing herself in a most appalling fashion. "Who are you two?"

"I am Sherlock Holmes and this is Dr. Watson," said my friend. "I must ask you two to clothe yourselves so that I may ask you some questions."

"You're Mr. Holmes, are you?" said Daisy, suddenly rousing herself. "I've got a letter for you."

"A letter?" said Holmes.

"That's right. Our gentleman said a tall, skinny chap named Sherlock Holmes might be coming round, sticking his beak in where it don't belong. But I've got it somewhere."

So saying, she rose to her feet and began wandering around the room in a state of complete confusion.

"I put it somewheres," she said. A special place so's I'd remember it."

"Of course," said Holmes impatiently. "Perhaps in a drawer."

"No, not in a drawer! You might help me look for it, you know. I've been out for a while. It's a big, proper envelope."

Holmes and I had no choice but to begin searching for this envelope, as our only means of escaping from this sordid scene and the company of these two vulgar, heartless creatures.

"Here it is!" cried Daisy, overturning a platter of fruit. "It's got some stuff on it, but you can read it all, I bet."

Holmes all but snatched the envelope from her hand and opened it quickly, taking out a single sheet of paper. He read the contents with an impassive face and then handed the page to me without a word.

> My dear Mr. Holmes,
>
> If you are reading this document, you are as shrewd as you are persistent. I congratulate you! And you, too, must be pleased—pleased, I mean, to learn that all your conjectures of fantastic and brutal crime have proved to be false. I am happy to be able to put your mind at ease on these matters, which I fear have troubled you far too

> long and have occasioned extraordinary exertions on your part, with no hope of compensation. You are, sir, a man of character, and it must be a comfort for you to discover that there is not a shred of evidence to demonstrate that any crime has been committed. You may return to your humble abode at 221-B knowing that you have done your duty as an Englishman!

Under ordinary circumstances, I am sure that the heavy-handed sarcasm of this missive would have amused my friend. However, to be confronted by these clumsy witticisms in the presence of these vulgar women could not but try his temper. I handed the letter back to him and he restored it to the envelope, placing it in his breast pocket.

"Will you fellows be staying?" demanded Daisy. "Because if you are, you'll be paying, and Daisy and me ain't cheap!"

"Certainly not!" I said heatedly, for I could bear their impertinence no more.

"Now, listen to that fellow," said Patricia, who appeared to be sampling the remains of their feast. "Everything's cold but the champers. How long have we been out?"

Daisy made no reply, but joined her companion at the table.

"We've got some quail at least," said Patricia, lifting the lid on a serving tray. "Do you fancy a quail, Mr. Holmes?"

She turned around, carrying half a dozen roast quail in her hands and smiling at us as insolently as before. Then she sat on the sofa, depositing the quail in her lap in a manner that was surely less than hygienic.

"Sure you don't fancy a nibble?" she asked.

Holmes turned to me, his face flushed with anger.

"Let us depart, Watson," he announced.

CHAPTER 5

Jennie Finds a Home

HOLMES MADE NO REMARK whatsoever on our return journey to London, nor did I expect him to. To be balked in our investigation in such a grotesque and humiliating manner must have tried Holmes's patience to the breaking point. I dared not broach the theory that inevitably suggested itself to me, that both the death of the servant boy and that of Mr. Jonas White had in fact been accidents, and that the "case" he had pursued so fiercely since our return from Loch Rannoch was not a crime at all but rather some involved and meaningless practical joke. The character of Sherlock Holmes consisted of many strands, but no one who knew him as I did could deny that he was one of the proudest of men. Nothing could gall him more than to be treated with the insolence we had received at the hands of Cecil Rhodes and Winston Churchill—nothing except the possibility that he had been wrong.

When we arrived in London, we discovered Mrs. Hudson rather impatient to be relieved of Jennie's care, for the child expressed very limited interest in any domestic duties whatsoever, other than the consumption of sticky buns and the sort of confection known colloquially as "gobstoppers." Mrs.

Hudson, for her part, expressed very little patience with children who do not do as they are told. Jennie, after all, came from the very bottom of society and was far more used to defying authority than complying with it. The vigor with which Mrs. Hudson delivered her sentiments on the matter convinced me that Jennie must quit her residence under our roof as quickly as possible. At the same time, the prospect of inducing Betty and Eunice to assume responsibility for the child came to appear correspondingly remote.

I decided to broach the matter with both women over a dinner of sprats and oysters at Molesworth's, similar to the one that had served Holmes so well during his interrogation with Miss Soames. I felt it best to provide the ladies with some understanding of the case that Holmes and I had been pursuing, knowing that its sensational nature would hold an irresistible charm for them. They also had an enormous curiosity as to the exact appearance of both the exterior and interior of Miss Marigold's house, and all it contained, and her clothes and the clothes and appearance of the girls in her employ, which I did my best to provide. After the waiter had delivered our third bottle of champagne, and after Eunice had consumed her second portion of charlotte russe, I deemed the time appropriate to change the topic of conversation to Jennie and her future.

"It is most remarkable," I said, "that the information that led us to Dolly Marigold was supplied by a young street Arab, a girl of no more than nine."

"Living on the street like that, it's so awful," cried Eunice.

"She's quite a bright child, really," I persevered. "Holmes and I believe she may be in danger. We believe it's necessary to take her in."

"What are you getting at, Johnnie?" said Betty, who was not lacking in shrewdness.

"Why, that she might be appropriate as a servant girl, at your house, perhaps, Eunice."

"Gordon Bennett! I should say not! Why should I want a lying, thieving little thing in my house?" said the lady.

"Yes, Johnnie, why should she?" said Betty, taking, so it appeared, no small amusement in my discomfiture.

"We could make a trial of the matter," I said, "giving both of you an opportunity to meet Jennie."

"So it's Jennie, is it?" said Betty. "You sure she's nine?"

"I am," I said stiffly.

"You sure she ain't yours?"

"I am," I repeated, even more stiffly. "Holmes and I would be glad to provide an allowance for the child, paid to you, I mean, so that there would be no cost. Rather, a small profit."

"I don't trust a street girl," said Eunice, obstinately, leaving me nonplussed. The substantial quantity of food and drink she had consumed had seemingly soured her temper as much as I had hoped it would have sweetened it.

"We could just have a look, Mother," said Betty, putting her hand in mine. "Maybe she won't be so bad."

I could not but respond to such thoughtfulness with extreme gratification.

"I run a refined house," said Eunice. "I won't have no wild creatures running about."

"Now, Mother," said Betty, who appeared decidedly to have switched sides, "you know you've been wanting someone to take care of things on the third floor for you. Maybe Jennie's your girl."

"She's *not* my girl," persisted Eunice.

"Perhaps it would be appropriate for me to bring her by in a week," I said, thinking that a delay would allow me to prepare Jennie, in some small measure, for life with Eunice. Yet the more I considered the contrary natures of those two proud spirits, the more difficult it became to imagine them beneath the same roof.

"Oh, Johnnie, you have bitten off a mouthful," Betty told me later that evening, after we had finished with Eunice's company. For reasons of her own, Betty had been in a high good humor throughout the evening, which had sometimes been to my advantage and sometimes not. But as we relaxed in the privacy and comfort that only a two-guinea hotel room can afford, I could only reflect that while the minx has quick, sharp teeth, she also has the softest and most luxuriant of pelts.

When the day for the transfer of Jennie's custody finally arrived, her mood was less than cooperative.

"I *won't* go!" she cried. "D—— me for a Jew!"

"Such an oath is most inappropriate for anyone, but particularly in the mouth of a young girl," said Holmes. "You must not speak ill of anyone in such a manner."

"D—— me for a Jew," she repeated, obviously pleased by the effect of her remark.

"Jennie," I said, "if you don't behave, we shall have to take away your new frock."

This last threat proved to be perhaps heavy-handed, for the child immediately burst into tears. In the time that Jennie was with us, it became obvious that, far more than food and warmth, the real charm that life away from the streets held for her was the opportunity to gratify her appetite for finery, which was remarkably developed. I have seldom seen such pleasure in a child when I took her shopping for the first time. I could not resist purchasing several outfits for her, and it was her greatest happiness to pose before a full-length mirror for hours at a time.

"You'll send me back!" she wailed.

"No, Jennie," said Holmes suddenly, kneeling before her and taking her by the hands.

"We will never send you back, no matter what you say, and no matter what you do," he said, looking straight into her eyes. "Now, do you believe me? Do you?"

Despite her agitation, Jennie was all but overwhelmed by the power of Holmes's assertion.

"Yes," she quavered.

"That is a good girl," he said. "Jennie, you must go and live with Miss Marbles and her mother. I cannot tell you that you will have an easy life. You are used to doing as you please. Now you will have to work, and I suspect that Mrs. Marbles will prove to be a stern mistress. You have endured much hardship in your life, Jennie, and it has not broken you. Now you will endure a different kind of hardship, and it will benefit you greatly. You will work, which you will find tedious, but it will benefit you. And you shall attend school as well."

"Won't!" burst out Jennie with sudden ferocity. "Won't!"

"Why, of course you will, Jennie, for two or three hours a day. You must learn to read and write."

"I can read as well as anyone," she said. She snatched an envelope from a table and held it before her eyes. "Mister Sherlock Holmes, 221-B Baker Street, London, England."

"Read the return address," prompted Holmes.

"Rev. Robert Ferguson, Loch Rannoch, Scotland," she said in a shaky tone, stumbling over the abbreviation for "Reverend" and the unfamiliar Scottish words as well, but sounding them out in quite a reasonable manner.

"That is very good, Jennie," Holmes said. "But can you write?"

At this remark her little face fell.

"I don't want to write," she said sullenly.

"But you must, Jennie. If you are to wear fine clothes, you must learn to read and write, so that you may exchange billets-doux with your admirers. You must learn to read and write, and you must learn to do many things. And you will do them. And we will never send you back to the streets."

At that remark, the child suddenly flung her arms around Holmes's neck. He held her tightly for a second and then disentangled himself.

"Come, Jennie," I said, taking her by the hand, "we must go now."

To soften the blow of departure, I had arranged for us to travel to Eunice's rooming house by an elegant brougham.

"Is this ours?" asked Jennie, obviously pleased.

"It is indeed," I said, "for the next hour."

"This *is* nice," said Jennie, seating herself on the thick, brown velvet cushions. She rubbed her hand back and forth on the plush to see it change color in the light.

"Now, Jennie," I said as we rode through the streets, "Holmes and I will pay Mrs. Marbles for taking you in, but you must work as well. You must mind Mrs. Marbles in everything she says, and address her as 'ma'am' at all times. If you behave yourself properly, you will receive an allowance of three pence a week. But if you misbehave, we shall withhold your pennies. So if you are a good girl, you will soon be able to buy yourself a fine velvet cloak of your own."

Jennie listened politely to my words, though I detected perhaps an ounce of skepticism in her manner. I could not but be impressed by her feat of teaching herself to read, but a quick mind is not always an obedient one. The collisions that were bound to occur between Jennie and Eunice were, I decided, nothing for me to worry about. Despite her advancing years, Eunice was a strong and vigorous woman. Jennie might elude her for some time, but ultimately there would be a reckoning.

The journey from Baker Street to the rooming house was not a short one, and to pass the time I could not forbear from raising the question of Jennie's command of the written word.

"How did you learn to read?" I asked her.

"Easy," she replied. "The coppers was always writing me up. I thought I'd better know what they was up to. I used to do sweepings at the Gaiety, and one of the girls took me in for a time. She taught me to read the bill, so's I could know all the swells—Tom the Terrible Turk and Mademoiselle Evette. She was a Frenchie. How they talk!"

"Did you live with this woman?"

"For a time. But Molly had a boyfriend who beat her fierce. Always drinking. So I left. I like the Gaiety. A girl can make a penny there."

"Would you like to see the show sometime?"

Jennie's face lit up wonderfully at this remark.

"Oh, could I?" she cried.

Such innocence and such joy in a child! My bachelor's heart trembled at its touch. As Betty had so shrewdly observed, I had bitten off a mouthful, far more than I had realized. Up until this moment Jennie had been a charity. I had comforted her as one might feed a hungry dog. But here the passion of her soul blazed forth, and I realized its power. Jennie, I instantly surmised, in her innocent joys and innocent rages, could be crueler than the cruelest mistress. I shook within my overcoat at the small child beside me and longed for our arrival at Bromley Street.

When we arrived, both Jennie and Eunice were fiercely suspicious of the other. I held Jennie tightly by the hand to prevent her from bolting, which, I feared, she was quite likely to do.

"Jennie," I said, "this is your new mistress, Mrs. Marbles. Say 'Good morning, Mrs. Marbles.' "

"Good morning," Jennie muttered, with downcast eyes.

"Good morning, Mrs. Marbles," I prompted.

"Good morning, Mrs. Marbles," she repeated sullenly.

"Good morning, Jennie," said Eunice primly. "I'm sure you'll be a good girl."

Such sentiments were, of course, guaranteed to arouse Jennie's ire, but she concealed her emotions rather more successfully than I might have expected.

"Now, Jennie," I said, "I have explained to Mrs. Marbles that for the first month, while you are getting settled, you will work here full-time, but afterward you will attend Miss Worsham's School for Girls for three hours each morning. And you are to obey Mrs. Marbles in all things."

"I don't want to go to school!" Jennie burst out, objecting, for some reason, to what was distant rather than to what was near.

"But you must go to school," I said. "You must become proper."

"I don't want to be proper!" she shouted, suddenly furious.

"Don't you want to be pretty, like me?" said Betty, entering the room.

Jennie stood transfixed, for surely Betty was pretty, dressed in her evening best, a shimmering pink satin gown that glowed against the unpretentious decor like a brilliant, solitary rose.

"Don't you want to be pretty like me?" she repeated.

"Oh, yes!" Jennie cried, running toward her but not quite daring to touch Betty's elegant gown, one that, I am proud to say, I had purchased.

"Then there is a great deal for you to learn, Jennie," said Betty, taking the child by the hand, "and you must do everything that Mother says. And if you are a good girl, I shall teach you everything I know about being pretty. Now, is that a bargain for you?"

Jennie nodded vigorously, holding tight to Betty's hands.

"I think now that I must depart," I said. "Jennie, I shall see you in a fortnight."

Jennie glanced back at me with some longing, but held tight to Betty. For a brief second Jennie looked rather nervously at Eunice but then returned her gaze to her newfound idol and champion. As I returned alone to the brougham I could not but feel profoundly touched by the experience of surrendering Jennie to the first day of her new life and by the extraordinary generosity shown by Betty to welcome her in. I bade the driver to return me to Baker Street, reclining on the velvet cushions to consider the workings of Providence, which had intervened in little Jennie's life in such a remarkable manner.

CHAPTER 6

A Visit from Two Peers

THE READER MUST NOT imagine that Jennie's life at 19 Bromley Street was always surrounded by such a nimbus of fine sentiment. Several days later I was informed by Betty that Jennie had hurled one of Eunice's favorite vases from a third-floor window. The vase's companion was similarly demolished a week later. Naturally, I was required to cover the damages and also chose to entertain both Betty and Eunice at a second dinner at Molesworths. At that time Eunice described Jennie as "quick but cunning," which was surely not the best of all possible worlds. However, it was clear that Jennie had displayed at least a modicum of competence and pertinacity in the completion of the many duties that Eunice was pleased to heap upon her. Jennie, it appeared, had won the conditional acceptance of the mother and retained the affection of the daughter, which, under the circumstances, could only be considered a remarkable victory. I took all three out for lunch the following week and found Jennie to be subdued but in reasonable spirits. It was more, really, than one could have hoped for.

I continued to work at Charing Cross, for the flow of casualties remained unstanched. In the notorious "Khaki Election" that brought the last year of the old century to a close, Mr. Churchill gained the seat in Parliament that he had sought. The first January of the new one was forever darkened by the death of our beloved queen. That sad reminder of the resistless passage of time was only counteracted by the pleasure I took in helping to provide for Jennie's new life. Despite her vivid and fantastic temper, one could see in her a determination to free herself utterly from the streets, even if that meant obeying the will, and at times even enduring the lash, of the hated Eunice.

Holmes spent much of his time on the Continent, where his great reputation preceded him. And so the months passed, until one morning in March 1902, when I read in the paper of the death of Cecil Rhodes, which returned my attention forcibly to the unresolved mystery of our strange journey to Loch Rannoch. Holmes arrived at the breakfast table while I was still finishing my coffee.

"Cecil Rhodes is dead," I remarked as he sat down.

"Common humanity forbids me to rejoice in the death of a fellow member of our species," Holmes said, accepting the cup I offered him. "Concealment of a murder is perhaps a trivial matter compared with the excesses Mr. Rhodes committed in the pursuit of his African empire. Yet as I suggested to Mr. Churchill, I doubt that this affair is at an end."

I made no reply, for I did not dare to suggest to my friend that his accusations of murder were unfounded. Another month passed with no further discussion of the matter. I arose one morning to discover that Holmes was out. Whether he had left that morning or had failed to return the night before, I did not know. I enjoyed a leisurely omelet while perusing the latest outrage of the kaiser in the *Times* when Gerald, our pageboy, appeared to announce the arrival of two gentlemen to see Mr. Holmes at ten o'clock.

"What are their names?" I asked the lad, who was, perhaps, not the brightest young man to enter our employment.

"The Duke of Ascot and Lord Sin Gin," he stated.

"Really?" I replied. "Well, show them to the waiting room. I will be with them shortly."

I was, in fact, in no particular hurry to do so, for my pocket watch assured me that the time was scarcely a quarter to the hour, and I had no doubt that our callers, whoever they might be, were not in fact peers of the realm. I finished my coffee and entered the waiting room and found myself in the presence of two very elegantly dressed gentlemen indeed, one of them middle-aged and one quite advanced in years. The elder gentleman rose cautiously from his chair as I entered.

"Are you Sherlock Holmes?" he asked in a nervous yet demanding tone.

"No," I replied. "I am Dr. Watson."

"Oh. But we had an appointment with Sherlock Holmes."

"Yes. Mr. Holmes will be with you shortly. Please join me in the sitting room," I said, leading them in. I conducted them to two of our armchairs and took a third for myself.

"Our interview is with Mr. Holmes exclusively," said the elderly gentlemen.

"I often assist Mr. Holmes with his cases," I explained.

"Well, you won't with this one," snorted the other.

"Ah, Watson, I see you have made the acquaintance of our visitors," said Holmes, entering.

"I was just leaving."

"Not a bit of it. Your presence is imperative."

"It is a most private matter," said the elderly gentleman. "Perhaps I did not stress that point sufficiently in my message."

"I have no secrets from Watson," said Holmes, with just a touch of sharpness in his voice. "If you gentlemen wish to engage my services you must be willing to place complete reliance in the discretion and common sense of Dr. Watson and myself. Otherwise this meeting is at an end."

The gentleman seemed to be caught off guard by the aggressive nature of this statement.

"Naturally," he said, stammering a little in his confusion, "there are limits, which need to be established."

"Oh, get on with it, then, Johnnie," snapped his younger companion. "We've no choice, and you know it."

The elder gentleman collected himself and sat down.

"Very well," he said. "Since you are to be privy to this

conversation, Dr. Watson, you should know that this is his grace, the Duke of Ascot, and I am Lord St. John of Brittleton."

Now, of course, it was my turn to feel confused, for I had not the slightest idea of how to confront an actual duke. My incompetence earned me a condescending, contemptuous glance from the duke, but fortunately Holmes seized control of the conversation.

"The duke and Lord St. John have come to us on an interesting matter," he said taking out a cigar.

"A very private matter, Mr. Holmes," said Lord St. John. "There must be no mention of this in the press."

"I understand your concern," said Holmes. "Let me be candid with you, gentlemen. I know why you are here. I know what you want. I can tell you a great deal, but I cannot tell you the one thing you most wish to know. If I tell you what I do know, it will cost you £500."

"You sound very sure of yourself, Mr. Holmes," said the duke.

"I have an unusual perspective on this case, Your Grace," my friend said.

"Very well. Pay him, Johnnie."

Lord St. John took out a checkbook while I watched, speechless.

"Thank you, Your Grace," said Holmes, as the duke passed him the check. "I believe you will have your money's worth."

Holmes took the check without glancing at the sum, folded it in half, and placed it his breast pocket. He took a long puff on his cigar and then placed it in the ashtray on the table before him.

"About twenty years ago," he said, "Mr. Cecil Rhodes effected the final consolidation of the De Beers Diamond Company when he purchased the holdings of his great competitor Mr. Barney Barnato."

"Yes," said the duke.

"Mr. Barnato's company owned land, equipment, mining rights, and many other things, but his most spectacular holding was the so-called Great Blue of Kimberly, an immense uncut blue-white diamond of more than five thousand carats, by far the largest diamond ever discovered. For complex financial reasons, Mr. Barnato did not own this diamond outright. To realize its value, it would be necessary for him to sell it, and a greater part of the proceeds would go to his creditors.

"Negotiations between Mr. Rhodes and Mr. Barnato occupied the greater part of two years. As I understand it, the financial pressures on Mr. Barnato to sell were immense, but he was a very stubborn man. Halfway through the negotiations, a catastrophic fire swept through a portion of Kimberly, burning to the ground the bank that held the great diamond. When the vault containing the diamond was opened, it was discovered that all of the contents had combusted, due to the great heat. The financial arrangements concerning the diamond were such that Mr. Barnato's creditors endured the far greater loss, but his own losses mandated the sale of his holdings to Mr. Rhodes almost immediately. In fact, the price that Mr. Barnato obtained was surprisingly small, while his creditors received only minimal compensation.

"When the consolidation was effected, Mr. Barnato moved to Paris, where he lived until, it is said, he was stricken by some disease of the mind and committed suicide by leaping overboard while at sea. But while he lived in Paris, some observers were struck by Mr. Barnato's wealth, which seemed to grow, and to grow markedly, rather than diminish with time, despite the fact that he took no interest in business but rather devoted himself entirely to pleasure. The rumor, which had always existed, grew that the Great Blue had not been destroyed in the fire. Mr. Barnato had saved it, and had sold it in a secret transaction to Mr. Rhodes for a very large sum."

"Paid for with De Beers stock," said the duke abruptly.

"Yes," said Holmes, "although the diamond, of course, was not reported as property of the company. Mr. Rhodes was notoriously an unromantic man, whose one consuming interest was the expansion of British power in Africa. You gentlemen knew him better than I, but anyone meeting Mr. Rhodes would easily conclude that he had little if any concern for outward display. However, I believe that Rhodes did conceal a sentimental attachment to that unique industry that formed the first basis for his wealth, and he expressed that attachment by acquiring the Great Blue merely for his own possession.

"If he had wanted to, Mr. Rhodes could secretly have disposed of the diamond by having it cut into a multitude of small, first-rate diamonds, which he then could have sold, with some difficulty, for an enormous sum."

"Several hundred thousand pounds, easily," the duke interrupted once more.

"But he did not," continued Holmes. "The years passed, and the diamond remained untouched. From what I have read, Mr. Rhodes felt acutely that he would not have a long life, yet he chose to make no movement toward cutting the diamond. Eventually, I believe, and quite recently, the rumors of its existence coalesced into fact."

"That damned woman," the duke interjected.

"The Princess Esterhazy," said Holmes with a nod. "The relationship between the princess and the archduke remains indistinct to me, even now. She was a woman far past her prime, but clearly still quite adept at intrigue. At any rate, it was she who first determined that the Great Blue still existed. One can conjecture that Mr. Rhodes removed the diamond from Kimberly to Scotland with the express purpose of guarding it against her, although both his declining health and the Boer War itself are respectable alternatives. In any event, the princess must have informed the archduke of this remarkable object's existence and of its location in Scotland.

"On the basis of this information, the archduke then fashioned this extraordinary plan, of which one can only say that so far it has proved extraordinarily successful. He arranged for an official tour of this country; he arranged for an unofficial visit at Mr. Rhodes's estate in Scotland, for an indeterminate length of time; he arranged for a double to appear at Mr. Rhodes's estate in his place, with the charge of stealing the diamond, which remarkable charge the double did carry out. The very fact that you gentlemen are now here before me makes it all but certain that the archduke has obtained the Great Blue, which, in all likelihood, has now been converted from a fabled lump into a king's ransom of glittering jewels."

"Impossible!" shouted the duke, clenching his fists in anger. "That diamond is the property of De Beers, and every jeweler in Europe knows it! No man who values his trade or his life would touch it!"

"Your company's reputation is indeed formidable," said Holmes. "However, there remain craftsmen beyond its reach. The jewelers of the Romanovs in Moscow, for example, or those in Constantinople, or even Baghdad or Tehran. You must remember that the archduke comes from the far reaches of eastern Europe. He has the very great privileges of his rank and family name, and access to the assistance of the Austrian government. In addition, of course, there is the simple fact that the archduke has far greater claim to the stone than anyone else."

"That is entirely untrue, Mr. Holmes," snapped Lord St. John. "The Great Blue was paid for with De Beers stock, and we can prove it."

"That would be very difficult to prove," said Holmes. "Mr. Barnato and Mr. Rhodes were both very cunning men. They covered their tracks well. And now both are dead. It might be possible, even now, to show that in the 1880s and 1890s De Beers effected significant transfers of stock to Mr. Barnato, under the direction of Mr. Rhodes, for no apparent benefit to De Beers. But Mr. Barnato cast himself into the sea in 1897 and Mr. Rhodes died in the past year. You may accuse the dead of fraud, but you cannot convict them."

"Then you have charged me £500 to tell us nothing can be done," the duke said angrily.

"I did not say that," replied Holmes. "I told you that I could not tell you the one thing you would most like to know, which is how to obtain the diamond. But there is something that can be done, and that is to reopen the murder of that unfortunate servant boy who now lies buried in a remote village in Scotland."

"That is impossible," said Lord St. John, entering the conversation once more.

"Not at all impossible," said Holmes. "It is always possible to overturn an injustice. If I were allowed to examine the evidence that surely remains at Loch Rannoch, I have no doubt that the local authorities would rule in favor of reopening the case."

"You must know that in Loch Rannoch nothing can be done without the consent of Cecil Rhodes's brothers," said Lord St. John.

"No doubt," said Holmes. "But I believe those gentlemen have also taken an interest in locating the missing stone."

"Those incompetents!" the duke burst out, savagely. "They have added nothing to De Beers!"

"I could imagine them making the same remark with regard to your grace," said Holmes dryly. "However, I quite understand Your Grace's concern. As both substantial stockholders in De Beers and heirs to their brother's private estate, they have dual options to pursue in claiming ownership of the stone. No doubt they would prefer to claim it as their personal property."

"No doubt!" said the duke.

"Yes. But as long as the archduke-palatinate is free and in sole possession of the stone, nothing can be done. In the eyes of British law, the Great Blue does not exist. If De Beers wishes to bring suit against the archduke, demanding that he give an accounting for any and all first-water blue-whites in his possession, it may surely do so, but I do not think the courts of Austria will look with much favor upon it. British notions of commerce and justice are not necessarily accepted in Vienna."

"Then you plan to indict the archduke for murder?" asked Lord St. John.

"I cannot indict anyone for anything. However, I can investigate. There is no doubt that a murder was committed at Loch Rannoch. The continued concealment of that crime assures the concealment of the theft of the diamond. I cannot promise you that if I am allowed to determine what happened at Loch Rannoch that the diamond will be returned. However, I can promise you that if I am not allowed to investigate, the diamond will not be returned. The Great Blue, if cut into a multitude of untraceable stones, would have a value of at least £200,000, as you have estimated, and possibly even twice that amount, if accounts of the diamond's quality are indeed accurate. However, a stone of such size could also be cut to create a single great diamond and a number of smaller stones. In an appropriate setting, such gems would be worth perhaps £250,000, although in fact such pieces become essentially impossible to value, and serve as vehicles of prestige rather than commerce. The company of De Beers is quite prosperous. You gentlemen, and the Rhodes brothers, are all extremely wealthy men. A decision to let the matter lie would be quite understandable, and, as a business proposition, surely the wiser choice."

"The company of De Beers will not allow itself to be victimized in such a manner," said Lord St. John decisively.

"Clearly, the company has the right to conduct an investigation," said Holmes.

"Under what circumstances would *you* conduct an investigation, Mr. Holmes?" Lord St. John demanded.

"You gentlemen would first have to reach an agreement with Mr. Rhodes's heirs. Since you have already shown me the kindness of a check for £500, I feel an obligation to warn you of the difficulties before you. To mount a proper investigation, that ridiculous coroner's report of an accident must be overturned, and replaced with a proper verdict of homicide. Since the original fraud was effectively perpetrated by Mr. Rhodes himself, his death makes such a reversal less embarrassing than might otherwise be expected."

"And what makes you think the authorities in Loch Rannoch would ever agree to such a proposal?" demanded his lordship.

"The Rhodes brothers would agree to it to obtain the Great Blue."

"There's no use talking to him, Johnnie," said the duke with disdain. "He's only trying to drive up his price."

"He's right, Mr. Holmes," said St. John. "You have no right to play us off one another this way."

"I assure you I have not spoken with the two gentlemen,

either directly or indirectly," said Holmes. "I have remarked before that possession of the stone is essentially a matter of vanity rather than profit, and vanity is a motive even more corrupting, perhaps, than mere covetousness. I understand, to some extent, the pressures you gentlemen are under. But the trail has grown terribly cold. To conduct a partial, or partisan, investigation would be worse than useless. Unless I am free to treat this case as though it were no more than a garroting in a Cheapside alley, we are simply wasting each other's time."

Holmes delivered this last statement in his most severe and uncompromising tone. The two aristocrats glared first at him and then at each other but said nothing. Finally Lord St. John spoke.

"We cannot approve of your attitude, Mr. Holmes," he said, "particularly in light of the fact that we have just given you £500."

"I shall be glad to return the sum if you feel I have not earned it," said Holmes, proffering the check before St. John's very eyes.

"D——ned cheek!" exploded the duke. "I'd rather drink a case of Gladstone claret than waste time with such a socialist!"

So saying, he fairly leaped to his feet and headed out the door.

"You may keep the check, Mr. Holmes," said Lord St. John, nervously eyeing his companion's departure. "The Great Blue belongs to De Beers and must be returned. The duke feels very strongly about this matter, you must understand. And so do I."

"Yes," said Holmes, "and you, Lord St. John, must understand that I feel very strongly about this matter. I was brought to the scene of a brutal crime and denied the opportunity to bring a murderer to justice. The most basic principles of British law were perverted to suit the purposes of one rich man. Now I find that man's business partners, and quite possibly his heirs, seeking to bend me to their purposes. I can assure you that if I am to initiate an investigation of the crimes associated with the disappearance of the Great Blue, I must first be given assurances by all parties involved that I will be allowed to continue that investigation to its end, no matter where it leads me."

"Very well, Mr. Holmes," said Lord St. John. "I think it best that we discuss this matter with the rest of the board. Sir Samuel must have a look at it, to be sure. He will get us what we want. He always does."

With that, his lordship rose as well, and departed from our humble rooms.

"Never let it be said that the English aristocracy has not adapted to the ways of commerce," said Holmes, reaching for his pipe. "Perhaps you would favor me with a glass of brandy and soda, Watson. I feel the need for refreshment."

CHAPTER 7

A Visit from the Board

I HANDED HOLMES A GLASS, which he took with obvious pleasure.

"This is an extraordinary turn," I said.

"It is indeed. I had begun to fear that I should never have an opportunity to settle matters with the archduke and his accomplice. Now I must ask you to excuse me, Watson. The two noble lords have given me much to consider."

I departed from our flat with no little displeasure at this abrupt dismissal. I had heard something of the Great Blue and Barney Barnato and the Princess Esterhazy. Stories linking that unfortunate woman with rumors of the continued existence of the great diamond, which had not been uncommon in the penny press, I had dismissed without a second thought. But now, fantastic as it sounded, there seemed to be no doubt that these rumors were true, and that they were connected to the strange events that had occurred some two years before at Loch Rannoch. I earnestly wished the opportunity to discuss these matters with Holmes, but he appeared equally anxious to avoid such an occurrence, for when I retraced my steps to Baker Street that evening I discovered that he had disappeared, leaving only a brief, penciled note, that informed me with scant courtesy not to expect his return for several days.

During Holmes's absence I settled into the routine of a man more at home at his club than his residence, for the Galenians' location, so near to Charing Cross, made it an ideal retreat. During that time I received frequent inquiries from an assistant of a solicitor, Sir Samuel Jenkins, in the employ of De Beers. My solitude at Baker Street extended itself from days to weeks, and it was almost three weeks to the day that I discovered my friend once more in our rooms. I returned quite late from surgery to find him engrossed in one of those chemical experiments that so intrigued him.

"Is that you, Watson?" he cried as I entered.

"Of course it is," I responded. "I hope I am not interrupting you."

"Indeed not," he said, turning around at my approach. "This tincture will require some time to settle."

He held up a vial for my inspection.

"I suppose I owe you some explanation for my abrupt and prolonged absence," he said, motioning me to a chair. "But perhaps I can get you a glass. You appear to have had a difficult evening."

"Yes," I said. "Several new arrivals that unfortunately required immediate amputations. How did you know?"

Holmes strode to the tantalus on the sideboard and removed the bar.

"When you keep regular hours it is your invariable pattern to repair to your club for dinner," he said over his shoulder. "The Galenians hold to the fine old custom of brushing the members' hats on each visit. But when your duties keep you late, your habit is to return straight to Baker Street and dine at Morphy's, where they are not so attentive. Tonight you return at a late hour with your hat unbrushed. Here, take this."

He handed me a glass and sat in the chair opposite.

"The generous contributions of the firm of De Beers to our accounts have encouraged me to upgrade our cellar," he said. "By the way, Frank and Elmhirst Rhodes will be calling tomorrow morning at ten. I hope it will be convenient for you to join us."

"Yes," I said, feeling both revived and relaxed by the brandy. "Do you intend to accept them as clients?"

"I am not entirely sure. I wished to investigate this matter from every angle before consenting to enter the employ of either De Beers or the brothers before being absolutely sure of my ground."

"During your absence I heard frequently from an assistant of a Sir Samuel Jenkins."

"I am not surprised. You may have forgotten, but Mr. Churchill mentioned Sir Samuel's presence at Loch Rannoch on the night of the diamond's disappearance. To the extent that Cecil Rhodes had a confidant, Sir Samuel was that man. He managed De Beers's affairs in London for more than a decade while Rhodes was in Africa. He knows both the City and Whitehall like the back of his hand. He has a finger in every pie, trusts no one, and is feared by all."

"It does not sound as though you trust him yourself."

"I do not," said Holmes. "I strongly suspect, though I doubt I shall ever be able to prove it, that Sir Samuel was aware of the diamond's existence during Rhodes's lifetime. I suspect as well that he worked with Rhodes in attempting to recover it after the theft. Now, however, Rhodes's death has released the secret of the stone's existence and its theft. It is a slight hope, but the brothers of the deceased may prove more honorable than either their brother or the two peers."

"A slight hope, indeed," I said. "What is the point of taking such clients?"

"The murders, Watson, the murders," said Holmes, his voice sinking in volume but rising in intensity. "I do not enjoy being baulked and turned aside when innocent blood has been shed. I must take my allies where I find them."

Even more than his words, Holmes's manner of speech convinced me that the temper of his outrage had not declined by a single degree since the time of our departure from Loch Rannoch. I finished my glass and retired for the evening, confident that I should learn more on the morrow.

The next morning, Frank and Colonel Elmhirst Rhodes arrived punctually at ten, accompanied, to my surprise, by the

Duke of Ascot and Lord St. John, as well as Sir Samuel Jenkins. The two brothers were well-dressed, prosperous men, looking far less driven than their late brother. Frank Rhodes, the elder of the two, clearly suffered from the same ill health that had destroyed his brother and had the fussy, sometimes sad mannerisms of the confirmed valetudinarian. Colonel Rhodes was younger and more vigorous than his brother, but it was evident that they had arranged to place the matter entirely in the hands of Sir Samuel, whose person I considered with some care. Though rather short and fat, he seemed to command the confidence of all four gentlemen. His dress, though less than tidy, was of the finest black broadcloth. His ruddy face and physical vigor suggested the character of the inveterate outdoorsman, and his casual appearance was offset by a pair of brilliant blue eyes that darted beneath his heavy gray brows. Throughout our visit he treated himself liberally to a fine, light brown snuff from a jeweled box.

Our five guests seated themselves in our sitting room, and Mrs. Hudson appeared with a tea tray bearing the fine porcelain Holmes had obtained during our visit to Singapore. When she departed, our conversation began.

"Sir Samuel," said Holmes, addressing the solicitor, "since you are trained in the law, you must be aware that your participation as an adviser in this case contains many difficulties."

"I am not so aware," said Sir Samuel smoothly. "A diamond has been stolen that was in the personal possession of the late Cecil Rhodes. In his will Mr. Cecil Rhodes stated that unnamed personal items of value, including both cut and uncut gems of all description, not otherwise disposed of, should pass to the joint custody of his surviving brothers, Frank and Elmhirst Rhodes. At the same time, Mr. Rhodes's will expressly separates from his estate all property of the De Beers Company, regardless of its physical location. As a member of the board of De Beers, an office that I share with all four of these gentlemen, it is my intention to see that the diamond is recovered and returned to its rightful owner."

"That is one way of stating the matter," said Holmes.

"However, there are many side issues that you have neglected to discuss. In addition to the theft of the diamond, there is the question of the murder of the servant boy. Mr. Rhodes applied outrageous pressure to obtain a false coroner's verdict describing the affair as an accident. I have said before that that verdict must be overturned."

"And so it has, Mr. Holmes, so it has," said Sir Samuel. "Here is the document that corrects that unfortunate judicial error."

As he spoke, the solicitor handed Holmes a document, which my friend perused in silence.

"This is progress," he remarked after a long pause. "I suppose it is too much to ask for an official reprimand of those who were party to the original fraud, much less a punishment."

"Coroner's juries do make mistakes, Mr. Holmes," the solicitor said. "To punish errors would only lead to their concealment."

"No doubt," said Holmes. "However, there remains another matter yet to discuss."

"You refer to the supposed division of interest between the De Beers Company and the heirs of Mr. Rhodes?" Sir Samuel asked.

"Yes."

In reply, the solicitor handed over a second document, considerably more lengthy than the first.

"I can give you the essence," he told my friend.

"Thank you, no," said Holmes. "I have an affinity for the printed text in its entirety."

Holmes placed the document on the table beside him and took his blackened churchwarden between his teeth, filling the bowl with navy cut. When he had the pipe properly lit he took up the document and read it through to the end, a process that consumed the better part of an hour, and all of our guests' patience.

"Are you satisfied, Mr. Holmes?" Sir Samuel demanded, when my friend at last put down the document.

"An ingenious arrangement," said Holmes. "I congratulate you, Sir Samuel. Though no man may foretell the future, you seem to have anticipated most of the conflicts that could arise in the conduct of this case."

"*Most,* Mr. Holmes?" said the solicitor, with a look of amusement. "Perhaps you could instruct me on the flaws of this contract. All of the parties involved, and their representatives, have found it to be both exhaustive and sound."

"It bears the great flaw of complexity," said Holmes. "I suggest that instead of attempting to anticipate every possible contingency and assigning a price to each, that the personal heirs of Cecil Rhodes simply sell all claims whatsoever to the Great Blue they might possess for the price of £25,000, payable immediately by the company in De Beers stock, and leaving the company as sole claimant to the stone."

"So that if the diamond is never recovered we will be out £25,000 for nothing?" snapped Lord St. John. "I hardly call that fair dealing, Mr. Holmes."

"Twenty-five thousand for a stone that is worth ten times that and more is not fair dealing but hard bargaining," insisted Colonel Rhodes, who appeared to direct his anger equally at Holmes and St. John.

"It was hardly fair dealing in the first place," interjected the duke. "Twenty-five thousand would scarcely cover the money your brother stole from the firm."

"Our brother," said the colonel sharply, "created De Beers, and created you. The Great Blue was my brother's most treasured possession, and he intended it to remain in his own family."

"Really?" said Holmes. "You knew of its existence?"

At this question the colonel faltered and cast down his eyes.

"I see," said Holmes, forming a pyramid with his fingers and sinking deeper into his chair. "Your brother was a complex man, Colonel. He left the bulk of his estate, not to his family, but to the creation of the Rhodes Scholarship Fund. The trustees of that fund, I am sure, will also be interested in the existence of the diamond, although Mr. Rhodes did go to the trouble in his will of enumerating all the assets that were to be transferred to it.

"Reviewing all the facts, I think it is impossible to say what Cecil Rhodes intended to do about the Great Blue. During his lifetime he seemed to regard any public attempt to recover it as counterproductive to his interests. His own right to the stone was questionable, and now that he is dead, true ownership is almost impossible to determine. The creditors of Barney Barnato have as good a claim as any."

"That eventuality has been taken care of," said Sir Samuel, reaching into his valise and removing a handful of papers. "Court records allowed us to determine a complete list of Mr. Barnato's creditors at the time in question. Each has sold all rights against Mr. Barnato's estate to either the Rhodesian Development Corporation or African Lands Limited."

"Which are, I presume, wholly owned subsidiaries of De Beers," said Holmes.

"Yes."

"That does simplify matters. If the colonel and Mr. Rhodes sell their claims to De Beers, it is possible for an investigation to go forward."

"I think that will be agreeable," said Sir Samuel, looking quickly from the duke to Lord St. John. The duke, his face still flushed and pugnacious, seemed on the verge of speech but ultimately remained silent.

"Naturally, we will have to discuss this matter with the full board," said Lord St. John, taking up the conversation. "However, I don't anticipate any problems."

"Then there remains the matter of my fee," said Holmes. "I suggest £2,000 to undertake the investigation and an additional £8,000 to achieve its return."

"Now, that's not quite reasonable, Mr. Holmes," said Sir Samuel. "De Beers has already paid you £500. And we already know where the stone is. The archduke has it."

"No doubt, or at least he knows where it is," said Holmes. "But at the present time there is absolutely no evidence recognizable in a court of law to show that a theft has occurred, and certainly no evidence to implicate the archduke. There is, in fact, no legal evidence that that remarkable lump of compressed carbon once known as the Great Blue still exists. Constructing a case against the archduke that will compel him to relinquish possession of the diamond will be no small feat and may involve, I might add, no small expense."

"Do not trifle with us, Mr. Holmes," the duke interrupted. "We intend to have that diamond."

The imperious tone in the duke's voice, and even more the anger in his face, I confess caught me by surprise. Despite the frequent outbursts of our guests, I had in fact regarded this dispute as little more than a set of country gentlemen arguing over the possession of a particularly fine salmon. For the first time I recognized the truth of Holmes's remark of the irrational allure of a great diamond.

"I am sure that Mr. Holmes would give his best efforts if hired," interrupted Sir Samuel. "And I am sure as well that he can recover it if any man can."

Holmes paused at the solicitor's words.

"I appreciate your confidence in me," he said. "You were originally employed by Mr. Barnato, in Kimberly, were you not?"

"I was," Sir Samuel replied. "I knew Kimberly before the first pit was dug."

"And then you saw the Great Blue."

"I did, more than once. And there is no diamond like it, for quality or size. We'll pay the £25,000, Mr. Holmes, but we'll take out £2,000 for your fee. We can have a meeting of the board in less than a week."

"Just a minute," interrupted the duke. "We can still outvote you. I don't see the point of paying this fellow £2,000 to smoke his pipe."

"I'm sure everything can be arranged in a private discussion," said Sir Samuel, putting emphasis on the word "private."

"Yes, I believe that as well," said Lord St. John quickly. "I think we've consumed enough of Mr. Holmes's time."

"Is that agreeable to you and your brother, Colonel?" asked Holmes.

"I do not believe that my brother intended the diamond to be disposed of in this manner, but perhaps the sum will be sufficient," the colonel said stiffly.

"I believe the board will reach a decision that will be satisfactory to everyone," said Sir Samuel smoothly. "Thank you for your time, Mr. Holmes. We shall inform you of our decision within a week."

And with that our five guests quickly made their departure.

"What do you think, Watson?" Holmes asked once we were alone.

"I hardly know if you will have a client," I said. "Sir Samuel has his work cut out for him. Neither the duke nor Lord St. John seems particularly amenable to the compromise you propose. But I was surprised that the two brothers did not put up more of a fight."

"Their brother was scarcely as generous with them as he might have been. An additional £25,000 would be welcome indeed. Besides, as shareholders in De Beers, they will still benefit from the recovery of the stone."

"And you think that Sir Samuel can persuade the board, with the duke and Lord St. John against him?"

"Peers seldom make policy," said Holmes. "Dividends are what matter. Sir Samuel appears to have a genius for compromise."

I finished my tea and stepped to the window. The fine equipages of our guests had disappeared, and Baker Street was filled with the usual flow of anonymous hansoms and growlers.

"Do you really expect to bring the archduke to justice and recover the stone?" I asked.

"It is a pretty task, I grant you. But the archduke is undoubtedly accessory to two murders committed on British soil. We were brought into this wretched case under government auspices. It would not surprise me if the government does take an interest in this case again. If we do have the government behind us, it may be possible to do something."

"Do you have any idea of where to start?"

"I shall begin in Paris. The handwriting in the note we received from the accomplice had a precision that bespeaks a French education. A cracksman with the skill to open a Goliath 1000 may have come to the attention of the Sûreté in his youth."

"Yet the English, as I recall, had nothing of the foreigner."

"True. I do not doubt but that our man is a perfect chameleon. He will be almost as hard to catch as the archduke himself. But since I have already been rewarded so handsomely, and have expectations of more, it only seems reasonable that I should share my good fortune."

So saying, he opened his notebook and took from it a check, which he handed to me, a check written for the sum of £250!

"Holmes," I said, "this is absurd!"

"Not at all. I have used you already to deflect the unwanted inquiries of our prospective clients and no doubt shall do so again. Besides, you have the extraordinary expenses of Jennie to consider."

That last remark was all too true, for Jennie's assertive spirit had not much been tempered by her new circumstances, and it required a generous hand to keep Eunice from evicting Jennie into the streets. Only a month before, I been forced to replace all the curtains in Eunice's drawing room, and pay for new carpeting as well, Jennie's attempts at emulating a conjuring trick performed by the Amazing Flamo having gone seriously awry.

"Taking that girl to the music hall every week is just asking for trouble," Eunice told me with some indignation when registering her complaint.

Her statement was true enough, but Jennie adored the stage, and the promise of a trip to the Gaiety, or the threat of withholding one, was the surest way to gain her attention and compliance. Her comportment since the disaster had been respectable, but hardly deserving of unusual reward. I decided instead that my first purchase with my unexpected bounty would be a new dress for Betty, who had not had a special treat in some time.

"Oh, Johnnie, you are such a one!" she said when I informed her of my decision. "Do you think we could go to the theater?"

For Betty, no treat could surpass a journey to the "theater," which she pronounced in an extraordinary manner, affecting an upper-class accent that she applied to no other word in her vocabulary. A night among the "swells" was her chiefest delight, so much so that her comportment on such evenings could hardly escape the censure of the well bred. But such is the charm of youth, and such the indulgence of age, that these evenings were my chiefest delight as well.

We chose for our evening a performance at the Drury Lane of *The Second Mrs. Tanquery,* featuring the estimable American actress Ethel Barrymore. Betty's gown was striking even for her, a gold and white creation "right off the boat from Paris," as she assured me, with a generous froth of Belgian lace that enhanced rather than concealed its equally generous *décolletage.* So attired, it could hardly be expected that Betty might escape attention, for which reason I had decided to accept the extra expense of a private box—the enchanted bower, one might say, of our modern civilization, where, for a brief moment and at a substantial cost, we are as gods.

In was in such a relaxed and exalted spirit that Betty and I descended to the foyer after the second act, Betty's fair white arm resting on mine as she discoursed on the excellence of Miss Barrymore's performance.

"Dr. Watson!"

The powerful figure of Winston Churchill stood before me at the foot of the stairs, parting the flow of elegant personages like a great rock dividing the progress of a stream.

"Dr. Watson!" he repeated. "It is imperative that I have a word with you."

"Mr. Churchill," I said, rather caught off guard. I fear I had not my wits fairly about me, for Betty and I had consumed the better part of a bottle of champagne during the first two acts, and I was a bit dazzled by all the brilliance of the occasion.

"Will you come along, Dr. Watson?" Mr. Churchill demanded, taking me by my free arm and leading Betty and myself to the edge of the great crowd.

"Betty," I said, "this is Mr. Winston Churchill. He is, that is—are you in Parliament, Mr. Churchill?"

My ignorance of Mr. Churchill's position was entirely feigned, of course, but I felt justified in provoking him. His treatment of Holmes and myself had been high-handed in the extreme, and some of his remarks on the Boer War during the election were, I felt, scarcely forgivable, in particular his statement that "a vote for the Liberals is a vote for the Boers."

"I have the honor of representing Oldham," said Mr. Churchill irritably.

"Yes, of course. Mr. Churchill is a member of Parliament, Betty. Mr. Churchill, this is Elizabeth Marbles."

"Pleased," said Mr. Churchill, taking Betty's hand, though keeping his fierce eyes on me.

"Goodness, Mr. Churchill, you're the feller in the papers, ain't you?" asked Betty, with all the lack of discretion that I could have anticipated.

"Yes, I have been featured in the popular press, young lady."

"Why, you are a fine gentleman, you are, Mr. Churchill," Betty said with a saucy curtsy that, I regret to say, had the rather obvious goal of drawing attention to her bosom.

"Thank you, young lady. I really must ask a moment alone with Dr. Watson, Miss Marbles."

"Well, of course, Mr. Churchill. But ain't you got a girl, a fine gentleman like you?"

"I . . . Miss Barrymore and I will be dining together," said Mr. Churchill.

"Really? Well, isn't that fine. What do you think, Johnnie? He's dating Miss Barrymore. Are you engaged, Mr. Churchill?"

"I should not put it in that manner," he replied.

I cannot deny that I enjoyed Mr. Churchill's discomfort, though Betty's exuberance, so utterly contrary to the atmosphere of the Drury Lane, or any other respectable establishment, did impose a marked strain upon my own composure as well.

"What's Miss Barrymore like?" continued Betty. "Why, I'll bet she just wears the most beautiful clothes, doesn't she, Mr. Churchill?

I fear that Mr. Churchill had lost all interest in continuing his conversation with Betty, for he was staring at me with such intensity that he appeared ready to explode before my very eyes. I was about to interject a remark in hope of checking Betty's relentless interrogation when we were interrupted from another quarter entirely.

"Winston!" a voice exclaimed.

I turned to the speaker, altogether the greatest lady I have ever beheld in my life, dressed in the very height of fashion and opulence. Though perhaps slightly past her prime, she was accompanied by an extraordinarily handsome young man.

"Mother!" exclaimed Mr. Churchill with what seemed to me to be a touch of horror.

"Miss Barrymore is so enchanting this evening," said Mrs. Churchill. "Such a remarkable artist. Please, introduce us to your friends."

From Mr. Churchill's expression, I felt sure that Mrs. Churchill knew very well that Betty and I were not her son's friends.

"This is Dr. Watson, Mother," he said, "and his friend Miss Elizabeth Marbles. Dr. Watson and Miss Marbles, this is my mother, the Lady Randolph Churchill, and her husband, Mr. George Cornwallis-West."

"Charmed, I'm sure," said Betty, extending her hand to the gentleman, who was truly an Adonis in evening dress. Both her words and actions appeared to be drawn from a scene in the play that we had just witnessed. Mr. Cornwallis-West took her hand with some amusement, his shrewd eyes shifting from mother to son in a manner that entertained the former as much as it distressed the latter.

Betty, I am pleased to say for her own sake, was entirely unaware of whatever slight, malicious, three-handed game was being played around her. What was happening around her she did not know and did not care to know. To have her hand kissed at the Drury Lane by George Cornwallis-West was for Betty if not heaven itself then a facsimile whose distance from the original was unworthy of notice.

"Your young lady is very charming," Mr. Cornwallis-West said to me with clear impertinence. I took Betty firmly by the arm in response, for she was in fact advancing rapidly on his person, with an intention, as unconscious as it was explicit, of transferring the kiss upon her hand to a more intimate and substantial portion of her body.

"Come, my dear," I said, attempting to direct her back up the stairs. "I fear we'll miss the start of the third act."

"But we must speak, Dr. Watson!"

Mr. Churchill interjected himself into the situation at this point, grasping me by my other arm and spinning me about, as though I were a character in a French farce.

"Perhaps the young lady would like to join me for a glass of champagne," remarked Lady Churchill, asserting her presence in a decided manner and capturing the attention of all. I gladly relinquished Betty to her care, whom she took firmly on her left arm. Then taking Mr. Cornwallis-West with equal firmness on her right, Lady Churchill departed with her retinue in search of refreshment. There was nothing for me to do but hope that that lady's sense of propriety, and her sense of possessiveness, would keep Betty's fierce attraction to her husband in check. I was about to make a remark to Mr. Churchill in praise of his mother's remarkable character and charm, but the furious scowl he favored me with when I turned to him deprived me of all inclination toward speech.

"I must talk with you, Dr. Watson," he said. "It has come to my attention that Sherlock Holmes is conducting an investigation of the archduke, which I had forbidden him to do. This is a most gross impertinence and interference in affairs of state. Mr. Holmes must desist in this activity at once."

"I don't believe that you have the authority to restrict the activities of Sherlock Holmes or anyone else," I said sharply for I had had enough of Mr. Churchill's imperious tones. "At least two murders have occurred on British soil, and perhaps more."

"If crimes have been committed, that is the affair of Scotland Yard and not Mr. Holmes," retorted Mr. Churchill. "You should not speak of such things in a public place."

"It is you who has initiated this conversation," I said.

Mr. Churchill liked few things less than contradiction. His eyes glowed at me as though incandescent. Having once provoked him, however, I was not inclined to break off my assault.

"It may interest you to know," I continued, "that Holmes has already left for the Continent and has begun his investigation. I am prepared to follow him. Where it will lead I cannot say."

Sadly, I had pushed things too far and in fact had fallen directly into the trap Mr. Churchill had prepared for me.

"He will get no farther than France," he said coolly. "Mr. Holmes will shortly be receiving notification from the embassies of Germany, Austria-Hungary, and Russia declaring him and yourself to be *personae non gratae* within the boundaries of those empires. You should know that the Foreign Office has given its full and explicit approval to these decisions."

I stared at the man, appalled.

"You dare to deny the right of British subjects to travel as they please!" I stammered in my rage.

"It is not my decision but the decision of four great empires," he said, enjoying himself immensely. "Affairs of state far outstrip the petty concerns of middle-class morality, Dr. Watson. In the future, it will be much better for you and your friend to confine your attention to matters suitable to your station rather than above it. And now you will excuse me."

And with those malicious words he made his departure. I could only stare open-mouthed at his effrontery. I walked to the bar in search of Betty and her companions, but could not find them, returning to my box when the house lights began to blink. Twenty minutes into the third act, Betty returned, aglow with pleasure after enjoying a glass with Lady Churchill and her husband in the privacy of their box and clearly determined to recount her adventures in the last detail. I poured us each a glass of champagne and, resolutely casting aside all the vexations I had so recently endured, allowed myself to be seduced by Betty's sweet effervescence, to the extent that I felt no real distress when, later that evening in the privacy of a more intimate setting, she loudly cried, "Georgie! Oh, Georgie!"

PART II

Aboard the Orient Express

CHAPTER 8

Aboard the Orient Express

A FINE WAY TO BEGIN an investigation, I must confess," said Holmes, toasting me with a glass of champagne. "The British voter should be induced to turn out the Conservative Party more often."

"He should, indeed," I replied. "I have never known such luxury."

Outside, the lights of Paris gleamed through the darkness. Sherlock Holmes and I were departing from the French capital in the most pleasant manner possible, traveling in adjoining first-class compartments aboard the Orient Express. We were en route to Constantinople at the expense of De Beers, all official barriers to our endeavor having vanished after the great victory of the Liberal Party at the polls in the opening months of 1906. More than four years had elapsed since Sir Samuel had first hired Holmes to investigate, but at last our journey had begun. I had departed from Victoria Station at four-thirty in the afternoon, arriving in Paris at about ten, where Holmes boarded the train. Holmes had been in Paris for several weeks, pursuing a smuggling case at the request of the French government.

"How was your journey from London?" he asked.

"Quite comfortable, except for the Channel," I said. We were held up for half an hour entering Calais, during the thick of the storm. My appetite has still not recovered."

"How unfortunate. What was the cause of the delay?"

"An enormous yacht was blocking the passage. The *Peregrine,* belonging to the American millionaire Horatio Thompson. She had turned sideways to the current, but the crew got her around at last, and we pulled through. In any event, I am here. What an extraordinary turn of events!"

"Yes. I confess I was amazed to receive a visit from Sir Samuel last week at my hotel. I did not expect ever to hear from him or De Beers again. But he was most insistent that we make the trip as soon as possible."

"Then Archduke Josef is in Constantinople."

"Yes. And the diamond has been cut, into a number of pieces, both large and small, by jewelers to the sultan. But the archduke is behind in his *douceurs.* He had to surrender the stone to have it cut and now may not regain possession. He has spent very freely in the past few years, based upon loans, but now he appears to have suffered a crisis in his financial affairs that I am at a loss to explain."

"Has this happened only recently?" I asked.

"I believe so. I have never abandoned the case entirely, but my files are all in London. But this is an extraordinary turn of events. The Liberal Party, it seems, is less obsequious to the Hapsburgs than the Conservatives, and we are allowed to join the chase."

"Do we know how many diamonds there are?"

"One great stone, of more than three hundred carats, one of ninety carats, one of seventy carats, two of fifty, three of thirty, twenty of five carats each, and more than seventy of two carats each, all of them stones of the first water."

"Remarkable!"

"Yes, the finest shop in Paris could not manage such a display, and all from one stone. I gather that Sir Samuel is particularly fearful of the impact of so many small, high-quality stones entering the market beyond the control of the De Beers monopoly."

"Indeed."

"Yes. According to Sir Samuel, De Beers has taken a particular interest in developing the New York market for engagement rings and is determined to prevent any interference in its growth."

I gathered from Holmes's expression that he did not entirely share our client's concern. He drank from his champagne and picked up a large, elegant folder from the small table between us. The folder, bound in supple, dark-blue leather and featuring a luxurious gold seal on the cover, featured a brochure that described the wonders of the Orient Express in the most extravagant language possible.

"It is kind of the railroad to provide us with a list of our companions for our journey," said Holmes. He removed three sheets of stiff writing paper from the folder, which contained the names of the passengers written in fine calligraphic script, and studied them carefully.

"Most interesting," he said at last, when he had completed his perusal. "We are traveling with three smugglers, two spies, and one suspected murderess, none of whom, fortunately, is likely to mean us harm."

"A suspected murderess?"

"Yes. Madame la Comtesse D'Espinau. Her husband, a brute of a fellow but enormously wealthy, drowned while attempting to swim the Bosporus. She visits the site each year in his memory. Surely you remember the case. Her beauty and exotic parentage were sources of inexhaustible interest to the daily press."

"No, I don't believe I can recall the name at all."

Holmes opened his cigarette case and passed me one.

"You must have been in South Africa at the time. Yes, of course. I recall the *Daily Mail* trumpeted it as the case of the new century, although the evidence was far from conclusive. The count was so vain as to indulge in several glasses of cognac prior to attempting to duplicate the feat of Hero and Byron. It was suggested at the time that the lady administered a drug in the cognac that induces severe cramping of the muscles a short time after ingestion."

"You were involved in the investigation?"

"Yes. The autopsy gave suggestion of foul play, and the countess had been in London a month prior to her husband's death. There is an apothecary in the East End, a Mr. Nolan Wells, who provides a variety of drugs for those who need them. I had hoped to end Mr. Wells's career with this case, but was disappointed. The countess insisted that the only drug she had obtained from Mr. Wells was opium, for her husband, and perhaps that is true. In any event, the count had remarkably few friends for a man of his rank, while the countess had many, among them the French premier. In addition, she was quite generous to the count's few living relatives, devoting an unnecessarily large portion of her husband's fortune to their care."

"Perhaps she felt it was her duty to do so."

"Perhaps, Watson. You are always inclined to chivalry. If you meet the lady, I suspect you will grow even more sympathetic to her cause, for she is very beautiful indeed. Her father was a French diplomat, an aristocrat with little more than a once-great name, while her mother was from a family of enormously wealthy Phanariot Greeks, with close connections to the sultan's chief vizier. Unfortunately, both her parents died at an early age, and a coup within the sultan's retinue deprived the family of all position. The countess came to Paris as an orphan at the age of twelve, enchanted everyone, made a splendid marriage, and now lives a life of semiseclusion due to the scandal. I understand that she is trying to reestablish the position of her family in Constantinople."

"I should hope that I would reach my conclusions as to the lady's guilt entirely on the evidence of the matter," I replied.

"Indeed," said Holmes. "Well, the lady may be worth avoiding."

"I am always cautious with a countess," I said, amused at the thought. "What of our other companions? Are there any others whom you suspect of being in league with the archduke?"

"An excellent question. At the present time I would say the answer is no. However, when we arrive in Vienna tomorrow morning I will not be so sure. There are a variety of military officers from the Austrian Empire scheduled to board. One can never know where the archduke will find a confederate. Even now, I would counsel vigilance. In any event, I am not entirely sure that this list is complete."

I was about to reply when I heard a knock at the door. I opened it to reveal perhaps the most elegant servant I ever saw in my life, a tall man in a dark blue uniform heavily trimmed with gold braid. It is utterly impossible to imagine such an individual on an English train.

"Mr. Holmes, Dr. Watson? Allow me to welcome you to the Orient Express. I am *le chef de train,* M. Lestrange. It is my constant duty to ensure that your trip will be the most enjoyable railway journey of your lives."

M. Lestrange spoke excellent English, with that special accent that a proud Frenchman affects to apply that special polish to our language that we unfortunately cannot achieve ourselves.

"The Orient Express is happy to serve a light breakfast in your compartment anytime after eight A.M., and lunch is available in the *wagon-restaurant* beginning at eleven. If you have any further requests, you may summon the *conducteur* for your *wagon-lit* through the speaking tube. Good evening."

We bid the estimable M. Lestrange adieu and resumed our conversation. It was clear from my friend's words that despite the passage of more than four years, his interest in the case of the Great Blue, and his memory of the harsh treatment he had received at the hands of Winston Churchill, remained as vivid as ever. He had devoted every free hour of the past week exploring new sources of information about our foe, and had brought a great mound of printed matter with him. As he expressed his desire to begin his researches immediately, I excused myself and thought to stretch my legs before returning to my own compartment.

I had scarcely exited Holmes's compartment when I was struck by the scent of a most exquisite perfume. Nor did I have to look far for the source, for as I turned around I found myself looking into a pair of magnificent dark brown eyes.

"Good evening, monsieur," the lady said. "You are English,

are you not? Forgive me for troubling you, but I am in search of the *wagon-restaurant*. Are you familiar with its location?"

"The dining carriage?" I asked. "Yes, it is three carriages forward."

"Ah, then I have come in the wrong direction."

"Perhaps I could accompany you," I said. "Permit me to introduce myself. I am Dr. Watson."

"Dr. Watson, the celebrated author?" she asked with a charming smile.

"Yes," I replied. "I am accompanying my friend Sherlock Holmes on a journey to Constantinople."

"Then we shall be traveling companions for the next three and a half days," she said, taking my arm in the gentlest possible manner. "I am Madame la Comtesse D'Espinau."

I could hardly believe the words that issued from such beautiful lips! Having quitted Holmes's company for less than a minute, I now found myself arm in arm with a suspected murderess!

I could hardly doubt that, were the countess as deadly as she was charming, no man could escape her. She very kindly ignored the fact that once she was headed in the proper direction, it was impossible for her not to discover the location of the dining carriage, and we chatted amiably as we strolled through the train. In any event, the pleasure of walking through the Orient Express with a beautiful woman on one's arm is a rare one indeed.

The countess wore a lovely evening dress of rich cream color, setting off the darkness of her beautiful skin, which held more than a suggestion of Levantine blood. She was tall and graceful, with a superb figure. Although no longer in the first bloom of youth, her thick black hair, exquisitely coiffed, showed not a strand of gray. From each ear there hung a magnificent black pearl, which glowed richly against the warmth of her elegantly curved neck. Dazed by her beauty, charm, riches, and rank, I fairly floated through the carriages beside her.

"How fortunate," she said when, all too soon, we arrived at the dining carriage, "to have encountered such a charming traveling companion at the start of a long journey. I hope to see you again soon, Doctor."

Reluctantly, I bid the countess adieu and returned to my own compartment. I had no desire to tell Holmes of our encounter. I was, I fear, utterly bewitched, but unwilling to acknowledge my fate, as a supercharged cloud, pregnant with lightning bolts, may appear neutral and harmless as long as it remains far from a conduit for the pent fury within.

I fidgeted for some time and then decided to seek out the gentlemen's lounge, two carriages back, which proved to be a shrine to the tobacco leaf such as I had never known. The moment I opened the door my nostrils were assailed by the aromatic essences of the finest and most intoxicating tobaccos one could imagine. The elegant marquetry of the wood paneling, the luxurious carpet, the rich Spanish leather of the chairs, the polished brass—all were mere offerings to the great god, whose heady incense filled the atmosphere and pervaded the senses. Half a dozen acolytes sat about the carriage, each nourishing a superb example of the cigar maker's art. As I settled into a vacant chair, an attentive waiter appeared instantly at my elbow and took my order for a glass of port. The atmosphere was such that I scarcely needed to light a cigar, and indeed the small señores in my cigar case would cut a poor figure in comparison to the great Cubans that flourished around me. I picked up the morning's copy of the *Times,* whose pages were largely devoted to the launch of the great new battleship *Dreadnought.* It was the unanimous opinion of all experts that the remarkably advanced design of this ship would guarantee British supremacy on the high seas for decades to come, leaving the kaiser and Admiral Von Tirpitz trailing haplessly in our wake and compensating decisively for the acknowledged superiority of the German port in Kiao-chau, China, as compared to our own in Wei-hai-wei. Furthermore, the experts joined in rejecting insinuations in the foreign press that both America and Italy had begun construction of comparable ships. "British steel, and British snap, remain unique in all the world," remarked Admiral Fisher with a truculence that was generally admired.

For my own part, my experiences in the Boer War had left me with a skepticism toward the fruits of imperialism that as a younger man I might have considered unpatriotic or even treasonous, despite the rigor of my experiences in Afghanistan. As I folded my *Times* and placed it beside me on my seat, I regarded the future with somewhat more trepidation than did the experts assembled by that newspaper. I was no more than halfway through the columns devoted to the topic of the great ship when I was interrupted by a servant whose rank, I later discovered, was *conducteur,* a sort of sergeant in the army needed to ensure the comfort of the guests aboard the Orient Express.

"Excuse me, My Lord," he said, "but the *chef de train* would have a word with you."

"I am hardly a peer," I responded. "Please address me as 'Doctor.' "

"All Englishmen traveling aboard the Orient Express are lords," he replied.

"I am afraid not," I responded. "But you say that M. Lestrange wishes to see me?"

"Yes, My Lord. M. Lestrange."

"I will be with him immediately," I said.

I followed the man to the baggage car, where I entered a special compartment reserved for M. Lestrange. There was a businesslike elegance to his compartment that suggested authority rather than opulence.

"Dr. Watson," he said, greeting me. "You are most kind to come on such short notice. I thank you for this opportunity."

"I am glad to be of assistance," I said. "Is there a problem of some sort?"

"Not a problem, sir, no. It is the constant endeavor of the Orient Express to fulfill each traveler's every desire. And we are, of course, men of the world, you and I."

"Of course."

"And on a journey such as this, there is no fairer desire than that for intimate companionship. We understand. We approve. And we will assist in every way. We only ask for the payment of a fare. You understand?"

"Not entirely," I said, for in fact I did not understand at all.

"The young lady," he said. "Mademoiselle, will you join us?"

The door from the adjoining room opened, and out stepped Jennie, dressed as a lady in the latest French fashion!

"This is, I believe, your daughter, Doctor?" asked M. Lestrange.

CHAPTER 9

A New Companion

"JENNIE," I SAID, IN amazement, "what are you doing here?"

"Well, I couldn't stay away, now, could I? They say travel is ever so broadening."

"Where did you get those clothes?"

She smiled at me with outrageous effrontery from beneath a bonnet seemingly contrived entirely from egret feathers.

"Why, I charged them to De Beers, of course. You told me they were the fellows paying the freight."

"It appears that the young lady concealed herself within a large trunk identified as your property, Dr. Watson," M. Lestrange remarked. "The trunk was embarked in London aboard the baggage car that accompanies the Calais *wagon-lit* in which you yourself traveled. The somewhat unusual instructions were to deliver it to your compartment after our departure from Vienna. However, when one of our baggage men had occasion to move the trunk, he detected indications that all was not as it should be. He relayed this information to me, and I was able to discover this delightful creature inside."

"And so you've been cooped up in a trunk all day?" I demanded of Jennie.

"It's not such a hardship. Anyway, I've come to see the Terrible Turk."

"There will be no Terrible Turks for you," I said. "M. Lestrange, I apologize for this inconvenience. Please add all appropriate charges to our bill."

"Of course, Doctor. And where will the young lady be staying?"

Jennie gazed at me with fierce eyes. I did not see how her presence on our journey would be anything but a major impedance to Holmes's investigation. But Jennie's remarkable charm and presence had become the great pleasure in my life over the past six years, and to disappoint her in this matter required more unflinching rectitude than I could muster. At the tender age of fifteen Jennie had managed to fashion for herself a remarkable career as a singer on the music hall stage, appearing for the past two years as a featured performer at Will Ramsey's *Arabian Nights*. She had as well filled her head with all sorts of absurd notions. To be riding on the Orient Express was a dream come true for her, and I had not the heart to make her dream vanish.

"Is it possible to find a separate compartment?" I asked.

"Of course," M. Lestrange replied. "For Mademoiselle Watson, all things are possible."

Jennie's eyes sparkled.

"Now, that is better," she said. "Can we get a bit of grub? I meant to bring some biscuits but I forgot all about it in the rush."

I looked at her. She had obviously prevailed upon M. Lestrange to allow her time to repair her appearance, for she did not resemble at all a girl of fifteen who had spent the past twelve or fourteen hours locked up inside a trunk. Nor, in fact, did she resemble a girl of fifteen.

"A midnight supper is available in the dining car," said M. Lestrange. "Perhaps you and the young lady would care to join me?"

"Thank you, M. Lestrange, but we shall find her carriage ourselves. I believe I need to speak to my daughter alone," I replied. "You have been most helpful."

"I am delighted to be of service, Doctor," said M. Lestrange, speaking ostensibly to me but staring directly at Jennie.

I took Jennie by the hand and led her from the compartment.

"Why did you tell him that you are my daughter?" I demanded as we headed down the corridor. I had, in fact, adopted Jennie, for a variety of legal reasons, but we both preferred not to emphasize this aspect of our relationship.

"Well, what did you expect me to say, that I was your chippie? Anyway, he certainly didn't believe me. But isn't he the charmer, though? He promised he'd teach me French."

"This is insupportable, Jennie," I said. "This is a most important case."

"Oh, I won't be in the way," she assured me, as though I feared she would deliberately obstruct the investigation. "I'll be a help. I helped you before, didn't I?"

"That was different," I said. "We are not in London now. Constantinople is no place for a young English girl like yourself."

"Constantinople's no worse than London, I'll bet you that. They'll slit your throat for a tuppence anywhere you go. Oh, now, look at this! Isn't this just the best of everything!"

She made this exclamation as we entered the dining carriage, and surely she could be forgiven for her sentiments. The tables of the car were covered with white silk and heavy with polished silver and cut glass. Overhead, dozens of small electric lights gleamed softly from chandeliers. Our table was decorated with a small elegant vase filled with freshly cut flowers, and we sat in chairs upholstered with finely worked leather.

"Oh, now I shan't get up, ever!" said Jennie once she was seated. "And you were going to keep this all to yourself!"

"That is not the point, Jennie," I said. "I'm sure Mrs. Marbles is worrying herself to death over you."

"That old cat," she replied. "She misses the scratch I fetch her. But you needn't worry about that. I left her a sovereign hidden away, and she'll find it quick enough. I pay my debts. May I have a cigarette, please?"

"Of course you may not."

She grinned at impish delight at my response.

"Well, anyway, here I am, safe and sound. Aren't you pleased I'm not hurt?"

"Since it was you who placed yourself in danger, you should not be congratulated for having escaped it."

"Oh, pooh! It was the most brilliant plan ever. Maximillian showed me how to work the lock from the inside. The Great Houdini couldn't have done it better."

"Maximillian is, I suppose, a theatrical acquaintance of yours?"

"Well, of course he is. Maximillian the Master of Escape. He's been on the bill with us for a month. He can get you out of anything."

"Then why did the baggage man have to rescue you?"

"He didn't rescue me—well, not altogether. You see, they wedged me in, so I couldn't open the door but a few inches. Well, I knew that if I came out before we reached Paris you'd just send me right back, so I waited just a bit. About eleven o'clock I heard a fellow moving about and I gave a yell, and here I am."

Jennie smiled complacently as she completed this tale. Despite her tender years she had become close to impossible due to her remarkable success on the stage. But never had she leaped so entirely over the boundaries of her life until now. I was struggling to gather my thoughts when M. Lestrange arrived, pleased to warm himself once more in the flame of Jennie's youthful charm. He read the entire menu to her, translating each item and delighting in Jennie's earnest mispronunciation of her choices. A liveried waiter stood by to record her selections, which I duly seconded, and we shortly commenced upon a fantastic midnight supper of iced cantaloupe, cold roast duck shimmering in aspic, and a salad of rice, tomatoes, and aubergine. I abjured all sweets at the conclusion of the meal and contented myself with a cognac, but Jennie was not so abstemious and enjoyed a soufflé flavored with anise, along with peaches and strawberries from Africa and a plate of elegant Parisian chocolates that gleamed like jewels. Such epicurean self-indulgence was perhaps not the best thing for a young girl who had spent the better part of a day being treated like a piece of baggage, but Jennie was not to be dissuaded, and in fact she consumed the whole with immense pleasure.

"This is better than Gunter's," she said when the meal was concluded. "I wonder if my compartment has been prepared."

"Please stop talking like a West End *soubrette,*" I said. "That is the one thing that will get you off this train. If worse comes to worst, I shall take you home myself."

This threat, which was not entirely idle, served its purpose.

"Well, can I at least say hello to Mr. Holmes?" she asked in a subdued tone.

"Of course you may. And if he insists that you leave, then you must go."

Jennie colored slightly.

"Sometimes you sound so serious."

"This is a serious matter. It is hard for me to resist indulging you in this manner, but I cannot allow my personal concerns to compromise the investigation. We are, ultimately, dealing with an utterly ruthless man for the very highest stakes."

"But Mr. Holmes will catch him, won't he? I mean, he never fails."

"Life isn't always what I put in my books, Jennie. You know yourself how hard life can be."

I looked into her clear blue eyes, which never seemed to waver. How our chance encounter on a dirty London street had changed my life!

"All right, then," she said, "I'll be good. Now can I see Mr. Holmes?"

"I shall first see if he is awake and if so prepare him for your presence."

"It isn't your fault that I'm here."

"I know it isn't, but it is my fault, or at least my decision, that you will remain here. Holmes would never have consented to your presence if I had suggested it prior to our embarkation."

"Don't you ever call him Sherlock?"

"The only person who addresses Sherlock Holmes as 'Sherlock' is his brother Mycroft, and that shall never change."

"Of course not."

She was smiling at me once more, but I stiffened myself against her wiles. I left Jennie in the restaurant car under the devoted care of M. Lestrange, who instantly began teaching her to say "My name is Jennie" in French, and made my way to our compartment. I found Holmes still awake, playing his violin in the softest manner possible. I reclined on the soft leather cushions and listened as the delicate music filled the compartment like an overflowing liquid. I waited until the last note faded away into silence before speaking.

"We have an unexpected guest," I said.

Holmes smiled.

"I presume that it is your young charge," he said. "No other individual can prompt that mixture of pride and frustration that I read in your expression. How did she make her way onto the train?"

"By packing herself into a large trunk, which she then had shipped to Victoria Station as part of my baggage. I fear she will add considerably to our expenses on this trip."

"If we come back with the diamond, I am sure Sir Samuel will not begrudge the cost."

"I left her in the restaurant car with M. Lestrange."

"The *chef de train?*"

"Yes."

"A remarkable individual."

"Jennie would like to see you before she retires."

The faintest of smiles betrayed itself on Holmes's lips.

"So often, in your earlier writings, you portrayed me as invulnerable to women's charms."

"I did no more than take you at your word."

"Indeed. I confess that I am as powerless before Jennie's charms as you, despite the fact that we are in pursuit of a heartless murderer. I should, of course, be delighted to greet her."

"I shall do so at once. I would not want M. Lestrange to neglect his duties on her account."

"That would be inadvisable."

I departed from our compartment and hastened to the dining carriage, where Jennie and M. Lestrange remained locked in mutual enthrallment.

"Thank you for caring for Jennie, M. Lestrange," I said, taking my charge by the arm.

"Mademoiselle is so remarkable," he said with a deep bow.

"Adieu, monsieur," said Jennie, presenting her hand.

"Adieu, mademoiselle," responded the *chef.*

"Really, Jennie," I said as I led her into the next carriage, "you should not encourage a foreigner in such a manner."

"Oh, M. Lestrange is *un* prune shoveler, don't you worry," she replied. "I'm as safe as sixpence with him. Besides, I've got my hat pin, don't I? And I know how to use it."

Having thus been reassured, I led Jennie down the corridor of our carriage to Holmes's compartment.

"Welcome, Jennie," said Holmes, rising. "I have not seen you for six months. How you have changed in that time."

"I won't be a bother, Mr. Holmes," said Jennie with a graceful curtsy. "Why, you and Dr. Watson won't even know I'm here."

"That would be disappointing if true," said Holmes. "I hear from Watson that your success as an entertainer continues to grow."

A burst of girlish delight overcame Jennie's pose of worldly sophistication.

"I'm top of the bill, I am!" she cried, her voice suddenly taking on a marked cockney accent. "Old Will don't know what he got! They all tell me I'm the next Marie Lloyd!"

Then she subsided into silence, though with a mischievous grin.

"Indeed," said Holmes. "I am sure Watson has impressed upon you the seriousness of our mission."

"Of course."

"Good. Now, it is late, and I am sure you are ready for bed. While you are on this journey, you must lock and bolt the door of your compartment on every occasion, and particularly at night. The Orient Express is no safer than London."

"I'll be careful, Mr. Holmes. I'm a very careful girl."

And with that, we departed. I took Jennie to her compartment in the carriage before us and paid Holmes one last visit before returning to mine.

"You do not fear that De Beers will object to bearing the expense of another compartment?" I asked.

"Not if we return with the diamonds," said Holmes. "I have been reacquainting myself with the archduke's career. It is most disturbing. You do have your revolver, Watson?"

"Yes, of course."

"I suggest you place it beneath your pillow. It will not take much to make this man desperate."

CHAPTER 10

The Royal Interest

"SO, WATSON, THE GAME is afoot?" asked Holmes when I entered his compartment on the following morning. Something in his manner suggested that he was not entirely in earnest, but I could not fathom his intent.

"What do you mean?" I asked. "Is the archduke aboard the train?"

"No. It is your pursuit that I refer to, not mine. A woman has entered the case."

"Whatever do you mean?"

"Come, Watson, save your craft for the ladies. The Orient Express supplies its guests with new razors made of the finest German steel. In any event, a stropping of thirty seconds restores the edge of even the commonest blade. This morning, I heard you strop your razor for at least a minute. Furthermore, you have waxed your mustache, you exude the unmistakable scent of Hamman Bouquet, and you wear that cravat given to you some years before by a lady whose name now escapes me, which I believe you associate with amatory success."

"It is only appropriate to appear at one's best in such

luxurious surroundings," I said. "However, I should mention that I did encounter the Countess D'Espinau."

"It does not surprise me," said Holmes. "The lady is well acquainted with the archduke."

"How absurd! What grounds do you have for that accusation?"

"Both own a villa, or *yali,* on the Bosporus. Both travel to Cannes, Baden-Baden, and Monaco on a regular basis, and, of course, to Paris."

"Why, by that reasoning, you could link her to the king."

"No doubt. I merely wish you to be careful."

"I shall be very careful."

Rather than endure any more of Holmes's persiflage, I decided to quit the compartment and pay a visit to Jennie. I found her in excellent spirits, as one could well imagine, and we enjoyed a fine breakfast of coffee and French rolls with strawberry jam. M. Lestrange, not entirely to my surprise, paid Jennie a visit, and, learning of Jennie's enthusiasm for *fraises,* promised her a *coeur flottant merveilleux aux fraises* for high tea. His entire manner was suffused with the sort of Gallic elegance that irritates the true Englishman as much, I fear, as it entrances the true Englishwoman. At any event, I had new reasons to regret Jennie's presence, and I experienced profound misgivings when she announced her intention after breakfast of repairing to the ladies' lounge. But, of course, it was impossible to physically supervise Jennie's behavior at every moment. We agreed to meet at twelve-thirty and we went our separate ways, she to the ladies' lounge and I to the smoking carriage.

The carriage was relatively unoccupied at the time, and as I watched the charming German countryside roll by, I took the opportunity to ponder Jennie's character anew. From the first time I had known her, Jennie had commanded an audience. Now that she was approaching womanhood, one could call her entirely a creature of the theater. Acting and being were one to her. She sought the spotlight as eagerly as a dog seeks the love of its master, the spontaneity of her pursuit equaled only by its pertinacity. In the eyes of the law I was Jennie's father, for I had adopted her to assure that in the event of my death my estate would pass to her without possibility of dispute, though under such restrictions as would be appropriate for a person of her age, sex, and temperament. At the same time, I felt it would be entirely unwarranted for Jennie to exhibit herself on the stage as my daughter, an opinion in which she concurred, rather to my surprise, for at that time I had not realized how acutely she studied the emotions of those around her and how easily she adapted her moods and desires to complement the will of her audience. With a gesture that I confess touched me deeply, she chose the maiden name of my wife and appeared on stage as Jennie Morstan.

Jennie's appetite for attention, at once innocent and all-consuming as a child, became more obviously calculating as she began to attain the mature charms of her sex. For the powers of attraction she herself felt an irresistible attraction. Upon the stage of *Arabian Nights* she was given to performing a song, "Every Little Movement Has a Meaning All Its Own," whose very title was an unmistakable invitation to physical innuendo of the most obvious kind. Jennie's youthful and graceful form, emphasized by a costume mature beyond her years and vivified by her extraordinary personality, could hardly fail to provoke a shamelessly carnal response, particularly when exhibited before an audience predisposed to supply a ribald interpretation to the most innocent gesture.

"They do like it, don't they?" she would say upon exiting the stage, her face glowing with a proud and somewhat malicious joy.

Explicit warnings, in such a matter, are the merest folly. My relationship with Jennie was hardly that of a true father and daughter. Her income, which I continued to manage, was already substantial, and Jennie agitated continuously for more. Having grown up in the streets, the question of money was never far from her mind, and it was my responsibility to deal with her employer Mr. Ramsay on this point. Jennie arranged her "cash talks" with me with great care, cordoning them off from our normal social intercourse, for this was the one time that she showed her will without reserve, and it was the one time I felt I earned my worth as a parent, for her suspicions and rages on such occasions could burst forth with appalling directness, showering me with expressions of the fiercest contempt for not obtaining for her what she conceived to be the true worth of her abilities.

I felt at such times the great value of my experiences as a physician. Having viewed the human frame, and the human soul, over and over again in the most tragic and pathetic circumstances, I could allow Jennie to rain her most heartless accusations against me without feeling their edge. So often had I, as it were, observed myself in the operating room, covered in filth, with no end in sight for my labors, and, too often, no true hope for a successful conclusion to my efforts that, even though these "cash talks" might leave me drenched with perspiration, I never doubted that Jennie and I would eventually attain a peaceful and just resolution, and in fact, when we were over and done, she would hold me tightly and press her head against my chest, with never a sound until she had recovered her composure. Then I would depart, and when we next met she would have assumed once more the guise of the enchanting performer with which she so loved to beguile the world.

I sat with my head filled with such thoughts as the train arrived at the station for Augsburg. There were few in that city who could afford the fares of such a luxurious mode of transportation, but the few who could, awaited in the morning sunshine, arrayed in all their finery. As the gleaming train rolled to a halt I could hear excited voices, speaking a language I could not understand, absorbed in the great ritual of arrival and departure. Once the passengers were on board, the shrieking whistle and puffing locomotive broke the morning quiet of that medieval town, whose narrow streets had given birth to one of the world's greatest revolutions in human faith and set nation against nation for centuries. I watched the quaint buildings slide by, one by one, until we were out in the German countryside once more.

When I had completed my reverie on Jennie's character, I sought diversion in the form of reading matter, chancing upon a copy of *The Egoist* in the small international library maintained aboard the Express. The novel, by Mr. George Meredith, proved to be a recent addition to that long line of domestic novels that constitute the English Comedy of Manners. Mr. Meredith addressed the well-worn topic of marriage among county families of unequal means with a method all his own, drawing out the fears and hopes of his characters in the most elaborate detail, in language that was often too fine for my comprehension, so that the thread of his exquisite embroidery sometimes disappeared entirely before my eyes. As the sun passed the meridian it was entirely unclear to me whom the protagonists should marry, or whether they should marry, or indeed whether anyone, ever, should marry anyone at all.

When I put Mr. Meredith's novel down, I could not say that he had satisfied me, but he had intrigued me. I decided to take the volume with me when I departed for Jennie's compartment, arriving to discover her in the last stages of the completion of her toilet. Her costume, which must have taken an hour to assemble and array, was entirely new to me. I had excellent indications that Jennie hoarded money in some secret fashion of which I was unaware, but surely she had exhausted all her resources in purchasing new garments for this trip. The twin forces of youth and a career onstage had given her an obsession with her appearance that I, who was certainly no stranger to female vanity, found at times frightening to behold. There was, outrageously, nothing that Jennie wanted half so much in life as a maid.

"Why, there you are," she said at my arrival. "My, don't you smell like a fine cigar. I could be a detective myself if I had a mind."

"I'm sure you could," I said.

"Well, I could. You and Mr. Holmes could use some help, and here I am. We'll go to lunch and I'll detect everyone in the car for you."

She paused for a minute to give a final caress to the billowing ostrich plume that crowned her hat.

"There," she said. "That will have to do. But I won't look half so grand as the other ladies."

"You won't be half so old, either," I replied.

"Well, that's true enough. But I did see one who's pretty enough to be a princess, and not two years past twenty. Let's hope she stays in her compartment."

I opened the door for her and we walked to the restaurant carriage. M. Lestrange greeted us upon our arrival and conducted us to our table.

"If there is anything that mademoiselle requires, she has but to ask," he said.

"*Oui,* monsieur," she replied, a little too loudly.

He made an elegant bow and departed, leaving Jennie suffused with delight.

"Isn't he wonderful?" she asked. "Englishmen are so wooden. Why can't you be *un* prune shoveler, like him?"

"The expression is *un preux chevalier.* It means 'gallant knight.' "

"Un preux chevalier," Jennie repeated several times, employing a different intonation with each repetition. "There, that's got it."

"I see this trip will turn you into a perfect Continental," I said, surveying the menu.

"Well, it will," said Jennie. "I'll be the finest young lady London ever saw. Oh, look at all this. The French do know how to grub, don't they?"

She nodded, not at the menu, but at a broad platter a waiter bore down the aisle.

"I thought you were going to be a detective," I said.

"Humph. Aren't you clever, now? A girl has to eat, you know. What's 'trut de riviera belly manure'?"

"*Belle-meunière.* Grilled brook trout, as cooked by the pretty miller's wife."

"The pretty miller's wife? Who's she?"

"It's a story. Napoleon stopped at an inn known as *La Belle-Meunière,* in honor of the pretty miller's wife who did the cooking."

"Napoleon! I suppose it's fancy?"

"Yes, of course it is."

"Then that's what I'll have. How do you know so much about French cooking?"

"For several months during my convalescence in India I was stationed in Calcutta. My colonel was a man devoted to French cuisine. He had the habit of entertaining us with stories regarding their origin."

"Well, then, you know everything. 'Desserts.' That's puddings, right?"

"Yes."

"What's 'glass'?"

"*Glaces.* Ice cream."

"Oh, goody. Fish and ice cream, then. Now you have something."

"I shall content myself with bread and cheese."

"No, you have to have something else, so I can have some."

"Very well. I shall have the green turtle soup and the *salade russe.*"

"Salade russe," she pronounced in an amused tone. "What's that?"

"Russian salad. Cooked vegetables bound in mayonnaise."

"That's better."

Our waiter arrived to receive our order, and departed.

"Now, look at that fellow," said Jennie as another gentleman entered. "There's a suspect for you."

"What makes you say that?"

"You'll see him in the theater, night and day. Look at the way he combs his hair."

The gentleman, one would have to say, was rather offensively well tailored and polished in his person.

"There is more than one fop aboard this train, I am sure," I remarked.

"A fop! Listen to you. That fellow is more than a fop, unless he's a fop duke. Oh, can he polish an apple! Just look how he talks to that waiter. They're two of a kind. He's the king of the headwaiters, he is. He's English, ain't he? Look at those eyes. They'd go right through you, but you wouldn't want them to."

"What are you talking about?"

"He's trouble, you'll see. I'm going to ask François to keep an eye on him."

"François?"

"M. Lestrange. I'm sure he'll do anything for me."

"You may find, Jennie, that there is a limit even to the power of your charms."

She flashed me a brilliant smile, almost unendurably charming, as if in implicit refutation of my statement.

"We'll see about that," she said with a slight flush in her cheeks. "But I'll tell you this. He ain't the only one to watch. That fellow with the brown velvet collar knows more than he's telling. He's been watching us ever since we came in."

"Perhaps he's merely admiring your hat."

"None of that. He's been looking at you. And he's not that sort of fellow. He knows who you are. He's a detective, all right. He's been sent here to spy on you. That must make you feel proud. You're so important someone would buy a ticket on the Orient Express and pay a fellow just to keep you under observation."

"How can you be sure he's a detective?"

"Well, he's no gentleman, is he? Not with those socks."

"I fail to see the problem."

"They don't match his trousers. Just a bit too flashy. He's a bit of a trouper, he is, and one trouper can always spot another. But he is smooth. He must be French, I'll bet. A policeman, for sure. Special Branch."

"Special Branch. Perhaps this is a play you have recently seen."

"I have not. Mr. Holmes will confirm my theory. You forget how much I know about policemen. Look at the way he moves his eyes. Very quick, but he keeps his lids down so that folks won't notice. He's not reading that paper. And his expression never changes. A copper's always too cool by half. He's a copper, all right, but a Special Branch man all the way. He's got style, and he knows his way around the ladies. Look at those hands, manicured and all. A manicured policeman. Yes, he's smooth. But he's got a bit above himself on this job."

I looked into Jennie's grinning, mischievous face. For a moment she looked like the little urchin she once had been.

"Very well," I said. "Perhaps you're right. What about the lady across the aisle from him?"

Jennie gave a snort.

"Her? Why, I know her, all right, and I bet she thinks she knows me. You are such a one, you are, acting like such a lamb. If I didn't know you better. She's only got one thing on her mind, and you know it. You haven't got the cash for a lady like that."

"She could be entirely innocent."

"That's how you do it, isn't it? You're such a gentleman. She ain't got her eye on the diamonds, I don't think. She's regular trade, and the diamond is something else. I'm surprised her man let her out. But she must be a regular. Otherwise he wouldn't pay for her grub. She's not just a chippie. Oh, goody, here comes lunch."

And in fact our luncheon did arrive just as she spoke, the green turtle soup wonderfully redolent of the sea, and her trout fresh from the grill.

"Isn't he beautiful?" she asked, sticking her fork into the trout. "Why, I could eat this all day. How's your soup?"

"Excellent."

"How do you say it again?"

"Say what?"

"The trout."

"Truite de rivière belle-meunière."

"Truite de rivière belle-meunière," she repeated. "I'll be a Frenchie before we're back in London."

"I shouldn't doubt it," I replied.

"Now read the whole menu for me."

"I think you should enlist the services of a native speaker for that. François, perhaps."

I saw her smile once more.

"Yes, perhaps that would be best. Are we going to meet with Mr. Holmes now? I mean, after I've had my *glaces?*"

"Of course. You must tell him what you've learned."

When Jennie's *glaces* appeared, they arrived on a silver salver, and the waiter who carried it was accompanied by M. Lestrange himself. The remainder of our meal threatened to prolong itself almost indefinitely as M. Lestrange did read the entire menu to Jennie, and she repeated each item several times, the lesson occasioning near-infinite delight in both teacher and pupil. When Jennie had mastered the menu—to her own satisfaction, at least—she adroitly changed the subject.

"M. Lestrange," she said in a cautious whisper, "My father and I have been amusing ourselves trying to guess the nationality of that gentleman in the fine black suit and the calfskin boots. Father says that he is Swiss, but I insist that he is one of our own countrymen. Could you settle the matter?"

"The gentleman with the faun waistcoat, you mean?"

"Yes."

M. Lestrange smiled.

"I can tell you that the gentleman boarded the train in London and that his English is impeccable. However, he has remained in his compartment until now, and has requested that no reference be made as to his identity."

"Why, then, he is English!" she exclaimed, but still quite softly. "You see, Father," she said, tapping my arm, "such a fine gentleman! He has the bearing of a duke, surely. He must be well known throughout Europe. Why else should such a man seek to conceal his identity?"

"Some gentlemen are as discreet as they are well born," replied M. Lestrange. "I can only say that it is the first duty of the staff of the Orient Express to respect the least wish of her passengers."

"Oh, M. Lestrange, you are such a gentleman! Of course, I am being rude. And he is so very charming. And so mysterious! Why, he might be the Duke of York!"

"The duke, I believe, is a considerably younger gentleman," said M. Lestrange, betraying a certain irritation with Jennie's continued fascination with the stranger. "This gentleman is, perhaps, not so young as he looks."

"Oh, but so distinguished! Such perfect manners!" continued Jennie, who kept her eyes discreetly fixed on the object of their discussion, who was in fact dismantling a partridge with remarkable aplomb.

"Gentleman of the court have a remarkable polish," said M. Lestrange, somewhat sharply.

"The court? My, my. A royal gentleman?"

"Not of the royal family. Now I must ask you to excuse me, for we are about to arrive in Munich, and there is much to be done."

And with that M. Lestrange took a most gracious leave from Jennie, allowing us to take our leave as well. Our departure was regarded with discreet amusement by the other diners, for Jennie's remarkably spontaneous personality could not but impress itself on the most blasé observer.

"Watch them look," she said softly as we exited. "It's a hard job keeping secrets on this train."

"Perhaps they have never seen a young girl with such an extraordinary hat," I suggested.

"Oh, now. When you give folks something to look at, then you've got them. Mr. Holmes will tell you that."

CHAPTER 11

The Unpleasantness in Number Seven

WHEN WE RETURNED TO Holmes's compartment, we found him immersed in a document that he had apparently plucked from a large leather envelope that lay at his feet.

"You should have been there, Mr. Holmes," Jennie cried. "We had the most charming time. I had *truite de rivière belle-meunière et glaces.*"

She grinned with pleasure at her pronunciation, which was in fact remarkably assured. Indeed, it seemed that her very English was beginning to assume a Gallic flavor.

"No doubt I should have," said Holmes. "Did you see anything interesting?"

"A French detective," said Jennie, "and a mysterious English gentleman, very fancy, in black with a faun waistcoat."

"That would be Lord Worthington," said Holmes. "He is a gentleman in very close connection with the king."

"The marquis!" exclaimed Jennie, as if she were quite familiar with the gentleman. "What is he doing here?"

"It is not impossible that the object of our quest has also attracted the attention of the throne," said Holmes, opening his cigarette case. "In fact, it is almost to be expected. The king, after all, has use for such baubles."

Jennie, rather to my surprise, flushed slightly at Holmes's words.

"But how did you know that it was Lord Worthington?" she asked.

"About an hour ago I repaired to the gentlemen's smoking lounge to stretch my legs. I observed a tall gentleman with remarkably blond hair wearing a ring inscribed with the legend *nemo me impune lacessit,* which proclaims him to be a member of the Order of the Thistle. Lord Worthington's discretion has given him the nickname in the press of "the Anonymous Marquis," but a man who has a nickname is not so anonymous after all, and I have read several newspaper accounts that refer to his personal appearance. He has been a close associate of the king for more than a decade and has served as his emissary on delicate missions to the Continent more than once. I doubt if his lordship had any real intention of keeping his presence here a secret."

"Well, he's a fellow that wants watching," said Jennie. "I'm going to change."

"Whatever for?" I asked.

"For the ladies' lounge. I can't show up wearing the same thing I wore to lunch. What would they think of me?"

"She takes very well to the privileged life," I remarked to Holmes as Jennie departed.

"Indeed," said Holmes. "I fear I shall make poor company for you this afternoon, Watson. The presence of both Lord Worthington and the Countess D'Espinau aboard this train require that I renew my attention to that large collection of periodicals I brought with me devoted to the activities of the European aristocracy. If you would be so kind as to hand me that Gladstone from the top shelf I shall begin my researches."

As I handed Holmes the Gladstone there was a knock on the door and we heard the infinitely civilized voice of M. Lestrange requesting permission to enter.

"Mr. Holmes, Dr. Watson," he said, addressing a brief bow to each of us. "I hope you are all well."

"We are indeed," said Holmes, "thanks to your perfect hospitality."

"Your kind words are most appreciated, Mr. Holmes. I fear that I am in the somewhat awkward position of asking a favor of the great Sherlock Holmes."

"Please do so," said Holmes.

A look of palpable relief passed over the features of the *chef de train.*

"There has been an occurrence, Mr. Holmes," said M. Lestrange, "a most unfortunate occurrence. A gentleman in the last *wagon-lit,* a M. Brilleton, in compartment number seven, is most sadly dead, and the circumstances surrounding his death are most unclear. I know that it would be too much to ask for you to consider the matter, but to place such an unpleasant affair in the hands of the local police would be most distressing to my superiors and most inconvenient to our guests."

"I will see what I can accomplish," said Holmes. "Please, let us begin."

We walked quickly through the carriages until we reached the last. An uncomfortable *bagagiste,* clearly the discoverer of the body, waited for our arrival, along with another, more formidable individual, introduced to us as *Chef du Brigade* André.

"It is best," said M. Lestrange softly, "that we discuss this inside the compartment, although I warn you that what you see will not be pleasant."

Entering the compartment, we discovered that the *chef de train* was as good as his word. Lying on the berth was the figure of a man covered with a blanket. His eyes stared at us blankly, the pupils dilated with the final relaxation of death. His face and beard were smeared with blood, as was the pillow that lay next to his head, and blood dripped as well from his nostrils and one corner of his mouth, but there were no cuts or other signs of violence visible on the face. The faint but unmistakable scent of opium hung in the air.

"Jacques says the gentleman had two suitcases with him, but you see that every personal item has been removed," said M. Lestrange.

"Yes," said Holmes. "Were any of you acquainted with this man?"

The three shook their heads wordlessly.

Holmes turned to the *bagagiste.*

"Was the body covered when you came in?" he demanded.

"No, My Lord," said the man nervously. "He is without clothes."

"I see," said Holmes. "Then we must have a look."

So saying, he removed the blanket, revealing the nude corpse of a tall, powerfully built man in his early thirties.

"Do you see a wound, Watson?" Holmes asked, taking out his lens and studying the man's face with extreme care.

"No, nothing. The blood on lips and nose suggest an internal hemorrhage, but I see no sign of an injury that would cause such a bleeding."

As I spoke, Holmes brushed a fly from the body and continued his examination.

"No," he said. "No injury to the face whatsoever. However, this fellow is a bit of an impostor. The beard is well trimmed, but it conceals several of the sort of facial scars associated with brass knuckles. Have a look for yourself."

I spread apart the whiskers with my fingers and saw the scars to which my friend was alluding.

"Yes," I said. "Though the scars look quite old. Perhaps his condition of life has improved."

Holmes took back the lens and began to examine the victim's hands.

"Our fellow has given blows as well as received them," he said. "Note the swollen knuckles. But, as you noted, none of the injuries is recent."

After this remark, Holmes fell silent as he studied the rest of the body. When he was done, he straightened and stared down at the corpse.

"It appears that he was smothered with the pillow, but there are no signs of a struggle at all," he said at last, more to himself than the rest of us. "I cannot understand how that should induce such a hemorrhage, unless he were suffering from some hidden complaint. Perhaps we had better turn the poor fellow over."

Holmes and I performed that grim task while the three servants stood aside. Holmes examined the body with great care, but it appeared to be entirely unmarked, save for a long scar suggestive of a knife wound on his lower back on the left side. When he had finished his inspection we turned the body upon its back once more.

"Tell me everything you know about this gentleman," he said, addressing the *bagagiste*.

"The gentleman boarded the train in Epernay with a ticket through to Constantinople," the man began nervously. "He had two suitcases, not large, which I carried into the compartment. He tipped me five francs—Belgian francs. But then he gave me an English banknote, for twenty pounds, and asked that it be changed for French francs. It was very new and stiff."

"That is most helpful," said Holmes. "Go on."

"He asked to be brought his breakfast at nine. I knocked, but he did not answer. I knocked again at ten and once more heard nothing. This afternoon I brought to him his suit that he had given me to be pressed and his boots, which I had shined. When he did not answer this time I thought that he must be elsewhere, so opened the door and found what you see."

"A woman has been in this room," said Holmes. "Did you see her?"

"I did not," said the man, obviously frightened. "There was no one to board the *wagon-lit* when we arrived in Chalons and Bar-le-Duc, and so I was occupied elsewhere."

"This woman," said Holmes, bending over the berth, "had long black hair and expensive tastes, at least in perfume."

He held up for our inspection a long black hair he had plucked from the pillow and sniffed the hair gently.

"It is a fine scent," he said, "subtle yet distinct. Perhaps I flatter myself, but I do not think that it is available in London, or even Paris."

"I believe I recognize the scent," said M. Lestrange, taking the hair and sniffing it as well. "There is a shop in Constantinople. The proprietor, Herr Strasser, is a most unusual and ingenious man. He devises his perfumes to order, but a number of his ingredients are quite unique."

"Is there a woman on board this train who uses such a scent?" asked Holmes quickly.

"There are several," replied M. Lestrange a little stiffly. "I cannot place them under suspicion without cause. In any event, a lady's choice of perfume should not be a subject of comment."

By Holmes's expression, one could conclude that he found the *chef de train*'s discretion on this point to be excessive.

"Very well," he said. "I shall conduct my own researches. From the evidence, it appears that M. Brilleton boarded the train and was shortly joined by a lady with no superfluous morals, for, as you have no doubt observed, the atmosphere of this compartment bears the scent of opium as well as perfume. M. Brilleton's lips bear the scent of cognac and his body the signs of coitus. It appears that, having reduced the gentleman to a stupor, she then either induced in him a fatal internal hemorrhage herself or admitted an accomplice who did so on her behalf. She then gathered together all of his personal items and discarded them, perhaps by the simple expedient of throwing them out the window."

"You say 'perhaps'?" asked M. Lestrange.

"Yes. The murderer is obviously intent on preventing us from knowing anything about this man other than that he is dead. If the suitcases were thrown out the window, it may be possible to recover them. But if the lady had an accomplice, as I suspect she did, he may have taken them with him, in which case they may never be recovered."

"Why do you say this woman had an accomplice?"

"If I were a woman, I doubt if I would have the confidence to assault M. Brilleton, regardless of his condition. What the devil is the matter with that fly? He keeps returning to the same spot."

Holmes took out his lens and examined an area just below the victim's rib cage on the left-hand side, squeezing the flesh between his thumb and forefinger as he did so..

"A definite wound," he said. "I should have noticed it before. Have a look, Watson."

He handed me the lens and I studied the spot, which was indeed a wound. Through the glass, I was able to see a distinct hole in the muscular tissue, scarcely larger than would be made by a syringe.

"Triangular in nature, you observe," said Holmes. "And, do you see, each side is slightly concave. What do you make of that?"

"It would certainly serve to stiffen the needle, if that is what is was. What extraordinary workmanship. But then it would be unacceptable as a syringe."

"Precisely. This implement was made to kill, not to heal."

"But what was the purpose? To inject poison? And then why was this chosen as the point of insertion?"

Holmes nodded silently, as if acknowledging the force of my objections.

"You are right," he said. "I am confident that this wound is the key to the man's death, but precisely how it was done is far from clear."

After this exchange, Holmes resumed his close examination of the corpse, which he concluded without further comment. The grim scene, and the small but vicious wound that Holmes had discovered played upon my nerves. Murder accomplished with such a secret and malicious implement as the wound implied was murder indeed.

"What shall we do, Mr. Holmes?" suddenly burst out M. Lestrange as Holmes replaced the blanket over the corpse.

"I shall tell you what you shall do," said Holmes. "M. Brilleton boarded this train in Epernay and was never seen alive again. We may assume, then, that he was murdered on French soil."

"Yes!" said M. Lestrange with remarkable enthusiasm. It suddenly occurred to me that M. Lestrange might not wish this crime to be investigated by the German police.

"Since that is the case," continued Holmes, "I believe this body should be placed in the custody of the Sûreté. I shall prepare a telegram, to be delivered at our next stop, to M. Compte in Paris. I have worked with the gentleman on a number of occasions, to what I believe is our mutual satisfaction. I will give M. Compte a brief description of the matter, which I then will describe in greater detail in a letter that must be hand-delivered by a trusted messenger. In addition, you must obtain a description of the two suitcases M. Brilleton brought with him, and have the track between here and

Epernay inspected for them. If they were thrown from a moving train it is quite likely that they burst open. Every item must be recovered."

"It will be done," said M. Lestrange eagerly.

"We must transfer the body to a train that will take it to Paris, and, of course, we must do this in such a manner that will not alarm the other passengers.

"Jacques!" commanded M. Lestrange. "Inform *le chef de cuisine* that I must speak with him here at once."

"Oui, mon chef!" replied the *bagagiste,* who was not unhappy to depart.

"Just a moment," said Holmes. "You said that M. Brilleton gave you a suit to be pressed and a pair of boots to be shined."

"Yes."

"And they had not been returned to him?"

"No, they have not."

"Did you find anything in the pockets of the suit?"

"Only a blank sheet of paper."

"Do you still have it?"

"I believe so."

"Excellent. Bring everything to my compartment."

"Of course, My Lord."

The man hastened off, and we turned our attention to the body once more.

"Our *chef de cuisine* may be able to assist us in caring for the unfortunate M. Brilleton," said M. Lestrange once the door to the compartment was safely closed and locked. "As a young man, he served as an *apprenti* in a hunting lodge maintained by the grand duke of Bavaria. He became quite familiar with methods for preserving large furred game, including deer, bear, and wild boar."

"No doubt that will prove useful," said Holmes drily. "Will we be able to make the transfer before Vienna?"

"I think not. I would not entrust this burden to a stranger. Fortunately, our sister train is en route from Constantinople. We will meet in Budapest. The *chef de train* is my brother."

"This would entail a delay of several days," said Holmes.

"Yes, but I think you would agree that our first concern is discretion."

From his tone, one could easily guess that M. Lestrange's first concern always was discretion. However, my friend did not take exception to this comment. Instead, he began to search the compartment for clues, but if he found any he did not say so, for he pursued his inspection in complete silence until the *chef de cuisine* arrived. This *chef* was quite elderly, a tall, thin, bloodless man at once completely deferential and entirely aloof. He seemed to have no emotions at all.

"Michel," said M. Lestrange, "our guest M. Brilleton has unfortunately been murdered."

"That is unfortunate," murmured the *chef.*

"Mr. Sherlock Holmes has most graciously consented to assist us in handling this unpleasant affair without distress to our guests and without dishonor to the Orient Express."

The *chef* turned to my friend and bowed deeply.

"Mr. Holmes has decided that M. Brilleton's body must be sent to Paris. However, we cannot place the body on a train traveling in that direction until we reach Budapest. Naturally, we wish to do all that may be done to maintain M. Brilleton's person until it is delivered into the hands of the authorities."

"Of course. I would suggest that we place a quantity of fresh sorrel and bay leaves on the body, and then wrap it first in parchment, and then in linen."

"I fear," said Holmes, "that we must omit the sorrel and bay leaves."

The *chef* bowed to Holmes's statement.

"Very good, sir. We will prepare room in the refrigeration unit, which maintains a constant temperature of forty degrees. I do not suppose that it would be possible to remove the blood from the body?"

"Unfortunately not," said Holmes. "We must preserve the evidence to every extent possible."

"I understand, sir. We will rotate the body every four hours to prevent the blood from becoming settled."

"You are confident that this treatment will maintain M. Brilleton for the next five or six days?"

"I am indeed, sir. When I served in the grand duke's chalet, the Archbishop Denis suffered a fatal stroke during the month of January in 1851. Due to a variety of circumstances, we were unable to move the body for several weeks, and we preserved it in just the manner I have described. After the funeral, the grand duchess was so kind as to inform my superiors that his eminence's appearance had been the subject of favorable remark by several persons of rank."

"One cannot ask for a better recommendation than that," said Holmes. "Very well. I shall leave these matters in your hands. Dr. Watson and I shall return to my compartment to inspect M. Brilleton's suit and boots. In addition, I shall begin composing my messages for M. Compte."

When we arrived at Holmes's compartment, we found Jacques waiting for us by the door.

"The suit and boots are inside, My Lord," he said as we approached.

"Very good," said Holmes. "Come in for a minute."

"Of course, My Lord."

The suit, cut from sober black broadcloth, rested on one of the seats, while the boots, also black and made from fine polished calf, sat on the floor. A white sheet of paper, folded in thirds, rested on top of the suit. Holmes took the paper and examined it carefully with his lens.

"Did you find this paper?" he asked.

"Yes, My Lord."

"Was it folded in this manner, or did you fold it?"

"It was already folded, My Lord, just as you have it."

"And in which pocket did you find it?"

"The side pocket of the coat, My Lord. The right side."

"Very good. Here is another five francs for your assistance."

"Thank you, My Lord."

As the man exited, Holmes unfolded the sheet of paper and held it up to the light.

"You have a clue?" I asked.

"I have several. This is very fine rag paper, and it bears a watermark, the initials 'GWR,' written in a stylized script. What does that suggest to you?"

"Great Western Railway, perhaps."

"Excellent, Watson. And notice the fold. Exactly the right size for a packet of twenty-pound notes. You see that the crease is not sharp, but quite rounded. This sheet could have held a thousand pounds easily, and more, if the notes were new. Ah, and what is this?"

Holmes held the paper quite close to his nose.

"Extraordinary," he remarked.

"What?"

"This paper bears a distinct scent of snuff. It is unfortunate that our own addiction dulls our senses to what is often the most informative of clues."

Holmes took out his lens and examined the paper with intense care.

"Most suggestive," he said at last. "I shall have to run some tests, but I believe that this sheet of paper was once in the possession of Sir Samuel Jenkins."

"My dear Holmes!"

"Sir Samuel is on the board of the Great Western Railway."

"But surely many individuals have access to that company's stationery."

"Indeed. But you recall that the solicitor is also quite generous in his use of snuff? A fine, light-brown snuff of unusual pungency? I grant you, the evidence is far from conclusory. But Sir Samuel strikes me as a man who is quite careful not to let his left hand know what his right hand is doing. His goal is to recover the diamond. If he may do so by staying within the law, he will do so. But if not, not."

"Perhaps not. Still, what evidence do you have to support such an accusation, beyond a watermark upon a sheet of paper and the scent of snuff?"

"Your skepticism is always refreshing, Watson, When you were examining the body, did you notice that there were circular markings around the dead man's right eye, markings consistent with the frequent and prolonged use of a jeweler's lens?"

"M. Brilleton, I should think, had scarcely the physique of a jeweler," I retorted.

"True. M. Brilleton was not averse to the use of physical

force under the right circumstances. But before we push our theories too far, we had best examine his suit and boots."

Holmes took out his lens once more and examined the suit carefully.

"There is nothing," he said at last. "It is quite new. I suspect that M. Brilleton was almost as anxious to avoid providing us with information about his identity as was his killer. Let us have a look at the shoes."

"They would appear to be as new as the suit."

"Yes, but this is better. Notice the height of the heels and the thickness of the soles. M. Brilleton scarcely needed to enhance his height. You have a penknife, Watson?"

"Of course."

"Notice that both the heels and soles are affixed by means of tiny screws, a quite unusual method. We shall see what we shall see."

Holmes set to work and quickly removed a heel.

"Do you call this evidence?" he asked, holding up the hollow heel for inspection. "One could carry a dozen fine diamonds in each heel without the slightest difficulty. And I fancy the sole may prove to be even more suggestive. You see, it is very firmly anchored."

Holmes removed fully a dozen screws before the sole came off.

"Now, that is ingenious," he said.

Both the bottom of the shoe and the inner side of the sole were fitted with black velvet. As he held the two pieces of the shoe up to the light, the fabric appeared to display rows of small dimples or depressions. Holmes touched one of them with his finger.

"Just the right size for a two-carat stone," he said. "You remember that according to Sir Samuel's information, a sixth of the Great Blue has been transformed into such stones."

"Was this fellow set on robbing us?" I asked.

"It would certainly appear so, though I am not sure why. If our client does not trust us with the diamonds, why would he trust a man who appears to be a professional thief? Is he intent upon obtaining personal ownership of all the diamonds? Surely that would impossible to conceal. There is much that is unclear."

As Holmes spoke, he took out his churchwarden and began to fill it with the rough-cut navy shag he preferred when considering the most abstruse problems. On such occasions it was always my habit to quit my friend's company, for the slightest noise or unnecessary movement was likely to stimulate an imperious rebuke.

"No doubt," I said, rising to my feet. "I believe I shall repair to the smoking lounge until dinner. May we expect you?"

"I think not. You must never say this to a Frenchman, but there are few things more deleterious to the proper functioning of the intellect than *grande cuisine*."

I took my copy of *The Egoist* to the lounge, where I continued to do battle with Mr. Meredith's prose until it was time to have high tea with Jennie in the restaurant carriage.

Whether "high tea" as it is practiced on the Orient Express exists anywhere else in the world I cannot say, for I am no frequenter of the exclusive West End establishments that first devised this ritual, presumably under the misapprehension that wealthy Englishwomen were failing to consume their proper allotment of butter and cream. As I entered the carriage I was confronted by a sight that, had I been honest, I might have predicted. Seated at the table of honor were Jennie and the countess!

"Dr. Watson!" exclaimed the countess, rising from her chair and extending her hand. "I have had the great joy of meeting your most charming daughter!"

There are few tasks for which an Englishman is less qualified than kissing the hand of a French countess aboard the Orient Express. Knowing that I had the attention of the entire carriage fixed upon me made the task no easier, but, inspired by the thought of touching that lovely lady's hand, I performed the act with a sort of giddy triumph, more excusable in a schoolboy, I fear, than a middle-aged man. All discomfort, however, soon vanished, for the countess proved the most charming of conversationalists. The extreme elegance of her person was most agreeably softened by an open and affectionate manner that was utterly devoid of aristocratic pretense while remaining entirely in the best of taste. I seemed fairly to float in a fine sea of feminine charm, buoyed by my luxurious surroundings. Persons passed by and food was presented to us, but the details of faces and dishes alike remained mysteries to me. Even the *coeur flottant merveilleux aux fraises,* presented with a great flourish, made little impression, for it was no more than what may happen to the simple, honest dish of strawberries and cream once it falls into the hands of a Frenchman.

After tea there was little time left—for the ladies, at least—to dress for dinner. Having had enough international conversation for one day, I avoided the gentlemen's lounge and returned to my compartment, for I was sure that Holmes would still be absorbed in contemplating the strange facts surrounding the murder of M. Brilleton. I reclined on my fine leather bench and resumed my study of *The Egoist,* whose intricacies, like the light of a fitful moon, always promised illumination but rarely supplied it. But for the time being the promise was enough, and I drove forward with the hope that Mr. Meredith would fulfill that promise and ultimately reveal at least some of the profundities of the human heart at which he was invariably hinting.

At seven o'clock I put aside the book to begin the process of donning that absurd costume required of any man who wishes to take part in official society after sundown. With the assistance of a deferential *bagagiste*, who not only addressed me as "My Lord" but actually appeared to believe that I was one, I managed to clothe myself without inflicting undue damage on either my garments or my temper. I set off for Jennie's compartment and found her in the last stages of her *toilette,* delighting in the ministrations of the countess' maid!

"Now, isn't *this* the best," she said, holding her head perfectly still as the young woman adjusted the cloud of flamingo-colored Prince of Wales feathers that floated above the broad brim of her hat. "What I would have missed if I hadn't packed myself away!"

When at last the glowing cloud was arranged to her satisfaction, we made our departure for the restaurant carriage, where we were greeted by the countess. We then spent the next three hours consuming a meal of grotesque opulence. Despite my service under General Cathgart, I had never before borne the full weight of haute cuisine. Each dish was more fantastical than the last. One can only conclude that it is the special purpose of French cookery to dissolve the entire substance of a dish into polish, so that no trace of the primeval beef, pork, or chicken remains, converting the whole into a sort of *purée raisonné* that can then be shaped and reshaped by an abstract and extravagant fancy far closer to architecture than cookery, a fancy whose sole intent is to remove from its creations all taint of the hearth and kitchen, not to mention pasture and field.

Our table, I fear, provoked no little envy in the other diners, for I can state without false modesty that Jennie and the countess outshone all the other ladies present, and, in a setting such as the dining carriage of the Orient Express, youth and beauty, when properly funded, inevitably take the palm. Although I look back now on that meal with some measure of embarrassment and regret, at the time I felt none. Jennie's innocent delight at each of the treasures placed before us was a constant pleasure, and the countess' attentive and witty conversation a potent intoxicant indeed. I fear I became entirely captive to her charm and happily concluded that I was in fact as young and handsome and clever as she pretended to believe me to be. I spoke with a degree of freeness not appropriate to a middle-aged man entrusted with the welfare of a fifteen-year-old girl and no doubt spent more time than was strictly necessary contemplating the beauties of the countess' lovely back and charming *décolletage.*

Such was my enchantment that the hours fairly flew by, and it seemed that we had hardly seated ourselves when the waiters arrived with the *pièce de résistance,* miniature railway carriages fashioned of marzipan and nougat and filled with ice cream. In honor, I suppose, of my masculinity, I was presented with an outsized *bombe* fashioned in the shape of a locomotive, its coal scuttle filled with elegant chocolates, which I gallantly distributed to the ladies. At that particular moment the countess, who had been the soul of vivacity, suddenly complained of a headache and departed for her compartment, after agreeing to meet for luncheon on the following day. Incredibly, Jennie's appetite had not yet exhausted itself, and she consumed two of the carriages, along with half a dozen chocolates.

"What do you think of her?" she asked.

"The countess?"

"Yes, the countess! Who else should I be asking you about?"

"Most charming."

"Is that all you have to say? She's set her cap on you, all right."

"Nonsense. A mere flirtation. That is her world."

"Really? Then why did she pass up all those fancy fellows for you? You're not rich."

"Indeed not. She is merely amusing herself at my expense."

"You think so? You'd best be careful, Papa. She's the kind of girl who might slit a fellow's gizzard if he wasn't careful."

"No doubt she will find some other way to amuse herself tomorrow."

Jennie smiled and said nothing. When she finished the last of her ice cream we rose and I escorted her to her compartment. Returning to my own, I confess I felt a certain restlessness and confinement. Though the night was hardly young, I felt not a trace of sleeplessness. However, I had no interest in a visit to the smoking lounge, and doubted that Holmes would welcome a visitor at this late hour. There seemed no alternative to the solitude of my own compartment.

When I entered I discovered that the illumination had unaccountably failed during my absence and the room was entirely dark. As I groped for the light switch I felt a light hand upon my shoulder and a gentle voice whispering in my ear.

"You will need no light tonight, monsieur."

It was the countess!

My shock at discovering her in such private quarters was palpable. Indeed, I almost fell to the floor, provoking in her that intense merriment that overcomes a woman when she senses she has a man entirely in her power. My befuddled attempts at protest were met with a passionate kiss that instantly destroyed in me all power of thought. The carnal desires that had tantalized me all evening took complete charge of my will and I shamelessly ran my hands down her beautiful back, quickly discovering as I did so that she had divested her graceful frame of all but the most intimate of undergarments! A heartfelt groan of both pleasure and disbelief burst from my lips and a surge of desire ran through my body as my trembling hands hungrily explored the infinitude of riches that had been bestowed upon me.

But even as I did so, she slipped from my grasp, disappearing into the darkness so suddenly that I could not stifle another groan, this one of despair, so easily did she play upon my desires. A second later the window shade slid upward, and the mysterious white light of the full moon poured through, and yet a third groan was wrung from me, for beholding such beauty was truly enough to pluck the reason from any man. The countess reclined upon the berth she had prepared for us with an air of voluptuous calm that would have caused Titian himself to throw down his brushes in despair.

"Gently, Doctor, gently," she whispered, her dark, beautiful eyes shining softly in the moonlight. "True lovers are never in a hurry, would you not agree?"

In silent answer I sank to my knees and took her lovely foot in my hand. I had heard of men who took an almost obsessive delight in women's feet, but never before had I encountered such emotions in myself. Yet somehow the countess' foot held me even as I held it, and to kiss her delicate toes, her charming arch, and her slender ankle was an intoxicating joy, and I found, rather to my amazement, that the pleasure she enjoyed from the receipt of these caresses exceeded even the delight I took in bestowing them, so much so that I almost feared I should render the rest of my person superfluous. Joy indeed it was to linger on this delightful part, but it was impossible to prefer the perfect part to the perfect whole. Insensibly my kisses led me upward, and I soon joined the countess on the berth, embracing her magnificence in full measure.

Throughout this encounter I was intermittently aware that

the very next compartment was occupied by my austere friend, who had warned me that the enchanting woman whose willing captive I had become was quite likely a murderess. To my shame, however, this knowledge served as a goad rather a check to my desire. I was so much a fool as to pretend to myself that any second I would flee from this Circe's embrace and reclaim my reason. It is, indeed, perhaps the shrewdest trick of Venus that nothing so inebriates the soul as the willful violation of propriety. The more I struggled to still the countess' silken whispers, and the more I struggled to shun her silken flesh, the more unendurably arousing they became. She, of course, knew this game as well as any woman could, and as only a woman could, delighting in her power over me, turning me this way and that as a skillful angler draws a fat salmon to his net, with the fatal difference that, as the salmon pursues his freedom, so I hungered for the countess' meshes.

But however eagerly I wished to be ruled by the countess, I had first to join her in her unencumbered state, and I was regrettably a great distance from that goal. However, the lady proved all too skillful in assisting me, so that even as I lay upon the berth my tie, my studs, my braces, my collar, my cuffs—all seemed to float from my body of their own accord. Furthermore, her removal of each fragment of my attire was accompanied by kisses and caresses, each more wickedly bestowed than the last, so that the warmth of my desire heightened even as the opportunity for gratifying it increased.

When at last I had shed the bonds of civilization and had joined the countess in that Edenic state she had so wantonly assumed, she grasped me by the most shameless of handles with no more preamble than a savage in the jungle, causing me fairly to shout with amazement. As soon as she slipped beneath me my frenzied flesh seemed to melt into hers, and I felt her knowing hands gliding like serpents toward a secret destination. Never had I known such wickedness! Deep within me I felt a wild flurry of dismay as my body protested against such unscrupulous use, but against such an adversary as the countess there could be no defense. Alas, my passionate alarm and resistance only confirmed the location of my weakness and made its conquest more sure! My body, and I fear my soul, quickly betrayed me and I fell, panting and gasping, like a great stag overcome by the hunter's craft.

After such an evening, the reader may well imagine that I fell into the deepest possible sleep. Yet I was not so deeply asleep that I was not roused when the countess sought to make her departure. Having been brought low, I was now as low as she who had made me so, and, catching her by the ankle as she attempted to flee, I resolved to serve her even as she had served me. She struggled to escape, but her efforts to do so only enlivened my desire, and as I drew her to me I felt the desire burning in my breast kindle in hers. For the heat of our debauchery was contagious, each drawing a lustful strength from the other, so that now the countess hungered for my triumph as I had hungered for hers, and surrendered that closest and most secret of redoubts even as I had surrendered mine. And as consciousness fled my brain I felt that our wantonness was at a balance, and I could sleep without fear of betrayal.

CHAPTER 12

Whist in the Afternoon

MY APPRAISAL OF OUR relationship, though conducted in the most primitive of circumstances, proved entirely correct. The countess aroused me with gentle kisses when the first hues of dawn had just illuminated the sky outside our window. Beholding her lovely, calm, smiling face, one would have thought her the most guileless of mistresses. She had that ability, so much more common among women than men, to manage all her moods with near-perfect nonchalance.

"If you were a true gentleman, monsieur," she said, "you would do me the infinite kindness of bringing me my robe and slippers. I fear my maid must be asleep."

As I smiled back at her in the soft light, I must have looked more like the world's happiest schoolboy than a gentleman. I took her beautiful head in my hands and kissed her, and she did not protest. But at length she pushed me away with a giggle, and I knew it was time to depart on my journey. I put on my own robe and slippers and set off, the key to the countess' compartment in my pocket. Fortunately, I did not encounter a member of the staff on my journey to the next carriage, and I found the countess' compartment without incident.

Once inside, I quickly found the items I sought in her closet and took them under my arm.

The countess, wrapped in a fine linen sheet, was the picture of imperturbable beauty. I happily assumed the role of maid and enjoyed casual yet supremely intimate glimpses of her nude loveliness as I removed the sheet and then bestowed the robe. With a perfect, feline calmness she first revealed and then concealed her exquisite person. Yet when she was done she extended her foot almost shyly and with the faintest of tremors in her voice asked, "Would you be my footman, monsieur?"

Such an invitation! I began to kiss her toes, lightly at first, as though purely in jest, but I soon found the practice so much to my taste that my desire, which I had felt after such a burning in the night could but smolder in the morning, burst forth with renewed heat. The countess, I found, despite her hauteur, was more than ready for my game, for my kisses, ascending with my ardor, soon conquered her defenses, which, indeed, were well calculated to provoke my desire rather than defeat it, and I soon found myself in full possession of the regions of Venus, which I then confidently explored to our mutual delight. And so we surrendered ourselves to a morning of sweet wantonness, a gentle conclusion to a night of rather brutal amour. At last the countess could tarry no more, and she stole away, leaving me at once satiated and inebriated with her love.

So I lay for several hours in a sort of half sleep of blissful exhaustion. I did not rise until ten, performing my ablutions in a leisurely manner and calling on Holmes no earlier than eleven. I found him immersed in the study of his society periodicals, and noted with disguised amusement that he had been utterly oblivious to the rapturous events that had occurred in the compartment next to his. It is, I suppose, both the secret and the flaw of genius that it concentrates all its power on a single problem and ignores all else. I resolved, of course, to perpetuate the secret, for Holmes's unreasonable suspicions of the countess would inevitably prompt him to adopt a censorious view of what was in fact the most elegant of gallantries.

I returned to my compartment and thought to resume once more my perusal of *The Egoist,* but the briefest glance was sufficient to convince me that it was no longer possible for me to take an interest in the county conundrums that so oppressed Mr. Meredith's lovers. A man who has spent the night with la Comtesse D'Espinau looks upon the world with different eyes.

I had no appetite for breakfast, and so journeyed to the smoking lounge, whose clientele was dramatically changed, for we had arrived in Vienna the night before and were shortly due in Budapest. The English language was rarely heard, largely replaced by the German, though the French still lingered. Glancing out the window, I also noticed that the speed of the train was greatly reduced. From Paris to Vienna we traveled with the celerity of an express on the Great Western. Now that we had passed into eastern Europe, we dawdled like a local on the London Chatham & Dover, the train rolling slowly yet smoothly over the tracks. Seating myself in one of the train's fine leather chairs, I relaxed with a cigar and a cup of tea, scarcely noticing the broad plain of Hungary through which we passed, so fixed was my mind on the events of the night before.

I could not but wonder, of course, what motives the countess might have in bestowing her bountiful favors on me. My relationships with women for the past decade of my life, which were decidedly less conventional than is generally considered appropriate, had convinced me that one adds rather than detracts from a passion to consider its merits in the cold light of day. Was it reasonable to believe that such a great lady should find herself the helpless prisoner of a middle-aged, middle-class practitioner of medicine? It is true that my authorship had given me some renown, but I doubted that my books had created much of a stir in the fine salons of Paris. I had, at least, received no invitations.

The more I closely I considered the matter, the more I felt myself being drawn into deep and dangerous waters. Could the countess actually be a murderess, as Holmes suspected? Or was she the innocent victim of brutal innuendo? Could such a dainty foot be the foot of a killer? It seemed impossible, but how could one be sure?

Such thoughts did little to calm my mind. Although I longed for companionship, there was no one I could repair to but Jennie, who was not such a one as to serve as a confidante for such sensitive matters. Instead, I could but dream of the delights I had enjoyed the night before, and wonder if I dared to enjoy them again.

At last the noon hour approached, and passed. At half past the hour I journeyed to Jennie's compartment.

"What have you been up to?" she demanded when I called upon her. "It's almost one."

"Well, you can't be hungry after last night's dinner."

"Don't change the subject," she said, touching me on the cheek. "Somebody gave you a shine, all right. I don't suppose you're telling."

"I enjoyed a supremely pleasant dinner and an excellent night's sleep," I said. "Nothing more."

"Nothing more," she said. "Oh, Papa, I thought you were going to behave."

I made no reply to this, for arguing with Jennie on these matters was futile. It amused her to consider me as incorrigible, and since in this case I was far guiltier than she could imagine, silence was by far the wiser recourse. Jennie had already chaffed me on the subject of the countess, and any denials on my part would only increase her suspicions.

The fierce rush of pleasure I felt at the sight of that lady as we entered the dining carriage washed away in an instant all qualms I might have felt about continuing our relationship. To suspect such a beauteous goddess of a crime was in itself a crime, and I resolved to trouble myself with such repulsive thoughts no more.

The infinite pleasure I took in her company was unpleasantly marred by the presence of a gentleman previously known to the countess, who upon entering the carriage insisting on joining our company. Samuel Patterson was a young American, tall, attractive, and well dressed, with a superficially charming manner, though ultimately self-important and shallow, like too many of his countrymen. He quickly informed us that he was a graduate of Harvard College, which distinction apparently authorized him to deliver the final pronouncement on every topic that came to hand. He praised the food but faulted the wines of the Express, found London dull and Vienna tedious, preferred Naples to Venice, and exalted Paris to the skies. He was polite enough to confess that his homeland was still "new," but informed us calmly that he wouldn't give up New York for all of Europe, for, so he claimed, we were all "done, from Curzon to the kaiser." Never, I believe, have I encountered a young man so utterly in love with the sound of his own voice.

Any intelligent man would have found this bumptious arrogance insufferable, particularly in one so young, but such is the perversity of the female sex, the more insolent his tone, the more Jennie and the countess delighted in it. Their flushed cheeks and sparkling eyes, their soft, quick cries of mock outrage, their delighted giggles that ran like silken, silver rivulets through the air, spoke more eloquently than words of their enchantment with this fair-haired young man.

I found myself tiring of his company very quickly, but with the ladies so delighted, it would be folly to allow myself to sink into sullen discontent with our new companion. I resolved to maintain myself in the conversation and, after a few minutes, I received the most welcome of rewards, the gentle but persistent pressure of the countess' foot upon mine. This gesture could not but relieve me of all care, and I scarcely even minded when Mr. Patterson invited us to his compartment for whist.

The American proved to be a remarkably skillful player, winning hand after hand while chattering away on every topic under the sun, even managing a *misère ouverte* while discoursing on the merits of pickled eels, disposing of his trumps with remarkable insolence and causing Jennie to denounce him as "*most* wicked," which denunciation was, of course, the highest possible praise. To please her, he attempted this difficult feat a second time only three hands later, and she rejoiced endlessly when his efforts concluded in a satisfying debacle. One could see that she was quickly falling in love with him, and the difference in their ages was unfortunately not so great as to render such a relationship an absurdity. Mr. Patterson was imperturbable in his triumph, and continued to converse blandly on the market for Greco-Roman antiquities, the invention of the airplane, and the architecture of the Hagia Sophia, promising to provide us with a guided tour of that fabled edifice when we reached Constantinople. He was, he explained with becoming modesty, an expert on every aspect of the new science of archaeology, in the manner of Schliemann, and was journeying to inspect a "dig" on the outskirts of the city.

I was, of course, not unhappy to see the game end, at five o'clock, to allow the ladies time to dress for dinner, and I was delighted to learn that our new acquaintance would not be available for dinner, pleading the press of business that he declined to specify. Once our little party broke up I took the opportunity to call upon Holmes, feeling that I should mention at least my social involvement with the countess and invite him to join us for dinner. Rather to my surprise, he accepted the invitation.

"You think that my suspicions of the countess are unjust?" he asked.

"She appears to me to be a woman of the highest character, and, considering her place in the world, remarkably gracious and unaffected," I said rather stiffly.

"Perhaps," he replied. "The fair sex, after all, is your department. But I would urge, if not caution, then discretion."

"I am sure I would never say anything to betray your interests. In any event, the countess has been most incurious as to our reasons for this journey."

"That, at least, is reassuring."

At seven o'clock Holmes and I each summoned a *bagagiste* to assist us in performing the ritual of dressing for dinner. Despite his enormous success as a consulting detective, Holmes had grown perhaps even more bohemian in his attire over the years, but in the pursuit of an investigation he took a special pride in discarding his personal preferences, and his appearance that evening was marked by the innate punctilio of a true gentleman.

We stopped first at Jennie's compartment, which necessarily occasioned more than a delay, for Jennie was ever a believer in provoking her audience. After a wait of perhaps fifteen minutes she appeared, in a shimmering pink gown that one could not quite call outrageous, at least if one did not know that its wearer was scarcely fifteen years old. There was a wonderful vivacity to Jennie's slender, graceful, and utterly feminine figure, the first, fairest flower of young womanhood, which I could not behold without experiencing the most intense and bewildering complex of emotions. She took my arm smartly and with an expression of limitless delight shining on her face, led the way to the dining carriage.

We arrived to find the countess already seated, a vision of loveliness in a silken gown of ivory and gold, which served as the perfect complement to her glowing skin and beautiful black hair. Despite her unquestionable sangfroid, she was not entirely able to conceal her eagerness to meet the great Sherlock Holmes.

"Mr. Holmes!" she cried. "It is a very great honor to meet such a champion of justice."

"It is a very great honor to meet such a lovely and distinguished lady," said Holmes, accepting her proffered hand with remarkable aplomb.

"I understand, Mr. Holmes," said the countess, once we were seated, "that you entertain the most remarkable suspicions regarding people in high places."

"I fear that it is impossible for me to discuss an open case," said Holmes smoothly. "In any event, the innocent have nothing to fear—from my hands, at least."

"Ah, if it were only you!" returned the countess, smiling. "Truly, the innocent have much to fear in this fearsome world. But not tonight, and not on this train. In any event, I am forever indebted to you and Dr. Watson for permitting me the acquaintance of your delightful *protégée*. In a few years, I know she will be the delight of all Europe, and Paris especially."

Jennie grinned with delight.

"Merci boucoups," she said, and then proceeded to speak French in the most alarming manner, interrupted good-naturedly

by the countess and by her own amusement at her errors. This rather deliberate sport continued until the *serveur* arrived and we placed our orders. After the grotesquely Lucullan feast of the night before, which had left me feeling rather debauched by my own appetites, I determined that, even at the risk of appearing middle-class, I would confine myself to a sensible meal, consuming nothing more than *soupe, salade,* and *le beefsteak,* which, I confess, proved to be the finest I had ever eaten.

Holmes joined me in this display of self-restraint, which naturally earned us a generous serving of Gallic raillery from both the countess and Jennie, who seemed to be pluming herself for a role in those French farces that constitute such an ineradicable feature of the British theater. They both dined lightly but extensively, consuming no less than ten gossamer courses during a meal that lasted more than three hours. The countess was clearly an expert in grand dining for a lady, and Jennie responded delightedly to her tutelage, committing, as had become her wont, the pronunciation of each dish to memory as the dinner proceeded. Throughout the dinner, Jennie and the countess provided a remarkable counterpoint to each other. The innocent flame of Jennie's youth contrasted extremely with the countess' perfect sophistication, yet also illumined it, so that rather icy diamond revealed both its brilliance and its depths in a manner that it could not have conceivably done if unassisted.

As before, the excellence of the wine and the beauty of our companions made an irresistible combination. Yet it was a wicked pleasure that I took in it all, for, unknown to both Holmes and Jennie, beneath the table I felt once more the unendurably delightful pressure of the countess's lovely foot! As I looked on the countess' polished features and breathed her delightful perfume, how I longed for another night of shameless and shameful debauchery! The fantasies of my morning reverie seemed pale indeed when confronted by the countess' beautiful person! How I was forced to dissemble, and how I enjoyed my wickedness!

"So, Mr. Holmes," the countess said after we all had had the pleasure of a few glasses, "all of Europe is waiting to know the answer to the riddle that only you can solve: What has become of the Great Blue, and who will be its final owner?"

"Two riddles rather than one," replied Holmes. "It is the archduke who can answer the first, and I suspect strongly that Sir Samuel will answer to the second."

"The archduke, so I am informed, denies all knowledge of the stone."

"You are acquainted with the archduke?"

"We have met on a few occasions. There are so many archdukes in Austria, and so often they are poor. Your country is more generous to its aristocracy. Austria gives titles freely, but little else. Of course, in my fair republic, I am fortunate to have my name, much less an estate."

"I understand that you enjoy the pleasures of several châteaux."

"More cottages than châteaux, I fear. But I do have a few treasures that give me comfort. You must come visit me, Jennie, in the spring! My chestnuts surpass anything that Paris has to offer! And oh, the amaryllis!"

"I should love to," said Jennie, affecting an upper-class English accent, which she apparently deemed appropriate for her role as a guest in the French countryside.

"Yes, it is the earth that gives us everything, although there is much to be found in the city as well. You have been to Constantinople before, Mr. Holmes?"

"Unfortunately not."

"You and the good doctor and Jennie must come to visit me in my *yali* during your stay."

"I hope that will be possible," said Holmes. "I may be occupied the entire time, but perhaps Jennie and Dr. Watson will have the opportunity to enjoy your hospitality."

"I am sure that we will," I interjected, a bit awkwardly.

The countess smiled.

"You will find Constantinople to be a most remarkable city, Mr. Holmes," she said, returning her attention to my friend. "We are very far from Europe. As unlike London as you can imagine. But you have been to the East, I know. In India, and Singapore."

"You are well informed, Countess."

"We are both well informed. There is much to learn in Constantinople. It is a city that is wise, but not wise as we are wise, and not wise as you are wise, Mr. Holmes. There is a knowledge that is not darkness and not light. In Constantinople, the spirit is often wakened by sorrow. One walks among the cypress trees in the presence of untold tragedies of untold peoples. There is a great deal of danger in Constantinople. A great man, a good man, may die for no reason, and a woman, too. And yet I am rarely more at home than in my *yali,* though the cuisine is simple, and there are no parties, and no theater but the shadow plays in the streets, which no woman can see."

"Far from London, indeed," said Holmes.

"Yes. I fear an Englishman, first coming to Constantinople, would be shocked first by the dirt, and then by the injustice. There are great distances in that city, and even the very rich enjoy more privilege than comfort. And yet, as I say, it is a city in which one may grow wise if one is not in a hurry. But Englishmen are always in a hurry."

"Perhaps that is true, Countess."

"Still, you should not be afraid. There is much to be learned in Stamboul. But you must be willing to unlearn much of what you know. I was once very French. But now I have let the East into my soul. I enjoy Paris when I am there, but I do not miss it. Soon, I think I shall go no more. Indeed, perhaps I should never have come back to Stamboul. Perhaps it was better not to know. But now that I have, I cannot go back to what I was. You, Mr. Holmes, in many ways are so simple, so strong. Perhaps it is better that you should turn back. London is a good place, a clean place. It is not everything, but it is your home."

"Perhaps," said Holmes with a smile. "However, if not a wanderer, I am certainly a traveler, although I have not been truly abroad for a decade. I have had more than a taste of India and the Far East. What is more, one can travel in spirit as well as flesh, although it is true that few things awaken the spirit more surely than physical encounter. As for patience, I am often more patient than my foes would wish. I find as I grow older that it is the pleasure of the hunt that is the one sure thing in life, at least for such a strange creature as myself."

Holmes spoke with such calm, and with such depths of meaning beneath his words, that I felt the countess must retreat. However, she did not, but rather matched my friend smile for smile.

"You have traveled, then, and you have a rare spirit. I am very glad that we have had this conversation, Mr. Holmes. This is, perhaps, the most fortunate journey of my life."

She seemed to glow as she spoke these words, with all the glittering elegance of France, and yet with something more, the sort of wordless wisdom that, so she suggested, awaited us in Constantinople. But remarkable as were her words, her actions were far more so, for as she spoke, she slipped the key to her compartment into my hand!

"Now I fear I must leave you," she said, rising to her feet. "I find that I tire easily, and easily become tiresome to those around me."

And with this elegant leave-taking, she made her departure. Our waiter appeared, offering to fill our glasses one last time, but we declined. The spell that had held us for hours was broken for the moment, and we were three people almost alone in a darkened carriage.

"Now, she is a remarkable woman," said Jennie, sounding as grown up as possible.

"Few indeed can match her charm," said Holmes.

"I'm going to be just like her, only I shan't drown my husband."

"Very good, Jennie. I should hate to see you hang."

Jennie smiled.

"Oh, you wouldn't hang me, would you, Mr. Holmes? And you mustn't hang the countess either, at least not until I've had the pleasure of her company for some time. I do enjoy this train! One meets the most extraordinary people!"

I could only smile at Jennie's naive enthusiasm. Our small party soon broke up and we returned to our compartments, though, needless to say, I remained in mine for only a brief time. The simple touch of the countess' foot had sent a species of electrical fire coursing through my body for the entire duration of the meal. And if that subtle titillation had heated my soul, the gift of her key had detonated it. I was utterly on fire to possess her. Her elegant toes, her dainty feet, her magnificent body would all be mine!

I slipped down the corridor, knocked discreetly at her door, and then entered. A single lamp illumined the compartment, but the light was more than enough to ignite my soul, for there, stretched on the broad seat, was the countess, in a posture that, by supplying no more than a hint of impropriety, did more to inflame my desire than the most explicit display. I fell to my knees and made that sweet journey to her beautiful feet. What delight to kiss that instep, to caress those toes! What bliss to make the most pleasant of all ascents, to burrow beneath her scented gown and to at last make open all that was hidden! And what heaven, after such rapture, to rest beside that beautiful body, in perfect forgetfulness, until sadly roused by a tenacious and unwelcome sun!

This time it was I who awakened first, and was able to gaze on her loveliness softened by the serenity of sleep. Masses of black hair fell over her beautiful shoulders, and a crumpled white sheet covered the warm, dark flesh of her bosom. I watched as the rising sun spread across the room, patiently dispersing the darkness and driving the shadows from her face.

"Ah, *bonjour, monsieur,*" she said, waking.

"Bonjour."

There was such warmth in her expression that I could not forbear kissing her.

"Morning already," she said, her voice assuming a more decisive tone. "Too bad!"

"Why is it so unfortunate? We arrive today in Constantinople."

A look almost of sadness passed over her face.

"Yes, my home! I should be happy! But life in Stamboul is so complex. I prefer to travel."

"You spoke of the city with such affection last night."

"Affection? No. Understanding. Understanding is deeper than affection, but not so nice. You English do not understand."

She said this with something more than coquettishness, and turned away from me. But I held her and kissed her neck.

"You are the best of doctors," she said, taking my hand and kissing it. "The only doctor who has made me feel happy. But journeys must come to an end. We cannot be in Constantinople as we have been here."

"Why not?"

This, I fear, made her laugh.

"Why not? It is impossible. I am known in Stamboul. I am watched everywhere. No, no. I have friends, and to have friends one must know how to behave."

She spoke in a confident, jesting tone that still held affection, worthy of a great woman of the world consoling a youth. Yet, as I watched, a tear trickled down the side of her cheek.

"You must go," she said suddenly.

"But I will see you in Constantinople?" I said.

"Yes, of course, and you must bring Jennie with you. You must never let anything happen to Jennie! You must promise me that!"

"Of course," I said, "although Jennie does have her own mind."

"Yes, she does," she said, laughing. "Yes. But still I will punish you!"

She was so beautiful here I sought to kiss her once more, but she eluded me, burrowing beneath the sheets, where I pursued her.

"No!" she almost shouted. "If you are a gentleman you will go!"

How I wished to have her once more that morning! Rarely has the joy of the chase spoken to me with such urgency! But she spoke, not with anger or fear, but with that special shyness of her sex that can live with the most brazen wantonness, and I had no choice but to obey. With very little grace I absented myself, washed briefly, and donned as much of evening garments as was consistent with both modesty and convenience. When I reappeared she was dressed in an elegant gown, with her lovely hair still about her shoulders.

"Your friend Mr. Holmes does not like me," she said, putting her arms around me.

"I would not say that."

"Will you defend me?" she asked.

I could not reply, for the sweet embrace of her body flowed right through me, and I felt as though my flesh were dissolved in air. For a long minute we held each other, and at last I felt my soul return to itself.

"Bonjour, monsieur," she whispered again. "Please, call on me when you are in Constantinople."

With that, she slipped away. I stumbled forth in considerable disarray toward my compartment, my body blessedly at peace from a night of sweet debauchery but my head filled with vague concerns from the countess' mysterious speech. In such a sweet, uncertain condition, a man requires solitude above all else. However, fortune was not with me. Though I had but one carriage to travel before reaching my compartment, I was so unfortunate as to encounter M. Lestrange, the *chef de train.* To my amazement, he put his hand on my shoulder as we passed.

"You are a remarkable man, monsieur," he whispered.

CHAPTER 13

Journey's End

I SAID NO REPLY TO this surprising compliment, but hurried onward, for I had no wish to display my mood. I undressed quickly and crept into bed, for I had had no more than three hours' sleep, and we were due to arrive in Constantinople by noon. Scarcely had my head touched the pillow when my delicious dreams faded into an unbroken sleep. A knock on the door awakened me at nine o'clock, and I bid the *serveur* to return in half an hour with tea and scones. I performed my morning ablutions and dressed in a hazy state of near-somnambulistic bliss until disturbed by the *serveur*'s knock on the door. Regretfully, I put on my robe and received my tea and scones. As the fellow was exiting, Jennie arrived, wearing her most elegant clothes in honor of our impending arrival in Constantinople.

"Another excellent night's sleep?" she asked as she entered my compartment.

"Most excellent," I said, calmly, for I resolved neither to deny nor affirm any accusation. "Would you care for a cup of tea?"

"Thank you."

She took the cup, the plumes of the Prince of Wales feathers nodding on her hat in the sunlight.

"Such a *bonjour!*" she exclaimed. "By the way, have you seen Mr. Patterson?"

"I have not. I believe he informed us yesterday that he would be occupied for the remainder of the journey."

"You are so stuffy! Perhaps we will see him at lunch. Antoine assured me last night that we may have *tripes à la mode de Caen*."

"I doubt if we shall have time," I replied. "I believe we are ahead of schedule. In any event, it's only tripe, which I believe you once told me you should never eat."

"It isn't tripe, it's *tripes à la mode de Caen,*" she said.

"Of course. Well, I, for one, have been on this train long enough."

"Oh, I could ride the Orient Express forever!" Jennie cried. "That is, if they had a stage."

"It is a shortcoming, to be sure."

"But they should. It isn't right to coop people up like this with no entertainment. Of course, you can't dance, not really. Why don't they do something about the track?"

"You must talk to M. Lestrange."

"You are so clever, Papa."

I failed to respond, which only amused her all the more.

"I have never seen you so happy. You must be very, very wicked."

"Not at all. Have a scone and we will go see Mr. Holmes."

The promise of a visit with Holmes always served to calm Jennie's high spirits. While she was capable of submitting me to the most merciless ridicule, Holmes remained for her that mysterious, all-powerful figure who had plucked her from the streets and given her all she now possessed. She ate her scone with fastidious care—in the manner, so she said, of the countess—and we then departed to join Holmes, whom we found immersed in a large pile of documents of a most obscure and official nature, all in French.

"Ah, there you are, Watson, and Jennie as well. I have just been reviewing a few records of real-estate transactions along the lower Bosporus. Most informative."

"What have you deduced, Mr. Holmes?" said Jennie.

"Nothing that I can share, unfortunately," he replied, emptying the ash from his churchwarden, which he then placed carefully in his pocket.

"Well, that's no help," she said. "How can I help you solve this case if you don't tell me anything?"

"The task is not so much to solve a case as to build one. To fashion a net both large enough to fit an archduke and strong enough to keep one is no simple task. And once we have our net, we must still craft a way to bid him enter."

Jennie's manner suggested a little impatience with this answer, for she much preferred direct action to subtlety, but she made no complaint.

"It is so early!" she announced with disappointment, consulting her watch. "I hoped we would have time for lunch!"

"Unfortunately not," said Holmes. "M. Lestrange informed me that our passage on this last leg of our journey has been remarkably swift and that we are due in Constantinople in less than an hour."

Indeed, outside our window we could already see ruined temples, shattered walls, and collapsed churches, signs that we were entering a land antique beyond imagination. All of Europe's past lay here, broken and scattered about by the heartless hand of time. The ancient road that ran beside our track could have borne the tread of Agamemnon and Achilles, Xerxes and the Persian horde, the chariot of a despairing Hannibal, the triumphant legions of Pompey, Caesar, and Constantine, Attila and his Huns, Richard the Lion-Heart, and Suleyman the Magnificent.

As the countess had warned, much of what we saw was worn, wooden, and banal. As any visitor to Constantinople soon learns, the city is fearsomely vulnerable to fire, and every decade large areas fall victim to the flames. Only the ancient churches and great mosques survive. For whatever reason, the Turks refuse to profit from their experience, and create the same crowded wooden tenements over and over again. Only the palaces of the great, and the "Pera" or European section, a strange blend of East and West, are exempt from the recurrent infernos.

"We really are here at last," said Jennie as the Express slowly entered a broad railway "yard," with perhaps a dozen tracks, laden, for the most part, with worn and antiquated equipment, which made the greatest possible contrast with the polished *wagon-lits* of our train. "Are you going to get the diamonds, Mr. Holmes?"

"I should not," said Holmes, "be at all surprised."

PART III

The Sublime Porte

CHAPTER 14

The Siereki Station

WE STEPPED FROM THE train and walked beneath the arches of the Siereki Station, a remarkable edifice whose mixed architectural heritage announced to the traveler that he was truly quitting the West and entering the East. All around us was that strange mixture that is so characteristic of Constantinople, a few elegant Europeans in a great hurry to get somewhere or other, pushing impatiently through the great, indifferent sea of the East. There were not a few Eastern nobles present in the station as well, each surrounded by a shabby yet multitudinous retinue.

As we made our way down the platform and into the main waiting room, the passengers insensibly sorted themselves into those who actually lived in Constantinople and those who were merely visiting it—the dark and the light. We, of course, were part of the lighter-hued contingent, and among the Europeans were all of our acquaintances, including Lord Worthington, who appeared to particular advantage, or so Jennie said, in his uniform of colonel of the Coldstream Guards.

As we walked, Jennie searched alertly for a glimpse of Mr. Patterson to no avail, and I confess that I took an unworthy delight in the absence of that young gentleman. For my part, I found I could not restrain myself from searching as well—unobtrusively, I hoped—for the presence of the countess. At last I observed her lovely form moving gracefully along the platform, followed demurely by a pair of traveling maids. As soon as I caught sight of her I felt my heart beginning to beat with an uncontrollable fervor. As I walked by my friends, I felt myself an absurd mixture of artful dissimulation and innocent, heartfelt longing. Such an unstable combination might be expected to detonate from the least jar, but when the countess approached, I felt myself surprisingly at ease.

"Madame le Comtesse!" cried Jennie, as though she had not seen the lady for several years. *"Bonjour!"*

As she spoke she dropped into a charming curtsy that had the no doubt desired effect of fastening every eye upon her.

"Bonjour, mademoiselle," replied the countess with no less elegance. "Mr. Holmes? Dr. Watson? It is so pleasant to have one's feet upon the ground at last. And I am delighted that you have agreed to accept my hospitality. I can only hope that your stay in Stamboul will be an extended one. There is no pleasure to compare with good company."

The countess shifted her charming eyes conscientiously to each of us as she spoke, and for my part I conscientiously refrained from even the most covert intimation of desire. Yet as she departed from us I felt a sudden surge of longing. Simply to be in the presence of the woman I loved was the strongest possible tonic to my confidence and my passion.

We rode to our hotel in a coach-and-four that bore the livery of the Pera Palace, a hotel that takes its name from the European sector of Constantinople and offers the very latest in luxury and comfort, so that the intrepid tourist may be spared the inconvenience of ever having to leave the silken cocoon of Western elegance. Yet if we cared to see it, the great, indifferent East stood all around us. Jennie was clearly disappointed by the drab, dusty, dispirited population that filled the streets, though the sight of an occasional great turban did lift her spirits.

"I'm going to get one of those," she announced.

"You must be careful, Jennie," I said, though knowing that Jennie cared for no word so little as "careful." "Muslims have very strict rules about the behavior of women."

"They'll put me a harem, do you think?"

"Indeed they would. They would think that very much the best place for you."

"Why do you think that's so funny?"

I made no reply and, though Jennie taxed me on the point persistently, declined to do so throughout our ride to the hotel. When we entered the lobby of that elegant establishment, Jennie savored her new surroundings with renewed delight.

"Now, this *is* grand, isn't it?" she said, leaning on my arm and whispering in my ear. Her delight was so palpable that the myriad cares and complexities of our current situation, which had all but overwhelmed my brain during the past two days, at once resolved themselves into thin air and vanished. Jennie was happy, and that was enough.

"Perhaps I may have a word with you, Watson, once we are settled," said Holmes, catching me quite by surprise.

"Yes, of course," I said, striving to recover my thoughts. I could not imagine what topic he wished to discuss, though there were several that I wished distinctly to leave unventilated.

We were obliged to exchange our assigned rooms for a small suite, to accommodate Jennie's presence. I spent some time getting her settled, going to the length of surreptitiously examining the windows to ensure that she would not find it possible to use them as alternative means of exit. I then embarked on the delicate enterprise of making the acquaintance of the chief of security at the hotel, who by a stroke of good fortune proved to be Major Harold Soames, Ret., of the British Army in India. I reminisced with the major for some time, and then made a sufficient number of indirect suggestions regarding Jennie, who at this time I preferred to identify as a niece entrusted to my care, to convey to him my concern that "propriety" be maintained. Rather to my surprise, the major intimated to me that his "native" staff required monetary inducements to ensure their alertness, though I wondered if the larger portion of the five pounds I conveyed to him might not end up in his purse rather than those of his subordinates. Still, when I left his office I felt sure that I could rely on his assistance.

Having thus hedged Jennie's freedom to the extent possible, I returned to our suite, where I found Holmes seated before the large bay window that constituted the most remarkable feature of our accommodations, seemingly pondering the contents of a telegram that he held in his hand.

"This is a message from Mr. Jenkins," he said as I entered. "I am to call on the English ambassador tomorrow, who is to offer us his assistance in obtaining the diamonds."

"That is a remarkable change," I said, remembering the contemptuous treatment I endured at Mr. Churchill's hands at the Drury Lane.

"It is indeed. Although I do not know why, it appears that the archduke has made great difficulties for himself. He recently took out a mortgage on his *yali* here on the Bosporus of almost £15,000, for what purpose I cannot understand, for he has not redeemed the jewels, nor has he made any outstanding expenditure in Vienna. His position both in that city and here in Constantinople seems to decline with each passing day."

"Do you have hopes of bringing him to trial?"

"Here in Constantinople? That would be impossible. And to have him extradited to Scotland, even more so. Besides, what evidence have I?"

"But what about the murder on the train?"

"That was surely the act of the double. My only hope is to gain possession of the diamonds. Unless the archduke is willing to relapse into the obscurity he has struggled so persistently to escape, he must come after them. And in the pursuit he may betray himself."

There was more than a hint of frustration and impatience in my friend's voice as he spoke of these matters. Although he did not say so, the possibility that we had made this long journey for no more purpose than to transfer a king's ransom in jewels from the hands of one rich man to those of another could not have been far from his mind. Rather than discuss these matters further, Holmes set himself to the task of tuning his Stradivarius, an activity more congenial to his ears than mine. I quitted our suite and visited the hotel's small library in search of reading matter to replace *The Egoist* but had not made a selection before I was accosted in a most jocular manner by Mr. Patterson.

"Dr. Watson! I hope you are well settled," he cried in a loud voice, as though he believed I suffered from deafness.

"As well as can be expected," I said.

"It was such a pleasure to meet your daughter on the train," he said, taking a chair beside me. "She's such a charming young lady."

"Thank you for your kind words," I said shortly. "I ask you to remember, Mr. Patterson, that Jennie is very young, very young indeed, and scarcely more than a girl."

If Mr. Patterson was intimidated by my brusque words, he concealed his dismay with perfection, for his ingenuously smiling countenance, so devilishly young and handsome, altered not one whit as I spoke.

"Yes, of course she is," he said, "a charming girl. You know, nothing would delight me more than the opportunity to show her around Constantinople—properly chaperoned, of course, and only those places suitable for a young girl."

"I shall take your kind offer under advisement," I said firmly. "The weather in these parts is inclined to be inclement, and Jennie's health has always been somewhat delicate."

"Of course," he said, agreeing with me once more. "But perhaps if the weather is pleasant? The Hagia Sophia, for example, though converted to a mosque, is really one of the great monuments to our faith. The antiquities at Kariye are quite remarkable as well, and access to the church has become quite easy since its restoration for the kaiser's visit last year. The mosaics are among the finest in the world. And, of course, the Greco-Roman antiquities are of immeasurable educational value."

"Yes, indeed," I agreed in my turn, though I could hardly refrain from snorting at the puppy's effronteries. Under normal circumstances, Jennie's enthusiasm for Greco-Roman antiquities was less than nil, though to hear of them from the lips of Mr. Patterson would, I had to admit, fill her with joy.

"I am unfortunately detained in the morning, but I would be most happy to call after lunch," he said. "Shall we say two o'clock?"

"Very well, then," I agreed, "though I fear the weather will not cooperate."

"One must be an optimist in these matters," he said, with a disagreeable tone of self-satisfaction. "Good day to you, Dr. Watson, and please extend my best wishes to Jennie."

As I watched his departing figure I felt a jealous fury rising in my breast that shook me to my soul. To let that cunning fellow have his hands on my Jennie! How easy, how pleasant did murder suddenly seem! To put a bullet in that man's head would be the most innocent act the world had ever witnessed! For a full five minutes my heart burned with a sharp anger that all but blotted out my reason. At last my reason recovered, though my fury did not subside, and I was able to observe myself close at hand. The incipient lechery that I despised in him I had already displayed myself. All of my own wantonness redounded upon me as the images of my lascivious encounters with the countess flew about my disordered brain. How those shameless joys now informed against me!

I found it impossible to concentrate on any book or magazine. I left the library and retired to the smoking lounge, where I sought to collect my thoughts with the aid of a glass of ale and one of the fine Havanas supplied to us by M. Lestrange. The pleasant surroundings and the passage of time helped to calm my temper but could not end my dilemma. It was more than natural for two young people such as Jennie and Mr. Patterson to wish to pass the time in their own company rather than that of their tedious elders. Yet no one could know as well as myself the unfettered and independent spirit that flamed within Jennie's bosom. She longed, above all, for adventure, and what adventure can compare with love, and what fitter object for that passion than a tall, handsome, accomplished young man of the world like Mr. Patterson? And as for Mr. Patterson, what young gentleman could find Jennie other than irresistible? Jennie and Mr. Patterson, I could only conclude, were a combination scarcely less combustible than gunpowder and a lighted match.

So then should I oppose them, either in the spirit of a conventional morality that I had violated myself a thousand times or in that of a jealous father determined to deny to others what he could not have for himself? So often I had prided myself on the mature pleasure I had given to young women. The barrier of years that separated Jennie from Mr. Patterson was trivial compared to the measure that stretched between myself and any of half a dozen of my lovers over the past decade. Though I condemned, justly, the spirit of the mere seducer, I refused to recognize virginity as the sacred idol that our society pretended to worship. I had no desire to take that which a young lady had no wish to give. But more than once I have taken what was offered and was blessed for having done so. If ever I prided myself on the knowledge of a woman's heart, I could not deny Jennie Mr. Patterson's companionship without committing the very basest act of hypocrisy.

And yet how feeble, how very feeble indeed, are the promptings of reason! Only those who know the flames of jealousy know how hot they burn! The grim and vicious tales of retribution that fill Boccaccio, which I once dismissed as hopelessly "Italian," now struck me in a new and different light. Fortunately, a message from Jennie interrupted my agony. I put aside my cigar and journeyed to her room.

"Where have you been?" she demanded. "I knocked on your door, but Mr. Holmes wouldn't answer. I could hear his violin."

"I have been enjoying a cigar," I said.

"Let's have a carriage ride," she said, looking out her window. "Isn't it wonderful?"

Her enthusiasm was so pure I could not help laughing.

"What's so funny?" she demanded.

"Jennie, you can see for yourself how poor and mean this city is."

"No, it isn't; it's adventure. I want to see the new mosque and the Hagia Sophia."

I looked at her eyes, brimming with intelligence and impudence.

"Very well, then," I said, "because you are so set on it. But I warn you that the Turks are very strict with their women, and you shall not be permitted to do as you like."

"But I'm not one of their women, am I? So I shall do as I like."

"You may not be one of their women, but you are in their city, so you shall behave yourself. I suggest that you change into something more subdued, while I summon a carriage."

She looked at me with the infinite amusement that the young entertain for their elders.

"Of course, Papa," she said with a curtsy.

"I shall come for you in an hour," I said. "And, by the way, Mr. Patterson asked me if he might call on you tomorrow after lunch."

"He did!" Jennie fairly shrieked. "And what did you say?"

"I said yes, of course, though I shall supervise you both closely."

"Supervise me! Oh, you are too absurd, Papa."

"Please, Jennie, do not speak to me in that atrocious accent. I can abide any impertinence but that."

"You prefer me in English?"

"I do indeed."

"Very well. You deserve a reward, I suppose."

Her eyes were sparkling as she spoke, and she gave me a quick kiss upon the cheek. And so I departed, marveling once more at her charm. The energy of her person was such a tonic to my spirit that it was difficult indeed not to do whatever pleased her best. And I felt almost a physical movement within me to endure if not to accept whatever might come to pass between her and the ineluctable, ineludible, ineliminable Mr. Patterson.

CHAPTER 15

A Boat on the Bosporus

OUR CARRIAGE RIDE WAS entirely uneventful, but had the supreme advantage of keeping Mr. Patterson out of sight if not out of mind. I realized, as I had not before, how difficult it would be to keep an adequate rein on Jennie's high spirits. The North and South Poles, I fancy, are closer together than Muslim notions of feminine propriety and those entertained by my charge. We did not venture beyond the Pera in our journey, but even so, the reactions of passersby to the sight of a young woman riding boldly in an open carriage made me realize how directly we were challenging the Muslim custom of closeting the weaker sex. I was happy to return to the Palace, even though I knew that Mr. Patterson lurked within. When we returned to our suite, we found Holmes deeply engrossed in the chemical analysis of the sheet of paper we had recovered from the murdered man's jacket pocket. He begged us to have dinner without him, but as Jennie disappeared to begin the laborious process of dressing, he motioned me aside.

"We have business later this evening," he said. "I have received a second telegram from Sir Samuel. We are to meet with a gentleman named Aristides Adanopholos."

"I confess that I do not recognize the name."

"Mr. Adanopholos would be dismayed if you did. However, despite his best efforts, he is well known to the police as far east as Calcutta and as far west as New York."

"And how should Sir Samuel know him?"

"Sir Samuel is a leading figure in the sale of licit diamonds. Mr. Adanopholos is the leading figure in the sale of illicit ones. I myself have had several dealings with him. He is a dangerous man, Watson, but sometimes a useful one. The Sûreté has been quite interested in his activities for years. I believe Sir Samuel has assisted them with information on Mr. Adanopholos's bank deposits in Paris, which would explain his willingness to cooperate. But we must be on our guard. The gentleman would be only too happy to repay us with our own coin."

"And you had suspected Sir Samuel!"

"And I still do. But we shall know more when the night is over. Now I must return to my filtration."

An hour later Jennie and I left Holmes adjusting the slow drip of an amber fluid through layers of filter paper into a beaker beneath. Dinner at the Pera was if anything more expansive than on the Orient Express. Fortunately, Mr. Patterson was nowhere to be seen, and the time passed innocently enough. When we returned to our suite, Jennie accepted with surprising meekness the news that Holmes and I were departing on a midnight journey without her, so much so that I half suspected a determination on her part to follow us from a distance, and I could not resist locking her bedroom door when she retired.

Once Jennie had retired, I changed quickly into clothes more suitable for a rendezvous with a smuggler. We then summoned a hotel attendant and suggested to him our desire to visit one of the less reputable establishments of Constantinople, maintained by a certain Madame Vincent.

"You understand, under the circumstances, that we wish to be discreet in these matters," Holmes said, handing the man half a crown.

"Of course, My Lord," he responded, in heavily accented

English that nonetheless suggested distinctly that half a crown did not purchase much discretion at the Pera Palace.

"Very good," said Holmes, adding half a sovereign to the man's collection.

"Indeed, My Lord," the man said, more enthusiastically. "I will be most pleased to reserve a carriage for your purposes for the entire evening. It will arrive in less than ten minutes at the rear of the hotel. The carriage will be closed, very discreet."

"Excellent," said Holmes. "We will await your call."

The man departed, and Holmes closed the door firmly.

"It is impossible to be too careful in this city," he said. "The death on the train troubles me immensely. What was Sir Samuel's plan? Why was the man murdered, and by whom? Why was he murdered, while we escaped? I cannot help suspecting the archduke. We must be prepared, at every moment, for the intervention of unknown forces."

"What about Mr. Patterson?" I asked. "He has come out of nowhere."

"Yes, but he did not board the train until Budapest. Surely the murderer boarded in France."

"We only have his word for that," I said, reluctant to let the idea go. "If Jennie concealed herself on the train, he could have done so as well."

"It is a possibility," Holmes admitted. "One can only hope that such a charming young man as Mr. Patterson is innocent of any involvement."

"I can only hope that Jennie does not find herself compromised by a ruthless scoundrel," I exclaimed, with perhaps more heat than was proper.

"Of course not, Watson," Holmes replied. "Surely, the young man requires watching. And then there is the countess. I find her presence suspicious as well. There are too many threads to sort them out thoroughly."

I was about to respond when there was a knock at the door.

"That will be our carriage," said Holmes. "It would be best not to discuss the case from now on."

The attendant conducted us to a small room that contained a private elevator with scarcely enough room for the three of us. We descended rapidly to what appeared to be the basement of the hotel, for when we stepped out, we were confronted by rude masonry rather than elegant paneling and fine paintings. The attendant led us through a narrow corridor into a sort of tunnel where a nondescript carriage waited.

"Excellent," said Holmes, handing the fellow another half sovereign. "It appears, Watson, that the Pera Palace is well acquainted with the needs of a gentleman."

We rode with drawn shades for more than half an hour through the unknown streets of Istanbul. Holmes lapsed, as he so often did, into silent contemplation, the darkness of the carriage broken only by the glow of his churchwarden. At length the carriage came to a halt and we stepped out before a large, unadorned wooden building. Behind the building one could see the gleam of the waters of the fabled port known to history as the Golden Horn. Holmes tossed the silent coachman a shilling and promised him another when we returned. His guttural response gave uncertain assurance that we would find him at his post.

"We can but entrust ourselves to the honor of the Pera Palace," said Holmes as we walked to the darkened entrance of our destination. He took the large bronze knocker that hung from the door and struck it twice in swift succession and then a third time. The door swung open almost immediately, and the soft light of an oil lamp confronted our eyes.

"We are friends of Adanopholos," said Holmes, addressing the figure concealing itself behind the door.

"You may enter," a male voice replied.

We stepped into a room whose dimensions were at first entirely mysterious to me, for the flame of the oil lamp scarcely illuminated the arm of the man who held it. We could do no more than follow the light before us, which soon displayed a second door. When that door opened, a flood of light revealed that we were in a short passageway that led into a large room lit with what appeared to be hundreds of oil lamps, which hung from the ceiling in chandeliers made of polished brass.

We then stepped into an extraordinary room, perhaps fifty

feet square and perhaps twenty feet high. The walls were completely covered with a highly glazed tile of the most remarkable patterns, entirely abstract, though suggestive of stylized vines and topiary. The background was a light tan, while the patterns were formed throughout in various shades of brown, of extraordinary richness, ranging from light camel to the darkest sable, which approached the absoluteness of black without ever surrendering to it. The walls themselves supplied almost the entirety of the room's decoration, for there was no furniture at all, with the exception of a collection of massive pillows that lay on the rich carpeting. On the carpeting and pillows, in turn, lay a dozen voluptuous creatures, arrayed in oriental finery that did much to enhance the inherent physical charms of the eternal feminine, but little to conceal them.

"Mr. Holmes and Dr. Watson," a voice said. "I have been expecting you. I am Madame Vincent."

We were confronted by a tall, thin woman in a long black dress, accompanied by two powerful manservants. She had the indefinable air of a woman of her profession, which I had previously remarked in Miss Marigold, an air of reticence, refinement, and command. Both her face and voice implied a blending of East and West, and everything about her suggested a complete understanding of the weaknesses of the male sex.

"We have an appointment," said Holmes.

"Yes, of course," she said. "My manservants will show you the way."

We followed these forbidding gentlemen, who led us to a curtain that concealed an exit to a stairwell whose steps descended thirty or forty feet beneath the floor of the great room we had just quitted. Although Holmes appeared to have every confidence in the power of the name of Adanopholos to secure our safety in these dubious surroundings, I could not resist the impulse to keep my right hand resting lightly on my belt, only inches away from the butt of the small revolver I carried in the pocket of my trousers. The two ruffians, however, appeared to intend us no harm, but simply directed us through a series of passageways that led us to a small dock concealed beneath the building. The smell of coal smoke and steam announced the presence of a small, steam-powered vessel that awaited us. Our escorts exchanged a few words of what I took to be Turkish with the three men in the boat, which proved to be sufficient to establish our identity. We stepped into the boat without speaking and concealed ourselves within its superstructure. In minutes we had crossed the Golden Horn and reached the opposite shore, an area that I later learned is called Galata, though to a casual observer it simply appears as part of Constantinople proper. We arrived at a dock quite similar to the one from which we had departed, and were ushered wordlessly out of the boat. At this point another pair of ruffians confronted us, and we were escorted up a stairway into a small, bare, windowless room illuminated by a worn gas chandelier, whose glowing mantles cast dark shadows upon the floor. A large man seated at a desk awaited our arrival. He dismissed the guards with a few harsh words in Turkish and spoke to us in excellent English, flavored with a slight French accent.

"Mr. Holmes," he said with a nod. "And this is Dr. Watson?"

"Yes, Mr. Adanopholos," said Holmes.

"Then sit down," he said.

Mr. Adanopholos was a large, powerfully built man whose richness of dress and polished appearance proclaimed him to be a man of the world. Yet despite the coolness of the night, his brow was covered with sweat, and he seemed to stare at us with a mixture of anger and fear. His manner and voice alike betrayed a man in the grip of an overwhelming emotion.

"You drive a very hard bargain, Mr. Holmes," he began. "Very hard indeed."

"We came at your request," my friend replied. "You expressed no rancor in our dealings in the past. Surely a man who makes his living as you do should not be surprised to find himself confronted by difficulties."

"Very well. I have done everything that you have requested, despite the danger. Here it is."

So saying, he took from the floor behind the desk a

Gladstone bag from which he removed a small urn made of bronze, quite covered with tarnish. He removed the lid and took from the urn a bundle of thick black felt. Wrapped in the felt was a bag made of the very same material. He spread the cloth on the desk before us and gently emptied the contents of the bag onto it. To my amazement, Mr. Adanopholos spread before us the most splendid collection of jewels I had ever seen in my life. Dozens of small brilliants gleamed like points of fire, but pride of place went to a dozen large diamonds and one great stone that outshone them all.

"The diamond has been cut," said Holmes, the simplicity of his words belying the emotion he must have felt at seeing the fabled stone at last.

"Yes," replied Mr. Adanopholos, strangely indifferent to the enormous wealth that glowed on the table before him. "I have fulfilled my end of the bargain. Now you must fulfill yours."

"You move so swiftly," said Holmes. "Legal matters in the control of another country cannot be dismissed at the wave of a hand. I assure you that I will do everything in my power to convince the Sûreté to show lenience in your case."

"I care nothing for the Sûreté!" shouted Mr. Adanopholos with sudden vehemence. "I demand that you return my wife and child immediately!"

"Your wife and child?" asked Holmes, who appeared stunned by this charge.

"I will not be toyed with, Mr. Holmes," the smuggler continued. "If you will not tell me now that my wife and child will be returned to me unharmed, you may as well kill me now, for otherwise I assure you that I shall kill you!"

Mr. Adanopholos flung these words at us with a rage and a desperation that was terrible to see. His apprehension for his own life was not altogether unreasonable, for at his first explosion of anger I had taken the precaution of drawing my revolver, which I now rested on the table.

"There shall be no killing," said Holmes. "Watson, please remove that firearm. Mr. Adanopholos, I assure you that I know nothing of the kidnapping of your wife and child. In fact, although I have had some knowledge of your activities over the past ten years, I did not even learn of their existence until recently. I can only ask that you will be good enough to explain to Watson and myself the details of the charges you make against us."

Mr. Adanopholos relaxed to the extent of removing a handkerchief from his pocket and wiping it across his face.

"My wife and child live in Cannes," he began, his voice still marked with agitation. "I am pleased to hear that you did not know of their existence, Mr. Holmes. I am accounted a ruthless man in my line of work, a reputation I admit that I have coveted and that I have earned. But my weakness is obvious. Several weeks ago, in Sofia, I became aware of the unusual exertions of the Sûreté against my interests in Paris. I did not know why this was happening, but I soon discovered that they were being aided and encouraged by the firm of De Beers, with whom I have had frequent dealings in the past, always on the basis of mutual respect and mutual profit. I often deal in gems, and diamonds in particular. De Beers is the one market for diamonds, and a man is a fool to cross his market.

"I sought to discover the reason for the company's animus against me, but received no more information than the strong suggestion that I should visit Istanbul. I do not like to be told what to do, Mr. Holmes, but my connections here are excellent. My arrest in this city would be most unlikely and I can rely on dozens of men to assist me, men who are not squeamish about the killing of infidels."

"Watson and I did not come here to threaten you, or to receive threats ourselves," said Holmes mildly.

"Of course not. When I arrived at Constantinople I heard much talk of what lies on the table before you. I have followed the archduke's career with both admiration and caution. I was aware of the issue of the diamond, although I found it hard to credit reports of its continued existence. A week after I arrived in this city I learned of the trap that had been set for me. A man whom I have dealt with in the past, whom I must respect but do not like, arrived at my villa bearing an envelope that contained this photograph."

He took from the desk a large envelope and removed from it a photograph, which he then showed to us. The photograph depicted a middle-aged woman and a girl two or three years younger than Jennie, quite fashionably dressed. The woman was holding a copy of *Le Monde,* and the photograph was large enough that the date, April 6, 1906, was clearly visible.

"Without going into details, Mr. Holmes," Mr. Adanopholos continued, "I can tell you that my wife and child occupied an exclusive villa in Cannes, with a staff of servants personally chosen by me to provide for their safety. I, of course, had received no word of their abduction. On the contrary, it is my routine to receive daily telegraph messages attesting to their well-being, messages that I have continued to receive—messages that were quite obviously false."

"The sixth was a week ago," said Holmes. "Whoever brought this photograph traveled from Cannes to Constantinople as rapidly as is possible. It should not be impossible to determine who purchased a first-class ticket for such a trip."

"You know little if you think a competent smuggler would leave such a trail," said Mr. Adanopholos sharply, his anger flaring once again. "Your employers set an impossible task before me, Mr. Holmes, and I fulfilled it. It is up to you to establish a time and place for the exchange of the diamonds for my family. I do not know the archduke well, but I can imagine he will not take this loss lightly. You had best move quickly. I will not accept failure on your part."

Mr. Adanopholos voiced this threat with a cold, implacable tone, far different from the desperate note he had previously sounded. His manner suggested to me that he had little faith that he would see his wife and child again and was already engaged in planning an extensive and savage campaign of retribution against all those he believed to be responsible for the great injury he apprehended.

"Mr. Adanopholos," said Holmes, "I give you my word of honor that I shall do everything in my power to assure the safe return of your wife and child."

"You will forgive me, Mr. Holmes," the smuggler replied, "if I place little trust in your word or your honor. But if you value your life, and that of your compatriot, please see that they are returned."

Holmes made no reply, but simply paused for a moment to stare at the vast treasure that lay before us, the cold, imperishable brilliance of the stones seeming to mock the brutal tale of human greed and cruelty we had just received.

"Come, Watson," he said, rising to his feet, "we have work to do."

As we began our exit, Holmes turned to our host and spoke once more.

"Mr. Adanopholos," he said, "will you kindly telephone me tomorrow afternoon at my hotel at four o'clock?"

"Yes, of course."

"Very well. I hope to have good news for you at that time. If nothing else, you will receive a message telling you when to call again."

"I will, Mr. Holmes. But I ask you to remember that I must hide myself to avoid arousing the suspicions of the archduke."

Holmes nodded his assent to these words, and we descended quickly to the dock below. Our trip across the Golden Horn was fortunately without incident, and we soon returned to Madame Vincent's. Although the hour was approaching three o'clock in the morning, that formidable lady was still awake and alert.

"I hope your journey was profitable," she said.

"It was, indeed," said Holmes. "Allow me to express our appreciation for your assistance in this matter."

So saying, he opened his purse to gratify the lady's concealed yet omnipresent avarice with ten golden sovereigns.

"English money is so beautiful," she said with the satisfaction of a connoisseur. "It would give me so much pleasure if you gentlemen would accept the hospitality of my *salon des odalisques,* if only for a few hours."

"I fear not," said Holmes. "Our time is precious. I should take it as a great courtesy, madame, if you could inform me if you learn of anyone making inquiries regarding our presence here. I understand that one cannot always say everything that one wishes, but this is a matter requiring the greatest discretion."

"I always extend my guests the utmost in discretion," Madame Vincent replied as she conducted us through that great hall of scented and refined debauchery that had greeted us on our first arrival.

When we arrived at the exit from Madame Vincent's establishment she spoke quickly in Turkish to one of the guardians of that portal, who disappeared to summon our carriage. We bade a quick farewell to our unscrupulous hostess and entered our carriage, which offered us our first opportunity for uncensored speech in hours, though even in the confines of the ancient four-wheeler I thought it best not to entirely forsake caution.

"What on earth do you propose to do?" I asked Holmes, my voice as low as possible.

"I propose to remedy matters," said Holmes, taking out his churchwarden and putting it between his teeth. "I can only pray that it is not too late."

CHAPTER 16

A Telegram to De Beers

BY THE TIME WE returned to our rooms, the eastern sky outside our windows had begun to brighten with the first light of dawn.

"A late night, Watson," said Holmes, "and much to do in the morning. We have been cruelly betrayed by our employers, and we must set matters right."

"You are convinced that agents of De Beers have kidnapped the wife and child of this man?"

"I have no doubt of it. As Mr. Adanopholos indicated, he has been on intimate terms with some of the less reputable employees of De Beers for many years."

"Then our presence here has been no more than a ruse."

"The company, I am sure, would rather call it a matter of insurance. In any event, the first order of business is to procure the release of the hostages. Because of the distances involved, this will require a certain attention to detail. I shall cable Sir Samuel at ten this morning. I detect his hand in all these matters."

"You paint his character in the blackest hues."

"I do him no more than justice. When one considers all that was done in Africa by Cecil Rhodes in the name of England, the mere kidnapping of a smuggler's wife and child can hardly be considered out of bounds, particularly when the failure to do so might endanger the market for engagement rings in Manhattan."

"And what shall you tell him?"

"I shall tell him that the goods are secure, and that they will be transported as soon as the agreed-upon remuneration has been received by the seller. I shall also inform him that M. Brilleton failed to make his connection."

"Brilleton? The murdered man?"

"Yes. You see, Watson, it was a clever plan, clever indeed. You and I were sent here to catch the eye of the archduke. If matters had fallen out a certain way, if Mr. Adanopholos had failed in his efforts to obtain the stones, we might even have played the role we thought had been given to us. But while we proceeded above the law, the company dove beneath it, kidnapping his wife and child and demanding that he obtain the diamond if he wished to reclaim them. Mr. Adanopholos did so, without shedding blood, remarkably enough."

Holmes sat in a chair and took out his cherrywood.

"The entire plan," he said, as much to himself as to me, "must have been conceived less than three weeks ago, for it was at that time that the existence of Mr. Adanopholos's family first came to light. The Sûreté was able to obtain certain documents from a banking establishment in Barcelona, a bank that ultimately proved to be the source of funds for the wife and child. I fear that somewhere along the line, within either the Sûreté itself or British Customs, the information was passed to De Beers. The company then set this nefarious plot in motion, using us as its cat's-paw."

"But why were we involved at all?" I asked. "Why send us to Mr. Adanopholos? Surely the intent must have been to have M. Brilleton acquire the diamonds, since a man of his character would not object to the manner with which they were obtained."

"Because Mr. Adanopholos would never have met such a cutthroat as M. Brilleton," said Holmes with some irritation. "Our reputation was an essential part of the plot. M. Brilleton,

I believe, was sent to keep an eye on us, and to interfere, perhaps even in a murderous manner, if we failed to play the role De Beers had assigned to us."

"You would accuse De Beers of plotting our murder?" I exclaimed.

"Oh, the American market is worth the lives of a few Englishmen who have outlived their time, I should imagine," he replied. "One could hardly call De Beers squeamish. The company currently employs thousands of Chinese laborers in its mines in Africa under conditions scarcely separable from slavery. Corruption, begun abroad, eventually finds its way back home. In any event, we have made ourselves the target of criminals before. We must simply keep our pistols about us as well as our wits."

He delivered this last remark with an amused smile, as though the ruthless deceit that had been practiced upon us were merely a spice to the chase.

"I take it that you will inform De Beers that you are withdrawing from the case?"

"I shall do no such thing. They have their purposes and I have mine. They sought to shape me to their purposes. I shall now do my utmost to return the favor."

That remark concluded our discussion for the evening, or rather the morning, and I departed for bed, pausing briefly to open the door to Jennie's room. In the faint light I saw her fair, brave features relaxed in sleep, the very picture of innocence and youth. Seeing her in such circumstances, one could hardly imagine the fierce will that animated her delicate body. Quietly, I stepped into the room and stole to the windows, where I gently pulled shut the curtains, to shut out the least light of the rising sun. She would be up all too soon, her head filled with the sort of ardent fantasies of which only a fifteen-year-old girl is capable. I could not help but dread what was to come.

I returned to my room and fell into a sound sleep immediately upon retiring, a rest from which I did not waken until almost eleven. Holmes was gone, of course, to his appointment at the British embassy. I found Jennie almost ecstatic with anticipation, with three whole hours to endure before the arrival of Mr. Patterson. I gave her *The Egoist* to peruse as a sedative to her nerves, though I doubted that Mr. Meredith's sentences would prove much to her liking, and stepped outside to enjoy a leisurely cup of Turkish coffee on our balcony, contemplating in the far distance the great dome of the Blue Mosque, which seemed to loom over the city almost like a second sun.

At twelve-thirty we enjoyed a peaceful lunch on the balcony. I told Jennie nothing of the events of the night before, but quietly resolved never to allow her out of my sight for the duration of our visit, and to keep, as Holmes said, both my wits and my revolver about me.

At last the great hour arrived, and Mr. Patterson presented himself in all his youthful splendor. He was accompanied, to my mingled delight and dismay, by the countess!

The object of our journey that afternoon was Kariye, a church of no little fame that had suffered greatly at the hands of the Muslim conquerors but that was now, as Mr. Patterson had previously informed me, significantly restored. The question of religion was obviously a great one in Constantinople, and, as I learned during our carriage ride, one of almost infinite ambiguity. Officially the Muslim faith enjoyed an absolute monopoly. The edifice known as Kariye was a mosque, not a church. But beneath this mask, intrigue was all-powerful, as long as it remained hidden. The countess, I came to understand, had had a hand in the restoration, and had in fact been a member of the kaiser's party during his visit in 1905, vivid testimony to the position she held in the city. It also became obvious that the countess and Mr. Patterson also had visited the church together that year subsequent to the kaiser's departure, information that caused me no little disquiet. To see them chatting amiably of the sights we were to see, and in particular to see the countess' charming feet peeping from beneath the folds of her elegant skirts, so tantalizingly close—these were not sights calculated to calm my spirit. My vows regarding the countess were far less constant than the weather, but to be with her under such circumstances served to stimulate the most primitive passions that may rage in a man's breast. To endure such emotions, while speaking casually of the spring flowers and an upcoming reception to be held at the French embassy, was less than pleasant, and I leaned heavily on my cigar for solace and support.

When we arrived at last at the church, I was surprised to see that it was scarcely remarkable in its dimensions, for I had been expecting a structure similar in size to St. Paul's or Notre Dame. Though far from grand, the church has a pleasing sense of completeness, built of fine gray stone at the lower levels, surmounted by one large, central dome and four smaller ones of differing sizes. The domes all rest on towers, with high, arched windows to admit light. If there is a plan for the arrangement of the domes I could not discover it, and it appeared that the church had reached its present dimensions through a process of accretion.

When we alighted from our carriage we were greeted with grave politeness by a figure draped in black, whose manner proclaimed him to be a priest of some sort, though whether Muslim or Orthodox I could never be sure. He greeted the countess, who certainly was known to him, in Greek, and she responded with that special pride of someone freed from the strictures of official civilization and allowed to converse once more in her native tongue. The priest did little more than usher us into the building, which was entirely unoccupied, silent yet eloquent testimony to the countess's position within Constantinople.

But if the priest was silent, Mr. Patterson was not. I had before conceived him to be little more than an idle young gentleman, but it appeared that he was in fact a scholar of no little learning. When we first entered, he squatted on his hams to point out to us a particularly worn and battered row of stones that he proclaimed to be part of the original foundation, put in place, so he said, some thirteen hundred years ago. I took a certain malicious pleasure in his chatter, for the more attention he paid to the stones, the less he could pay to Jennie, and Jennie did not easily forgive such neglect.

We first entered into a section of the church that Mr. Patterson identified for us as the Parecclesion, whose walls and ceilings were covered with frescoes that I am sure Mr. Patterson found very remarkable, though I confess that I did not, and neither, I suspect, did Jennie. I can never recall a time when I did not find the interior of a church to be depressing, the hymnals, pews, vestments, and indeed the very air to be filled with a vaguely censorious and suffocating presence that chilled my heart and oppressed my brain. My parents were quite dutiful Presbyterians, which is the only part of my upbringing that I ever regretted. It was at university that I first tasted the bracing tonic of free thought, and I have never forgotten nor regretted the joy of that sweet libation.

To my great surprise, the countess was very otherwise to my thinking. She took great pleasure in hearing Mr. Patterson discourse, and the young man could never provide details sufficient to please her. These stiff, solemn, hieratic figures spoke to her of the past glories of her race, when Greece and Rome were one, when Constantinople still held itself to be the city of the Caesars and the center of the world. She delighted in the obscurest detail that Mr. Patterson could uncover and asked me repeatedly if I were not charmed by the fiery stream that descended from Christ's feet to form the lake of flame that consumed the damned and if I were not overwhelmed by the portrait of St. Cyril, whose rigid, condemnatory features seemed to sum up all that I found distasteful in Christianity. However, I could take honest pleasure in the depiction of the angel who bore the scroll of heaven, which was inscribed with the sun, and the moon, and the stars. The sun, at least, smiled with a pagan generosity, as if to say that he would warm all mankind, regardless of their follies. Oh, for a religion with a good heart instead of cold fingers!

From the frescoes we then passed to the mosaics, which were exclusively found in the inner recesses of the church. Here undoubtedly were subjects for wonder. The myriads of tiny glass cubes, set in the walls and ceilings far above our heads, seemed to burn with an eternal flame, catching the light in the most remarkable and unexpected ways. The brilliant figures, set against backgrounds of pure gold, had a silent, massive power, utterly unlike that of the soaring cathedrals of the West but just as convincing.

The countess read us the Greek inscriptions, and Mr. Patterson supplied the details of the various incidents from the Bible that were depicted for us with such earnest and literal detail. The effect, though not one very much to my taste, exerted a persistent influence upon the imagination, forcing even such an impatient skeptic as myself to consider the long centuries during which the lamp of the Christian faith was held aloft in the East rather than the West. For how long did troubled souls seek resolution beneath these solemn personages, who wheeled above our heads like the eternal constellations! How many prayers were said within these scarred walls! And yet this was a new church! Very new!

As we craned our necks, I gained an inkling of the importance of the figure of Mary in the Eastern Church, who has, of course, been exalted even more greatly by Rome, much to the righteous disgust of those of us who spring from dissenting stock. Jesus appeared frequently above our heads, but always as creator or judge, and even the saints seemed to have discarded any human vulnerability during their ascent. Mary alone appeared human; and the poor peasants and townspeople who had gathered here in times past, so ignorant of the workings of the world and so helpless before it, must have clung passionately to that hope and that peace that she alone offered.

The mosaics were much despoiled by thieves, the golden cubes eagerly wrenched from the walls, more by Christian fingers than Muslim, said the countess, who had unkind words for both Venice and the pope. Indeed, it is difficult not to conclude with Voltaire that religion and thievery often join hands, though, of course, I was too polite to say such things in such surroundings. So Catholic stole from Orthodox, and Protestant stole from Catholic, and so does the new religion of equality steal as well.

"Are we going to stay here forever, Papa?" demanded Jennie.

I had, in my reverie of past revolutions of the spirit, been so unconscious of my companions that I had wandered into a separate room, where Jennie might accost me without fear of being overheard.

"Oh, it is Mr. Patterson who is enamored of such things, not I," I replied.

This witticism was not well appreciated.

"He does go on, doesn't he?" she said in a cautious tone.

"Americans have all sorts of vices."

"Too many! Look what the damp is doing to my shoes."

"I shall call it to his attention."

"Ha, ha. Do say that we must leave, Papa. I would so rather play whist or sing a song for him!"

She spoke with the perfect urgency of the young, who, of course, cannot be denied. Even the saints in heaven must give way to the desires of a young lady. I approached Mr. Patterson and explained that the hour was getting late and that I was scheduled to meet with Holmes on an urgent matter. I gathered that the request was not entirely welcome, for gaining such unfettered access to the church was no easy task for someone lacking the rank of a kaiser, but Mr. Patterson, with all his airs, did have the manners of a gentleman, and was quick to place our needs above his. He graciously took Jennie by the arm, which brightened her spirits noticeably, and I extended a similar courtesy to the countess.

"I fear our antiquities must bore you," she said. "Our traditions are so very much different than yours."

"On the contrary, I found the mosaics quite fascinating," I said, pleased to be able to make both a favorable and an honest reply.

"You don't know what it means to me to see a church again in Constantinople!" she said with sudden exultation. "Of course, I cannot say that publicly, for officially it is still a mosque. But I retain the hope that someday Constantinople will again be the great city it once was, the great meeting place between a new East and a new West!"

She spoke with such urgency and such sweep that I was quite amazed. Who could have imagined that a great society lady would conceal such strange passions?

"That is indeed a remarkable goal," I replied at last.

"Yes, and for you a strange one. London is your world, I know. Everything pales in comparison."

"I would not say that at all. The more I travel, the more London shrinks, though I must say that I prefer it. The tube and the *Times* and a decent steak and kidney pudding are all I require."

The countess seemed amused by this reply, but made no response until we had passed into the sunny courtyard in front of the church.

"Really, Doctor?" she said when we had quitted the holy surroundings. "I do not think you are so bourgeois as that. You are a man of adventure, as I know to my cost."

"Your cost, Countess?"

"Yes. My cost and your delight. You are a most wicked man. How a man with your sins hopes to control his daughter is beyond me. She could make a fine match if you set your mind to it."

"I dictate to Jennie? And find a fine match for her? Her career is her world. However handsome Mr. Patterson may be, and however rich, she would not consider marriage if he thought to bar her from the stage. You do not know what applause means to her."

"You study her so closely. And no doubt you are right. I fear you know far too much about my sex than any man should."

"However much I know, I remain its slave."

"Indeed? Someday I shall put you to the test."

"I can only hope that that day will be soon."

At this point we were obliged to put an end to this raillery, which surely bordered on the indecent, and joined Jennie and Mr. Patterson in the carriage. After such a conversation, to sit in the sunlight and behold the countess' beauty was as sure an intoxicant as ever has been known to the mind of man. I could not but marvel at the subtle passions that animated her soul. She was a wise woman, even profound, and yet as wanton a creature as one could imagine. She seemed utterly at her ease, and discoursed amiably with Jennie and Mr. Patterson on all that we had seen. I myself said little, for my spirits had been amply stimulated by the lady, and I was happy to let them cool, or perhaps rather simmer, in her sunlit presence. Mr. Patterson, to my displeasure, had lost that religious note in his conversation that Jennie had found so trying and had reverted to his tediously American, cocksure manner, which unfortunately met with her consistent approval. And so we journeyed, a very curious foursome, back to the Palace, arriving too late for the ostentatious "high tea" made available to guests, and so the countess took her leave, saying that she must dress for the reception. I was so selfish, and so appetitous, that I resented bitterly the fact that she did not see fit to invite me, as though that would have been appropriate. Most fortunately, Mr. Patterson had social obligations as well, connected with his "dig," so we were free of him for the evening, though he promised that he would return in a day or two.

"He talks so much better when he isn't in church," said Jennie gratefully.

"Archaeologists are very strange people, Jennie," I suggested, an observation that did not meet entirely with her approval.

"He has excellent manners for an American," she said, as though she were a duchess extending a gracious sympathy to our awkward cousins across the sea.

"I am sure he would be pleased to hear that," I said as I opened the door to our suite.

As we entered, I received an acute surprise, for seated in one of the overstuffed chairs that decorated our drawing room was a tall, thin Turk, with a massive turban surmounting his head, puffing contentedly on one of the pipes of a large bubble-bubble!

"Ah, Watson!" the fellow cried out, "And Jennie as well! Did you enjoy your excursion?"

CHAPTER 17

A Curious Device

"HOLMES," I SAID, "WHY have you assumed that remarkable disguise?"

"I have been to the bazaar," he said. "I wished to observe rather than be observed. Fortunately, one of the pageboys at the hotel was willing to assist me in this charade, for of course I never could have managed the language on my own. I made a study of some of the Turkic dialects in Mongolia years ago, but my accent is irredeemably European."

"I must have that turban!" cried Jennie. "I must!"

"Jennie, ladies do not wear turbans," I said, striving to correct her enthusiasm.

"Oh, that shows how little you know," she replied, eagerly removing the spherical object from Holmes's head. "Why, I shall be the finest Turk ever, with my turban and my scimitar. But it does not go with this dress."

And, bearing her prize in her hands, she departed into her room.

"I thought you had an interview at the British embassy," I said.

"And so I did. Lord Adcock proved to be a most cautious host."

"You met with the ambassador himself, then."

"Yes. I was surprised to do so, but it suggests how close an interest the authorities are taking in this case. Naturally, I did not tell him that I had seen the diamonds in the possession of a noted smuggler, but pretended my goal was to acquire them honestly through direct negotiations with the archduke. He assured me that the embassy would do all it could to assist me, but offered nothing specific."

"Has he ever met the archduke?"

"Yes, he has. I know for a fact that he has been a guest at the archduke's *yali* more than once. It would not surprise me if the ambassador does not wish us well. In any event, after I left the embassy I was determined to see another side of the city. I disguised myself in the manner you see and made my way to the bazaar with Ari. Among the Turks of the city there seems to be little awareness of the momentous transactions that have recently occurred. We asked for jewels, but saw only a few items and had few offers. Naturally, I must return tomorrow in a different guise. However, I did find something. What do you think of it?"

He took from the worn cloth bag that sat at his feet a wooden stick, perhaps two feet long, made of two pieces fitted together, less than two inches in diameter, resembling to some extent the "swagger stick" of an officer.

"It is a curious device," he said, removing the larger of the two ends. "If you reverse the ends and give it a clap, you see what happens."

As he spoke, Holmes gave the butt of the stick a light blow with his hand, and immediately a long, cruel blade sprang from the mouth of the stick.

"Good lord," I exclaimed.

"The puissant pike in miniature," Holmes said, displaying the tool for my inspection. "The blade is fitted with a powerful spring, you see. One can deliver a killing blow at close quarters with very little effort and no sound at all, other than the cries of the victim. And the handle is fitted so that one can reset the spring with no danger of injury."

"An assassin's tool," I said.

"Precisely."

"But why did you think to purchase it?"

Before answering, Holmes drew thoughtfully on the bubble-bubble.

"The blends here are quite striking," he said, indicating that I should sample one of the other stems. "Having forbidden themselves alcohol, the Muslims have made a fine study of nicotine. But to return to the matter at hand. Do you remember, on our first meeting with Mr. Churchill, how he told us of the false archduke's swagger stick, which he liked to call a 'coup stick,' made, I believe, of polished walnut?"

"Vaguely."

"Do you remember how he said that, at the moment the impostor realized he had been discovered, he clenched furiously at the stick and made as if to remove the cap?"

"No," I said, rather embarrassed by my faulty memory.

"Well, perhaps you did not compose an extended account of the interview. But I assure you that he did describe this action on the part of the impostor. Now, imagine a device such as this, fitted, not with a knife blade but a thick, rigid needle, such as the one that must have penetrated the body of the unfortunate M. Brilleton."

"Certainly it is possible, but the penetration of a needle, even into the vital organs, even the heart itself, while surely damaging, would be unlikely to be fatal."

"Under ordinary circumstances, yes. But I will tax your memory a second time by referring to the autopsy performed on Mr. Rhodes's servant boy, which found that he had died of internal bleeding, though it could not identify the source of the internal wound, nor external wounds suggestive of any blows or other injuries that could induce such internal bleeding. A similar case had occurred in France several years earlier—a maid at the Hôtel Bristol who was dismissed several weeks after she had reported seeing a man she believed to be the Archduke Josef on the fourth floor of that hotel, a statement she made during a private inquiry into a sensational theft of some £70,000 in jewels from three different suites. Supposedly the woman had been drinking and fell down a flight of stairs."

"And had she been drinking?"

"Her stomach contained no more than two glasses of wine, scarcely enough to intoxicate any Parisian over the age of five. M. Compte, at that time a junior detective in the Sûreté, wished to classify the death as a homicide under investigation, but was overruled by his superiors. The theft has never been officially acknowledged, but M. Compte assures me that the jewels were ransomed for some £40,000."

"Forty thousand pounds!"

"Yes. The archduke, of course, was excused from any suspicion, both on account of his rank and the fact that he was present at a private party held in the suite of the Duke of Newcastle for the entire period during which the robberies could have occurred."

Holmes paused to apply a match to the bowl of the bubble-bubble, drawing gently on the stem.

"Consider those deaths in light of what we saw while examining the corpse on the train," he resumed. "By the merest chance, we observed the entry point of an extraordinarily crafted needle. It is easy to conclude that a close examination of the other two bodies would have discovered similar wounds."

"But the hole we saw was no more than twice the diameter of a normal hypodermic, if that," I interrupted. "Surely blood clots would block such wounds, even in the heart itself."

"Yes, unless the device were used to inject a potent anticoagulant. I have analyzed the blood sample I took from M. Brilleton's mouth and nose and have isolated an organic substance that I believe is not a component of human blood. But I am scarcely an expert and have not the tools for such fine research. M. Compte has far greater resources, but the challenge of managing an investigation over such large distances is not a pleasant one. He should have received the body only yesterday. I dare not entrust this information to the telegraph office, even in code."

"What can you do?"

"I shall continue my analysis of this substance. In precisely one week, our estimable *chef de train* will return on the

Orient Express. By that time I shall have prepared a monograph on my findings, which I shall entrust to him for conveyance to M. Compte. A thorough autopsy and analysis may identify the anticoagulant that was used."

I listened to my friend's statement with some skepticism, for as a physician I was well aware that an anticoagulant of the strength required to allow an individual to bleed to death from an internal pinprick, even to the heart, did not exist. Anticoagulants are, of course, invaluable in the laboratory, but remain painfully volatile and unstable. However, his words prompted a recollection of one of my encounters in the smoking carriage aboard the Orient Express.

"Perhaps I can save you some time," I suggested. "During our journey here I encountered a most unusual man, Dr. MacLaurin, a Scot who has spent his entire adult life in France. He is a gifted surgeon and his specialty is cancers of the stomach, but what is of particular importance is that he had just attended a week-long conference in Vienna on the very subject of transfusions and anticoagulants. He was traveling to Belgrade, and the purpose of his visit is to operate on a local grand duke. I don't suppose the facilities in Belgrade are distinguished, but he surely would have access to the best available."

"Do you think he would cooperate?"

"Of course he would. He is a man of science."

"Of course. But I would be reluctant to place myself within the jurisdiction of Austria. Still, it would save time. On the other hand, there is Mr. Adanopholos' family to consider as well. Perhaps if you could send the good doctor a telegram, seeking his assistance without going into details. You do not know perchance the name of his hotel?"

"No."

"Then simply locating him will occasion delay in the first place. In the meantime, I must assure myself that De Beers and its minions are making good on their promise to deliver Mr. Adanopholos' wife and child."

"Surely there will be no delay, when the lives of two human beings are at stake."

"So one would wish. But I suspect that the gentlemen

involved are more concerned with their own safety than that of their prisoners. It is my understanding that they travel by boat, and are not expected for at least a week."

"A week!"

"Yes. It is a dirty business, Watson, very dirty indeed, and it will be a time before we are out of it."

"Then perhaps I should send a telegram to Dr. MacLaurin immediately," I said.

Holmes nodded his assent and I departed with some haste, returning to find him sprawled on the sofa, his long legs stretched out before him and his beloved Stradivarius tucked beneath his chin. His posture would hardly have won the approval of a Paganini, but the diabolical melancholy of his tone had much in common with that dark and brooding maestro. Since Holmes seemed entirely unaware of my presence, I was debating whether to leave or remain when the door to Jennie's room opened and she entered in all her pride, dressed as a boy in what appeared to be black silk pajamas, with her prized turban perched upon her head.

"Have I come at a bad time?" she whispered to me

"Not at all, Jennie," cried Holmes in a loud voice, evidently determined to discard his low spirits.

"What do you think, Mr. Holmes!" Jennie responded as she promenaded about the room. "We're a pair of proper Turks, you and I, and we'll skin Papa for an infidel if he doesn't mind what he's told."

"That remains to be seen," I told her. "Now, if you want your supper, you must change."

"I shall dine à la Turque," she retorted. "Besides, I feel like staying here."

And with that, she hopped first upon a chair and then upon a table, and began to sing "Every Little Movement Has a Meaning All Its Own," amusing herself with the task of capering as she sang while balancing the turban on her head.

"It's perfect, don't you think?" she asked. "I shall have to learn the hootchy-kootchy."

"Please do not use such vulgar expressions, Jennie," I commanded. "This is not America."

"You are so fussy," she said, leaping to the ground. Scarcely had her feet touched the carpet than there came a knock on the door. I answered it and received a message from a liveried servant who bowed graciously at the receipt of a shilling.

"It is from Mr. Patterson," I said with some dismay. "He expresses his appreciation for a pleasant day and asks if we should care to visit the Hagia Sophia in the morning at ten."

"That's a church, isn't it?" said Jennie suspiciously. "I should prefer a pleasant walk, or perhaps a journey on the Bosporus."

"What have you been reading?" I demanded.

"I haven't been reading anything," she replied, parading elegantly about the room as before.

"We shall see," I said. "In any event, I am not sure that it would be proper for you to visit the Hagia Sophia. Turks take a very dim view of women appearing about in public. Our visit to Kariye was an exceptional favor."

"Then I shall go in disguise, like Mr. Holmes. With this turban I can go anywhere I please."

"Deception has peculiar risks, Jennie," remarked Holmes. "Honesty is most often the best policy."

"Yes," I said, "and in this land you cannot rely on the police for protection."

"That shan't be a problem," retorted Jennie, who was clearly determined to defy any restriction on her person. "The countess has given me protection. I'll show you."

She departed from the room and returned a minute later carrying her handbag, from which she extracted an alarmingly large derringer.

"Two barrels, you see," Jennie said, holding it up for our inspection. "Bang, bang! That will stop any fellow. The countess gave me this one and kept one for herself."

"One must be cautious with firearms," said Holmes, taking the weapon from Jennie's young hand. "It is well made, at least, and with a safety catch. But loaded weapons and handbags are a dubious combination, Jennie."

"But what if I am attacked all at once?" Jennie asked. "Can you stop a Turk with a hat pin?"

"You shall have to trust to Dr. Watson and myself," said

Holmes. "I suggest that you give custody of this firearm to your father."

He handed the derringer back to Jennie, who dutifully handed it to me.

"I suppose you will be wanting the bullets as well," she said, taking a box from her handbag. "But you must give it back to me in times of great danger."

"We shall see, Jennie," I said, taking possession of both the gun and the shells.

Deprived of her derringer, Jennie's mood seemed to shrink.

"I suppose we must go to the Hagia Sophia after all," she said. "It's better than nothing. But Father, you must invite the countess for a cruise. She will be sure to invite us in, and at her *yali* we can do as we please."

"Possibly I shall," I said politely. Jennie had no way of knowing what a temptation her saucy words posed for me. To visit the countess in her *yali,* to caress her feet and to kiss her glorious toes! Rather desperately, I pushed the temptation away.

"Of course," I said, "it is unlikely that we shall have much time for visits and sightseeing."

"More time than we would wish," said Holmes irritably. "The more I consider it, the more I wonder if I must not seek out Dr. MacLaurin in Budapest. I fear I must ask you both to withdraw. There is much here that must be resolved."

CHAPTER 18

The Great Church

JENNIE AND I ENJOYED a subdued dinner by ourselves and then played two-handed whist for several hours while Jennie analyzed Mr. Patterson's person and personality in almost infinite detail, noting the fineness of his hands and the particularly unpleasant tone his voice assumed while discussing the dormition of the Blessed Virgin. When I remarked that, to my understanding, the Muslims had stripped the interior of the Hagia Sophia of all images, and those of the Queen of Heaven in particular, her mood brightened appreciably.

"Well, that's good," she said. "The less to talk about, the better. Is the countess coming? Did he say?"

"You know the countess finds you most refreshing."

Jennie smiled at this compliment. She displayed at times a most remarkable and most becoming modesty, as though she possessed a full understanding of her own self-regard and hunger for recognition and applause.

"What about you, Papa? Do you find her refreshing?"

"What man would not? A glamorous, titled widow who combines the mystery of the East with the polish of the West, who has been everywhere and done everything?"

"You don't think she did the count in, do you? I mean, not unless he deserved it."

"Of course not. She is entirely innocent."

Jennie said nothing, but the sparkle in her eyes suggested much. I had no desire to speak extensively of the countess, for I felt that one way or another I would be sure to betray my passion, which flourished unrestrained in the deep recesses of my heart. I was reluctant to retire, knowing that when I did so it would take full possession of my consciousness once more. After sating our appetite for cards, Jennie and I returned to our suite, where Holmes was kind enough to accompany Jennie in a number of songs, though the repertoire of the music hall was very far indeed from his habitual taste. In the middle of our recital he received a telegram from Dr. MacLaurin, responding favorably to his inquiry.

"I fear I must cut short our recital," he announced. "If I hurry, I may make the Express tonight and be in Belgrade tomorrow."

No sooner had Holmes spoken than he summoned a servant to bear his bags, which stood packed by the door, leaving Jennie and myself with no recourse but to retire for the evening.

Sleep, however, did not come easily to me that night. In the darkness and solitude of my bedchamber, my longing for the countess reasserted itself with a fury. Never, I believe, had the desire to possess ever taken such full possession of my soul. How I longed for the logical severity of Holmes, the girlish charm of Jennie, the smug prattle of Mr. Patterson—anything, rather than the sharp tooth of desire, which left me tormented and sleepless. After an hour of shameful fantasy, I finally regained some control over my wanton spirit and took up a recent copy of the *Lancet*. A long article examining patterns of necrosis in the phalanges of frostbite victims helped to soothe my temper and, with the assistance of a glass of warm milk, I was at last able to retire with calmer spirit at no later than two in the morning. I awakened the next day at half past nine, embracing my pillow but otherwise in restored spirits. My heart, I fear, was as wicked as the night before, but my eye was clearer and my hand steadier. I found Jennie, who was, of course, already awake and fully dressed, waiting for me impatiently.

"Where have you been?" she fairly shouted. "You know he will be here at ten."

"Mr. Patterson may wait," I said firmly. "If you will be so good as to order me a breakfast of kippers and coffee I shall be with you shortly."

"There isn't time for kippers," she called, but I refused to be hurried. I felt confident that the countess would be a member of our party, and I was determined to prepare myself for her company in a manner that would leave me entirely at my ease. A man prepared to embrace his fate, after all, should do so looking his best. A half hour later I emerged, feeling fresh and self-confident. My breakfast, presented with all the sumptuous charm of which the Palace was capable, awaited me, and I sat down in my chair with an air of measured leisure quite intended to provoke Jennie to the point of exasperation.

"You think you're so clever," she said, holding herself in check.

I made no reply but simply enjoyed my kippers. A servant's knock announced the arrival of our guests, and Jennie impatiently descended to the lobby to greet them. As she left, it occurred to me that excessive cleverness on my part could easily prompt Jennie to commit actions that we would both regret, and I decided that it was best to leave my breakfast and join the party.

By agreement, both the countess and Jennie were dressed in a most sober manner, but the very severity of the countess' dress, when combined with the special warmth and freshness of her complexion, made her presence as charming as if she were wearing the most fashionable of evening gowns. I presented my arm with honest pride and was rewarded with the intoxicating touch of her delicate hand upon mine. So blessed, I advanced through the lobby of the Palace with all eyes upon me. When we were seated at last in our carriage, Jennie threw me a glance of censure, but I smiled grandly and stared her down.

We arrived at the vast structure of the Hagia Sophia by a circuitous route, which did not allow a full view of the exterior. Great walls of ancient stones loomed before us like weathered cliffs, for the Sophia, though very much repaired through its long life, had endured for well over a millennium, and was far closer in age to the Colosseum than Notre Dame. When we arrived we were greeted by a number of Turks in traditional dress, who would accompany us into the mosque and by their very presence dilute and disguise our foreignness.

We entered the great structure in a manner appropriate to supplicants, by a side entrance, without the slightest display. Although surely once adorned with far greater glory than the Kariye, the interior of the Sophia today presents a blank and confusing face to the visitor. If any Christian decorations still lie beneath coats of paint and plaster, the Turks refuse to allow them to be revealed. Although several of the mosques built since the Ottoman conquest rival the Sophia in size or even surpass it, pride of possession has determined the Turks to allow no concession to the tastes of European tourists, and those who venture into this structure may do so only upon Turkish terms, or, as they would have it, in submission to the will of Allah.

My first impression, I confess, was entirely one of disappointment, for the interior seemed to be no more than a great, blank thing, a piling of stones upon one another to no purpose or effect. I was, indeed, somewhat amazed that my reaction was so tepid, for the least curious eye could see that an immense amount of skill had gone into the construction of the church. The building of such a structure with the meager tools, and even more meager science, available to mankind less than six centuries after the birth of Christ could only be considered a miracle, but however much Mr. Patterson discoursed on the achievement, and on the lost glories of the interior decor, I remained unmoved. The broad dome above my head was no more than a vast bubble, and the ineffable beauties of the great cathedrals of the West were entirely lacking.

For more than an hour we strolled cautiously within the Sophia, and during much of that time the countess and Mr.

Patterson spoke Greek—a great pleasure, surely, to the countess, but to Jennie it was Greek indeed. I feared that at any moment she might do something outrageous, if only it would reclaim Mr. Patterson's attention, but remarkably she did nothing more than cling ever more tightly to his arm, seeking to remind him, so I would guess, that he was her only protector in this fearsome and frightening world.

My own patience was scarcely less worn than Jennie's, and I was about to suggest that we depart for luncheon when a remarkable event forever changed the way in which I viewed the Sophia. The sky had been well clouded as we rode over to the church, and while we were inside the light was even and subdued. But as I turned to the countess to speak I was aware of a sudden lightening, and looked up to see the sunlight bursting through the series of high windows immediately beneath the dome. The great shafts of illumination sped through the air and struck on the walls opposite as one window after another became bright with sun, until at last light came streaming forth from all the windows, though most brightly from the south. And it was then that I saw the great space the church had created, the stone walls soaring upward, dividing and then joining into the unity of the great dome, while the half domes and smaller domes that clustered around it echoed its completeness, as the salt waves of the sea follow one another to crash endlessly on the shore and yet stretch to the horizon as far as the eye can see. And as I saw the church I saw as well how mankind, Greek and Turk, Christian and Muslim alike, might wish to let such a mighty truth slip from their hands, preferring, more by neglect than abuse, to allow its clarity to descend to a common meanness, worn and unremarkable, rather than permit its power to transform them into something greater than they knew.

"You know so much, Doctor," said the countess, slipping her arm around mine.

"Such loss, and such greatness," I said in reply.

"Life is so brief, and so incomplete. At least here in Stamboul we know life's harshness, and life's truth."

She spoke in such a wondrous manner, with her lovely eyes

so full of mystery, hinting of limitless depths—and yet, what monsters might those depths not contain! Once more, as I had done a thousand times, I went back on my resolve. In fact, I scarcely knew what resolve I now was breaking, to be rid of her forever or to sell her my soul! But in my heart of hearts I knew well enough: whatever matter there was between the countess and myself, I could never leave her, never free myself from her power, until I brought that matter to a close, if it cost me my life. And so with such satanic resolve I stood in God's greatest church, hardly daring to hope that there might be grace enough for even a villain such as I!

CHAPTER 19

The Charms of the Orient

"YOU HAVE BEEN AMUSING yourself in my absence, Watson?" Holmes asked as he seated himself once more in our suite at the Palace.

"Within reason," I replied. "We have spent the past three days visiting the Hagia Sophia and the Blue Mosque. Earlier in the week we took a boat ride in the harbor to observe the arrival of the *Peregrine*."

"Indeed? The same vessel that you saw in Calais, belonging to the American millionaire?"

"Yes."

"Mr. Thompson travels at remarkable speed. You were not allowed on board?"

"No, of course not. Afterward, we continued up the Bosporus to the countess' *yali,* which is a charming villa in all respects. She invites us there for dinner this evening."

"Unfortunately, I must decline. Dr. MacLaurin's advice and assistance were invaluable, and I must begin my researches at once."

"Surely our schedule is not so rigid. I understood you to say that Mr. Adanopholos's wife and child would not be arriving until Friday at the earliest."

"That is true. And I have already made arrangements for the transfer to occur in Sophia on Saturday morning. Sir Samuel will arrive later in the day to take possession. But I cannot allow the secret of M. Brilleton's murder to remain a mystery. With Dr. MacLaurin's help, I now possess a perfectly adequate laboratory to support my researches. I have everything, in fact, except time. The distillations involved cannot be rushed, and the samples I have of M. Brilleton's blood are highly perishable. There is simply no time to waste."

It was, of course, useless to attempt to dissuade Holmes once he had applied himself to a case. His intellectual instincts were focused to a single point, as a lens focuses a beam of light, and he would not rest until a solution—the correct solution—had been discovered. With strong misgivings I next applied to Jennie to accompany me, for I could easily tell what her response would be. Mr. Patterson had announced at the conclusion of our visit to the Sophia that he would be entirely occupied in his researches for the next several days and would not be available for social events of any kind. Under such circumstances, to invite Jennie to accompany me to dine with the countess was to invite a form of derision that a man cannot welcome from his daughter, a form of derision that Jennie was incomparably suited to supply.

"Me, Papa? How could I presume to trespass upon your amours? You cannot be serious."

Jennie's raillery, malicious though it was, contained a large kernel of truth. Though I felt obliged to ask for her companionship—and she surely would have ridiculed me if I did not—in my heart I did not wish it. To dine alone with the countess was a temptation to which I was determined to succumb. Though I might have hoped to prefer Jennie's company as a shield against corruption, that hope was a mere mask for my true intent, to descend once more into that maelstrom of desire that the countess had roused in my soul. Mr. Patterson's announced absence from the proceedings deprived Jennie of any incentive for attendance, and thus I was left at the mercy of my desires, as I so devoutly wished. After kissing my lovely trophies for good luck, I departed with a heart at once cold, light, and passionate, contemplating life, so I fancied, with both the desire of youth and the wisdom of age.

I traveled first by carriage and then by boat, a sort of waterborne omnibus, where I mingled for the first time with the populace of Constantinople, many of whom affected a mixture of Eastern and Western dress. Around me were the soft murmurings of Eastern voices, and the few lights of the great, darkened city. A full moon silvered the domes of the great mosques and the Sophia, and gleamed on the water as well. On my right lay somewhere the ruins of Troy; to my left, the homeland of Alexander. The great spirits of the past seemed to ride with me on my own pilgrimage of conquest. The countess! Oh, the countess!

The joy I felt at my arrival at her vast villa was somewhat tempered by the fact that, instead of the intimate meal I had anticipated, a full-scale dinner party was in session. The weather was clement enough to permit the guests to use the grand patio, which overlooked the Bosporus and provided a remarkable view of the setting sun. At first I felt very little at my ease among the elegantly dressed, cosmopolitan crowd, where French was easily the preferred language, followed by Greek, Turkish, and Russian. Those who upheld the banner of the English tongue were few indeed.

I was, however, not entirely obscure, for, as I discovered, "the archduke's diamonds," as they were called, were a topic of great interest among the cosmopolitans of Constantinople, and it was well known that Holmes and I were engaged in their pursuit. Fortunately, discussions of the stones were conducted in veiled tones. Not seldom is the oily smoothness of the Levantine preferable to the manly directness of the Englishman. I said little but heard much, and no doubt my interlocutors felt the same. I could gather, more by manner than speech, that Holmes and I were regarded as men of true resolve, for it was naturally assumed that we were the animating spirits behind the abduction of Mr. Adanopholos' family. To be admired for being a hardened criminal is a curious distinction, but in Constantinople, at least, quite real. I remembered the countess' words on the train about the nature of life in her city, and found that all she said was true. No one doubted that life was brutal and cruel, and bound to pass soon away. Only the saints in heaven, wheeling above our heads like the softly gleaming stars, were exempt from life's fierce chase, where even the greatest victor soon fell prey to defeat.

I acquired a taste for this harsh fatalism with remarkable quickness. Once I was recognized as the mysterious Dr. Watson, I had no shortage of charming companions. We dined alfresco under the stars, the tables illuminated by the light of great brass lanterns. I was careful to consume no more than two or three glasses of wine, for the ladies in particular, though entirely indirect, were remarkably persistent in their conversation with me. They were never so rude as to actually ask a question, yet there always seemed to be a space after their remarks that it only seemed appropriate that I should fill, a confirmation, perhaps, that might confirm far more than I wished to say. This sort of fencing may quickly grow tedious on its own, but when it is accompanied by fine food and fine wine, and beautiful eyes and beautiful bare shoulders, one does not tire of it so quickly.

The evening progressed, and the hour grew late, and my hostess seemed to busy herself with every guest but me, until I wondered if this party were not a graceful way to end an affair that, once taken from its natural setting, seemed awkward and graceless. I put these unattractive thoughts firmly from my mind but they returned to me as the number of guests dwindled. Few things are less attractive, after all, than an unwanted lover. My early vainglory diminishing, I was considering whether I should not beat an unforced retreat while there was still time to quit the field with honor when a tall and solemn servant approached me.

"*Madame la comtesse* has asked that you accompany me to the library," the fellow said when he was sure that none would overhear.

Despite the vagueness of the errand, I was more than ready

to comply. We passed silently through the great house, which offered remarkable extremes of opulence and disrepair. The great entrance hall gleamed with polished black marble, but sections of the intricately carved ceiling had fallen in, and the missing pieces were replaced with nothing more than bare plaster. The marble steps of a beautifully curved staircase bore the stains of rotted carpeting. On the second floor, the hallway was entirely bare of furnishing, and the walls stained with damp.

"The library is in here, monsieur," the servant said at last, opening a massive wooden door and standing aside.

The library proved to be a welcome relief from the disrepair I had elsewhere observed. The floors, ceilings, and walls all appeared to have been restored to their original richness, yet I seemed to be at once outside and in at the same time. Great glass windows, surely fifteen feet high, overlooked the Bosporus. Above my head, a circular, domed skylight admitted the light of a full moon. Dozens of thick candles set in grand candelabras added their warm glow to the richness of the room. And there, on a grand sofa, in the very center of the room, lay the countess!

In such a setting we surrendered to a passion as vast and mysterious as Constantinople itself, a passion whose flame burned with such intensity as to consume my consciousness entirely. I awakened in the morning with no more recollection of the events of the previous night than an infant or an inebriate. Nor did I care, for I had the most supreme of all blessings, the countess in my arms! In our cozy bower on the floor, contrived from a glorious silk sheet and warm woolen blanket seemingly conjured out of the thin air, we could ignore the traces of the night's debauchery, which no doubt presented a rather absurd and disconcerting spectacle when viewed in the cold light of day.

"You must promise me," whispered the countess, gently kissing my eyes.

"What can I promise?" I replied. "I have given you everything."

"You!" she laughed. "You English know nothing of giving. You must promise me."

"Very well, Countess. I promise you."

"You must promise me never to leave."

I shook my head.

"The one vow I wish with all my heart to make, I cannot," I said.

"A year then. You cannot leave earlier."

What delight to lie there beneath that glass dome and be teased in such a manner by such a woman!

"A year! If only I could! We must depart Constantinople in three days."

"No! You cannot!"

"You will find a dozen men to replace me, younger, handsomer, and richer by far."

"There is no one who can replace my doctor," she whispered, pressing her wonderful body against me. "Six months. Promise me."

"I fear I must rejoin my companions today."

"Impossible! But if you must, you must. I understand your English need for appearances. But perhaps in two days? I have a friend, very discreet, with a lovely apartment in the Pera."

I trembled at the temptation she put before me.

"Perhaps," I said. "We will not remain in Constantinople much longer."

"Really? What does the clever Mr. Holmes have up his sleeve?"

"You must tell no one, but soon we travel to Sofia to obtain the diamonds from Mr. Adanopholos before surrendering them to that d——d fellow Jenkins."

"You curse your employer?"

"Indeed I do," I said severely. "It was Holmes's intention to use this errand to initiate a case against the archduke. Instead, we find ourselves party to a kidnapping."

"I see. But you English are so impatient."

It was useless to argue with such beauty. I ran my fingers through her thick black hair, marveling at its satin richness.

"If we have so little time," I said, my voice husky with desire, "we should not spend it speaking of what cannot be changed."

And so our passion reawakened, to burn as brightly in the morning light as ever it did in the sweet darkness of night.

CHAPTER 20

A Sudden Departure

IN SUCH FASHION I lingered until well after the noon hour, at which time I realized sadly that I must depart. On my return journey down the Bosporus I rode as it were on a cloud of satiate bliss, filled with a benignant affection for all mankind, and indeed for all creation, as who would not be after such a night of all-encompassing gratification?

When I arrived in our suite I saw no one. Since the evening was exceptionally pleasant, I chose to sit on the balcony with a glass of wine and bask in the warmth of all that I had so recently experienced. A slight tapping on the window brought my attention back to the present.

"Watson, there you are," said Holmes. "I have been searching for you."

"You might have found me here," I replied.

"Indeed. I trust you had a pleasant day. I must inform you that we have a change of plans. The wife and daughter of Mr. Adanopholos will be arriving in less than an hour. We meet with Mr. Adanopholos at eight and depart tomorrow."

"Here?" I cried. "I understood we would meet them in Sofia."

"These matters are difficult to arrange," said Holmes evenly.

"Mrs. Adanopholos and her daughter have made the journey from Venice more rapidly than anticipated. It is only humane to make the exchange as quickly as possible. One cannot plan too far in advance. I have had one of the servants tend to the packing. Our luggage has already been taken to the station. I fear our accommodations will not be so grand as anticipated."

"But why it is necessary to leave Constantinople so soon?"

"Once we have the diamonds it would not be wise to tarry."

"Yes, of course. And Mr. Jenkins is agreeable to this?"

"He is indeed. But I have no time to discuss the matter further. Jennie is not here?"

"You see she is not."

"Then you must find her. Her presence here is vital."

"I must first send a message to the countess," I said. "I have an engagement with her tomorrow."

"I shall tend to the matter, Watson," said Holmes coldly. "First you must locate Jennie."

"I shall do so in good time," I replied with not a little sharpness, rising from my chair as I spoke. There were matters I felt needed to be addressed.

"Your suspicions of the countess are entirely unfounded, Holmes," I said. "I shall not allow the name of a woman of such noble character as the countess to be marred by your insinuations, nor would I allow you to usurp my duty to express my deepest regret at not being able to fulfill a commitment I made to such a gracious person. A servant may find Jennie. I must tend to my correspondence."

And so I departed to my room, vexed indeed at my friend's strange and condescending manner. I took my pen in hand and thought for some time before daring to express myself on paper. I could not, of course, give more than a suggestion of all that the countess had meant to me. To be wrenched from her company without even the briefest notice was a terrible hardship, and I could only hope that circumstances would soon allow us to be reunited again.

Yet even as I wrote, I wondered. How could I appear otherwise than as a bumbling bourgeois, falling on his face by striving to rise above himself, reaching with his clumsy hand to grasp a goddess by the hem as she rose infinitely far above him? The nights I had spent, the gratifications of the most private and wanton desires, was this anything more than a dream fetched from *The Arabian Nights,* a dream destined to vanish like the morning dew? What I had written seemed little enough, but was it not far too much? I hesitated, but then sealed the envelope and fixed it with wax. A lover unwilling to appear a fool is no lover at all.

I took the envelope in my hand and strode into our sitting room, to discover Holmes seated at the walnut table, a jeweler's scale and other implements of the trade placed before him.

"You have completed your correspondence?" he asked with some amusement. "I hope you extended my sympathies to the lady as well."

There was a tone of self-deprecation in Holmes's voice that I took as an apology for his ill-considered words regarding the countess. In any event, the supreme moment of our journey was arriving, when we would actually gain possession of the diamonds, and there could be no rift between us at such a time.

"I believe I have explained our sudden departure in an appropriate manner," I said lightly. "You will be pleased to know that I have said nothing that might compromise our plans."

"Excellent."

"Of course. Where are the mother and daughter?"

"They will soon arrive," said Holmes softly. "Once they are here I shall summon Mr. Adanopholos and we will make the exchange of the unfortunate ladies for the diamonds. When that is done, we will present Sir Samuel Jenkins with his ill-deserved prize and at last make an end to this wretched business."

Even more than his words, my friend's demeanor expressed the deep anger with which he regarded the duplicity of our erstwhile employers. Yet in an instant his mood changed, and he sat in an easy chair with the air of a man with nothing on his mind but leisure.

"We have some time before their arrival," he said, taking

out his cherrywood and stretching out his long legs before him. "We may as well enjoy a pipe."

Somewhat bemused, I complied with his suggestion.

Jennie entered the room, mischievously dressed as a boy in the black page's outfit she had worn before, with her hair pulled up beneath a snug-fitting cap.

"Right-ho, Guvnor!" she said, affecting that ridiculous "stage cockney" accent that is the bane of the London theater. "Everything's tip-top. Now, Mr. Holmes, you just give me my pistolo there and I'll be on me way."

Holmes could not forbear smiling at her outrageous cheek. When playing a role, Jennie's impudence knew no limits.

"Do you object to my arming your daughter, Watson?" my friend asked.

"If you think it is appropriate," I replied. "The derringer and the bullets are in the cabinet."

I took the key from my pocket and handed it to Holmes, who produced the gun and two bullets, which he then handed to Jennie.

"You may load your weapon now," he said, "but please remember to conceal it from our guests."

"Right-ho, Guvnor," said Jennie, loading her gun with immense delight. "I'll just keep it here in me vest."

"Really, Jennie," I said, provoked beyond endurance. "You must display some restraint."

My remark provoked such a look of calculated amusement that I could only dread her reply, but instead she checked herself.

"It's only play, Papa. I shall be as good as gold when the time comes."

"Thank you for speaking English," I said, for my temper was still somewhat less than happy.

"Oh, Papa. Perhaps Mr. Holmes could play his violin for us while we wait for the ladies."

"An excellent suggestion," said Holmes. "I imagine an air from Purcell would be appropriate."

Holmes tuned his Stradivarius and then began an ancient, supple tune that, as I relaxed beneath its gentle spell, did indeed cause the tension to depart from my troubled spirit.

Soothed by both Purcell's art and a fine cigar, in the company of Holmes and Jennie, I could forget, if but for a moment, the burden of Circe's spell. I had thrice tapped my ash when a soft knock at the door interrupted my reverie.

"This must be our guests, if I am not mistaken," said Holmes, instantly ceasing his playing. "If we but dim the lights, I believe all will be ready. Jennie, you are prepared to play your part? And you, Watson, as well?"

We both assented confidently to Holmes's question, though what my part was other than to assist my friend in any manner that he might request remained unclear to me. Holmes reduced the gas in the fine chandelier above our heads until the flames barely flickered, and bade me rise and take a position in an obscure part of the room where I might survey the doorway without being observed. For her part, Jennie crouched against the wall near the door, almost disappearing into the darkness, with one hand thrust melodramatically into her vest to grasp her derringer. When we were both placed to his satisfaction, Holmes opened the door, admitting a gush of light from the hallway.

"Our visitors are here, Maurice?" he asked, addressing an individual whose tall figure I could see but indistinctly. "Let me see the rings. Yes, excellent, and now the faces as well. Very good."

With that, two women in Turkish dress entered our suite, their faces entirely veiled.

"My apologies, ladies," said Holmes, "for the unfortunate manner in which you have been treated for the past week. I assure you that your ordeal will be over shortly. I ask only that you refrain from speech and obey our orders precisely for the next few hours."

The taller of the two figures, whom I could only assume to be Mrs. Adanopholos herself, nodded in the affirmative at the conclusion of this extraordinary statement by Holmes.

"Very good," he said. "Jennie will take care of you in her room. We have food and drink if you require it. Please take this opportunity to compose yourselves."

Jennie led the two women away.

"It appears that they have suffered no physical harm, at

least," said Holmes once the door to Jennie's room was firmly shut. "I suppose we should thank Mr. Jenkins for the refinement of his associates."

"What were the rings that you spoke of?" I asked.

"It is Mr. Adanopholos's pleasure to lavish jewelry on both his wife and daughter. I had descriptions of their rings from him, as well as photographs."

"And who is Maurice?"

Holmes smiled.

"An individual who has been of assistance to me in this city more than once. I cannot say whom I fear more in this case, Mr. Jenkins or Mr. Adanopholos, for I suspect that both would rather slit our throats than not. Fortunately, Maurice is unknown to either, and is unshakably loyal as long as he is well paid. We have the ladies, and soon, if all goes well we shall have the diamonds. Would you care for an encore?"

"Yes, of course."

With that, Holmes resumed his serenade, playing with perfect serenity for the greater part of an hour until another knock sounded on our door.

"Mr. Adanopholos will be with us shortly," he said, putting down his violin. "The gentleman is alone. Please have your revolver about you, but do not employ it or even show it unless I give you the command."

Five minutes after Holmes spoke, we heard yet another knock on the door. Holmes opened it to reveal Mr. Adanopholos, dressed in the manner of a prosperous tourist and carrying a Gladstone bag.

"I am pleased to see you, Mr. Adanopholos," said Holmes, locking the door and sliding the bolts after our guest had entered. "I am happy to inform you that your wife and daughter are in perfect health."

"I shall be the judge of that, Mr. Holmes," said the Greek gentleman coldly. There was no doubt that our guest was a dangerous man, in a dangerous mood, and, despite Holmes's words, I could not resist clutching the butt of my revolver in my jacket pocket. Mr. Adanopholos was not a man who could be stopped by anything less than a bullet.

"Then you must see them," said Holmes, knocking on Jennie's door.

The door opened at his knock, and the two ladies entered, dressed now in European fashion. Though their relief was palpable, their reunion could not be other than restrained in light of the awkward circumstances. They conversed rapidly in Greek for some minutes while Holmes watched carefully.

"You are satisfied?" he said when the pace of the conversation began to slow.

"Yes," said Mr. Adanopholos, though his tone made it clear that he was very far from satisfied indeed.

"Then I must have the diamonds."

Abruptly, Mr. Adanopholos tossed my friend the Gladstone he carried. Holmes caught it up and took it to the table, where his scales and other equipment lay at the ready.

"Please have a seat," said Holmes to our guests. "This will take some while. Jennie, perhaps you could play the hostess."

Jennie departed to her room and returned almost instantly with a fine silver tea tray with a teapot and cups and saucers, along with a fine array of cake and biscuits. She set these before the three and then departed. I guessed that it was my duty to watch our guests, while Holmes identified, examined, and counted the many gems, large and small, that had been born out of the Great Blue, a task that occupied him for fully an hour. As each stone was verified, Holmes placed it in a small velvet bag, which was then stored in a sealskin pouch.

"That's done," he exclaimed at last, holding up the swollen pouch and then laying it on the table. "You may have your Gladstone, Mr. Adanopholos, and be on your way."

"Fair enough, Mr. Holmes," said the smuggler, rising to his feet. "You have caused me more than your share of worry, but things have come round in the end. I have no complaints."

I could find no trace of guile in Mr. Adanopholos' speech, but a man such as he may say one thing and do another. Yet I was ill prepared for his next action, for just as Holmes handed him the Gladstone, his hand fairly flew inside and emerged with a small, black revolver, which he pointed at us with enormous satisfaction.

"You think you are a clever man, Mr. Holmes," he said in a soft, malicious voice. You should have searched the bag more thoroughly. Now, you will oblige me by handing over those diamonds."

"It would be unwise to discharge a firearm in this hotel," said Holmes mildly.

"No doubt. But if you think I do not want to kill you, you are greatly mistaken. Give me that bag."

"Of course," said Holmes, picking up the sealskin. But as he did so, instead of handing it to the smuggler, he tossed it with a flick of his wrist out the window.

"Are you mad?" cried the Greek. "We are five floors up!"

"The jewels will assuredly survive," said Holmes. "Whether they will still be there in ten minutes is another question."

Mr. Adanopholos struggled to maintain his composure, but in a few moments his agitation overcame all restraint, and he flung himself to the window, waving his pistol aimlessly in his excitement.

"Yes!" he cried. "They are still there! Come, children!"

So saying, he seized his wife by the hand and raced to the door, with his daughter chasing after. In an instant, they were gone.

"An excellent farce, was it not?" said Holmes to me, his shoulders trembling with suppressed amusement.

"But the jewels, Holmes! The jewels!" I exclaimed.

"Why should I or you care which gang of smugglers owns them? But their possession does offer certain advantages. Ah, here comes Jennie."

As he spoke, Jennie did enter the room, but she did so flying through the window on a rope!

"Do you have the jewels, Jennie?" Holmes asked.

"Right-ho, Guvnor," Jennie replied, "soft and smooth as a baby's bottom. Here you are."

And at the completion of this absurd speech she tossed Holmes a sealskin handbag that resembled exactly the one he had tossed through the window.

"Ten-pound test leader," he said, showing me a fine thread attached to the bag. "A trout fisherman's best friend, and utterly invisible except in bright sunlight. The true bag went up, not down, and Jennie dropped a duplicate to complete the deception. And now I fear we must make haste. Mr. Adanopholos surely has confederates about the hotel. We must make a clandestine exit from the rear."

"We leave now!" I exclaimed, in some confusion. "I had informed the countess that we would not leave until tomorrow."

"It will not distress the countess unduly to be unaware of our correct location for a day or two" said Holmes with some asperity. "The Orient Express does not leave for several hours, but I am sure that a local will suffice to begin our journey. Once we reach Büyükçekmece we shall be free to transfer to grander accommodations. Jennie, now we must have your gun."

"Oh, but can't I keep it?" she cried. "You can have the bullets."

"Very well," he said, amused by her determination to remain "armed."

Reluctantly, Jennie unloaded the derringer and handed the bullets to me.

"I wish I could have seen Mr. Adanopholos's face!" she exclaimed, recovering her spirits. "Was he fierce?"

"Very fierce, Jennie. But we will discuss this another time."

With these words Holmes hastened us to the rear passage at the hotel that he and I had taken to our first meeting with Mr. Adanopholos, where a closed carriage of nondescript appearance awaited our arrival. I felt no little frustration at the fact that Holmes had made Jennie rather than myself his accomplice in these matters, but also felt the need to conceal my choler, if only to avoid fresh raillery from Jennie, who remained exultant over her role in the recent deception.

To avoid possible observation by Mr. Adanopholos, we denied ourselves the comforts of the Siereki Station and were transported instead directly to the rail yard, where the local awaited us. We passed, not without some difficulty, directly from the coach into our carriage, a shabby castoff from the earliest days of luxury train travel, at least thirty years old and perhaps forty, with worn and torn seats, faded carpets, and tarnished, sputtering gas lamps. The fine cabinetry had been sadly abused by vandals, while the corridor bore both the scent and even the residue of the barnyard. Our compartment offered privacy but nothing more. Because there were no curtains to draw, we dispensed with illumination entirely, and sat in darkness for the entire trip, and in silence as well, for Holmes feared that the sound of foreign voices might somehow arouse suspicion.

We endured this tedium for the better part of three hours. The speed of our engine rarely surpassed that of a trotting horse, a quite reasonable precaution considering the abysmal condition of the rails on which we rode. At last we halted, at an obscure station whose platform was illuminated by no more than half a dozen fitfully burning oil lamps. Holmes cautiously raised the window and looked out into the dark.

"There is no one," he said. "Our wait here should not be long."

We stepped from the carriage onto the decrepit platform and waited while the train made its slow departure. Perhaps a dozen other passengers alighted from the train and quickly dispersed, leaving us quite alone. On the other side of the platform lay the gleaming rails of the main line. In about twenty minutes a bright headlight shone in the distance, and soon the great, polished locomotive of the Orient Express rose up before us. When the train halted, Holmes led us to the first carriage, whose door opened at our approach.

"Mr. Holmes, Dr. Watson, and Miss Watson. It is so good to see you again."

M. Lestrange, resplendent as always in his gold-braid uniform, greeted us with an elegant bow.

CHAPTER 21

The Second Coup

HE LED US TO our compartments and instantly began plying Jennie with compliments as only a Frenchman can. She, of course, responded with all the coquetry at her disposal. It would be difficult to say which was the greater actor and which the more delighted audience. We had scarcely settled in our seats when the train began its smooth glide from the station.

"Jennie," said Holmes, "there are a few matters that Dr. Watson and I must discuss with M. Lestrange. Perhaps you would not mind retiring to your own compartment for a few minutes?"

From her expression, Jennie did mind, but she retreated quickly enough, through the inner door that linked our compartments. Once the door had shut, Holmes addressed himself to the *chef de train*.

"Now, M. Lestrange, I hope you have been able to complete the arrangements I described to you earlier?"

"Everything is done, M. Holmes, as you requested. We will arrive in Belgrade in less than twenty-four hours. Until that time, all the amenities of the Orient Express are at your disposal. Now, if you will excuse me, I must pay my respects, first to Mlle. Jennie and then to the other passengers."

"I thought we were making the exchange in Sofia," I said, once M. Lestrange had departed.

"Yes, that was the plan," said Holmes, taking out his churchwarden and charging it with the fragrant Turkish blend the Pera Palace supplied to its residents. "However, the new schedule allows us to make the exchange in Belgrade. Mr. Jenkins is happy not to travel so deeply into eastern Europe."

"What 'arrangements' has M. Lestrange made on our behalf?"

"Ones that I sincerely hope shall prove to be sufficient. Now, if you will excuse me, Watson, I have much to consider."

Sherlock Holmes often proved to be a poor traveling companion, but this implicit rebuke, coming as it did on top of the deception I had already endured, held a particular sting. After one of the most pleasant days of my life, I had been denied the opportunity to bid farewell to the most charming and elegant woman I had ever known. Even if I would be so fortunate as to encounter her once more, either in London or Paris, I doubted that, without the generous funds of the De Beers Mining Company at my disposal, I could hope to encounter her as an equal. It was most foolish of me, having received so much good fortune so far above my station, to demand more, but such is the peculiar nature of the human spirit. Our vanity, unlike our stomachs, can never be filled.

Under the circumstances, there was no better choice than to seek out Jennie's company. Her vivacious good nature, brought to the very highest pitch by the events of the evening, was the perfect solvent for my ill temper, which, after all, deserved no indulgence. We soon set off for the dining carriage, where, over the course of a midnight supper, I described for her over and over again the utter consternation of poor Mr. Adanopholos at the disappearance of the diamonds. Fortunately, we had the carriage to ourselves, allowing Jennie to laugh to her heart's content over the confounding of our enemies, though in fact Mr. Adanopholos was far more friend than foe, for it was he who had delivered the diamonds to us. As I retired that evening I could not but feel a sharp resentment toward Sir Samuel, who had made us scarcely more than errand boys in his unsavory scheme, and

I wondered if the "arrangements" to which Holmes had so obliquely referred might not refer to a plan to thwart the millionaire, though how he might accomplish the feat I could not imagine. Such thoughts, however, faded from my mind as soon as I placed my head on my pillow. I fell asleep at once and had dreams for no one but the countess.

The next morning I attempted to engage Holmes in conversation, but he remained immured in an impenetrable silence. I cautiously offered to guard the diamonds myself to allow him to seek some respite in the smoking lounge, but he courteously refused. When he did so, I made the journey myself. Long experience had taught me that solitude was my friend's preferred companion, and never more so than when a crisis impended. The Case of the Great Blue, to give this collection of curiously related events a name, had stretched itself over six years, and had brought Holmes little but frustration and even humiliation. We had been bullied by Cecil Rhodes and Winston Churchill, baffled by the archduke, and now found ourselves the pawns of the insidiously cunning Mr. Jenkins. We were committed to delivering the diamonds to a man who had engineered the kidnapping of two innocent women. Whether the several deaths associated by Holmes with the diamond were in fact murders I could not say, but surely the mysterious man in compartment seven had been murdered, and the wife and daughter of Mr. Adanopholos had been kidnapped. Yet such was the uncertain legal status of all of the parties involved, including our own, that no recourse to the legal authorities seemed possible. We were far from London; far, indeed!

After a pleasant hour with my cigar and a copy of the *Strand,* I called upon Jennie, whom I found flamboyantly dressed for lunch and engaged in the perusal of a back issue of the *Morning Post.*

"You'll never guess what young Lord Rosford has done!" she cried as I entered.

"No, I shan't," I said. "Why do you read such nonsense? Aristocrats are all useless, frivolous people."

"Oh, but you don't think so, do you, Papa? Shall you ever see the countess again?"

She looked at me with wicked eyes.

"That is none of your concern," I replied. "Where did you obtain this paper?"

"M. Lestrange saved them for me. I liked the Palace but I love the Orient Express!"

She looked up at me, the very picture of a young lady of fashion, and I wondered how it would be possible ever to return her to Mrs. Marbles's rooming house on Bromley Street. Fortunately, it was a matter whose consideration could be postponed for several days.

We departed for the dining carriage, where we quickly made the acquaintance of a well-bred young French couple, the Latrobes. They were naturally delighted by both Jennie and her French, and we passed the next several hours pleasantly enough, dining on *potage queue de boeuf à la parisienne* and *beignets de ris de veau*. When we returned to our compartments Jennie allowed that she must begin dressing for tea, so I joined Holmes, whose mood, I discovered, had become distinctly less taciturn.

"What do you think of this, Watson?" he said, handing me a telegram as I entered.

" 'Presence of Dutch relative assured,' " I read. "What an obscure message!"

"Yes. M. Compte is nothing if not discreet. As I remarked to you earlier, the suggestions of your Dr. MacLaurin were invaluable. Are you familiar at all with the properties of a substance known as coumarin?"

"I believe I have heard of it," I said. "A lactone, is it not?"

"Indeed it is, a white crystalline lactone employed in the manufacture of perfume, easily derived from both the Dutch tonka bean and yellow sweet clover."

"I did not know that," I said, searching my memory. "But it has been used successfully in the laboratory as an anticoagulant. There were great hopes for more extensive use at first, I believe, but the problems of maintaining an effective concentrate in solution proved to be insuperable."

"Those problems have been overcome," said Holmes. "Dr. MacLaurin informed me that while he was at a recent conference in Vienna he learned of the possibility of maintaining a stable concentrate of coumarin in a private conversation with a physician who consulted with the Austrian Army's medical staff, a physician who disappeared from the conference the following day. When MacLaurin sought to obtain the doctor's home address from the directors of the conference, he was given an evasive answer. And as a private physician rather than a laboratory scientist he has had no opportunity to test the matter scientifically."

"But an effective anticoagulant could have a revolutionary impact on blood transfusions," I said.

"Indeed it could, which is precisely why the Austrian Army might easily regard it as a state secret."

"How outrageous to corrupt the practice of medicine in such a manner!" I cried. "I can only hope that it is not true."

"I fear that the twentieth century will have little time for such noble sentiments," said Holmes. "The Boer War was hardly an auspicious inaugural. In any event, it quite appears that the archduke, or rather his double, has already begun the process of corruption."

Holmes paused and took out his cherrywood, charging it with navy shag.

"In our conversations," he said, "Dr. MacLaurin told me one more interesting fact about coumarin. Do you recall, Watson, the testimony of the maid at Loch Rannoch, now more than six years ago, of how Jonathan, the servant boy, fell asleep in the archduke's room, dreaming of a meadow in haying time?"

"I do," I said. "The remark seemed so fanciful at the time."

"The boy was speaking no more than the truth. Coumarin has the scent of newly mown hay."

"Extraordinary! Then they have held the secret all this time!"

"Yes, and this evidence unites all the murders, conclusively, although no court of law in all of Europe would agree. The decision of the archduke to kill the innocent lad, merely because the boy had remembered the identifying scent of the substance, suggests how closely the secret was held, and suggests as well that the substance had already been used. In addition, an examination of the mortality patterns among the

Hapsburgs reveals more than one suspicious death—three, in fact—all tending to advance the rank of the archduke. I do not think that that gentleman's coup stick has been idle."

"But surely such a pattern would have been discovered?"

"Hardly. The aristocracy's appetite for dissipation, the extraordinary privileges given to rank, the ever-present fear of scandal, all combine to create a positive fear of the truth. The dead cannot be revived, after all. Why pursue inquiries that only inconvenience the living?"

"And yet you say you have no evidence."

"None that I could present to a magistrate or a jury. My only hope is that the archduke will overreach himself. Deprived of his diamonds, he may do so."

I was about to respond when there was a knock on the door that connected to Jennie's apartment.

"May I come in, please?" she asked.

"Of course, Jennie," said Holmes.

Jennie entered, presenting herself in a subdued, dark blue dress of surpassing respectability, a quality not often evident in her wardrobe.

"Do you like my bustle?" she asked, as though amused by her sudden conversion to propriety.

"Jennie, the manner in which clothing is worn is as important as the clothing itself," I said rather sharply, for as she posed before us she could not resist assuming an air of burlesque refinement, a sort of mock innocence that hinted all too strongly at its opposite.

"Oh, Papa, you are most proper! But I shall behave myself," she replied. "Shall we join the Latrobes for tea?"

Jennie and I journeyed once more to the gilded dining carriage, which Jennie had pronounced more than once to be her favorite place on earth. The Latrobes accommodated themselves graciously to this strange English custom and afterward joined us at the card table. The impending delivery of the diamonds to Sir Samuel played persistently on my mind, and I proved an indifferent partner for Jennie, who impatiently traded me for Mme. Latrobe. At last the evening hour arrived and passed, and the Orient Express slowly rumbled into the ancient town of Belgrade. Jennie and I courteously quitted our game and joined Holmes in our compartment.

"I think you had better come with us, Jennie," Holmes said. "Sir Samuel has surprised me before. I should not like to have you pay the price for my lack of precaution."

"Shall I bring my revolver?" I asked.

"I think not," said Holmes. "Sir Samuel is traveling by private car. He most assuredly will have guards with him, who I imagine will inspect us closely."

"You mean they will examine our persons?" I asked incredulously.

"Sir Samuel has already shown that he will violate any propriety to obtain the stones. You had best turn out your pockets beforehand, to avoid arousing suspicion. I wish Sir Samuel to believe that we are still his willing employees."

With that, we made our way from the carriage. An attentive *bagagiste* was awaiting our appearance, and quickly conducted us to an elegant private carriage that sat alone on a siding some distance from the main track. Shades were drawn on all the windows of the carriage, and it presented a somber appearance as we approached. The *bagagiste* conducted us to the near end of the carriage, where a tall, stolid fellow, whose manner, despite his fine broadcloth, was far more that of a prizefighter than a servant, allowed us to climb the steps and enter.

The first half of the carriage, though well appointed, lacked the opulence of the *wagon-lits* of the Orient Express, and was obviously designed more for commerce than luxury. A pair of desks sat on either side of the carriage, along with several club chairs, placed close to the door that led to the remaining portion of the carriage. A pair of well-dressed ruffians, quite similar to the individual we had lately encountered outside, lounged boorishly in the chairs, not bothering to rise at our approach. Holmes ignored them and led us to the door.

We entered and found ourselves in an elegant stateroom. Sir Samuel, seated on a fine leather ottoman, greeted us with unmistakable condescension.

"Mr. Holmes! And Dr. Watson! And a young lady as well! And such a lovely young lady! What an unexpected surprise!"

Jennie curtseyed in response to Sir Samuel's praise and seemed quite pleased to have his attention.

"This case has contained a number of surprises," said Holmes coldly. "This young lady is Dr. Watson's adoptive daughter. For a number of reasons, it became necessary to bring her along."

"At De Beer's expense, no doubt," said Sir Samuel. "Well, no matter. Such beauty and charm are always welcome."

"Oh, Sir Samuel," Jennie replied with a palpable simper, "you are such a fine gentleman to say so."

Jennie's coquetry, I suspect, had the strange effect of warming what otherwise would have been a cold and correct meeting. Her presence seemed to induce in Sir Samuel a spirit of rather calculating magnanimity that had been quite absent from our previous encounters.

"I doubt if the board will scruple over a few hundred pounds," he continued. "You and Dr. Watson have done your part, Mr. Holmes, and that is what counts."

I said nothing at this point, though I suspected that Jennie's free spirit with regard to other people's money had run her bill well over a thousand. Yet if it were ten times that sum it would scarcely recompense for having been made accomplices in a kidnapping.

"That is most kind, and would be most appreciated," said Holmes.

"Now," he continued, reaching for the sealskin purse within his jacket, "it is my pleasure to surrender these. I must admit that despite my misgivings, you handled the matter quite successfully."

"Thank you," said Sir Samuel smoothly, withholding, so it would seem, complete acceptance of my friend's words of approbation.

"We are fortunate to have the stonecutter's complete list, so that you can verify that nothing is missing, as I did when I received the diamonds from Mr. Adanopholos," said Holmes.

He opened the purse and took out a folded sheet of paper, which he handed to Sir Samuel. That gentleman perused the document with extreme eagerness. His hard blue eyes glittered, and his red face was flushed with avarice. Seated in his sumptuous, mobile parlor, he seemed the very god of greed.

"Three hundred and seventeen carats!" he cried, almost in ecstasy. "You have that diamond?"

"Yes, of course," said Holmes.

My friend took out the small bag that held the greatest of the jewels. Sir Samuel fairly snatched it from his hand and undid the silken drawstrings that held it shut. He took out the diamond and held it to the light. Once more I was amazed at the richness of the jewel, the dark, glowing brilliance of its deep blue core that seemed to burn with an electric fire plucked down from the heavens.

"Oh, now, that is beautiful!" exclaimed Jennie.

"Yes, yes, indeed," Sir Samuel replied rather irritably, as though no one but himself should be allowed to take pleasure in the jewel. Wrapping it tightly in the fingers of his left hand, he placed a jeweler's eyepiece in his eye and scrutinized the gem with enormous care. While he was so occupied, the carriage gave a start, which gave Sir Samuel a momentary alarm.

"Ah!" he said. "They are attaching us to your train. I shall be pleased to find myself west of Vienna as soon as possible."

And, as he spoke, the carriage began to move, lurching slightly as it passed over the points.

"And now the others," announced Sir Samuel, quitting his inspection of the great diamond.

Without comment Holmes passed the sealskin purse to the cunning solicitor, who opened the small bags with the unhurried delight of a connoisseur, exploring the beauties of each gem down to the last detail before passing on to the next. While he was engaged in this silent and sybaritic task, the carriage, propelled by an unseen engine, paused and reversed itself several times before coming to rest with a solid thud as it was attached to our train.

"Very good, Mr. Holmes, very good," said Sir Samuel at last when he had completed his survey of the gems and returned each to its velvet bag. "We have had our differences, but the diamonds are here, and that is what matters."

"Yes, indeed," said Holmes. "And now I think it best that I receive my fee. There have been extraordinary expenses associated with this case, and we are yet several days from London."

"Do you fear intervention from the archduke?" demanded Sir Samuel, his smooth words not quite concealing a flash of both temper and suspicion.

"No, I do not. We are more than one step ahead of his grace. However, while in the Balkans, money dissolves all obstacles."

"Very true, Mr. Holmes," said the solicitor with a slight snigger, as though he interpreted my friend's request as prompted by avarice rather than anticipation of actual dangers. He took from his coat pocket a wallet of the finest calf and opened it, revealing a sheaf of banknotes such as I had never seen.

"Oh, my!" cried Jennie. "That is a wad!"

"Yes, my dear," said Sir Samuel, obviously pleased with the impression he had made. "As Mr. Holmes says, money dissolves all obstacles in the Balkans."

"It is perhaps dangerous to carry such large amounts in so casual a manner," observed Holmes.

"My person is well guarded," said Sir Samuel serenely, counting out £100 notes as another man might count shillings. "There you are, Mr. Holmes. Three thousand pounds, with an extra five hundred for your troubles."

"Oh, my!" cried Jennie once more, rising to her feet with a confused look on her face.

"Is anything the matter, young lady?" asked Sir Samuel.

"I feel so—"

To my horror, Jennie pitched forward, her eyes rolling backward in her head in a most extraordinary manner.

"Dear, dear," exclaimed Sir Samuel, rising quickly from behind his desk and rushing to Jennie's aid. "What could be distressing her?"

I rose to assist Jennie as well, but as I did so she seemed to revive herself, taking the hand proffered by Sir Samuel and slowly regaining her feet.

"I am so very dizzy," she announced, taking a step and then half swooning into Sir Samuel's arms.

"You poor girl!" he cried, embracing her slender figure with perhaps too much energy, considering her unstable condition. "You must sit on my couch here!"

He carried Jennie quickly to the couch, where she seemed to alternately collapse and then revive herself in a most unlikely manner.

"My—my smelling salts," she murmured, struggling to open her purse.

"If I may help you," said Sir Samuel, opening the polished leather bag.

"Yes, yes, of course," said Jennie.

She reached into the bag, taking out a small glass vial and a handkerchief. She doused the handkerchief liberally with fluid from the vial and then, to my utter surprise, pressed the handkerchief firmly against Sir Samuel's face! The solicitor naturally began to struggle in protest against this bizarre conduct when suddenly his arms fell to his side and his entire body went limp on the couch. The solution to this mystery came only when I happened to inhale the telltale odor of chloroform.

"Excellent, Jennie," said Holmes in a low voice, rising instantly to his feet as soon as Sir Samuel had been rendered unconscious. "Now, Watson, we must work quickly."

Jennie reached into her purse and withdrew from it a large square of adhesive bandage, which she placed firmly over Sir Samuel's mouth. Then she stood erect and removed her jacket. Tied around her waist were several lengths of silken cord, which she undid and passed to Holmes, who used them to bind our adversary, now our victim, both hand and foot. The next part of the plan was clear to me, and I assisted Holmes in taking Sir Samuel's unresisting person to the bedroom of the carriage. Holmes pulled back the sheets and blankets from the bed and we placed the solicitor on the bed, face down. Holmes then drew the sheets and blankets back over the man, and Jennie neatly tucked him in. Jennie then took several additional lengths of cord from her waist, which

Holmes and I then wrapped entirely around the bed, drawing them tight and knotting them securely.

"That should keep him from harm, and us as well." whispered Holmes when we were done.

We returned to the sitting room, where Holmes reclaimed the jewels.

"Help me with my bustle, Papa," Jennie announced.

"What do you want me to do?" I said, confused by this strange request.

"Take off the bow. There's ever so much room inside."

I lifted up the large bow that decorated the back of her dress, revealing a spacious compartment concealed by several folds of fabric. Holmes placed the sealskin purse inside, and I quickly restored Jennie's costume to the dictates of propriety. When I was done, she held herself briefly in an elegant pose, looking back over her shoulder at her bustle, with mischief shining in her beautiful eyes. I was appalled, though not surprised, when she gave that artificial appendage a slight but entirely improper shake.

"Lordy, what I couldn't sell it for now," she remarked.

"Jennie!" I demanded. "That is most inappropriate."

"Oh, Papa, let me have a little fun. But I suppose we must be going."

"Indeed," said Holmes.

He opened the door, and we passed through the carriage, under the close, contemptuous surveillance of Sir Samuel's assembled bodyguards, who made no effort to rise to their feet and left us to exit the train entirely on our own.

"We are well quit of those ruffians," said Holmes as we descended the steps, which led, not to a platform, but rather to hard, uneven ground laden with gravel and cinders. I leaped to the earth and looked about in confusion, for I found myself in an almost stygian darkness. In the distance I could see a gleaming, well-lit train that could only be the Orient Express, bound for Paris. But Sir Samuel's elegant *wagon-lit* had been coupled to a string of gloomy carriages that showed scarcely a spark of illumination.

"I say, Holmes," I said, "this train is not the Orient Express."

"Very true. M. Lestrange was so kind as to agree to attach Sir Samuel's carriage to an east-bound local. If we are fortunate, the ruse will not be discovered for another five or six hours. Now we must make haste, for the Orient Express will soon depart. Jennie, can you walk on this gravel?"

"No, but I can walk on the rails," she replied, placing herself on one like a tightrope walker, her arms stretched out for balance.

As she did so the engine that stood at the head of Orient Express gave voice to a shrill whistle, as if to signal its imminent departure. The three of us hastened our pace, Jennie flying ahead of us despite her cumbersome attire. We had scarcely gained the platform when the cylinders of the engine released an explosive burst of steam and the massive drive wheels commenced their first revolutions. We flew past it to the first of the *wagon-lits,* where, remarkably, a door opened at our approach. As it was at the far end of the carriage, we had to sprint another twenty yards before boarding. Fortunately, the Orient Express is noted for the smoothness, rather than the celerity, of its acceleration, and we were able to step easily inside. As we did so, the door was instantly shut behind us by a waiting *bagagiste.* We scarce had time to collect ourselves when the train's *contrôleur,* M. Lestrange's deputy, greeted us with a deep bow.

"Mr. Holmes, Dr. Watson, Mlle. Watson," he said. "It is a great pleasure to have you with us once more. Allow me to escort you to your compartments."

We followed him through the train at an easy pace, which allowed us to regain some of the composure appropriate to our grand settings, and finally arrived at our compartments. Once we were inside, Holmes quickly relieved Jennie of the burden of the diamonds.

"These stones are a fearful responsibility," he said, placing the sealskin purse in his jacket pocket. "In case of a disaster I should prefer to be the one who bears them."

"Then I shall be well quit of this," said Jennie, giving her bustle a slight shake. "How the ladies sit upon them I shall never know."

Even as she spoke, there was a knock at the door. I opened

it to discover two liveried *serveurs,* one holding a silver ice bucket that bore a bottle of Mumm's, while the other carried a silver tray with the glasses.

"Place them right here on the seat," said Holmes. "Excellent. I will attend to the bottle myself."

He handed a florin to each of the *serveurs* and uncorked the champagne with a loud pop that sent the cork ricocheting about the compartment. Jennie shouted with delight and snatched the flying cork out the air.

"Well done, Jennie!" cried Holmes. "Watson, would you take it amiss if I asked your young charge to join us in a glass of champagne?"

"I would not, though I would certainly like to know why you excluded me from your arrangements. I might have given everything away."

"On the contrary. It is essential in matters of deception that at least one person be entirely without guile. Sir Samuel could never suspect you of concealing anything, for you had nothing to conceal. Your unfettered behavior allowed us to pursue our duplicitous intentions unobserved."

I could not but wonder if my friend was not simply continuing his deception with this suspiciously artful speech, but I could not gainsay the fruits of the evening—Sir Samuel's craft thwarted and the diamonds secure in our possession. There was no purpose in maintaining my sense of resentment under the circumstances, so I discarded it to join in the evening's merriment, savoring the glass of champagne that Holmes provided and relaxing while Jennie exulted in her triumph.

"He was fooled, wasn't he?" she exclaimed, reliving the encounter with Mr. Jenkins in its every detail. "Such a hard, clever man! A solicitor and a millionaire! Show a fellow a pretty foot and you have him!"

"Now, Jennie," I said, "you sound rather hard and clever yourself."

"Oh, he loved to hear himself talk, didn't he?" she continued, ignoring my comment. "So sure of himself! Well, let him keep it shut for a while, and see how much he learns! He's in a fine mood now, I shouldn't wager!"

In her delight she seemed to speak with several different voices, as though a number of her favorites from the stage were vying for the sole possession of her faculties all at once. I quickly discovered that it was useless to protest her exuberance, and could only choose to become her audience, a decision I did not regret, for Jennie never left an audience unappeased. She continued to delight both herself and us for more than an hour, when I took a slight hesitation in the otherwise ceaseless flow of her high spirit to suggest that the hour for rest had arrived.

"I must second your father's statement," said Holmes. "While we have accomplished much, we are still far from London."

Jennie was naturally loath to quit the stage. When she was gone I confronted Holmes on the matter.

"You told Sir Samuel that you did not worry about the archduke," I said. "But now it appears that you do."

"I do indeed," he replied. "The archduke or his double. We shall be passing through Austrian territory for another thirty-six hours. The possibility of an assault upon our persons remains a very real possibility."

"I shall sleep on my revolver," I said.

"Under the circumstances, that would be judicious."

CHAPTER 22

A Rude Awakening

I RETIRED THAT EVENING MORE than a little overwhelmed by the rush of events over the past two days. My exquisite idyll with the countess had been followed by our abrupt departure in the middle of the night aboard a miserable train, followed by our transfer to the polished elegance of the Orient Express and then our less-than-legal confrontation with Sir Samuel. I still experienced some vexation over Holmes's decision to exclude me from the details of the ruse he had conceived with Jennie to outwit our erstwhile employer and in fact wondered if I had seen an end to his schemes. But having concluded that rest was the best preparation for whatever lay ahead, I dismissed all resentments, questions, and suspicions from my mind and was soon rewarded by a sound and dreamless sleep.

That sleep, however, was not destined to remain unbroken. Indeed, it seemed to me that I had scarcely laid my head upon my pillow when I was awakened by Holmes's hand upon my shoulder.

"Rouse yourself, Watson!" he commanded. "I very much fear we have company!"

At these unwelcome words I awakened in a darkened compartment, with the curtains drawn, though the sill was illuminated by the first rays of the morning sun.

"Are we at a station?" I asked, rising to my feet.

"No," he replied. "Have you still your revolver beneath your pillow?"

"Yes."

"Leave it there, but do not neglect it. You had best wake Jennie. Tell her to prepare for guests but to keep all of her doors locked unless we tell her to admit someone."

I put on my robe and slippers and knocked repeatedly on the door to Jennie's compartment before entering. As I expected, I found her fast asleep, and being wakened did not much please her. But once she was awake she set herself fairly to preparing for company. I returned to my compartment. Outside the window I could hear voices speaking in the German tongue, followed by a metallic clang as the carriage door was flung open and then the sound of heavy boots in the corridor. At last there was a loud knock upon our door.

"Mr. Sherlock Holmes?" a harsh voice demanded.

"Yes," said Holmes, switching on the lights. "Whom do I have the pleasure of addressing?"

"You have the pleasure of addressing Hauptmann Gerhard Schwartz of the Imperial Austrian Army," replied the voice contemptuously. "And you are commanded to open this door in the name of the emperor!"

Holmes raised his eyebrows in amusement but made no reply other than to obey this arrogant demand. When he opened the door we were confronted by an Austrian officer of gigantic stature.

"You are Sherlock Holmes?" he said fiercely.

"I am," replied my friend. "And this is Dr. Watson."

"Stand aside for His Grace, Josef Anton, the Archduke-Palatine!"

As he uttered this ridiculous command, the officer himself pivoted sharply to the side, and there appeared before us that mysterious figure who had eluded us for so long!

The archduke was much as I had imagined him from the photographs that Holmes had obtained, a slender, imperious figure in an elegant, dark blue uniform hung with gold braid, the precise muttonchop whiskers now streaked with slight touches of gray. He surveyed us with a haughty eye, and a sardonic smile played about his lips.

"This is an honor, Your Grace," said Holmes. "Allow me to congratulate you on your recent promotion."

"Thank you, Mr. Holmes," the archduke replied in excellent English. "I should like half an hour of your time."

"I would be pleased to have you as my guest," Holmes said.

The archduke entered and closed the door.

"You will forgive the halting of the train," he said, taking a seat next to me and across from Holmes. "There have been reports of unsafe conditions on the tracks ahead."

"It is pleasant to know that the imperial government takes such a close interest in matters of railway safety," said Holmes. "I hope that we will resume our journey shortly."

"The train will depart. However, there is a possibility, Mr. Holmes, that you and your friend will have to come with me. I believe that you are traveling with a young lady as well."

"My adopted daughter," I interjected.

"Of course," he said with an insolent tone.

"On what grounds would you seek to detain us?" asked Holmes mildly.

"You know what I have come for, Mr. Holmes," the archduke replied. There was a bland, almost genial self-confidence in the archduke's voice that, despite my confidence in my friend's powers, made me fear the worst.

"Do you have legal justification for such a request?" Holmes responded.

"I do indeed," said the archduke, taking a large envelope from his breast pocket. "You will find that this document describes the jewels in detail and notes that they are the property of the Hapsburg family, entrusted into my care. You will note as well that it is signed by the chief justice of the Court of High Appeals in Vienna, which, of course, has final authority in these matters."

Holmes stared uncomfortably at the document, fingering the wax of the thick red seal affixed to its lower right-hand corner.

"I am not overly familiar with the German language," he said at last.

The weakness of this response brought a smile to the archduke's lips.

"That will not be a problem. One of my officers is explaining the matter to *le chef de train*. If necessary, we will search the entire train."

Almost as he spoke, M. Lestrange entered the compartment. He bowed low in the presence of the archduke, and the two chatted fluently in French. They spoke for several minutes, and then M. Lestrange bowed deeply once more and took his leave. I gathered as much from his manner as his speech that the archduke was master of the train.

"*Le chef* has been kind enough to affirm my authority to search the entire train," the archduke said, turning his attention to us once more.

"That will not be necessary," said Holmes.

"What is going on?" cried Jennie, suddenly entering the compartment. She was wrapped in a fine silk gown.

"Jennie, this is no place for you," I said, rising to my feet.

"So charming!" exclaimed the archduke. "How pleasant to have the tedium of duty enlivened by such a lovely creature. Hauptmann Schwartz!"

"Jawohl, Herr Graf!" the giant captain cried.

"Inform *le chef* that we must have refreshments suitable for such a charming young lady."

"I'm not hungry," said Jennie fiercely.

"Ah, the English lady is so cold. But such beauty deserves to be wooed."

"You need not trouble yourself with such gallantry," said Holmes. "I am prepared to comply with your wishes."

"Thank you for your common sense, Mr. Holmes. But there is no need for animosity. As a matter of fact, I will be remaining on the train, and you and your friends must join me for breakfast."

The archduke spoke mildly, but beneath his words was a tone of peremptory command.

"If you so wish," said Holmes. "But first things first. Here are the jewels."

As he spoke, Holmes took the sealskin purse from a pocket of his robe and handed it to the archduke.

"As simple as that!" the archduke cried. "If only all of life's troubles could be solved so easily. You will forgive me if I have a glance."

"The stones are all there," said Holmes.

"No doubt. However, with objects of such value, absolute surety is the first consideration. My jeweler will make the determination. Each stone will have to be examined in detail."

"Then you are traveling with us?"

"Yes. There are urgent matters of state that I must attend to in Paris. The emperor was kind enough to allow me the use of his private car. It was attached during the night. I was engaged in military maneuvers and was only able to intercept the train at this point. Now I believe we will be moving again."

As the archduke spoke, the engine's whistle hooted and indeed a minute later we were under way. I, however, was little aware of either the archduke's words or the train's motion. Instead, I was staring hard at the object he held in his hand, a thin, highly polished stick of wood.

"You admire my swagger stick, Doctor?" the archduke suddenly asked, aware of my fascination. "An amusing trinket. The grain is most attractive—Circassian walnut, I believe."

He held the stick out for my observation with an odious smile. I noticed almost in passing that his hands were discreetly covered by fine kid gloves.

"But I must apologize for intruding on you in this manner," he continued. "You have kindly given me what I sought, and the rules of hospitality demand that I repay you. Please join me for breakfast in my carriage in an hour. I hope that *truite au bleu* will suit your appetites. And the mademoiselle must come as well."

Jennie stared sullenly at the archduke throughout his speech.

"You must not look so fiercely on me, mademoiselle," the archduke continued with the utmost insolence. "The English have so much rectitude. A young lady so able to please should not be afraid to be pleasing."

"I please those worth pleasing," said Jennie sharply.

"Indeed! Well, a little spirit makes the finest game. In an hour, Mr. Holmes."

"In an hour, Your Grace," Holmes replied.

With that, the archduke made his exit.

"What a horrid man!" exclaimed Jennie, scarcely waiting for the door to close.

"He is horrid indeed, Jennie," said Holmes, "but one cannot catch a monster without coming to close grips with him. It will be worth our while to spend an hour with the archduke."

"But what can you do, Holmes?" I cried. "He has the diamonds. Is it possible to arrest him when we arrive in Paris?"

"No, for he travels as a diplomat. Besides, we have no office, no standing, no legal position. For a variety of reasons, De Beers has been unwilling to bring this matter into open court. In fact, they have been almost as unscrupulous as the archduke. So we must be willing to listen to what he has to say. It should be interesting."

"Interesting!" I replied. "Do you call it interesting to listen to such a wicked man taunt and insult all that is decent?"

"There are drawbacks, to be sure. But the archduke obviously desires an audience, and I intend to give him one. He holds so many high cards that he scarcely can be defeated except by his own vanity. You may remain here if you wish, but I shall beard the monster in his den."

"Then I must come with you," I said.

"Good old Watson! And you, Jennie? I know he is quite disagreeable."

"Oh, Mr. Holmes," burst out Jennie. "You know I must come when you put it like that! You should be ashamed of yourself! Really you should! I know what you are!"

And with this fierce statement she returned to her compartment. But an hour later she returned, dressed most elegantly and displaying the coolest composure one could imagine. The three of us proceeded to the archduke's private carriage, which provided a setting and atmosphere of almost inconceivable luxury. The ostentation and elaboration of every feature, from the lighting fixtures to the fabric used in the furniture, suggested, to me at least, a decadent obsession with privilege and the past, an almost desperate denial of the freedom and mobility that a railway represents, a longing for darkness rather than light and death rather than life. The carved, polished inlays that decorated the walls, the thick carpet on which we trod, and the massive furniture on which we sat, all seemed ready to collapse from the burden of their own extravagance. And at the very center of this self-condemning ostentation sat the archduke, like a polished and poisonous spider whose gleaming exterior scarcely concealed the venom within.

"Ah, my guests," he cried, rising from his chair as he spoke. "Please, be seated. Mademoiselle Watson, if you will permit me the honor?"

Addressing this last remark to Jennie, he drew back the chair at his right with his own hands, now clad in fine, white cloth gloves rather than kid. The breakfast that followed was surely the most splendid I have ever consumed. Those who have not had the pleasure of consuming wild strawberries, *brioche, truite au bleu,* and scrambled eggs with truffles have no idea of what they have missed. Throughout the meal the archduke played the role of the perfect host, with exquisite manners. The malicious condescension he had displayed only an hour before disappeared, and he seemed to have no concern other than to entertain us. It was altogether the strangest two hours that I had ever experienced in my life.

At the conclusion of the meal we sat with our coffee in fine old chairs of Spanish leather bearing the Hapsburg crest. A servant approached the archduke and handed him a card.

"Ah, the marquis," he said, grinning easily. "You would not object to a brief visit from a countryman?"

"Of course not," said Holmes.

"Excellent. We will ask the marquis to join us."

The servant disappeared, returning almost immediately with the gentleman whom Holmes had identified to us as Lord Worthington, a well-known confidant of Edward VII. The archduke rose and introduced us to his lordship, who seemed not terribly pleased with our company.

"Perhaps this time is not the most convenient," he said to the archduke.

"It is most convenient," the Austrian replied. "I have a gift for his majesty that I hope will be deemed acceptable."

So saying, he summoned a servant, who returned with a silver salver bearing a gleaming jewel box wrought of ebony and gold. The marquis opened the box and took from it a beautiful stone, one of the Great Blue's finest offspring.

"You may assure his majesty that the stone is at least twenty-three carats," said the archduke. "I hope he will have use for it."

"This is very fine, very fine indeed, Your Grace," said the marquis, but his manner was not so easy. "I am instructed by his majesty to inform you that he extends his deepest appreciation for your generosity in this matter. I should hope to have an opportunity to speak with you further, when you are less occupied."

"Unfortunately, my time is very short," replied the archduke. "I am entirely occupied in my business until I return to Vienna."

"Then perhaps . . . I believe it was my understanding that another diamond had been under discussion . . ."

"Yes, of course, but the workmanship on the fifty-carat stone is not yet complete. Please inform his majesty that the stone will be conveyed to him as soon as it is ready. In the meantime, we look forward to his company this autumn in Carpathia. We hope our stags will prove a worthy quarry."

"I shall inform him, Your Grace," said the marquis with a deep bow. "I shall leave you to your guests."

And so he departed, holding the jewel box firmly in his hand. The sight of the bearer of one of the oldest and proudest names in the annals of our nation cringing before a man who was a murderer many times over was not at all to my liking. And the thought that our sovereign should place himself in this man's debt I liked even less. I glanced at Holmes, who sat slumped in his chair, apparently lost in a fit of abstraction. Yet I noticed that beneath his languid, half-lidded gaze, his sharp eyes were focused exclusively on the features of the archduke.

"Please accept my profound apologies for this interruption," said the archduke as the marquis departed. "The exigencies of railway travel are most destructive to good manners and common courtesy."

"But Your Grace, I should imagine, is no stranger to the Orient Express," interjected Holmes suddenly. "I understand that you possess both a *pied-à-terre* in Paris and a *yali* on the Bosporus."

"Your friend is supremely inquisitive," said the archduke, turning to me as though we were somehow allies. "Mr. Holmes, you seem to know everything, and yet you never stop asking questions."

"Not at all, Your Grace," returned Holmes imperturbably. "Like Socrates, I am certain only of my own ignorance. To overcome this ignorance is both my joy and my labor, and my greatest joy is that my labor shall never be done."

"Spoken like a true bourgeois," said the archduke, with the sort of gentle but unmistakable condescension that a grown man might show for the thoughts of a child. "The middle class must have its work to have its purpose. But only those whom inheritance has endowed with the gift of privileged leisure find their purpose within themselves. And only those few are fit to rule."

This abrupt provocation did not fail to meet with a reply.

"The middle class," said Holmes smoothly, "may have all the faults you decry, and more, but you must acknowledge that it is a healthy plant, flourishing on both sides of the Atlantic and, what is more, both sides of the Channel."

"A brief interlude, Mr. Holmes, very brief. The sun of the masses, whose rise was suffused with blood, shall soon disappear, and its death, I fear, will not be less sanguinary than its birth. The American Civil War, and your own Boer War, are symptoms of an unnatural civilization, without discipline, that can find no way to exert itself other than self-destruction. England has much to answer for. You made your king into a servant and pretended to be shocked when France killed hers. The many have but one instinct and one role, that of obedience. But in your vanity and folly you have taught them that they are worthy to command themselves. No! A dog is only a dog, and must be taught, if necessary, with a cudgel."

"What nonsense!" cried Jennie, causing the archduke to burst into laughter.

"You see, Mr. Holmes!" he said. "You will be ruled by petticoats! The final madness of the middle class! Ah, to be lectured by such loveliness! It is great sport, but in the end, the master will be master!"

My impatience with our host's insolence grew with each passing moment, and I was longing for an opportunity to interject some comment that would initiate our departure, yet I knew that Holmes wished to hear the archduke out. Such was the tenacity of my friend that he was willing to endure the gloating triumph of his adversary in the hope of obtaining some faint clue that would enable him to achieve ultimate redress. But this last rudeness I found intolerable, and I was about to speak, when a liveried servant entered, bearing a silver salver that bore in its turn a calling card. The archduke took the card from the plate and surveyed it with some amusement.

"By all means," he said to the servant. "Tell the gentleman that he is invited to join my guests."

The servant disappeared and then returned with a handsome, well-dressed young gentleman whom I knew all too well.

"Robert!" cried Jennie, flying to her feet.

"Jennie?" he responded. "Why—perhaps I've come at a bad time."

"Not at all, Mr. Patterson," said the archduke suavely, rising to his feet with a sardonic grin. "Our schedules are both difficult. Please, do not hesitate to speak freely. I have no secrets from Mr. Holmes."

The sangfroid of our host seemed to grow with each passing moment. Never had I seen Mr. Patterson so uncomfortable, and Holmes appeared hardly less so.

"Then the . . . transaction was successful?" stammered Mr. Patterson as he took a seat.

"Extraordinarily so," said the archduke in a silky voice, taking obvious pleasure in the recapitulation of his triumph. "Mr. Holmes obtained the jewels without the slightest loss, outwitting both Mr. Adanopholos and Sir Samuel. Poor Sir

Samuel, in fact, seems to have disappeared from the face of the earth, although I am sure that he will soon reappear. Is that not the case, Mr. Holmes?"

My friend managed a faint smile but said nothing.

"I know, Mr. Patterson, that your employer will be dismayed by Mr. Holmes's impertinence," resumed the archduke, "but Mr. Thompson could scarcely expect such a champion of justice to acquiesce to such a harsh bargain. Indeed, he must have employed you on the supposition that Mr. Holmes would succeed in outwitting Sir Samuel, is that not correct?"

"Mr. Thompson believes in preparing for every eventuality," said the young man calmly.

I could scarcely believe my ears! Mr. Patterson's employer could only be the American millionaire Horatio Thompson. He had been pursuing us in his yacht! I struggled to conceal my amazement as the archduke continued the conversation.

"Yes," the archduke said. "And as a sensible businessman, Mr. Thompson is always ready to compromise, I am sure."

"The devil, as you Europeans say, is in the details," replied Mr. Patterson. "I must have some understanding of your terms."

"I understand that some concern had been expressed with regard to Mr. Thompson's marital plans. Some concern, I mean, within the royal family."

"I would hardly know of such matters," said Mr. Patterson smoothly. "I am only an American."

"Then allow me to enlighten you. Mr. Thompson has been seen—very discreetly, of course—in the company of Lady Helen, the first daughter of the Duke of Fife, for the past eighteen months, his earlier pursuit of the Lady Margaret, the second daughter of the Duke of Clarence, having unfortunately fallen through. Your employer appears determined to graft himself onto the Saxe-Coburg stock, though I understand that several members of the royal family have been less than enthusiastic at the prospect."

"This is mere gossip," Mr. Patterson responded, in an even tone.

"Indeed. Then it will be of no interest to you or your

employer to learn that not an hour ago I entrusted Lord Worthington with a stone of no less than twenty-three carats to bear to his highness. Mr. Thompson also will take no interest in the fact that his majesty will be joining my lord and master, His Imperial Highness Francis Joseph, for stag hunting in the autumn."

Mr. Patterson stirred uncomfortably.

"Naturally," the archduke continued, taking obvious pleasure in the effect his words were having on the young American, "a commoner such as Mr. Thompson could have no place in such a gathering. However, a kind word, perhaps even the absence of an unkind one, might have an impact. I am given to understand that the English king has expressed some concern over the reception that a marriage of a bearer of royal blood to a commoner might receive among the European royalty. Naturally, he would not wish to be seen as a supplicant to such an upstart as the kaiser, and the czar is a great distance from London."

"This is all quite new to me," said Mr. Patterson.

"No doubt. But I have a proposal for Mr. Thompson. I will be happy to be his ally, his enthusiastic ally, and to demonstrate the honor of my intentions, I will propose this gift."

With that he nodded to the most distinguished of the servants standing in attendance. The fellow departed to the rear of the carriage and then returned, bearing another jewel box, this one even more elaborately wrought than the one before. He presented the box to Mr. Patterson, who opened it without revealing its contents to us.

"Slightly less than fifty carets, I fear," said the archduke. "The perfection of the cut demanded some sacrifice in size. But the effect, you would agree, is quite remarkable. You may satisfy your curiosity as to the quality of the stone, and then report to your master."

A flicker of irritation crossed Mr. Patterson's smooth features at the mention of his "master," but he made no reply. He removed a jeweler's lens from his coat pocket and began an intense examination of the stone, which he continued to conceal from our sight. He occupied himself in this task for at least a quarter of an hour, to my ever-increasing consternation. I would have spoken had not Holmes, by his calm and unruffled demeanor, convinced me that he was pleased to observe this drama play itself out, regardless of the tempo.

"It is a first-rate stone, reasonably so," the young American said at last, as though disappointed by the results of his own analysis.

"It is more than first-rate, it is superb," rejoined the archduke. "No duke's daughter could resist it, if only her family approved. I have no doubt that Lady Margaret would have succumbed, if only Mr. Thompson had had such a sparkling inducement at his disposal."

"That is all very well, and this is a very fine stone, and you place it in a very fine box," said Mr. Patterson in a tone of contempt. "But the fact is that this is only one stone among many, and a far greater one exists."

"Then it is up to Mr. Thompson to decide what he wants," said the archduke. "He is fifty, is he not? He was childless by his first wife. He would like, of course, to have a son. He is so far fond of himself that he wishes to be the father of a son with royal blood in his veins. Such a corruption of the line of Saxe-Coburg is, of course, a sad outrage, but these are sad times. Yet Mr. Thompson's time grows short. Lady Margaret is married. Lady Helen has admirers, and Lady Helen is Mr. Thompson's one hope. Great marriages, particularly those surrounded by such difficulties as those confronting Mr. Thompson, take time. And though you are young, Mr. Patterson, you must know that no man can purchase time."

Mr. Patterson's expression gave ample testimony to the harshness of the dilemma confronting him.

"I have, of course, no authority to enter into such an agreement," he stammered.

"Of course not," purred the archduke. "However, Mr. Thompson is currently resident in Venice, is he not?"

"Perhaps he is."

"Why this pretense of secrecy?" said the archduke, amused. "The cards are on the table, Mr. Patterson, and any man can ascertain their value. Inform your master of my terms and he may inform me of his decision."

Mr. Patterson placed the diamond back in the jewel box and then gripped the box in his hand with an almost compulsive gesture.

"It is a very fine stone," he said. "Very fine."

The archduke grinned broadly.

"Then Mr. Thompson accepts my offer?"

"I did not say that."

"Of course not. But I will give you papers for Mr. Thompson to review. If he consents to sign them, then the diamond will be his."

Mr. Patterson hesitated for a long moment and then placed the jewel box reluctantly on the table beside his chair.

"I shall present your offer to Mr. Thompson for his consideration."

"Excellent," said the archduke. He signaled the chief of his servants with a snap of his fingers, and the man recovered the jewel box and bore it quickly away, disappearing once more into the rear of the carriage. A minute later he returned, bearing several large envelopes sealed with wax. Mr. Patterson rose to his feet and took the envelopes.

"I cannot be certain of Mr. Thompson's decision," he said awkwardly.

"Please inform Mr. Thompson that his decision, whatever it may be, must reach me in three weeks. I shall be in Paris for two weeks, returning to Vienna on the twenty-third. Good day, Mr. Patterson, and may good fortune accompany you on the rest of your journey."

And so Mr. Patterson departed, with very little grace, and not one word for Jennie.

"So, Mr. Holmes," said the archduke, when we were alone once more, "I hope I have not bored or offended you with this business."

"Not at all," Holmes replied. "You have been exceedingly generous with your hospitality. But surely it is time for us to leave as well. You bear very heavy responsibilities, and there is much for me to do as well."

"Of course," said the archduke. "I have been desirous of making your acquaintance for some time, Mr. Holmes. I must thank you for the assistance you have extended to me in this matter. I am not sure that I could have achieved such a felicitous outcome without it."

For my part, I doubt if my friend had received such a dubious encomium in all his life. The guilt of the archduke appeared blacker than ever, yet all our efforts to deny him the fruit of his crimes had redounded to his advantage. As a final touch, he had, in our presence, effectually bribed our erstwhile employer, the De Beers Company, which was, after all, scarcely less corrupt than he, and arrayed the British royal family against us as well.

"Unfortunately," said Holmes, in a voice that barely hinted at the anger and frustration he must have felt, "I cannot take such a sporting view of this affair."

"But you come from a sporting nation, Mr. Holmes."

"No doubt. You have had your triumph. We must go."

And so we made our awkward departure. I could not blame Holmes for refusing to bandy words with a murderer. I could only hope that this disagreeable interview might have provided him some clue that might ultimately be used against the archduke, however impregnable his position now appeared to be. I followed Holmes from the gilded carriage with Jennie before me, anxious to escape from its poisonous atmosphere of privilege and intrigue. But my haste was not so great that I did not notice, resting on a seat cushion of a small chair tucked in a corner, a curious piece of jewelery—a great, jet-black pearl in a golden setting. It was the earring of the countess!

PART IV

The Hapsburg Tiara

CHAPTER 23

A Renewed Acquaintance

MR. CHURCHILL'S FACE REDDENED.

"It is your duty as a British subject!" he said angrily.

"That is surely a topic for debate," said Holmes, setting down his teacup. "I see no reason to reopen this matter merely because you request that I do so."

"This 'matter,' as you call it, has assumed an entirely new dimension over the past several years," said Mr. Churchill. "The security of our empire and the safety of our people are at stake. It is imperative that we in the government maintain a free hand to act as the interest of England requires."

"Then do so," said Holmes. "You have the entirety of Scotland Yard and the Foreign Office at your disposal. My services can surely be dispensed with."

Mr. Churchill glared at my friend. The politician's face, which was as expressive as a baby's, was flushed with extreme exasperation.

"Surely my presence here testifies to the high regard with which your talents are held by his majesty's government," he said after a long pause.

"It is a regard not untinged with suspicion, Mr. Churchill," said Holmes. "I am happy to be made a tool of justice, but not one of intrigue. It was you who first summoned me to this case, almost eight years ago. My services were then dispensed with in a most summary manner. I warned you at the time that to allow such a crime to go unpunished would redound against you. Now you would set me on the case again, with infinite specifications of what I may and may not do, and whom I may and whom I may not pursue. I am a man of science and a man of justice, and what you propose, Mr. Churchill, is a perversion of both."

"Your attitude I find unpleasantly insouciant," replied our guest. "Would it be trespassing on your hospitality to request a glass of brandy?"

A flicker of a smile played at Holmes's lips. I half expected him to reject Mr. Churchill's unexpected request with the unthinking brusqueness and lack of tact that he so often displayed, but to my surprise he did not.

"Will you favor Mr. Churchill with a glass, Watson?" he asked. "I believe the '97 would be appropriate. And feel free to join him. I myself will be content with tea."

I went to the tantalus and inserted the key. Two years had elapsed, almost to the day, since Holmes and I had returned from our uniquely unsuccessful journey to Constantinople. On the few occasions when I had attempted to raise the topic of the archduke with Holmes I had been met with almost disdainful expressions of uninterest. It was apparent, from Mr. Churchill's agitation, that the case had taken yet a new turn. But the young cabinet minister's truculent manner seemed almost to guarantee my friend's refusal to reopen the case.

The bottle that I took from the tantalus was the last of five bottles of that fine vintage, obtained from M. Compte as an expression of gratitude for the assistance Holmes had given him some years before in connection with a smuggling case. It seemed a pity to waste such golden liquor on such an ungracious guest, and so I was perhaps less than generous as I filled Mr. Churchill's glass.

"Our supplies do dwindle, don't they, Watson?" Holmes observed as I passed the snifter to our visitor. "One can only pray that M. Curé will resume his trade once he has his freedom. But now, Mr. Churchill. You may tell us your story, but you must tell it completely, without omission. And if I do consent to participate in an investigation, it must be understood that justice will come first, and the diamonds second. Let me be explicit. I fear I must press you for a written statement, whose text I shall provide, signed by both Sir Robert Johnson and the prime minister, setting forth the basic premises of this investigation. In the event of any significant interference with my investigation, it will be my intent to reveal this statement to the outside world, and let the chips fall as they may."

Mr. Churchill quickly gulped the brandy I had given him, as if he feared that otherwise the course of the conversation might not afford him the chance of finishing it.

"I . . ." he began. "No. You shall have it, Mr. Holmes. But even before we reach a formal agreement, let me explain to you the more recent developments in this case in their fullest detail. I am about to reveal many state secrets, and many political ones. Every fiber of my being protests against this action, but it is absolutely vital that I obtain your complete cooperation. You could bring down a government if not an empire with what I am about to reveal to you now. I can only trust to your discretion and only hope that my magnanimity in this matter will find its brother in your response."

"With regard to the government, I never vote myself, but Watson here is a confirmed Liberal," said Holmes with a smile. "I have often heard him speak in praise of Mr. Asquith, although I believe his attitude toward Mr. Lloyd George is one more of admiration than trust. With regard to the empire itself, I believe we are both quite reasonably reliable, with some qualifications."

"Very well," said Mr. Churchill, ignoring my friend's humor. "I can only hope that you will choose to hold in confidence the information that I am about to convey to you. You are aware that this nation is involved in an intense naval rivalry with the German Empire."

"I had believed that excitement over the matter had been declining."

"Believe me, it shall shortly grow more intense. You are aware that the Germans have developed dreadnoughts fully the equal of our own. However, by weight of numbers the superiority of our navy remains absolute and unchallenged. But for certain members of the cabinet, whose names I will not mention, this superiority is not enough. They are demanding that we expand our rate of construction, with a reckless disregard for all domestic considerations. With regard to Mr. Lloyd George, one may quibble about certain aspects of his character, but there is no doubt whatsoever that he is a great man. We have worked together to create plans of the widest scope to ease the crushing burden of poverty that afflicts many unfortunate members of the working classes of Britain. These plans will be shattered if the warmongers get their way. If you gentlemen hold in your hearts any desire to bring succor to the third of our nation that lives almost without hope or pleasure, you will listen to what I have to say and you will help us recover the diamonds from the archduke."

I confess that I was quite surprised by Mr. Churchill's words. I knew that he had aligned himself with Lloyd George in the cabinet, but I had found it hard to forgive his earlier language as a Conservative. That first ill impression, compounded by the personal abuse that Holmes and I had endured at his hands, left me with little patience for him as a public figure.

"It is a fantasy that Germany's interests are opposed to our own," Mr. Churchill said. "Unfortunately, the personal ambitions of Archduke Josef are playing right into the hands of those who would embroil us in a ruinous arms race against the kaiser."

"So the archduke has resurfaced," said Holmes. "I consult the Austrian press on occasion. My understanding was that he had remained outside of politics. In particular, he has taken a persistent interest in the affairs of the Catholic Church."

"Indeed he has," said Mr. Churchill. "However, what I am about to tell you has not appeared in the press. The archduke's involvement in church affairs takes him regularly to Rome. It appears that he has taken advantage of these visits to pay court to Princess Lucia, sole daughter of King Emmanuel of Italy. And it appears that there is great danger that his efforts will be crowned with success."

"Now, that is remarkable," said Holmes, taking out his cherrywood. "I hardly thought private initiative had a place in such dynastic arrangements."

"These are not normal times," said Mr. Churchill. "In the past, Italy and Austria have been bitter enemies. Any match between a Hapsburg and the Italian royal family would seem impossible. But there are advantages. The church would be strongly in favor of an alliance between the two great conservative Catholic powers. In a spirit of goodwill, Austria could surrender her remaining possessions on the Adriatic coast that are deemed Italian. These lands are held for purposes of prestige only, and cost Austria dearly. To obtain this territory would enhance enormously the prestige of the Italian monarchy with the Italian people."

"No doubt. And why would this harm the domestic program of Lloyd George?"

"Because, Mr. Holmes, Italy is currently in an informal alliance with Great Britain and France against Germany and Austria. The Italian fleet is not impressive, but it exists, and it exists in a state friendly to Britain. As a result, we are able to concentrate our forces in the North Sea, where they are arrayed in opposition to the German Imperial Fleet. We hold an advantage against the Germans of more than two to one, which serves to check in some measure Admiral Fisher's insatiable lust for ships. They are all mad at the Admiralty. Lord Tweedmouth was a lunatic, pure and simple. I half miss him, in hindsight. He had an innate stupidity that was really quite endearing. But now that McKenna has replaced him, we are in real danger. The man is a menace. Ruthless! Implacable!"

Mr. Churchill raised his voice almost to thunder in our small sitting room. I really thought it inappropriate for a junior cabinet minister such as himself to speak in such unburdened fashion of his colleagues, particularly to outsiders, and particularly in such a loud voice. But in his emotion our guest seemed to forget himself entirely. He rose from his chair and began to pace the floor restlessly, in a manner reminiscent of his behavior at Loch Rannoch eight years before.

"They multiply dangers, for reasons of finance and promotion entirely! Our navy is a cesspool of intrigue! Incompetence at all levels! Mutiny the order of the day! Fisher and Beresford would eat each other alive if they could, and England would be the better if they did! Please, another glass!"

"Yes, Watson, another glass," prompted Holmes blandly.

I hastened to comply with my friend's command, emptying the decanter. Mr. Churchill took the snifter and drank gratefully. He returned to his chair and produced a silver cigar case from his breast pocket, from which he extracted a large, dark brown Cuban. The process of trimming and lighting such a trophy seemed to serve as a sort of pacifier for his emotions.

"In the cabinet," he said, once he had the cigar properly lit, "Lloyd George and myself are able to hold the line against them. Asquith, with all his faults, is for the most part amenable to reason when correctly handled. However, an alliance between Italy and Austria would upset everything. Fisher would use it as an excuse to double or even triple our current commitment of ships to the Mediterranean. If that were done, the balance between Germany's ships in the North Sea and our own draws almost equal. If the balance between our navies should become equal, no force on earth could resist the admirals. That d——d eunuch Haldane has defeated us on the army estimates. We hold our own against that madman Fisher by the slimmest of margins."

"And you see prevention of the marriage between the archduke and the princess as a sure means of forestalling the alliance," said Holmes.

"Yes. Without the international prestige accruing from the marriage, Austria could never accept the sacrifice of its Adriatic territory."

"And, why, precisely, would the return of the diamonds prevent the marriage? Would it not be more effectual, as well as more just, to expose the archduke as the accomplice in half a dozen murders?"

"In the first place, for the British government to make such charges, which could never be proved in a court of law, would expose us to the just contempt of the entire diplomatic community. More importantly, when I spoke of 'the diamonds,' I was not being completely honest. We know for a fact that the archduke has had the diamonds, almost all of them, set in a brilliant platinum tiara."

"Remarkable. Who has seen this object?"

"The princess certainly has," said Mr. Churchill with some irritation. "According to all reports, she is quite enthusiastic about the match. It is not her place to decide whom she will marry, of course, but her enthusiasm weakens our position. Our ambassador in Rome, Lord Millworth, obtained the specifics of the tiara when he was allowed to examine the marriage contract. There are elements in Rome, strong elements, that are quite republican in nature, anticlerical as well, that are strongly opposed to the marriage. But the politics are complex. The princess is young and beautiful. The archduke bears an Italian ancestry, however remote. And there are the Adriatic territories as well. The Italian people are notoriously romantic and sentimental, as well as madly nationalistic. Lord Millworth fears that a brilliant marriage, combined with territorial acquisition, could easily shift Italy into a de facto alliance with Germany and Austria, to our infinite detriment."

"And yet you think this will all come crashing to the ground if we deny the princess her tiara."

"The princess is widely recognized as headstrong and self-indulgent. According to Lord Millworth, the archduke has been showing the tiara at select gatherings of members of royal families for the past year. Austria has been happily encouraging the myth that the tiara dates back to the days of the Holy Roman Empire and was once in the possession of Maria Theresa. Apparently her name still holds resonance among the royalty of Europe."

"They cannot look forward, so they look back," said Holmes unexpectedly.

"Why, yes," said Mr. Churchill, who seemed to be surprised, even as I was, by this suggestion of republican sympathies in my friend. "At any rate, such people keep their secrets well, and it has only been in the past month or two that the existence of the tiara has become more widely known. Possession of some of the finest jewels in Europe would add a certain luster to the House of Savoy. There is no doubt that the tiara is valued highly by the Italian royal family. The terms of the proposed marriage contract are insistent that the tiara will become not simply the property of the princess during her marriage or even her lifetime, but that it becomes the property of the Italian royal family effective upon the date of the marriage. Both the archduke and King Emmanuel of Italy can trace their ancestry to the Italian house of Bourbon-Parma. If the princess were to die on her wedding night, the archduke would have no claim on the tiara. In any event, we must move swiftly. If the match is announced publicly, it will be extremely difficult to prevent the union from occurring."

"We knew the archduke to be a gambler from the first," said Holmes thoughtfully. "He has assembled a strong hand and played it well. It seems impossible, at this time, to bring an ordinary legal action against him and his associate, for purposes of forestalling the marriage."

"It is entirely impossible," said Mr. Churchill shortly.

"Then why do you need a detective? Surely it is the diplomatic corps that should handle the matter. Has the government not sufficient resources to discourage the match?"

"Diplomatic pressure can only go so far before it recoils upon the user," said Mr. Churchill. "If it were possible to threaten the archduke with exposure—not directly, but covertly—we might have an opportunity. If we could locate the double . . ."

"Who now, one must believe, no longer resembles the archduke to any marked degree," said Holmes.

"How can you say that?"

"The removal of the beard alone would be sufficient to deceive any layman," said Holmes. "It is quite possible to alter one's appearance significantly, given sufficient time and sufficient motive. Furthermore, it is quite possible that this gentleman is no longer alive, for he has certainly outlived his usefulness to the archduke."

This statement, so coldly analytical, produced a sudden change in Mr. Churchill's mood.

"Do you really mean that?" he cried. "Impossible! No, this fellow exists, Mr. Holmes, and you must find him! I shall not tolerate an evasion!"

Mr. Churchill's outburst met with a sharp response.

"I shall consider your request at my leisure," said Holmes coldly. "I shall inform you of my decision in three days."

"Three days!" exclaimed Mr. Churchill, who seemed very much in danger of exploding like a balloon.

"Yes," said Holmes mildly. "Watson, will you be so good as to accompany our guest to the street?"

This method of concluding an interview was not to Mr. Churchill's liking, judging from the expression on his face, but his need for my friend's assistance was evidently sufficient to silence his tongue. I led the young statesman from the sitting room and accompanied him down the stairs. The passing years had thickened Mr. Churchill's once slender figure, but he still moved with the aggressive impatience of what he had so often been called, a "young man in a hurry."

"I ask you to impress upon Mr. Holmes the absolute necessity of halting this marriage," he said as we descended the stairs.

"My friend has long been a declared enemy of the archduke," I said. "If he accepts the case, you may be assured that he will prosecute this investigation to the limit of his abilities."

Mr. Churchill glowered at my words.

"These matters require a delicate hand, an understanding of the great world," he said. "I shall have to supervise matters here with a close eye. I shall be in touch with you and your friend shortly, Dr. Watson."

I made no response to this statement, though I could have reminded Mr. Churchill that it was his "delicate hand" that had allowed the archduke to escape all responsibility for his extensive criminal career.

"I must caution you," Mr. Churchill continued as we stepped out onto the pavement, "against speaking with any member of the press about this subject."

"You may rely on our discretion," I said, striving to conceal my impatience, for the touch of Mr. Churchill's "delicate hand" was already beginning to grow heavy. A large, silver motorcar sat gleaming at the curb, evidently awaiting Mr. Churchill, for when we appeared, the chauffeur sprang from his perch and hastened to open the door.

"Very good, Rogers," Mr. Churchill said. "Here, what's this?"

He raced around to the rear of the car and I followed, where we saw a young woman crouched behind the vehicle, in the act of writing the familiar rallying cry "Votes for Women" on the boot in vivid red paint.

"D——n you for a suffragette!" roared Mr. Churchill. "What do you mean, defacing my automobile, you vixen?"

"Oh, now, Winnie, don't make a fuss," the woman said in a well-bred voice, turning her head so that we could see her face.

"Rachel!" cried Mr. Churchill. "This conduct is reprehensible to the utmost degree! To be preyed upon by my own flesh and blood! I shall speak to your mother!"

"Do as you please," said the woman, screwing the lid upon the pot of paint she carried with her and tossing her brush in the gutter. "Votes for women, Winnie, votes for women!"

And with this taunt ringing in our ears, she hurried off.

"Remove that filth, Rogers," said Mr. Churchill to his chauffeur, pointing to the painted slogan.

"Very good, sir."

"This Rolls-Royce is a very expensive piece of equipment, and it is your responsibility. You must be more observant in the future."

"Of course, sir," said Rogers, kneeling on the street as he wiped off the paint. Mr. Churchill supervised this operation so closely that I feared he might topple onto his chauffeur.

"D——d harpies would make geldings of us all," said Mr. Churchill once the paint was completely removed. "When women of good families behave in this manner, what hope is there?"

"It is distressing," I said, although, in fact, for the first time in my life I was beginning to warm to the suffragettes' cause.

"A firm hand is what a woman wants," continued Mr. Churchill. "You will express my concerns to Mr. Holmes?"

"Of course," I said.

I waved a polite good-bye to our visitor as he mounted into the backseat of his great car and departed from our door. When I returned to our flat at 221-B I was surprised to discover my friend dressed in his long gray traveling cloak, with his Gladstone in his hand.

"I am off for the Continent, Watson," he announced. "You will not be averse to joining me in a few days, or perhaps a week?"

"I am sure I could arrange that," I said, somewhat bewildered by his haste. "I was not aware that you were planning to travel."

Holmes paused at my words and placed the Gladstone on the floor. When he looked up at me, his eyes were glittering with excitement.

"My diffidence in the matter of the archduke was entirely assumed," he said, not without a touch of malice. "I have kept myself well acquainted with his career, although much of what Mr. Churchill had to say was previously unknown to me."

"Then why did you tell him that you were not certain that you would accept the case?"

"I will not negotiate with Mr. Churchill until I am sure of my ground. It is useless to argue with a man who listens only to himself. I prefer to have my case complete before I agree to investigate. I apologize for leaving you to fend off Mr. Churchill's queries. Please assure him that you know nothing of the matter, and assign all blame to my impossible nature. Perhaps I could trouble you for a few spare coins?"

I emptied my pockets, producing a half sovereign, two crowns, and a sixpence, which he eagerly swept into his purse.

"I shall probably be in Paris," he said, "but do not say so. Wish me luck, Watson. The penny has come round at last."

CHAPTER 24

Unexpected Guests

SHERLOCK HOLMES DISPLAYED UPON occasion an almost perverse love of mystification for its own sake, and this was one of those occasions. His immediate departure left me with no inkling of what was to come next. The luncheon hour was approaching. I had little appetite and contented myself with a bit of bread and cheese before leaving for Charing Cross. As a senior surgeon I now only worked a half schedule, though I supplemented my hours in surgery with instructional courses in field medicine for military surgeons, based on my experiences in the Boer War.

I did not finish at the hospital until after eight, enjoying a leisurely dinner at the Galenians and returning to Baker Street at close to midnight. I had the following day to myself, and in the hour after breakfast I was engrossed in the *Times,* warming my feet before a small coal fire when Warren, our latest pageboy, entered the room.

"Mrs. Assquick!" he announced with a nervous shout.

"Asquith, my boy, Asquith!" said a sharp, feminine voice.

I stumbled to my feet, uncertain if I was in fact about to encounter the well-known wife of the prime minister. An instant later a small, vivacious, and expensively dressed woman strode into our humble sitting room, a woman who could only be Mrs. Asquith.

"You are Dr. Watson!" she declared.

"Yes, I am."

"Please dismiss your boy. I wish to speak to you of private matters."

Warren, like every pageboy employed by Mrs. Hudson, was always happy to disappear. He quickly fled to his nook below the stairs, bearing an order for tea.

"I can only stay a short time," said Mrs. Asquith, glancing about the room. "Mr. Holmes is not here?"

"No," I said.

"But you are his confidant?"

"Yes."

Mrs. Asquith nervously removed her bonnet and then replaced it on her head, observing herself in the mirror over the bureau. She seemed to have forgotten my presence entirely. Then she seated herself and stared at me with her hawklike eyes.

"The princess will not listen to reason!" she said explosively.

"So Mr. Churchill explained," I replied.

"You are familiar with the details of this matter?"

"I have accompanied Holmes throughout this investigation. However, until yesterday, nothing had happened since we returned from Constantinople two years ago."

"You actually saw the diamonds?"

"Yes. They were loose stones."

She clenched her fists.

"Those jewels belong to England!" she shouted. "It is impossible that we should be abused in such a manner by foreigners!"

I sought to express sympathy for her distress, but this outburst seemed so unrelated to the facts that I was rendered speechless. Fortunately, Mrs. Hudson appeared with the tea tray and I busied myself with preparing a cup for our strange guest. While I did so, Mrs. Asquith darted about the room, examining its contents as though hoping that the diamonds might somehow be here, mislaid perhaps beneath an old letter and covered with dust. When I placed the cup before her chair, she quickly resumed her seat.

"You must be cautious with Winston," she said after taking a large draft from her cup. "This is an affair *d'une longue haleine.* One must make haste slowly. Winston has great spirit, but he does not think. Only Henry can handle him, and Henry is so busy. Lloyd George is the great danger. He has Winston under his spell. But I say too much. You must assure me that Mr. Holmes will succeed in this matter."

"I can only tell you, Mrs. Asquith, that Sherlock Holmes will do everything in his power to defeat the designs of the archduke."

"That is good. That is very good. The conduct of the court has been unconscionable. The king is growing old, and relies too much on his advisers. Yet Lord Worthington thinks the archduke means England well and would not abuse his position."

"Lord Worthington?" I exclaimed.

"Yes, the marquis," she said, with a distinct tone of condescension in her voice.

"I should not place my entire trust in Lord Worthington," I said.

My impertinent words had a suitable effect on Mrs. Asquith. Her eyes bulged out toward me in amazement.

"I should expect you to justify that statement, Doctor," she said.

For a moment I quailed beneath Mrs. Asquith's furious gaze, but I pulled myself together and dared to speak truth to power.

"His lordship has received favors, for himself and on behalf of the king, from the archduke. I can only say that I think he speaks as an interested party and should be recognized as such."

"What favors? What do you mean?"

I realized, too late, that someone so humble as myself could not simply offer advice on matters of concern to the great world, particularly not to someone such as Mrs. Asquith. I had no choice but to tell her in detail of the extraordinary interview that Holmes, Jennie, and I had witnessed between

Lord Worthington and the archduke. The reader may condemn my indiscretion if he wishes, but I can only say that no one who has not been in the position of seeking to keep a secret from Mrs. Asquith can imagine the dilemma I faced.

"What you say is impossible," she announced when my tale was done. "The British monarchy cannot be bought with trinkets."

"Of course not," I said. "But the archduke has at least purchased sympathy. You see the obstacles that Holmes faces."

"You must tell no one of this," she said. "Winston in particular. He is a dear boy, but he cannot keep a secret. The Americans are behind it all, I am sure of it. That marriage!"

"The archduke certainly played a role," I said cautiously.

"Yes. They meddle, and they meddle, and what are they good for? I have never known an American fit to ride an English horse. They have no right to speak our language! They should speak Apache, or, or Caribbean, or some such—something barbarous that would suit them."

Having delivered herself of these sentiments regarding our American cousins, she fixed me with her extraordinary eyes once more.

"Well, what do you intend to do?" she demanded.

"Why, to assist Sherlock Holmes."

"He has a plan? We must have no secrets, Dr. Watson. Henry trusts me implicitly in these matters. Official action would be worse than useless. The Tories would tear us apart!"

She slapped the arm of her chair in anger.

"A solution, Doctor, a solution!" she cried.

I shook my head.

"I can only tell you, Mrs. Asquith," I began, "that my friend is dedicated to achieving the ends you desire. He holds the archduke responsible for as many as six deaths and is determined to bring him to justice by one means or another."

"Yes, but what about the jewels?" she demanded passionately. "You see the problems they have caused already. In any event, it is the marriage that must be prevented, and with absolute discretion. The slightest scandal would be fatal to our cause. Above all, we must avoid the press!"

I realized that I should never give Mrs. Asquith the answers she wanted, and that my efforts to do so would, in all likelihood, only make matters worse. However, ending a conversation with that lady, I soon discovered, is no easy task.

"Perhaps it would be best for you to discuss this with Mr. Holmes when he returns," I said. "It is impossible for me to speak for him. All I can say is that he is fully engaged in this case and that I have never known him to fail when he is so engaged."

"You have said that before, Doctor," she countered. "Your loyalty is commendable, but it is not you who will be standing before the House to explain what has gone wrong. However clever your friend may be, he has no entry into the great world. He will always be seen for what he is, a man on a mission. To know what is worth knowing, one must move in such circles by right, not by duty. I will be in Paris next week myself, and there is much I could learn if I knew how to listen, and what to listen for. You have been helpful, but you need to do much more. This is no job for a policeman. There will be no arrests."

"I think I have said all I can say, Mrs. Asquith," I replied.

"But you have told me nothing!" she snapped. "I will not have Mr. Holmes blundering about, offending the countess—"

"The countess?" I exclaimed.

"Yes, la Comtesse D'Espinau. A remarkable woman, with extraordinary *ton*. She has been miserably used by our press, but she never complains."

"She is here in England?" I asked.

Mrs. Asquith raised her eyebrows in amusement.

"Really, Doctor, you know nothing of these matters. The countess and I have been quite friendly for several years. She was so kind as to extend to Herbert and myself the use of her fine château last spring. The Loire is so pleasant at that time of year. Between the two of us, I think she fancied herself a match for the archduke. By a great chance, her *yali* lies next to the archduke's along the Bosporus, and she knows him well. In any event, it was she who first told me what was afoot in Rome. She has guile, it is true, a woman of her background cannot escape it, but she means England well. She is happy to serve us, though she hopes to serve herself. But she has warned me that if the marriage is to be prevented, no harm must come to the archduke."

"I can hardly see how she should be the one to determine the outcome," I said.

"She should because she understands. It is she who can tell us the cards the archduke is holding. But I can tell you much as well, for I have dined with him myself on several occasions. You know, I felt there was something sinister about him from the very first."

Mrs. Asquith stared at me with her eyes wide open, as though demanding that I should admire her prescience.

"When . . . when did this occur?" I stumbled.

"Why, in the last several months. He was here for some time, you know. I believe there was mention of it in the *Tatler.* I never read such publications myself, of course, but if I worried about what other people might say I should accomplish nothing. And, of course, I had him to lunch at 10 Downing. But you must never tell anyone of that."

"No, of course not."

"In any event, to know someone properly you must dine in his home. He sets a most charming table, though I can't say that I admire his taste in *foie gras*."

"No?"

"Indeed not. Far too spicy. Now, Dr. Watson, as I have been fair with you, it is only right that you should be fair with me."

When she finished this statement, Mrs. Asquith looked at me with a fierce glitter in her eyes, as if I should instantly divine what it was she wished to know and then tell her. But what I could tell her and what she wished to hear were two very different things. From the course of our curious conversation, I could only conclude that Mrs. Asquith wished to be assured that Holmes would infallibly extract the jewels from the archduke and prevent his marriage to the princess, all without a public scandal or even the slightest resentment on the part of the archduke. And yet I knew that Holmes's intent departed very far indeed from those lines. I was about to construct another clumsy, diplomatic statement that would be sure to further provoke Mrs. Asquith's ire when she suddenly seized my hand.

"We must pray, Dr. Watson!" she exclaimed, sinking to her knees and dragging me down with her.

And so I found myself on my knees with this elegant society woman, who addressed the deity with stentorian tones.

"O God who watches over all, extend thy special care to thy servants, Dr. Watson and Margot Tennant Asquith, and Herbert Henry Asquith, and find it in thy bounty to guide their hands and ease their hearts. Give them patience to do thy works! Bring peace to this land and confusion to her enemies. Turn the violent man from our door and let us dwell in your house. Let princes hear your wisdom, and let the poor man prosper. We ask you to listen to our words and we promise to obey your will. Amen."

She prefaced this last word with a vigorous shake of my hand as a prompt to join in. Afterward she regained her feet and brushed the dust of 221-B from the folds of her skirt with an exclamation of disgust.

"Doctor, this is terrible!" she cried. "Look at my skirt!"

Her distress was so absolute that I hastened to my bedroom and returned almost instantly with a clothing brush, applying it to her fine dress.

"Surely you have a servant for this!" she said, somehow scandalized by my actions.

"Poor Warren is the most rudimentary of servants," I replied. "I cannot believe that he could perform any task to your expectation."

"Then I shall do it myself," she said, seizing the brush from my hand. "A Tennant can keep herself clean!"

She then employed the implement upon her dress with a kind of fury, as though demonstrating the independent nature of her heritage. When she was done she handed the brush to me.

"Remind Mr. Holmes of my words, Doctor. I shall expect a report as soon as he returns."

I nodded helplessly, realizing that there was nothing to be gained from contradicting Mrs. Asquith, for whatever purpose she had was sacred to her as long as she held it. She adjusted her bonnet in the mirror and turned to go. At that exact moment the door opened and Warren appeared once more.

"Lady Churchill!" he announced.

I do not know who was more alarmed by this new arrival, Mrs. Asquith or myself. The confines of our sitting room were scarcely competent to contain such remarkable figures, and the two ladies maneuvered with caution.

I had not seen Lady Churchill since our memorable encounter at the Drury Lane some eight years before. Her beauty now belonged to a previous generation, and her elegant person had both filled and softened since that time. She halted for a moment, as if to absorb Mrs. Asquith's presence, and then extended her hand.

"Margot!" she exclaimed "How pleasant to see you here!"

"And Jennie!" returned Mrs. Asquith. "I was just speaking of you yesterday to your son!"

"And he was just speaking to me of you," said Lady Churchill, with perhaps an undertone of wit.

"I should be enchanted if you could join Henry and me for lunch next Tuesday," Mrs. Asquith continued. "We have not seen you at 10 Downing for far too long!"

"That would be enchanting, but unfortunately we leave tomorrow for France."

"That is unfortunate," replied Mrs. Asquith, weighing this piece of information with some thought. "I am afraid that I am already late for another appointment. Please give my regards to your firm young husband!"

And with those words she made her departure, leaving me alone with the formidable Lady Churchill.

"Please, sit down," I said. "I shall have some fresh tea brought in."

Lady Churchill regarded my confusion with some amusement.

"There is no need," she said. "I gather that Mr. Holmes is not in."

"No, he is not."

"Then you must take a message, though I fear you are already overburdened with advice. Please inform Mr. Holmes that whatever resources I have are his. I know I cannot prove it, but I can lay claim to a greater share of discretion than either my son or Mrs. Asquith."

As she spoke, Lady Churchill's intelligent gray eyes looked deeply into my own. I saw traces of more than just worldly wisdom in the gaze of this aging society beauty, and for a brief moment I wondered if she might not know more than I wished about my relations with the countess.

"I am sure that Mr. Holmes will appreciate greatly whatever resources you may have to offer," I said.

"Excellent. I do have one question for you, Dr. Watson. The diamonds themselves. I understand that not all of them were used in the tiara."

"I cannot answer that," I replied, happy to have the excuse of ignorance. "As I am sure you know, Holmes and I saw the complete offspring of the Great Blue several years ago, but I have never seen the tiara itself, and furthermore I have no idea of what the archduke may have done with the remaining diamonds. There were many small stones that he may have simply sold on the commercial market. The larger ones that were not used in the tiara have quite possibly been distributed among members of the Hapsburg family."

"A reasonable supposition indeed," said Lady Churchill with a smile. "It has been so good of you to entertain me, Doctor. These matters are of the greatest importance, and I am sure that you and your friend will handle them in the best possible manner."

Lady Churchill's compliments formed the greatest possible contrast with Mrs. Asquith's peremptory advice, which the former lady no doubt intended. As she rose she extended her hand, and I kissed it lightly in farewell. When she was fairly gone the sitting room door opened once more and Warren appeared.

"Are there any more ladies coming today?" he demanded.

"I don't think so, Warren," I said. "Why do you ask?"

"Because I don't like 'em," he said earnestly. "They look at me awful fierce, specially that Mrs. Quickass."

" 'Asquith,' Warren. If you butcher a lady's name that badly, you deserve far more than dirty looks. Say it for me."

"Asquick," he stumbled.

"No, 'Asquith,' with a 'th.' "

"Asquith," he said sullenly.

"That's better, though you should practice some more. Mrs. Asquith is the wife of the prime minister."

"The prime minister? Then why hasn't he got an English name? That's no name for an Englishman."

"It *is* an English name, Warren. There are many English names beyond Smith and Jones."

Warren received this information reluctantly and then departed for his post. Outside, the sun, which had been entirely hidden all morning, had burned away the fog and now shone with a vigor that suggested a final end to winter's grip. A brisk walk would awaken my appetite for lunch and preserve me from the questions of additional society ladies drawn by the scent of the archduke's diamonds. The arguments in favor of this course of action were overwhelming, and I quickly departed for a pleasant tour of Regent's Park, traveling to the Galenians for lunch and retiring to the library for the rest of the afternoon, immersed in one of Russell's sea stories. At dinner I shared a leg of mutton with several of the younger members and enjoyed a genial discussion of pancreatic tumors that lasted for several hours, after which time I deemed it safe to return home. Yet even as I ascended the familiar steps to our flat I felt a vague foreboding, a certain something in the air that caused me to quicken my pace. I opened the door to 221-B and entered the sitting room, to behold the countess!

"How did you get in?" I demanded.

"What does it matter," she asked, "now that I am here?"

Never to my eyes had the countess looked more beautiful than that night. An extravagant gown of the richest pink wrapped her superb figure in a luxurious froth that caused her beautiful skin to glow with the warmth of a perfect pearl. With infinite wickedness she had chosen to rest one of her elegant feet on a small footstool. I was compelled to bite my tongue to regain my self-possession.

"I must ask you to leave," I said.

"Does my presence offend you?" she asked, amused.

"It is offensive to enter rooms that are not yours," I said with a trembling voice. I discovered to my distress that I was beginning to perspire freely.

"You have not always been so censorious, Doctor," she replied. "Perhaps it is your English climate that makes you so dull."

"It is not the climate but your conduct," I said sharply.

This clumsy accusation, which I delivered with far more anger than I should have wished, naturally amused this woman, who was the complete mistress of her own passions.

"Yes, Doctor, you have found me out. I have been most wicked. Perhaps you should take this occasion to punish me."

She smiled with perfect innocence as she uttered this cunning taunt, and touched her hand to her bodice.

"Warren!" I shouted. "Warren! Warren!"

"What are you doing, you poor man," whispered the countess, her eyes blazing with shameless delight at my near panic.

"Warren!" I repeated, dodging behind a chair.

"You think to evade me in such a manner?" purred the countess, continuing her pursuit.

"Warren!" I cried. "Confound it, boy, come here at once!"

Despite my desperate plea, it was several minutes before I heard Warren's awkward tread up the stairs, during which time I cowered before the countess, stooping so low as to arm myself with a poker from the fire. So little faith had I in my own resolve that I dared not lay a hand on her. To touch her beauteous form even with one finger would surely have transmuted my trembling courage to helpless desire.

At last poor Warren entered, holding what appeared to be half a baked potato in his hand.

"You wanted me, sir?" he asked.

"I did indeed, Warren. This fine lady would like to be escorted to her carriage."

"I have no carriage," said the countess.

"Then she would like to be escorted to the door," I said.

Warren stared at the countess. He was of that age when the

male sex tends to view a beautiful woman more with confusion and terror than desire. A weaker reed I could not have found to assist me in this preposterous yet decidedly dangerous confrontation.

"Take her arm, Warren," I commanded.

The pitiful boy dropped his potato and advanced toward the countess, yet avoiding her eyes.

"Take her arm," I repeated.

At last he grasped her arm.

"Farewell, Countess," I said. "I must ask you not to call again."

"Such a sad end to such a delightful friendship," said the countess, allowing herself to be led to the door. "Please allow me to recover my cloak."

She took the garment, a magnificent fur, from the back of the settee and flung it easily over her shoulders. As she departed, she turned to me and bestowed a magnificent smile.

"You wrong me, Doctor, but I forgive you. I mean you well."

I refused her the courtesy of a reply, and instead watched with a wildly beating heart as she disappeared through the doorway. When she was well gone I went to the door and locked it firmly. I then went to the window and watched her emerge on the curb. Despite her statement, an elegant brougham quickly appeared before her and she entered, riding off quickly into the night.

I went to the tantalus and prepared a strong brandy and soda, draining half my glass with one draft. As I did so, there was a knock on the door.

"Who's there?" I demanded.

"It's me, sir, Warren," came the reply.

"Are you alone?"

"Why, of course I am, sir. Will you be wanting anything more?"

I went to the door and opened it. Warren, obviously shaken by what had occurred, stared up at me.

"That lady gave me a sovereign," he said, stunned.

"Did she?" I said. "I'm not surprised. She is a very great and a very dangerous lady, Warren. You must never admit her again."

"But I didn't, sir. I don't know how she got in."

"No doubt. But you must never let her in, Warren, no matter how much money she gives you."

Warren gave no response to this earnest command, and I could tell from his expression that he was even more susceptible to the countess' wiles than I. There was no purpose in trying to stiffen such a helpless spirit, and I let the boy go.

After Warren departed I sought to temper my unruly passions by taking up the latest copy of the *Lancet*. Although an extensive article on new treatments of cholangio hepatitis caught my eye, I tossed the periodical aside after no more than fifteen minutes and embarked on a swift walk through London's darkened streets. Fantasies of an imagined encounter failed to materialize, however, and I returned to 221-B in an hour, cold and out of sorts, but still unready for bed. I relaxed with a glass of brandy and a cigar until well past midnight and then tossed for hours once I did retire, haunted by wanton images of the countess. How the passions rage when corrected by reason!

CHAPTER 25

Escaping the Countess

I AWAKENED IN THE MORNING utterly exhausted from the emotional turmoil inflicted upon my soul by the countess' visit. I decided that I must at all costs deny her the opportunity to make a second assault on my sanity and so resolved to take up residence at the Galenians for the remainder of Holmes's absence, however long that should be. Such a move would have the additional benefit of shielding me from inquiries from Mr. Churchill and Mrs. Asquith. I arranged with Mrs. Hudson that all messages from Holmes should be instantly directed to me at the Galenians, while all visitors should simply be informed that I was traveling. This simple ruse had the desired effect, and I was able to concentrate on my work, though the mere sight of a pretty foot was still enough to send my heart racing. I had been at the Galenians for a week when I received a cable from Holmes forwarded by Mrs. Hudson that informed me of his address in Paris. I replied with a brief note explaining in guarded terms my decision to vacate our rooms in Baker Street. I then heard nothing more from Holmes for perhaps three weeks, at which time I received a second cable, summoning me to Calais. We met at the railway station and adjourned to a hotel room where we might speak freely.

"Our prospects dwindle, Watson," said Holmes, his long legs stretched out before him. "The archduke's suit is very far advanced. I have been in conversation with the assistant ambassador from our embassy in Vienna. He informs me that not a few members of the Hapsburg family are quite jealous of the archduke's success, but even to suggest a charge of murder or other crime against him would be worse than useless. If we do not find some lever against him, the marriage will be announced in two months' time. Once the announcement has been made, there will be no turning back."

"And you have found no trace of the accomplice?"

"None, nor did I expect to. M. Compte has given me invaluable assistance in developing a dossier on M. Brilleton, but as to the murder itself, there is nothing. Our killer, and the lady who aided him, have vanished into thin air. But I understand from your note that you have been having your own difficulties in London."

I flushed a little at his remark.

"I thought it best to avoid the countess," I said. "No one knows more than I what a cunning woman she is. And to satisfy Mrs. Asquith I should have had to spend hours in conversation. She does not strike me as a reticent woman."

"Perhaps not," said Holmes with a smile. "I understand that she has an aggressive tongue."

"She does indeed. However, she has seen the archduke a number of times."

"Indeed? What did she have to say about him?"

"That he has excellent manners and that his *foie gras* is overly spiced."

"Did she, by Jove," he cried, rising to his feet. "Did she?"

"Yes, she did," I replied, amazed by his sudden emotion. "Does that mean anything?"

"It could mean everything," he replied. "What is the hour?"

"Only one o'clock."

"Then we have plenty of time. But we must depart for Paris at once."

I could not begin to imagine why Holmes was so struck by this trivial detail, and he was unwilling to enlighten me, but he had undoubtedly seized upon it as the key to the entire mystery, for he fell into a profound reverie of thought on the cab ride over to the railway station. Once we boarded the train he spoke not a word for the entire length of our journey to Paris, immersing himself in the study of a large sheaf of documents he took from his Gladstone. When we arrived at the Gare de l'Est in Paris at half past six he immediately led me to the track where the carriages of the Orient Express were being groomed for departure.

"Do you intend to travel to Vienna?" I asked.

"No. But if we are very fortunate we may be able to have a word with M. Lestrange and the *chef de cuisine.*"

Holmes knocked sharply on the door of the first carriage, summoning a *bagagiste* who naturally informed us that the train was not yet ready for boarding. For the price of a half sovereign Holmes purchased an interview with the *chef de train,* who in fact proved to be M. Lestrange.

"Mr. Holmes," he cried upon meeting us, "and Dr. Watson. It is a great pleasure to meet you gentlemen once more."

"Thank you, M. Lestrange," returned Holmes. "If it is at all convenient, my friend and I would very much appreciate a brief conversation with you in private. And I must ask if you are traveling with M. Rabin, the *chef de cuisine* who prepared so many fine meals for us on our journey."

"Indeed I am. I cannot feel comfortable without Michel."

"Excellent. It is imperative that I speak with him."

We journeyed to M. Lestrange's private office aboard the train, where we relaxed for a few minutes' time on the *chef de train*'s fine leather sofa until we were joined by the austere Swiss chef.

"Michel," said M. Lestrange, "you remember Mr. Holmes and Dr. Watson."

The chef performed a brief, precise bow.

"Of course," he said.

"I apologize for intruding in such a manner," said Holmes, "but by an extraordinary coincidence the opportunity now exists for solving the murder of M. Brilleton that occurred on the Orient Express almost three years ago. However, the questions that I must ask are not ones that gentlemen in your position will be pleased to hear. I can only hope that you will have faith in my discretion and my intentions."

"Mr. Holmes," said M. Lestrange, "you took it upon yourself to perform a great favor on behalf of the Orient Express and of Michel and myself. Your great career is proof of the power of reason to provide justice for humanity. Michel and I will answer truthfully whatever questions you have for us."

Whether the chef felt himself bound so entirely I could not say, but his bland, aloof features betrayed no distress at his chief's sweeping pronouncement.

"You are very kind," replied Holmes. "Now, then. I have been interesting myself in a variety of matters that I hope will prove not to be so trivial as they first appear. The Archduke Josef Anton Salvator of Austria has been a frequent traveler on the Orient Express for many years, has he not?"

"Indeed so, Mr. Holmes," said M. Lestrange. I believe the archduke purchased a *yali* in 1901 and frequently traveled between Vienna and Constantinople. And of course he often traveled to Paris as well. We have had the honor of his company perhaps ten or twelve times a year for close to a decade."

"And what would you say of his accent?" asked Holmes.

"Why, he had none—that is to say, he had the accent of an Austrian nobleman. He spoke Viennese French—very fine, though with a slight lack of definition for the vowels. It is a common error."

"Have you noticed any change?"

"In his accent?"

"In his accent or his choice of words. Anything, really, in his manner of speech."

"Well, the archduke is not a terribly outspoken man. He travels alone."

"Really? He never has a manservant with him?"

"Not that I can recall. It is his habit to engage a *bagagiste* for his exclusive service when he travels. He is, naturally, quite formal with all those beneath his rank."

"Does he employ the same individual on each journey?"

"No. He simply asks for the best man. In fact, it has been my impression that he does not enjoy a familiar face."

"That is interesting. M. Rabin. Perhaps you can help us. If no change has occurred in the archduke's accent, perhaps you may have observed one in his palate."

Holmes's extraordinary question immediately focused the attention of one and all upon the unbending chef.

"It is an unusual question, Mr. Holmes," the chef replied after a brief hesitation, "but extremely well placed. About two years ago, I noticed a distinct change in the archduke's dining habits, one that I found impossible to explain."

"Really?" said Holmes. "Please continue."

"The archduke," said the Swiss, with a peculiar intensity, "had a classic palate, and, as is befitting in a gentleman of the first rank, preferred game above all dishes. He understood sauces very well, and ordered wines as a Hapsburg should. But for the past two years he has shown the palate of a countryman, while ordering wine like a bourgeois on holiday."

This last charge, hurled with exquisite malice and uttered in a perfectly flat tone, somehow implied that the archduke was not the only person to have displayed this failing. As soon as the words were out of his mouth, M. Rabin's lips snapped shut, in the manner of a servant who has just said something that he should and yet should not have said.

"Did you find this conclusive?" asked Holmes.

"I found it very strange. Two years ago I myself carved for him a most excellent *sanglier,* a dish that in the past he never failed to request in season. He asked for only a moderate portion and failed to finish it. I thought that perhaps he was ill or else dissatisfied with my service. However, later in the meal he consumed three large servings of *tripes à la bordelaise,* which he ate with mustard, a dish that I do not recall he ever ordered before. And he has ordered *tripes* on every occasion since."

Holmes smiled.

"Thank you, *chef,*" he said. "There really is no substitute for the eye of a master. You speak of this man as a countryman. Could you be more specific?"

"He is from Alsace," the chef said abruptly.

"You are sure?"

"He requested allspice for his *foie gras.*"

"Ah. Then I fear we must conclude that the true archduke is dead. He created a monster, and the monster has consumed him."

As he uttered these remarkable words, Holmes rose to his feet.

"I believe, gentlemen, that you have provided a very great service to the countries of both England and France. I must ask you to keep this interview entirely private. I do not know when the accounts for these matters will be settled, but until they are, I must maintain a policy of complete mystery, for which I apologize in advance."

"No apologies are needed, Mr. Holmes," said M. Lestrange. "Michel and I are proud to have been of assistance, and we wish you and Dr. Watson Godspeed on your journey."

Both chefs bowed before us and we departed from that most elegant of trains. I followed Holmes as he walked silently along the platform, his head bowed in thought and his churchwarden between his teeth.

"I must go to Zurich," he said suddenly.

"Zurich!" I exclaimed.

"Yes. Neutral territory is best when dealing with well-connected murderers. If I am fortunate, I should be able to spike the archduke's guns in a week, or even less."

"How is that possible?"

"There are fully a dozen archdukes who outrank our Josef. This marriage would place him before all of them except the heir apparent to the imperial throne. Convincing evidence that Archduke Josef is in fact dead would cause the marriage plans to collapse in an instant."

"And you feel that the testimony of a chef will be conclusive."

Holmes smiled.

"No. But M. Rabin's observations have given me the key to half a dozen mysteries. If we can find a decent café with a quiet table, perhaps I can explain my thinking more clearly."

We made our way into the station and located an establishment that met Holmes's requirements. We sat and ordered a glass of wine.

"You see, Watson," Holmes began, once the waiter had left us, "ever since I understood the dimensions of the strange alliance between archduke and thief, I wondered if such a partnership could survive the accomplishment of its purpose. The thought of two cunning and ruthless men, with a single great diamond to share between them, seemed to me scarcely less than a recipe for murder.

"The possibility existed, of course, that the ability to continue the imposture in the future might prove to be of value, but that seemed to me unlikely. They could end their partnership by splitting the revenue obtained from the sale of the diamond, but disposal of the uncut stone for even a tenth of its value would be difficult, due to its notoriety. It would be a brave jeweler, after all, who would risk the wrath of Mr. Rhodes. That gentleman, I believe, expected that ultimately the thieves would be forced to sell the stone back to him for a fraction of its true value.

"But the archduke and his accomplice eluded all the nets that were spread before them. Mr. Rhodes died, and the stone was cut. Yet just as the archduke triumphed, he lost control of the gems. Why? How could he have been so careless as to allow his debts to overwhelm him, forcing him to pledge the jewels for which he had risked everything?

"I concluded that his accomplice must have been subjecting him to blackmail. But he had concealed his traces so well that neither the archduke nor I could discover his whereabouts. And I felt certain that the accomplice was no longer in Europe. The combination of modern communications and discreet Swiss bankers could easily allow one to administer extortion in Constantinople from New York City."

Holmes paused to light a cigar.

"But the murder of M. Brilleton on the Orient Express convinced me that the accomplice must still be here in Europe. The archduke could never have dared to undertake such a deed. The risks of recognition and discovery would have been overwhelming. But why should the accomplice care whether M. Brilleton, or Sir Samuel, or Mr. Thompson, or the archduke himself ultimately controlled the diamonds? He had so far exploited the archduke's resources as to drive him into bankruptcy. It would be best for him to quit Europe entirely and seek happier and safer climes on the other side of the Atlantic.

"M. Rabin's testimony has explained the mystery. For there was another Alsatian aboard the Orient Express—the unfortunate M. Brilleton. It is likely that two clever thieves from the same province would be acquaintances. I doubt that we shall ever know if M. Brilleton knew that his countryman was involved in the theft of the Great Blue, but he must have had his suspicions. He would have done better to stay away instead of accepting Sir Samuel's employment. M. Brilleton was the one link to our thief's past. When our man murdered M. Brilleton, he set himself free to assume the role of the archduke."

"But the man we saw on the train. Surely he was the true archduke?"

"I was, and am, almost sure that he was. It was a clever trick indeed to have that swagger stick, and an even better one to wear gloves. I cannot believe that we saw the impostor that day, but how can I be sure?"

"In any event, how could the impostor dare to impersonate such a public man?"

"For precisely that reason. The archduke is a very public figure, and only a public one. He has no intimates, and had none in the past. As a young man he dared not show his face in Vienna, due to his own sense of disgrace. After the theft of the Great Blue he resided for years in Constantinople, quitting it only months before we arrived, to elude his creditors. It is no coincidence, I am sure, that the archduke's mother died in the fall of 1906. It was her death that allowed the accomplice to strike. I believe he acted almost immediately after her death, for the story given to the press was that the archduke had retired to his *yali* in Constantinople for several months to recover from the loss. When he reappeared, he had changed his appearance entirely, shaving his beard. Here is a recent photograph."

Holmes handed me a large photograph of a young man, of handsome, almost elegant features, dressed in military uniform and standing at attention. His cold eyes stared out at me with an almost frightening arrogance.

"I could not recognize him, and yet I know him," I said. "But how do you propose to convince anyone of this fantastic story?"

"The archduke's adversaries will not require absolute proof. In fact, they would reject it if I gave it to them. They wish a secret scandal rather than a public one. I have known for some time of several suspicious deaths among the Hapsburgs in the past several years, deaths that improved the archduke's rank. I would not be surprised if autopsies would discover, even now, the presence of coumarin."

I could not help regarding Holmes's expectations as overly sanguine. That Austria's royal family would even entertain such extravagant suspicions against one of its own on the basis of obscure allegations from an Englishman seemed absurd. However, his confidence in the matter was unshakable, and there was no point in attempting to argue the alternative. I felt there was real danger that his long frustration with the case had prejudiced his extraordinary intellect, which, as he told me more than once, only drew necessary conclusions. Experience alone, I decided, could convince him of the error of his hopes, so I kept my own counsel.

When we finished our wine I accompanied him to his hotel, where I spent the night, returning to London the next day, leaving Holmes to pursue the case alone. I decided that my absence from Baker Street had been sufficient to discourage a second visit from the countess, so I returned to the comfort of our old lodgings. I did not hear from Holmes for another two weeks, when to my great surprise a diplomatic courier arrived at our door and handed me a letter from Holmes, whose text was as follows:

> My dear Watson,
>
> Our case has gone well, but not so well as I had hoped. Opposition to the match has grown in Austria, but the prospective bride has proved not so malleable. Please join me in Rome, and bring Jennie with you. The British embassy will be able to inform you of my whereabouts.

I made no reply to this curious message other than to indicate that I would assent immediately to Holmes's request. Jennie and I departed on the following morning.

CHAPTER 26

A Mediterranean Holiday

FEW THINGS, I SHOULD imagine, make an Englishman feel more English than a journey to Italy. Everything that an Englishman values is ignored, and everything he ignores is valued. Jennie was first enraged and then amused by the tranquil pace of life, where the future always seemed so far off that it was unreasonable to assume it would ever arrive. In her first bloom of youth she was, of course, far less affected by the rigors of three days of travel on indifferently kept trains, but the real tonic to her spirits was the endless attentions showered upon her person by virtually every member of the male sex. Her glorious blond hair, more than a little enhanced, I regret to say, by chemical means, affected Italian men rather as a red cape affects a bull.

"They aren't shy, are they?" she asked after our first trip to the dining carriage after crossing the Alps.

"You are hardly shy yourself," I replied. "You must moderate your behavior, Jennie."

"Moderate nothing," she replied. "I could make a fortune here. I'm going to tell Herbie to book in Rome the first chance he gets, the biggest hall they've got. I wonder if they've got any good songs down here."

"Italy is the land of songs, the most musical nation on earth."

"I suppose that's so. Well, I guess I'd better give a listen."

When we finally did arrive in Rome we were fortunately met by a representative of our embassy, for I was scarcely prepared to cope with the exuberant laissez-faire of the Italian temperament, particularly as stimulated by Jennie's presence. We were taken quickly by carriage to a small villa on the outskirts of the city with a brisk efficiency that suggested to me the importance that the government attached to Holmes's mission. This impression was reinforced when we arrived at the villa itself, which featured an enclosed courtyard whose gate was manned by a young Englishman with a marked military bearing and a Lee-Enfield resting in his sentry box. As we passed through the gate I observed a great, silver motorcar, a twin of Mr. Churchill's Rolls-Royce, sitting in the drive.

Holmes greeted us as we entered.

"My dear Watson," he said, "I fear you have found your journey wearisome. I apologize for subjecting you to such haste, but delays have become dangerous. Perhaps you would like to take a nap before dinner."

I disliked being addressed as though I were an aged valetudinarian, but in fact I had had no more than eight hours' sleep over the past several days. I complied with Holmes's suggestion, and once I had fallen asleep did not waken for almost four hours. When I recovered myself I joined Jennie and Holmes on a spacious veranda that looked out over a darkened plain to a city in the far distance whose lights suggested that it could only be Rome itself.

"It was kind of the embassy to give you such splendid accommodations," I said. "The view is remarkable."

"Remarkable and useful," said Holmes. "Sit down, Watson, and I shall tell you how matters stand."

"You said in your letter that progress had been uneven."

"Yes. There has been a great deal of progress, but there has also been a severe obstruction. Our diplomats in Vienna were already quite aware of members of the imperial family who were quite eager to prevent the marriage. The heir to the throne, from all I have been told, is particularly hostile to such a union. I spoke at considerable length with the private secretary of his highness, who I feel took a very cold view of the matter. The man is avidly searching for some method to confirm the impostor's identity that would convince the upper reaches of the Austrian bureaucracy."

"Do you think they would expose him?"

"That is hard to say. It would make them look like fools to all the world. I think they would prefer simply to force the archduke into exile and make him a virtual prisoner on some small, obscure estate. Unfortunately, our adversary has been one step ahead of us, as usual. He has already given the tiara to the princess, and she declines to give it back. She is quite amenable to marriage, but will have the tiara, marriage or no. The tiara's supposed rediscovery has already received a great deal of publicity in Vienna, as Mr. Churchill noted. The Hapsburgs cannot simply allow it to disappear again."

"Then what do you propose to do?"

"The princess is extremely given to self-indulgence. In particular, she enjoys being driven with several of her attendants over the back roads of this area in a large touring car manufactured by the firm of Isotta Fraschini. During these excursions, she wears the tiara."

"And you are proposing to steal it," I said, my mind recalling the image of the Rolls-Royce in the courtyard.

"Precisely. I hope you have no objection to theft in the cause of England?"

Holmes's obvious pleasure in the scheme was disarming.

"Does a guard accompany the princess?" I asked.

"No. There is a chauffeur, of course, and a footman, to assist them. However, any serious violence would compromise our position fatally."

"And how are we to proceed?"

"You shall be the driver and Jennie shall be the thief. We are approximately five miles from Rome. You will steal the tiara and bring it to me in the port of Santa Marinella, some twenty-five miles up the coast. In a week's time, a British cruiser will be waiting for us, just outside of Italian territorial waters. In that time, my dear Watson, you must become an expert chauffeur."

And so for the next week I awakened at six o'clock in the

morning to master the vagaries of that remarkable vehicle known as the Rolls-Royce Silver Ghost. I fear that few of my readers can know the selfish yet superb pleasures of operating such a machine. The mere touch of a finger places the power of forty-eight fine Cleveland bays at your command. By depressing a device known as a "clutch" and manipulating a lever that adjusts a complex series of gears, one can deploy this enormous power in such manner that the vehicle will accelerate from a dead stop to a speed of twenty-five miles an hour in less than thirty seconds! And once the motorcar is in motion, one can achieve speeds that approach, and sometimes even exceed, fifty miles an hour! Irresistible and omnipotent, you travel with the thunder of Zeus, the fury of Mars, and the speed of Mercury. Perhaps most intoxicating of all, everyone else on the road must get out of your way!

Naturally, no little skill is needed to operate such a formidable machine, and I must acknowledge that my years as a surgeon were a great help to me in mastering the techniques required to allow the Rolls-Royce to reach its full potential. For a week I practiced, and for a week we observed the routes of the princess. Holmes scouted their routes in the guise of a cyclist and eventually presented Jennie and myself with a detailed plan of attack. We should overtake them at a lonely stretch of road at the crest of a hill, where their momentum would be exhausted. My identity would be obscured by goggles and a duster, and Jennie would be dressed in a similar manner, though wearing the tights of an acrobat beneath her garment.

"I shouldn't be surprised if I shan't be needing this," said Jennie as we rode out that lovely spring morning.

"Won't be needing what?" I asked, my eyes fixed necessarily on the road.

"This," she said, waving her hand in an obscure manner.

"Jennie, I cannot see what you are doing while I am driving."

"Then pull over. Mr. Holmes said to wait about here."

"There is a better place just ahead. We shall be more concealed."

I continued to drive for another ten minutes and then brought the motorcar to a halt. By reversing the operation of the gears I drove the vehicle backward so that we were concealed from the road by a stand of olive trees.

"What is it you wish to show me?" I said, removing my driving goggles.

"This," she said, holding up the derringer that the countess had given her in Constantinople.

"Jennie," I said, "if any harm should come to the princess, or any of her companions, our entire undertaking will be ruined."

"Oh, I wouldn't shoot a fine lady like her. It's her lads that I'm worried about."

"They ride in the front seat. You must be upon her before she knows what you are doing."

"But what if they start shooting?"

"Then that will be your misfortune. In any event, you cannot steal the tiara and fire your derringer at the same time. Please give me that weapon."

Reluctantly, she complied with my demand, and just as she did so we heard the sound of the princess' Isotta Fraschini. The massive, dark green vehicle had its full complement of passengers—two liveried servants in the front seat, and the princess and her two young companions in the back. The top was down, and one could see even at a distance the sunlight glinting off the fabled jewels that we had so long pursued. I felt my stomach tighten and my heartbeat quicken. We had begun the hunt!

I let the Isotta advance past our position by about ten yards before engaging the Rolls-Royce's initial gear. We accelerated smoothly to perhaps five miles an hour, and then I shifted into the second, or "climbing" gear.

"Faster, faster!" insisted Jennie. "They're getting away!"

"They shan't get away," I said. "You take your position."

The Isotta was in fact traveling at scarcely more than ten miles an hour, sufficient to provide exhilaration but not so much as to provoke the dust that might disturb the courtly ladies' bonnets. Italian roads are a continuing disgrace to that nation, and macadam is a substance still unknown. To travel at speeds of more than twenty miles an hour on an Italian road is a severe ordeal. At this point, however, the entire width of the road was smooth and safe for high speeds.

I supplied increasing petrol to the Rolls-Royce's engine, and we began to gain speed. Jennie crouched in the backseat and removed her duster. As the bonnet of the Rolls crept past the boot of the Isotta, she first dropped lightly onto the running board of the Rolls and then leaped to the Isotta. At this point I could no longer follow her progress, for it was my duty to bring the bonnet of the Rolls level with that of the Isotta, and this demanding maneuver required my full attention. The shouts of the other vehicle's passengers and the honking of its horn informed me that they were aware of our presence, but I had no inkling of Jennie's activity until I felt a sudden start as she leaped back onto the Rolls and climbed into the backseats.

"I've got it!" she shouted into my ear. "Let's go!"

As she spoke, I shifted into the starting gear and boosted the flow of petrol to the engine. This is necessary because the starting gear, while limited in its top speed and excessive in its consumption of fuel, offers the most rapid acceleration at lower speeds. As our velocity approached fifteen miles an hour, I rapidly changed to the climbing gear, and we shot forward ahead of the Isotta. The high-pitched screams of rage that I could hear, even above the din of our roaring engine, assured me of the success of Jennie's mission.

"Keep going!" screamed Jennie. "Shift, shift, shift!"

It is the false assumption of the amateur that one must arrive in the top gear, or "overdrive," as quickly as possible. In fact, to derive the maximum advantage from the ingenious craftsmanship of the modern motorcar, one must work through the gears for an extended period of time. Optimizing acceleration and speed is a demanding art, requiring deft coordination to manipulate the various pedals and levers that control the engagement of gears, the supply of fuel, the proper air mixture, and the perfect functioning of the electrical system. I am proud to say that I quickly opened up a lead of perhaps a dozen yards in advance of the Isotta, a lead that would grow sensibly as we careened through the rolling hills outside Rome, for the Isotta was definitely inferior to the Rolls in its ability to maintain speed upon an upgrade. When we arrived at the coastal plain, with yet twenty miles to go before we arrived at Santa

Marinella, I was able to steal a backward glance and could see that we were easily a hundred yards ahead.

"They're eating our dust," said Jennie with malicious pleasure.

And indeed they were. The road, though rutted, was quite dry, and I was able to hold to a speed in excess of forty miles an hour! To maintain control of an automobile at such speeds, one must remain in a state of perfect concentration at all times. The howl and the rush of the wind, the roar of the huge engine, and the constant jolts and lurches must all be ignored if the speed of the vehicle is to be kept at the absolute maximum. As we thundered toward our goal, my mind was like the still point in a typhoon, instantly guiding the Rolls around the obstacles that sprang up before us—dangerous boulders, treacherous hollows, and unstable patches of gravel. It seemed but a moment since Jennie had snatched the tiara, and already the low silhouette of Santa Marinella was visible on the horizon.

But as we approached, a very real and seemingly inescapable danger appeared before us. A long stretch of the road had been flooded by an overflowing stream. I slowed desperately and shifted into a lower gear, so that I might maintain the forward drive needed to push the motorcar's tires through the soft earth without losing traction or control. Few tasks that confront the operator of a high-speed motorcar are more demanding, and it was impossible under the circumstances that our lead over the Isotta should not shrink. In her excitement, Jennie was scarcely understanding of my dilemma.

"Faster, d—— you!" she cried. "They'll be here!"

But it was impossible under the circumstances to maintain a speed of more than twenty miles an hour. I dared not look around to discover the progress of our pursuers, but the volubility of Jennie's agitation was more than sufficient to convince me that the gap between the two automobiles was narrowing, a conclusion that was confirmed in the most dramatic manner—by the sound of gunfire!

"D—— it!" shouted Jennie with fury. "They're shooting at us!"

"How close are they?" I demanded.

"Thirty yards," she replied.

"Are they using rifles or pistols?"

"What difference does it make?"

"It makes all the difference. If they have rifles we shall never escape."

I was about to say more when another shot rang out.

"Well, they haven't got rifles," said Jennie, rising far up in her seat. "Who do you think you're shooting at, you d——d rascal?!" she bellowed.

"Quiet, Jennie! They have every reason to shoot at us. We are criminals."

"Oh, don't be so proper! We've got the diamonds and we're going to keep them."

"Yes, of course, but how close are they now?"

"No closer."

"Good."

Despite the dangerous road conditions, I was traveling at more than twenty miles an hour—a reckless pace indeed, but entirely necessary. We were still more than a mile from Santa Marinella, and if we entered the port with our pursuers so close behind it would be difficult indeed to dispose of the tiara without detection. The flooding of the road continued for perhaps another three hundred yards, and over that distance it was impossible to increase our lead.

"Do hurry!" demanded Jennie. "They're gaining now!"

Another shot rang out, shattering our windscreen.

"D—— your eyes!" cried Jennie, and as she spoke, she plunged into the backseat.

"Are you hurt, Jennie?" I exclaimed, suddenly terrified.

"No, I'm not hurt! I'm shooting back!"

"Jennie, you mustn't hurt the princess!"

"I won't hurt the b—— b——," she sneered, in less than complimentary tones.

I fixed my eyes upon the road as one shot after another whizzed above my head. The loud reports of Jennie's derringer echoed in my ears, accompanied by shouts of frustration.

"Slow down!" she commanded.

"But if I slow down—" and as I spoke I heard the impact of a bullet upon metal.

"Are you all right?" I shouted.

"Yes! You've got to slow down. If I shoot from here I might hurt your precious princess. Yes! He's reloading. Give it the brakes as hard as you can!"

I knew better than to comply with Jennie's command. Instead of braking, I returned the gear assembly to its starting gear, which had the instant effect of violently reducing the speed of the Rolls without locking the wheels into a dangerous skid. As the Rolls plowed forward I dared to turn around and could see the distance between us and the massive Isotta shrink to less than ten yards. Jennie, wild with excitement, poised herself on the backseat, her derringer clasped in both her hands, and held her fire until the last possible second. With my heart in my throat I heard first the crack of her derringer and then the explosion of the front left tire of the Isotta.

"There! That's done it! Hit it, Johnnie!"

But I had already turned to the wheel and set my foot on the acceleration pedal. The Rolls leaped forward through the treacherous mire like a great stallion as the engine roared. Despite the risk, I flung one last backward glance and saw the Isotta turned sideways and already far distant.

"Dished and done!" cried Jennie. "Oh, it's a fine day for diamonds, my pretty princess! You see what comes from messing with an English girl!"

She vaulted into the front seat beside me and kissed my cheek.

"You're a fine chauffeur, Papa, a fine one indeed! I shall buy myself a Rolls when we return to London and you shall drive me everywhere in style."

I made no reply to this puffery but shifted into the climbing gear. We were finally free from the mud and I was able to work into the third or "upper" gear and thence into the overdrive, maintaining a speed well in excess of thirty-five miles an hour.

"Can't you go faster?" Jennie demanded.

"Of course I can, but now we are home free. If you would, you could wipe the mud from my goggles."

"Yes, Daddy dear," she said. "My, we both look a fright, don't we? I hadn't noticed."

Indeed, both the Rolls and ourselves had been subjected to a fairly brutal mud bath, but there was no time to consider a remedy, for we were fast approaching Santa Marinella. I downshifted once more as we entered the ancient, narrow streets, more suitable for Caesar's chariots than a modern automobile. We traveled slowly to the docks and found a large carriage house, marked, as Holmes had told us, with freshly painted red doors. At our approach, a young man sprang from a stone stoop and swung the doors open. I entered and brought the great motorcar to a halt. As the doors swung shut the entire room was plunged into darkness.

"You are all right, Watson?" asked Holmes in a quiet voice.

"Indeed we are," I said. "Jennie was splendid."

I heard the door of the Rolls open and Holmes took me by the arm. I removed my goggles and, as my eyes grew accustomed to the half light, I could see enough to put one foot in front of another.

"We must go down here," he said, directing me to a staircase with the beam of a small electric torch. "Are your pursuers close behind?"

"We left them about a mile back," I said. "Jennie shot out their front tire."

"Excellent, Jennie. The Rolls will be cleaned and sent upon its way this evening."

"Unfortunately, we suffered a bullet hole somewhere in the boot that will have to be tended to."

"Of course. We are well within our schedule."

We descended the steps to a narrow stone pathway that led directly to the harbor. A covered steam launch waited for us, and we crept aboard. In minutes we were bound for the open sea. Once we were free from the harbor, Jennie removed the tiara from her bag and placed it on the table before us. It was a simple, gleaming circle of platinum encrusted with the great gems we had seen two years before.

"I don't blame the poor girl for being upset," said Jennie, stroking the great gem at the front of the tiara. "But she shouldn't take things that don't belong to her."

While Jennie and I recovered from our wild adventure, Holmes conducted a careful examination of the magnificent gems that encrusted the tiara and pronounced them all genuine. To behold the marvelous stones once more, after having won them so briefly, and having lost them so cruelly, some two years before, was reward indeed for our labors. We had defeated the cunning Austrian at last!

An hour's travel brought us to the open sea, and we made the transfer to the battle cruiser HMS *Quarrelsome,* whose mighty steel walls rose above us like a great cliff. We were hoisted above like so many crates of produce, a perfectly safe yet thoroughly harrowing mode of travel, though the great ship was almost entirely motionless, indifferent in its huge bulk to the gentle swells of the Mediterranean. On deck we were greeted by the captain, a naval officer of intensely aristocratic bearing, whose manner toward us was a curious mixture of deference and condescension. He surely had been informed that we were on a mission of great importance, but apparently did not know what it was, for he did not ask us for the tiara. But regardless of his orders, the burden of showing courtesy to a trio of shamelessly middle-class landlubbers, one of whom had the supreme misfortune to be a young woman, clearly exceeded his powers of dissimulation. Upon being assured that all was well with us he instantly departed, leaving a young ensign to conduct us to our quarters, which proved to be spacious and well appointed in the extreme.

"Now, this is living," said Jennie, opening a porthole and observing the calm, brilliant sea before us. "From now on, I shall always winter on the Côte d'Azur."

"In any event, we shall be quite comfortable for the next several days," said Holmes. He disappeared into a bedroom and returned carrying a tray that bore a bottle of champagne in an ice bucket, along with three glasses.

"I know that we celebrated prematurely once before," he said. "But I feel safer now that we are under the protection of the Royal Navy. Watson, would you care to do the honors?"

I gladly popped the cork and poured three glasses. As I did so, Holmes took the tiara from its carrying case and placed it on Jennie's head.

"It is an ill wind that blows no good," he said. "The archduke has been an ill wind indeed, and yet he has done great good, for he has brought sweet Jennie from the streets and made her our own."

No man, I think, could have listened to that speech without tears in his eyes, and certainly I did not. The long frustrations that we had experienced, the great changes in our lives that had occurred over an expanse of almost ten years, all of which had culminated in the furious experience of the past few hours, were summed up in those few words. And we drank a glass to the obscure who had suffered, and to the obscure who had been saved.

CHAPTER 27

In the Company of the Prime Minister

WE ENJOYED THE HOSPITALITY of the *Quarrelsome* for some time, in splendid isolation from the entire crew, much to Jennie's vexation. What most vexed her, however, was not the lack of company but the lack of clothes, for her vast wardrobe had of necessity been left behind when we made our departure from Santa Marinella. Her persistence in this matter knew no bounds, and, to my amazement, the great trunks that accompanied us on our journey eventually arrived, courtesy of a speedy "torpedo boat," dispatched by the Royal Navy. Nothing gave Jennie greater pleasure than to dress in her finest gown and promenade the decks of the *Quarrelsome* at midnight, with the Hapsburg tiara resting on her head, its great jewels gleaming in the moonlight. Yet even this unspeakable luxury was incomplete.

"If only I had an audience!" she cried. "What good are diamonds when there's no one to envy them?"

At last we were transferred to another vessel, the *Enchantress,* the fine yacht the Admiralty is pleased to provide for the convenience of the prime minister. We were greeted there with every possible respect and conveyed to our quarters. An hour after we arrived, we were brought into august company indeed: Prime Minister Asquith; Lord Grey, the foreign minister; Mr. David Lloyd George, the chancellor of the exchequer; and Mr. Winston Churchill.

"It is a pleasure to meet you gentlemen," the prime minister said. "Please sit down."

The prime minister had every appearance of being a man of high intellect, unruffled self-confidence, and a fondness for luxury. There was a certain sheen about him, as though he had found the very best way of living and was determined never to depart from it, rather like one of those great bears of North America who feast on fat salmon every day of their lives. Lord Grey, on the other hand, was a small, delicate man, almost wrenlike, yet with an unmistakable aristocratic hauteur that inhabited his every expression and gesture in such manner as to forever separate him from the great mass of mankind. Compared to these, Mr. Lloyd George and Mr. Churchill were as noisy as volcanoes, seemingly in constant eruption even when they were most silent. As we sat before them, all eyes were fixed on the small leather satchel that rested on my friend's knees, for there could be no doubt in the minds of our hosts as to its contents.

"We are pleased to inform you, Mr. Asquith," said my friend, "that we were entirely successful in obtaining the tiara."

"So I understand," said the prime minister with some amusement. "Your actions, Mr. Holmes, have provoked a great deal of consternation among diplomatic circles. A stone dropped in still waters provokes a succession of circular waves that weaken as they disperse. However, the waves created by your actions seem certain to gain in force as they travel. They have disconcerted Rome; they impinge upon Vienna; and now they strike the *Enchantress*."

"Indeed," said Holmes. "Is it too soon to say whether their impact shall have the desired effect?"

"It is not too soon," interjected Lord Grey. "This entire affair was a most unfortunate and unlikely turn of events, Mr. Holmes, and never would even have manifested itself as a possibility were it not for the extraordinary wickedness of the individual whom you have unmasked, and the sad willfulness unfortunately displayed by a certain person in high places.

"I am confident that the passage of time, together with a suitable replacement for the archduke, will eventually calm that person's distress, though the party that attached itself to her cause feels a greater disappointment. The Austrians, however, have stated a specific grievance regarding the loss of the tiara, which they have officially proclaimed to be the ancestral possession of the Hapsburgs."

"No doubt they should," said Holmes.

"Yes, Mr. Holmes," said the prime minister. "And it has been my understanding that your one condition for your services was the tiara itself."

"Not to claim as my property," replied my friend, "but rather to determine its fate."

As he said this, he removed the tiara from the leather satchel and placed it on the prime minister's desk. No sooner had he done so than the prime minister, with what could have been construed as indecent haste, took it up in his own hands.

"It is a beauty," he said, affecting the indifferent tone of the connoisseur.

"Indeed," said Holmes. "Like many great jewels, the history of the piece scarcely bears examination. Fortunately, one equitable solution does suggest itself."

"Really?" said the prime minister, somewhat disappointed, I expect, to learn that the disposal of the tiara had already been decided upon.

"Yes. It is my understanding that Cecil Rhodes left the bulk of his fortune to provide scholarships for young men in Germany, England, and the United States, with the intent, I suppose, that they would continue the work of imperialism."

"That is correct," said Mr. Asquith.

"Then it is my desire that this tiara should be sold to the Austrian government for the sum of £200,000, which sum shall serve as the principal for a fund to establish scholarships for the education of young men of the African race."

"You want to educate the savages?" cried Mr. Churchill, ending what had been for him a most protracted silence.

"Indeed I do," said Holmes. "We speak of civilization as a blessing. Let us share its blessings as well as its burdens."

"Surely the disposal of such a, a remarkable treasure as this one should be done with especial care," said Mr. Asquith.

"I assure you, Prime Minister, that I have done so," said Holmes.

"Well, if you aren't going to give it to Wales, I don't care what you do with it," said Mr. Lloyd George. "If we keep it, we'll have to give it to the queen, and the Saxe-Coburgs have jewels enough as it is. Let the Hapsburgs have it back for two hundred thousand. And if Mr. Holmes wants to spend it on the Hottentots, let him do so. He's done his job and deserves to be paid."

If Mr. Asquith felt any resentment for this outburst from his ambitious junior, he gave no evidence of doing so. Instead, he turned to Lord Grey.

"What do you think, Eddie?" he asked.

"There is no question that the Hapsburgs want it back, though they will not appreciate paying £200,000 to get it."

"Do you think they will pay the two hundred thousand?"

"Yes, I do."

"Then I think we should get it and establish the little fund that Mr. Holmes has in mind."

"It seems an unsuitable conclusion for so varied an adventure," Mr. Churchill said angrily. "A game well played deserves a trophy, and this is a fine one indeed."

"I understand your feelings, Winston," said Mr. Asquith, and his tone, though both dry and judicious, encouraged me to believe that in fact he did. "But if we keep it whole, we should have to give it to the queen, which I fear would satisfy no one. If we could break it down, we could make many fine ladies happy. But it is a pretty piece whole, too pretty to break down. Perhaps if I hadn't seen it I should be of a different mind. But I have seen it, and I have no other solution than to sell it back to the Hapsburgs. Perhaps if we are polite to them they shall let us have a look at it now and again."

"It seems unfortunate that such a great natural treasure, brought from the depths of the earth by British wit and industry, and recovered for our nation by Mr. Holmes's acumen, should be basely surrendered to a reactionary dynasty located in an obscure corner of Europe," persisted Mr. Churchill.

"Indeed," replied the prime minister. "But I have found that the half loaf makes the better meal nine times out of ten. We shall go with Mr. Holmes's suggestion."

"Thank you, Prime Minister," my friend replied. "I appreciate your decision."

"It is you who deserves to be thanked, Mr. Holmes. This was a dangerous, ill-tempered affair that placed the concerns of great nations in the hands of an impostor and a giddy young woman. The people of England are in your debt."

"You are too kind, sir."

"Not at all. I hope that you and Dr. Watson and his charming daughter will consent to remain with us for the remainder of our cruise. The Mediterranean sun is the antidote for so many things."

"What do you say, Watson?" asked Holmes.

"Of course I could not object," I answered. "Jennie will be so appreciative."

And so we took our leave from that remarkable quartet of men, who seemed to have so little in common other than the pleasure they took in being at the very center of things. We found Jennie supervising the unpacking of her garments, adapting quite well to the new luxury of servants.

Life aboard the gilded salon of the *Enchantress* proved to be quite extraordinary, and entirely different than I could have imagined, though I was not surprised that evening to see the tiara resting atop Mrs. Asquith's head. It was her intention, so she said, that every lady should have a chance, but as the evening progressed, the tiara showed no sign of ever departing from her tresses. On the following evening the tiara failed to make an appearance, and I surmised that Mr. Asquith had deemed it wiser to remove that apple of discord from the company, a decision that, I should say, all but Mrs. Asquith applauded. That lady appeared particularly voluble and animated, perhaps in compensation for the grievous loss she had suffered, and I had the misfortune to sit between her and Mr. Churchill, who, I surmise, was still irate at the prime minister's refusal to claim the tiara for England. A conversation between Mr. Churchill and Mrs. Asquith is rather like the passage of two express trains on adjacent tracks in opposing directions: there is a great noise and rush of air, but neither has the least impact on the other.

Mrs. Asquith was full of plans for the marriage of the princess, suggesting that a match might be made with one of the lesser members of our own royal family. It is just as well that I am generally ignorant of these individuals, for Mrs. Asquith expressed her views of their various shortcomings with great freeness. She had, it seems, a list of aristocratic ne'er-do-wells whom she hoped to fob off on the lesser states of Europe "if only they will not embarrass us." She was confident, and with good reason, I thought, that many a royal fingerling would leap at the chance of a palace in Rome, but she worried about the temptations of a Mediterranean climate. "We do need a fellow with some backbone, after all."

Mr. Churchill, for his part, was seated astride a far more personal hobbyhorse. The *Enchantress* had touched at the port of Siracusa in Sicily that morning, which event had precipitated a near avalanche of classical quotations on the part of the prime minister and Lord Grey. Surprisingly, Mr. Churchill proved to be entirely ignorant of both Latin and Greek and, I discovered, possessed an intense animus toward those who prided themselves on their knowledge of the classics. We agreed together that Cicero was vastly overrated and doubtless could have risen no higher than president of the Board of Trade in modern England. Mr. Churchill then went so far as to say that even Homer himself, being blind, had never actually seen battle, though clearly he was a gifted rhymester.

However, the great surprise of our journey occurred five days later. We passed through the Strait of Otranto and made our way up the Italian coast toward Venice. One day short of our destination we enjoyed, or perhaps endured, a most elaborate dinner party at which we were joined, to my intense surprise and discomfort, by several members of the Austrian diplomatic corps! I could not imagine that any of these individuals might wish to speak to so undistinguished a personage as myself, but after the dinner concluded I was fairly well cornered by a young, shrewd-looking gentleman who introduced himself blandly as the Grand Duke of Carinthia. Naturally, I sought to confine the conversation to banalities related to the excellence of the weather, but the duke quickly took matters to the other extreme.

"It may interest you to know, Dr. Watson," he said, "that the Archduke Josef has had an unfortunate accident while hunting. He stumbled while pursuing a stag and his rifle discharged."

"That is unfortunate," I said, stumbling to keep my wits about me. The delicate smile on the young duke's face was sufficient to convince me that he took great pleasure in delivering this information.

"Yes. His condition is quite serious. However, the decision has been made not to release any information to the press at this time."

"Yes," I said.

"Once the issue has been decided, one way or another, of course, a public announcement will be made. The imperial family feels that this is a very delicate matter."

I nodded, feeling a deep sense of anger and even shame. If Holmes's deductions were correct, the real Archduke Josef was long since dead and it now appeared that his murderer had received the punishment his crimes so richly deserved. But to be told of another human being's death, even one so wicked and corrupt as this mysterious impostor whom we had pursued for so many years, in so gloating and self-satisfied a manner, was truly unpleasant. The crimes of both men should have been brought to light; instead, both crime and punishment were concealed behind walls of impenetrable privilege. I wished to be quit of this luxurious yacht and all its inhabitants and to return to our simple rooms at Baker Street and resume my duties as a physician, where I might in some small degree alleviate the sufferings of mankind rather than delight in them.

When I discussed the encounter with Holmes later that evening he had a similar reaction.

"A sad end to a sad business," he told me, clipping the end of a cigar. "The fellow was a monster, without a doubt, but we have accomplished no more than to deliver him into the hands of his fellows. A public trial, of course, would have been too great a scandal for the Hapsburgs to bear. This is very ill-flavored justice."

"There is the scholarship fund, at least."

"A small seed, very small. And who can tell how it will blossom? No, Jennie is the triumph of this case. You plucked her out of the burning, Watson. It was a rare triumph."

Holmes's kind words allowed me to see the matter in the best possible light, and I retired that evening with a spirit refreshed. The next day we had the perfect good fortune to behold the incomparable architecture of Venice silently rising before us in golden morning light. What pleasure it was to stand on the bow with Jennie, comparing the imperishable beauties crafted by the hand of man and the living beauties of her lovely young face, and to see her gentle features glow with delight as the glorious facades rose before her! What a debt I owed to the doges, master builders, and artisans long past!

CHAPTER 28

The Final Card

THE SPLENDORS OF VENICE proved to be the perfect solvent for the frustrations I felt over the brutal, hidden death of our foe. By the third day I had recovered my spirits entirely, and the night promised a special treat, a performance by a promising young violinist, a native of Vienna by the name of Fritz Kreisler.

"Depend upon it, Watson," Holmes told me as we dressed that evening, "the man is a genius. To have one Ysaye is more than any civilization deserves, and now we have two!"

For Holmes there could be no higher praise, for he placed the Belgian virtuoso above all others, even Vieuxtemps, whose magical skill with the bow had first prompted him to take up the study of the violin as a boy.

On the evening of the concert, the majority of the passengers of the *Enchantress* were attending a diplomatic reception, so Holmes and I had only Jennie as our companion when we traveled to the concert house, whose interior, though sadly worn in places, was a delightful jewel of the baroque, one of those wonderful efflorescences of Italian spirit that, in their spontaneity, individuality, and unforced profusion, seem almost a product of that nation's climate and soil rather than its genius.

"Why don't *we* ever do anything like this?" demanded Jennie as we walked along the broad corridor to our box.

"Each nation must cultivate its temper," said Holmes. "We English are chilly creatures and must learn to live with that."

"Well, I'm not," said Jennie. "I'll bet I'm Italian."

"You look entirely English," I said, not being able to resist pinching her pink cheek.

"Careful what you do to a girl's face," she replied. "I'm Italian inside, I bet, Italian through and through. This is where I'll live when I retire."

We took our box and, in keeping with the splendor of the night, ordered a bottle of champagne. From the very first, the genius of the young artist was manifest, and rarely can I recall seeing Holmes so transported. His intense receptivity to music allowed him to relax the demands of that stern and even imperious intellect that otherwise appeared to constitute both the essence and the entirety of his soul. His face softened, and his eye brightened, and his long fingers stretched forth as though bewitched and given individual life by the rich, dulcet sounds drawn from four taut strands of catgut.

For my part, I was equally as bewitched, or even more so. Never, I believe, have I ever given myself over so entirely to an evening of music. The young virtuoso had me entirely in his spell, and as the concert progressed I seemed to float from the darkened elegance of the concert hall into the warm stillness of an Italian landscape. I lay on rich, sun-dappled grass. Above me, the spreading branches and foliage of an ancient, gnarled olive tree shielded me from the noon heat. In the distance, white, fluffy clouds floated against the brilliant blue of the summer sky, hovering above the rolling hills of the piedmont. Transported by the music, I seemed to dwell in an ecstasy of silence, in a perfect, unchanging world. The faintest of breezes stroked my cheek, and a sweet, delicate aroma pervaded the air—the scent of newly mown hay!

I lurched to my feet like a man hurled from sleep by a nightmare, staring wildly about while my wits struggled to make sense of the inarticulate, almost animal alarm that had seized control of my person. Somehow my eyes caught sight of a young man in evening dress, and in his hand, the glimmer of polished wood!

Instantly, I plunged toward him and grasped the wand in his hand. I sought desperately to tear it from his grip, but though

I was his superior in size, his strength and agility gave him the advantage. I bore him backward but he twisted around and pressed me hard against the railing of the box. At every second I expected to feel the quick, sharp pain of the needle, for I could feel my strength weaken and my head grow dizzy as he pushed me farther and farther over the railing, the steel bar cutting deeply into my back. Darkness clouded my vision and my voice gurgled incoherently in my throat when all of a sudden I felt more than heard two brief blasts of thunder in my ears. At this point my consciousness faded entirely, and when I awakened I was sprawled on the floor, the strong odor of hartshorn filling my nostrils and Jennie holding me in her arms.

"Oh, Daddy," she cried, "are you all right?"

"I wish I could say," I said, my voice trembling with weary confusion. "What happened?"

"There has been a shooting," said Holmes. "You have quite a bit of blood on you, but I don't believe it's yours. Do you feel fit to stand?"

"Yes, of course."

Jennie and Holmes assisted me to my feet, but I instantly sank into a chair.

"That's better," I said. "I don't think I'm wounded, but I have had too much champagne. What happened to the fellow with the knife?"

"He is dead," said Holmes. "You had a sharp eye to spot this in the dark."

He held out the slim, deadly stick, and I took it carefully in my hands.

"It's quite safe," he said. "You can't release the blade unless you reverse the handle."

"I smelled the coumarin," I said, examining the polished wood. "It was all like a dream."

"A deuced useful one," replied Holmes. "I fear I was entirely unprepared for an assault."

Jennie handed me a warm, wet towel.

"Here you go," she said. "Clean yourself up. You look a fright."

I wiped my face and hands and noticed for the first time that my face and clothing were in fact smeared with blood. I began to daub at it with the towel.

"Here," said Jennie, taking the cloth from my hands, "I'll do that. You just sit there."

I paused until she finished with her ministrations.

"I should like to have a look at him," I said, rising to my feet.

Holmes and Jennie led me outside the box. The hallway was crowded with officious persons, half in uniform and half in formal dress.

"Mr. Holmes!" cried a uniformed gentleman, whose profusion of gold braid proclaimed his position of authority. "Your friend is all right?"

"Dr. Watson is unharmed," said Holmes.

"Such great fortune!" the gentleman exclaimed, taking me by the hand. "You are so brave!"

"Where is the young man?" I asked.

"Your assailant? He is here."

He led me to a knot of men, who separated at his command. There on the floor lay the body of the young man who, minutes ago, had done his best to take my life. Blood covered his shirtfront, mute testimony to the terrible wounds he had received. I could scarcely recognize him from the photograph Holmes had shown me some weeks before. This man seemed far younger, and the cold arrogance that so struck me had vanished from his face. His regular features, relaxed in death, gave not the slightest hint of the furious ambition and cruelty that had dominated his career, a career that had won him the world's greatest jewel; that had driven him to slay a helpless boy and half a dozen others; and that, rising to its highest pitch, had shaken the government of England before collapsing. On a sudden instinct I grasped his left hand and turned it palm upward. There was no scar.

"Then the archduke really is dead," I murmured.

"Yes," said Holmes, "and so is his murderer."

I looked back at the man's face. His sightless blue eyes stared at me now with the innocence of a child, and, performing a doctor's duty, I closed them, that none might disturb his peace.

"He looks like an angel," said Jennie, taking my hand.

"He was devil enough," I said, rising to my feet.

"He was indeed," said Holmes, "and he died with a thousand secrets."

"But who saved me?" I asked suddenly, a little stunned that in all the excitement I had not even thought to ask. "Was it you, Jennie?"

"Not me, I was asleep," she confessed.

"It was a woman!" exclaimed the Italian gentleman. "Most beautiful! And dressed all in black! She reached from the next box and fired with her derringer! Two shots!"

"A woman?" I said. "I must thank her."

"She has disappeared, signor. There was terrible confusion. Terrible!"

"But is there no sign of her at all?" I demanded.

"None, signor!" cried the official. "She was a woman of great mystery and elegance, masked, or so I am told!"

By both his words and manner this fellow manifested that fantastic temperament so prevalent in his nation, so I turned to Holmes for more elucidation, but he could do little more than shrug his shoulders.

"I fear I was of no more use to you than Jennie," he said. "I heard sounds of a struggle, saw two flashes of gunfire, and rushed to assist you. By the time we had ascertained that it was your assailant who had been shot, it appears that your savior had long since vanished."

As Holmes was delivering these remarks, vague shouts could be heard from one of the uniformed guards of the concert hall. Out of the corner of my eye I observed him as he approached his commander and handed him a small object.

"A clue, signores," he called. "A clue!"

"What is it?" asked Holmes.

"A shoe, Sr. Holmes," the commander said, "a fine lady's shoe. The carabiniere says he saw the lady throw it from her carriage."

The gentleman passed Holmes a fine lady's shoe indeed, a delicate, dainty shoe of gleaming patent leather and surpassing purity of design, suffused in its every aspect with the delicate wantonness of the eternal feminine, made for the prettiest foot in the world. No man could look upon that shoe without a heightened pulse.

"That shoe is not for me but my friend," said Holmes with a suspicion of a twinkle in his eye. "The fair sex is his department."